EMP RESURGENCE
Dark New World: Book 7

JJ HOLDEN
&
HENRY GENE FOSTER

ISBN: 197973111X
ISBN-13: 978-1979731119

EMP RESURGENCE

- **1** -

0800 HOURS - ZERO DAY +599

MARK BATES STRODE down the unadorned, sterile-looking cement corridor illuminated by glow strips embedded into the ceiling. With each step, his tasseled leather shoes clicked on the cement and echoed down the hall. He adjusted his silk tie with his left hand and held his reports in a manila folder in the other. When he reached a T-intersection, he turned left. He passed four doors on his right side, then stopped at the fifth and knocked loudly.

There was no immediate answer, but Mark knew better than to knock again, so he waited with as much patience as he could muster.

Thirty seconds later, the General's voice came through the door, calling him in.

Mark put his palm on the biometrics reader box next to the door, palm first, then he pressed down with his fingers, one at a time, in a particular order. The General didn't mess around when it came to security—you not only had to have the right fingerprints, you also had to touch each finger to the pad in a specific order, like a PIN. It wouldn't be enough to simply cut off his hand, if someone wanted to gain entry illegally.

When Mark's index finger joined the rest in touching the pad, the light on the door handle switched from red to green. He pushed down on the handle, the lever depressed, and the heavy steel door swung open. It glided silently and easily, despite its obvious mass, perfectly balanced on flush-mounted hinges.

He stepped inside and saw the General's room, immaculate as always, and a young woman lying naked in his bed. She was only partially covered by the blanket, but made no effort to cover herself when Mark came in. When his gaze met hers, she smiled at him while biting her bottom lip.

The General stood by his writing desk in his boxers, pouring two shots of whiskey. At sixty, having spent almost the last two years sitting at a desk, Houle's once-great physical conditioning wasn't so superb anymore. The distances around his waist and chest had switched places. Mark tried not to shudder at the sight of the General's pasty white, flabby body.

Houle took a sip of whiskey, then handed the other cup to his visitor. Mark knew better than to insult him by declining. "General, thank you for seeing me."

Houle replied, "Of course, my friend. How's the wife? And your son is, what, seven now?"

"Yes, sir," Mark said. "Lucy is fine, as is Junior."

Houle nodded, then raised his cup to Mark and said, "So what news do you have for me? I assume you aren't here to tell me the war is over." The General chuckled.

"No such luck." Mark looked again at the woman in Houle's bed. He raised an eyebrow and said, "Sir, listen—"

Houle cut him off. "*Psh.* She's got clearance. She's in the Intel pool for God's sake, and she probably already knows what you're about to tell me." He took another sip from his glass. "Hell, she probably knew it before you did."

"Of course, sir. I have a report from firebases Lincoln

Four and Lincoln Seven. Both were raided again last night. No casualties on either side. Only minor damage to property, easily repaired."

Houle frowned. "That's the third time in two weeks that a Lincoln base has been raided. Same M-O?"

Mark nodded. "Before dawn, an unknown number of raiders opened fire on the wall sentries at both locations. At Lincoln Four, they somehow launched a propane-tank bomb at the main gate. Fortunately, that gate was made of steel, so it didn't burn, unlike Lincoln Two last week."

Houle replied, "What did the department chief say about why Louisiana is getting hit so much lately?" His voice was even, jaw relaxed, and he calmly sipped his whiskey.

Mark knew better than to trust that image of calm. Houle could be unpredictable. "He says that since most of the armored vehicles were stripped from the territory for last year's... other campaign, they're stretched thin on their patrols of the local settlements. He also says it's only a distinct minority who resent your benevolent guidance at the local level."

Houle set his cup down and took a deep breath, then let it out slowly, like a balloon deflating. "Why do they feel the need to kiss my ass and tell me what they think I want to hear? Damn civilians. But we placed bounties on rebels, and we do still perform patrols. If we're getting raided like that, it's only because the civilian populace is protecting the opposition fighters. And that means the problem will only grow."

Mark shrugged. "Yes, sir. I'm sure you're right. They'd like to receive updated orders when you next meet with them." He drank the last of the whiskey in his glass, as there wasn't any to be had from the commissary. He hated to be wasteful. "Thank you for the drink," he said, giving Houle his most winning smile.

The General grinned back. "Yeah, you're welcome. If you want a bottle for yourself, or anything else, you let me know."

"I appreciate that."

Houle nodded. "I don't consider most people worth calling a friend, Mark, but you're a straight shooter and loyal."

"Thank you, sir."

Houle nodded and waved a dismissal as he poured himself another shot.

Mark set his empty glass down on the small table by the door and left with a grin. When the door closed behind him, however, his smile instantly vanished.

He hadn't told the truth about the extent of the raiding, but he had said enough to avoid trouble or raise any doubts in Houle's mind about his loyalty when the real extent of the problem was discovered. He could just say he didn't understand the raids' true importance.

The longer it took Houle to deal with Louisiana in the meantime, the more out of control things would get, the weaker Houle looked, and the more resources the General would have to spend on ultimately pacifying the area. That meant troops would be busy in Louisiana, in territory already controlled, instead of off trying to conquer what was left of America again.

Of course, the war wasn't over. Houle had made sure of that, Mark felt certain. He didn't yet have proof enough to go public with his suspicions to NORAD's many civilian and military residents, but he was gathering evidence and felt like he was on the right track.

Mark hustled toward his quarters to mull over how to help the Louisiana situation develop faster. His private brainstorming sessions had been crucial to his success at this little Fifth Column campaign he'd been running against Houle.

"Time to get to work," he muttered as he raised his hand to the biometrics box at his door.

* * *

1230 HOURS - ZERO DAY +599

Cassy smiled at Frank as he came in for their usual lunch meeting. In truth, the "meeting" label just gave them an excuse to shoo away anyone they didn't want to talk to over lunch. Days were busy, after all, and since spring had sprung, the pace was quickening every day from the slow winter doldrums. The Spring Equinox Festival had been a huge success with entertainers and traders from all over the region, games, and of course, the uncorking of the first barrel of autumn's apple cider production.

Frank grinned back at her and set his tray on the table. They now used a much nicer plastic table and chairs from a restaurant, which replaced the old wooden picnic tables. Those, they had given to some newer Clanholds.

"You look spry," Cassy said. "How's your new foot working out?"

Frank pulled up his pants leg to reveal a hammered, welded collection of metal strips, springs, and gears. "Really well. I don't need the crutches anymore, which is fantastic. I'd forgotten what it was like to walk through the Jungle without tripping on everything."

Cassy chuckled. "Dean did a bang-up job on it. It looks like something out of the Road Warrior movies."

"Kind of appropriate," Frank replied before sitting and taking a drink of cider. "So how are you doing?"

"I'm hanging in there. I still miss her, of course. Bri and Aidan are holding up, too."

"They were lucky to know her before she passed. We all

were lucky to have Grandma Mandy."

Cassy smiled, and let the moment of silence linger comfortably between them. They both seemed content to just enjoy each other's company. Together, they could sympathize with each other's problems and the stresses of the work they did. They were both leaders, and faced similar pressures. It was nice to talk to someone else who understood, and she suspected Frank felt the same.

He finished the last of his lunch, then set his fork down. "Lunch gets better and better every week, it seems."

Well, he wasn't wrong about that... Cassy knew it was the greenhouses that kept them in lots of fresh produce. It was nice how much they extended the growing season. She said, "I think the new fish are the key to it all."

Frank laughed. "Who knew keeping fish in those cheap above-ground swimming pools could make such good salads? And the herbs... better than any supermarket stuff we used to get."

Cassy looked at her plate and raised one eyebrow. "You mean we're eating fish-poop vegetables?"

Frank rolled his eyes. "Oh please, the whole thing was your idea. What did you call it?"

"Aquaponics. Hydroponics with fish and worm tea instead of chemical fertilizers. Not as healthy as the dirt-grown produce, but we can keep the aquaponics going year round. It's nice. Remember when that constant stew, looking more like tea than stew, was all we had to eat?"

"Ha! Don't ever mention constant stew again. Although at the time, as I recall, we counted ourselves blessed to eat that food-flavored water."

Cassy raised her cup of cider. "To the end of the Dying Times."

Frank returned the gesture. "So how are the Clanholds doing? Any big changes?"

"Nope. We're still building the earthbag dome complexes as fast as we can. We've got each new complex down to a routine now. Like a blueprint. Michael says that with the way they're scattered and how they're so defensible, Clan territory is almost completely castellated."

Frank nodded and looked as happy to hear that news as she had felt when she heard it. "And the weekly Clan Days were genius, Cassy. Getting everyone available together at a new Clanhold to build houses, or teach how we farm. It speeds everything up and gives the new holdings exposure to Clan culture, if you can call it that."

"I do call it that. It's important for us to have a unified culture, though it will take time to really grab hold. Still, we're successful at living, and they're desperate refugees, so they seem highly motivated to imitate what we do. Ethan's so-called Founder's Principle at work. It speeds up their assimilation."

"Do you trust them?" Frank eyed her, face expressionless.

Cassy frowned. With a frustrated huff, she said, "I don't trust them fully, but we've been careful so far. There are always some issues when you ask self-important people to give up their authority, but mostly the new Clanholds are policing themselves in that regard."

"Kind of your job to govern that mess, isn't it?" Frank swirled his cup around, though Cassy suspected it was empty.

"Frank, don't start that again. I'm the governor of the Confederation, the secretary of agriculture for New America, and a mother. You're the Clan leader. Clanholds report to you."

"Okay," Frank said. "Calm down. I was just kidding."

"Well, what's left of the Gap is now a new Clanhold, so we're expanding southward again."

"Isn't everyone else expanding, too?"

"Yeah, including New America. They have spread to cover everything from our east border to the coast, and from Scranton down to just before the outskirts of Philadelphia. Superior cultures absorb the inferior ones."

"Still worried we'll get swallowed up in New America?"

Cassy nodded. "Yeah. We're a part of New America now, so we can't rely on distance to keep our newborn culture separate long enough for it to stand on its own."

"Unless it happens to be the stronger of the two."

"True. But New America isn't the only possible way we could get swallowed up. The Mountain still controls a huge swath of the U.S., from Utah to Louisiana, and eventually, they'll spread their own version of culture."

"Most of Houle's control is tenuous at best. I'm more worried about the north Pennsylvania 'vader enclave. They've been silent for a year, other than that huge lot of supplies they sent us to help fight off Houle's troops. We'll eventually get some blowback from that; you know that, right?"

Cassy frowned. "It's been six months. Who's going to tell Taggart? Besides, it worked. We defeated the Mountain."

"Yeah, well, the Pen-York 'vaders are at least as strong as New America."

"I guess the only saving grace is that they don't have anywhere else to expand, so the more we expand, the more we'll eventually grow larger and stronger than them."

"On the downside," Frank said, "that means they might look to expand in our direction before we're ready for them."

"It seems to me that, so far, they are content to just rebuild in their own territory, ever since their failed invasion of Brickerville."

"You don't really think that was their best effort, do you? That was something weird, something we can't explain, but it wasn't an invasion. It was a migration, at worst. We were small, so they were dangerous, but those troops were a drop in their bucket."

Cassy sighed. It was an old argument. "Anyway, I can't wait for elections. Taggart is looking forward to stepping down as president, I know."

Frank shrugged. "*General* Taggart shouldn't be president anyway. I figure the new Constitution will crystalize that idea, though. We're pushing hard to make sure there is no election until we all have something ratified. I gave our envoys very specific instructions to stand fast on that issue."

Cassy pursed her lips. "Speaking of envoys, I miss those two."

"The warrior street girl and the Buddhist chemical engineer immigrant."

"Second generation immigrant," Cassy said. "I could talk about those two all day, but I have to go—I have a meeting with my farming instruction team in a bit."

Frank smiled. "I need to meet with the Council anyway, to go over a tribunal. That man who didn't do his assigned work last week demanded a tribunal instead of accepting ten hours of extra duty."

"Dumbass." Cassy laughed. The Dying Times missed a few who needed culling, she mused. She rose from her seat and bid Frank farewell.

Heading toward her house, her mind turned to the meeting coming up—dull, but important, like so much of life since the Confederation had defeated General Houle, the so-called Mountain King. At least that asshole wasn't a threat anymore since he had lost all his war machine toys last year.

* * *

0900 HOURS - ZERO DAY +600

Ethan wandered through the Clan bunker's barracks bay. As he passed through, he leaned over Amber and kissed her on the forehead, then continued onward to the expansion chamber. A select, loyal crew had dug it out over the winter, so now the "living room" didn't contain all his radio and computer equipment, freeing it up for actual living space. Amber had sure appreciated that.

He entered the new chamber, which had walls and a floor lined with cinder blocks. The ceiling was shored up, reinforced, and strong, but from the inside one only saw the drywall they'd stapled to the joists. He turned on his HAM radio and downloaded a couple of HAMnet files from friends, mostly logic puzzles from other geeks like himself, a few more of whom had made it back online over the winter.

He sat in his office chair—a new one without the annoying squeak—and leaned back. He spared a moment to look at the simple paintings on the cinder block walls. A smile turned up the corners of his mouth. Butterflies, fairies, castles, unicorns—which looked, he thought, like Narwhals more than unicorns. He had told Amber's daughter, Kaitlyn, that they looked amazing because, to him, they were. All twelve of them.

Once the slow HAMnet connection finished downloading the files, he flipped open his laptop and booted it. He always had a twinge of fear each morning when he did this, half expecting the dreaded green chatbox to pop up. His 20s handler, Watcher One, was the last person Ethan wanted to talk to after he'd randomly slaughtered a fifteen-year-old girl last year, using a 20s agent armed with a missile-launching quad drone. The agent had paid with his life, but that didn't help the poor girl Watcher One had killed.

Screw every last one of them, Ethan thought. He had

once thought the 20s were a patriot hacker group, but in the end, the 20s turned out to be nothing more than General Houle's private intelligence network, and they'd made Ethan help them to kill the world. The EMPs he had helped them deliver had messed up almost every place on Earth just as badly as the first enemy EMPs had ravaged America.

However, no green box popped up that morning, just as with the last six months of mornings. Whew. He flipped his messenger app on with a quick double-click, but no one was online. He'd hoped to talk to his friends in Florida again, but since they'd kicked the 'vaders out of that state, the whole situation there had gone FUBAR. Florida was completely balkanized, and every day he wondered if his hacker friends had survived another day. Thinking of their possible deaths made him sad.

A ding alerted Ethan to someone popping into his chatroom, snapping him out of his somber thoughts. He didn't recognize the name. "Well, well. Who do we have here?"

> **DarkRyder** >> *Howdy. ASL? Lol.*

> **Aeon_Wretch** >> *Hello. 30s, male, Virginia. U?*

> **DarkRyder** >> *20s, male Pennsylvania. How did u find this place?*

> **Aeon_Wretch** >> *PinkToes told me about it. You can thank him.*

Ethan frowned. PinkToes was suspect. Specifically, suspected of being Watcher One. Ethan had no proof, but when you played Cloak 'n Dagger, you listened to your gut, or you died. Still, that didn't mean this Aeon Wretch guy was bad, but it was a definite strike against him.

DarkRyder >> *That's not a ringing endorsement.*

Aeon_Wretch >> *Maybe u should change ur / handle to Dark Ruder.*

DarkRyder >> *LOL ok fair enuf. So what do u want?*

Aeon_Wretch >> *...*

Aeon_Wretch >> *PinkToes said Watcher1 is trying to contact u*

DarkRyder >> *So? He knows where I am @ if he wants 2 chat.*

Aeon_Wretch >> *He has a message*

DarkRyder >> *so what is it, I have things 2 do*

Aeon_Wretch >> *PinkToes said, 'Remember code Bravo 1-9-7-2? It's playing on a loop.'*

Aeon_Wretch >> *Whatever that means...*

>>DarkRyder has Disconnected<<

Ethan stared at the screen. No flipping way. His heart began to race. This was damn well not what he wanted to hear first thing in the morning. B-1972 was a 20s internal code for "get the hell out, they're coming for you." Who was coming? Watcher One wouldn't have said anything so useful as the damn identity of who was coming for him. If anyone truly was—it could just be a trick to try to flush Ethan out of Clanholme. Why else would Watcher One warn him at all?

He thought of the jet fighters supporting Houle's troops during the last battle for Harrisburg and shuddered. Though there had only been a few of them, they had almost overwhelmed the Confederation defenders in minutes once they began to launch missiles. Only another EMP had saved Ethan's people, blessedly at the expense of half of all Houle's machines of war. Ethan thought it too bad he couldn't have taken out the other half, too.

But no, he didn't think Houle would risk another fighter sortie. So it was either Houle sending some sort of death squad after him, or the 'vaders coming. He didn't figure the 'vaders would announce their intentions to Watcher One. That left General Houle in NORAD, Watcher's boss and the 20s leader. The note about "playing on a loop" seemed to indicate this as well since Houle had tried that once before, but that wasn't a certainty. Stupid cryptic references.

Shit. If Houle was again after him, that was almost worse than 'vaders. Houle's SpecOps guys were among the best. Not as good as Michael, the Confederation's general—a Marine major and SpecOps master—but almost as good and with many more of them.

Ethan picked up one of the dozen hand radios nearby. "Charlie Two to Lincoln One Actual, come in. We need to talk." He hoped Michael would know what to do.

- 2 -

1000 HOURS - ZERO DAY +600

CHOONY WALKED INTO the living room, which was still painted white despite Jaz's continual complaining about the color all winter. How many times had he pointed out that paint was free and could be found almost everywhere? Yet she had never gotten around to it. Jaz had so much she wanted to do to that house to make it into a home, however long they would be in Hackensack, but their responsibilities kept her far too busy to play homemaker.

Yes, Choony mused, it really would be playing—Jaz wasn't the homebody sort of woman, but she idolized the sort of quiet, domestic existence that would have driven her insane if she ever actually got to have it.

He sat on the brown leather sofa next to Jaz, who was reading through a stack of papers. "Anything interesting in there?"

She looked up, dazed and confused for a moment. She'd been so deeply into her reading that she must not have noticed him come in.

"Huh? Oh, the contracts. Well, Taggart's secretary of

state is demanding way too much in the way of tariffs. In the old days, we'd take him to court and then be bound by its decision."

"And now?" Choony looked into her eyes.

"Just like the Confed's deal with Bergenfield—we'll walk away until New America gives us a solution that works for us both, Doug's 'protectionist policies' be damned. The Confederation didn't have enough of anything back then to just hand it over to Bergenfielders who were too stupid or lazy to provide for themselves."

"We were still willing to trade."

"Yeah, but we weren't their nursemaids. And I feel the same about the secretary of state's demands."

Choony nodded. The Bergenfield thing was now an old argument, which they'd had to listen to all winter. Bergenfield wanted everyone to share everything equally, and the Confederation wasn't about to do that. Even if some court said the Confederation, as a territory within New America, must comply with its new demands to support Bergenfield, how would the court enforce it? Not like Taggart would send his army in to enforce such a decree. He'd lose the whole Confederation if he did that, so he had helped delay the issue indefinitely. Cassy's leadership had made sure the Confederation could go it alone at any time.

Jaz said, "Times are different now than before the war. There are no courts yet. But the idiot Taggart picked for SecState is one of those old-school local politicians. The guy was practically drooling at the thought of enforcing 'federal authority over interstate trade.' Screw him."

Choony shrugged. "Doug Holloway seems to think things will go back to the way they were. I have tried to explain to him that it won't happen."

"You should have explained to him that survivor communities these days have no problem shooting up 'federal agents' who try to overstep their bounds or take what isn't theirs. The Clan doesn't pay taxes and never will. It's theft. When they threaten to take your property or your liberty if you don't hand over what's yours, then you have the right to blow their damn heads off."

Choony didn't like when Jaz got this worked up. It caused her to be off balance—violent—which was never good for one's Chi.

"Funny," Jaz continued, "like, a couple of years ago I would have said the feds should have authority over everything if they could keep us safe, fed, and housed. Now it's hard to believe people ever had relied on resources from thousands of miles away."

Choony remained silent. He found it better to let her get it all out.

"Anyway," Jaz said, "I have to write a polite 'fuck you' to Doug and explain that he can shove his tariffs and 'mandatory' trade agreements up his ass. He can take a hundred paper cuts to his butthole as far as I'm concerned."

Choony thought it best to divert the conversation. She was getting downright brutal now. "Jaz, we sent a message to Taggart about the situation with Mr. Holloway. Has he replied?"

Jaz nodded, shuffling through the papers. After a few moments, she found what she was looking for and pulled out a single sheet of paper. "Here we go. He says that, while in principle he supports the idea of free trade with only government *oversight*, not regulation, such oversight requires tariffs to pay for it. However, he 'understands' that some communities may not yet be in a position to absorb tariffs. He welcomes a statement-of-facts from the Confederation about why Doug's tariffs should be waived."

Choony let out a low whistle. He could only imagine how Jaz wanted to respond to that.

Jaz continued, "He can welcome a few of my 'statement-of-facts' with a side of—"

Choony took the paper from Jaz. "Maybe that response is something I'm better suited to write."

Jaz frowned. "If you want." She paused for a moment and then said, "But if Taggart supports this guy's agenda, he can kiss New America's expansion goodbye, and both the Confederation and the Free Republic with it."

Choony's eyes glazed over as he became lost in thought about how best to respond. The answer that kept coming to mind was to simply deny anyone's authority to impose a tax of any kind, and that until the new Constitution was ratified —*with* the Confederation's signature—then the Confed maintained its right to refuse trade agreements, or even to refuse to remain a part of New America. Regretfully, of course.

He had no doubt that the Confederation would walk away from New America membership before going back to the old ways. Encouragingly, from what he had heard over the winter in Hackensack, other survivor groups pretty much all felt the same.

Choony didn't allow such problems as tariffs to rile him up, however. Things were what they were, and there was no point in getting upset over it. Doug Holloway would either go away or change his mind, or the Confederation would go it alone. Nothing Choony could do would force a particular outcome. Thus, he stayed calm.

Jaz, who had been silent for a while, looked up from her papers. "Doug is saying that we must return the two battalions of troops New America stationed with us last year."

"What? Half of those men and women are married to locals now. They have homes. We can't force them to leave." Choony took a few deep breaths trying to stay, at the very least, even-tempered.

Jaz growled, "And we won't. I know Cassy would punch Doug in his fat, red nose if she were here. That's totally not even an option for us. It's not like home is one non-stop flight away, these days. If they leave, they won't get to come back."

Choony shrugged. "It seems to me our only real option will be to release those who want to go and offer citizenship to those who stay in Confed territory. That's as close as we can get to doing what Taggart says without causing a riot at home."

"Good point, Choon."

"Well," Choony said with a wan smile, "one of us should write a letter to Taggart to let him know our official position on this issue."

Jaz pursed her lips, then said, "I'll send a letter to Cassy informing her of what we've done and ask for further direction. You send one to Taggart about the troops, along with the trade tariff thing."

Choony nodded and slightly bowed. Grinning, he said, "As my moon and stars wishes."

Jaz laughed; he loved how her face lit up. Her only answer was, "Nerd. You do know you'll never see that show again, right?"

Choony knew. But it was worth the sadness that came from reminding himself of that fact, just to see her smile so brightly.

* * *

0700 HOURS - ZERO DAY +601

Nate Runke strode through the battlefield with his rifle over his shoulder, the very picture of confidence, heedless of the danger all around him. Months ago, when all this began, he had quickly decided that his militia fought better when he led from the front.

Doing so had been terrifying at first, but since then, he'd seen so many cowards hiding behind cars or rubble still get taken out by a stupid stray bullet, even as he walked untouched in the open among them to bolster his troops' courage. When it was one's time to go, it was their time, no matter what anyone did to avoid it. Fear only crippled people in the meantime.

Today, however, Nate felt much safer than he had in so many other skirmishes. This one had seen his enemies slaughtered, instead of standing victorious at the end. In the back of his mind, he had a feeling, a tingling of his senses, which told him the tide had finally turned against the invaders. The 'vaders were being pushed back all across the city, and with every skirmish the Arabs and Koreans lost, Nate's militia gained more guns, ammo, Intel, food, and enemy uniforms to use in upcoming raids. It felt good to no longer have to hit the enemy fast and then run for their lives. Now, as the commander of the entire Philadelphia resistance movement, he felt like a lion with his pride, devouring a Korean gazelle. The thought made his heart race from the sheer thrill of it.

Nate nodded at his bodyguard. "I gotta say, Robert, I'm pleased at all the land we took back from the invaders today. Half of it is already planted, and the other half has the seeds and gear right here. It'll feed another hundred people if we can figure out the Clan's methods."

Robert smiled. "Maybe we should capture one of their teachers."

Nate laughed out loud. "Yeah, right. That would sure piss them off. New America, too. Besides, I'm not convinced it's in our best interests to ally with either of them when we finish liberating Philly."

Looking at the squad of ISNA soldiers they'd just ambushed in the mostly-open land east of Philadelphia, Robert grinned. At six foot six, he towered over Nate, but it was his intelligence and cunning that made Nate consider him to be such an effective second-in-command. "And to think, two years ago, you were a construction foreman," Robert said.

"And one year ago, we were slaves. What's your point?"

Robert shifted his weight but said nothing.

Nate continued, "Now, we can arm another dozen militia with AKs instead of zip guns and rocks."

"You can't ally with the 'vaders," Robert said out of the blue, frowning. "This is the birthplace of America. It'll piss off George Washington's ghost or something."

"Then let *New America* join *us* if they wish. But right now, the 'vaders have more of what we want. When Philly is liberated, and the East Territory is ours, we'll have something to trade to New America—food. Their general is a pragmatic guy. He'll see the value of an alliance with us. Let him and the 'vader general have a bidding war for our friendship, though, so we get the most we can for our efforts."

Robert shook his head. "Doesn't feel right even talking to the Korean bastards, much less considering an alliance with them."

Nate shrugged and nodded. "Yeah. I get that. But I have to be ruthless and just as pragmatic as they are if we want to survive in the long run, Robert. Trust me. Would I steer you wrong?"

Robert shook his head but didn't reply.

After that, they finished their tour of the land they'd taken in this battle. Nothing was written in stone yet, anyway, so he let the topic drop. But Nate had sworn he'd not only free his people, but one way or another he'd give them a better life, too. Philly and the East Territory had everything he'd need to accomplish that.

He had to finish taking it, first.

* * *

1100 HOURS - ZERO DAY +610

"Come in," Gen. Taggart said. He looked up from his papers to glance at the door, annoyed. When the door opened, he saw that his visitor was Doug Holloway. Oh great, this day was just getting better and better. He forced a plastic smile.

Doug walked in with his usual easy smile and waved at Taggart. "How is your day going, sir?" The man was a reptile, cold-blooded, and his perfectly-performed smile made Taggart's skin crawl.

Taggart needed the man's services, so there was very little to do about the situation. "I'm doing alright, I suppose. To what do I owe the pleasure of your visit this fine morning?"

Doug had a stack of papers in one hand, which he waved in the air as though they were very important.

Taggart was certain it was nothing he wanted to deal with, but such were the burdens of leadership. The way Doug focused on those papers reminded him of old McCarthy videos, and Taggart was certain his day was about to be ruined.

"Sir," Doug said with a pitch-perfect voice, "we've got to discuss these upstart Confederation people."

Taggart decided Doug must practice his lines in front of a mirror. His delivery was camera-ready. Perfect.

Doug continued, "If you want to be able to launch patrols to make travel safe for traders—who come from every region that claims loyalty to New America and beyond, I remind you —then it's imperative that we raise at least a *few* tariffs."

Taggart resisted the urge to sigh. "Doug, the thing is—"

"You and I both know that the cost of providing safety for these people have to be paid somehow," the snake-man interrupted, "but they don't seem to understand the costs and effort required to keep them safe."

Taggart grasped the bridge of his nose with his thumb and forefinger and let out a deep breath. "Doug, do you really think it's best to antagonize these people right now? Things are at a delicate balance with the invaders north of Scranton. This may not be the right time to upset the applecart. Not only that, you've had it fairly easy since the beginning of the war."

"I've seen my share of trouble, sir." Doug sounded righteously indignant, but then again, he sounded that way half the time.

Taggart felt his irritation rising at being interrupted. Fine, it was time to set him straight, Taggart decided. "No, you haven't had your share of trouble. Not really. You can't understand how bad things got. Those people survived and thrived on their own, and it wasn't until late in the game that I provided any support, much less troops."

"But, sir—"

"*Lock it up!* Pay attention. Even the troops I did provide were mostly retired and reservists. The government did *nothing* to help them survive. I hate to tell you this, but they aren't likely to see the need for tariffs, nor any need for our protection. Demanding one to get the other will sound like exactly what it is—a protection racket. Coercion. Hell, extortion."

Doug frowned and his cheeks flushed. His chest seemed to inflate as he wound himself up. "General, if we let this go, it sets a bad precedent. What will happen when the nation recovers and these independence freaks feel they owe us nothing? How can we keep them safe unless everyone pays for that safety?"

Taggart held up his hand. "Stop. Doug, you're a bureaucrat. You're not a survivor, much less a warrior. The survivors out there in the real world have no use for bureaucrats. In fact, they intensely dislike bureaucrats. And you know why that is?"

Doug's cheeks went from pink to bright red, and a vein on his right temple stood out, but he said nothing.

"Because it was bureaucrats like you who let the country fall apart in the first place. People like you knew the invasion was coming and did nothing to stop it because it wasn't politically expedient. You just didn't know how bad it would get."

"But now it's time to rebuild, and—"

"And I hate to tell you this, but the people who survived the Dying Times not only survived without government help, they're the ones who beat the odds. They were smart enough to survive and thrive. They'll see no reason to give that up just to appease a bureaucrat like you. Don't get me wrong, Doug, this new nation truly needs people like you to organize and run it. The day-to-day operations are something I can't manage well. I need men of talent, men who are loyal, if we are to rebuild New America. Men like you."

Doug nodded, and a bit of the rose hue left his cheeks. "Of course I'm happy to serve in any capacity you need, sir. The problem is, I'm telling you what we need, and I don't think you're listening. We can't afford to fight off invaders north and south, plus send aid to Philadelphia, plus defend this Confederation you seem to love so much. The only way to do it is through taxes. We need those to operate a government."

"We haven't needed them so far, have we? Why do we

suddenly need to change everything?"

"It's simple. What we're doing now is fine because we're in early rebuilding, and we're at war. It's expedient. But what about tomorrow, when people expect to get paid for their work, and we need to provide something to replace the dollar? We'll have to print or mint a currency. That will require employees. They'll expect to get paid."

"Doug, we pay them already."

"Right now, we pay them in goods from trade tariffs. Everyone wants to trade with you because it's profitable to do so, but that can't be counted on to last. We have much that they need, but they don't have much that we need. Now is the time to raise tariffs, because now is the time when it won't hurt them much and will help us the most. While the flow of trade is so one-sided, tariffs only lower their profit a bit. I don't think that's too much to ask, and speaking as a so-called bureaucrat, this really feels like simple common sense."

"We aren't going to raise taxes or tariffs. Not yet. This is a conversation that needs to get tabled until after we ratify the new Constitution. Until then, we don't have the authority to tax other groups. Technically, we are no more of a legitimate government than they are. I'm not alienating every ally we have over this issue. Find something else, get creative, do what you have to do, but no tariffs."

Doug clenched his jaw and narrowed his eyes. He gave Taggart one curt nod, then said, "Yes, sir. I think I do understand. There is, however, one more issue that we need to deal with."

Taggart closed his eyes for a second and took a deep breath. Then he opened his eyes, put on a faint smile, and nodded. "Okay, fire when ready, as long as I've got you here."

"Thank you. So, I've sent orders to the Clan to return our two troop battalions. The Clanners sent back a letter—

basically, they refuse. They say the troops have lived among them for a year, many have married into the Confederation, and so they don't want to leave."

"I expected as much. You do remember me saying that when we wrote up the order, right?"

"Of course. The problem is, we're at war. We're under Martial Law. The military has full authority, and that means they need to obey *you*."

Taggart snapped, "The Clan isn't under my authority, not in practice."

"Maybe not the Clan, not yet, but the soldiers themselves have a duty to obey. We need reinforcements against the forces that stand against us in Scranton, or to even have the option of helping resistance groups in Philadelphia. Meanwhile, the Confederation isn't in any danger right now and can easily afford to give up those troops."

"So you feel I should order all of them to return?" Taggart frowned.

"When you speak to them on your little radio, sir, it is my strong recommendation that you instruct them to have our soldiers returned to us. Do what you will with my advice." Doug then turned on his heels and strode out of the office, closing the door quietly behind him as he left.

Taggart let out a long, frustrated breath. "You can come out now."

His office side door opened slowly, and Sgt. Major Eagan poked his head in. "I really don't like that guy, sir."

Taggart understood the sentiment. "Still, he has a couple of valid points. We'll have to raise taxes at some point if the government is to rebuild this country. Not only that, we need those soldiers back."

"Yes, but what are you going to do, send troops to retrieve our troops? Those people spent far more time with the Clan than they ever did in New America. Of course they don't want to leave. You heard what he said about the Clan's letter. Most of them have married into the Confederation. Their families are Confederation citizens."

Taggart nodded. "Regardless of its legality, I'm not about to create tensions with the Confederation right now. If we want to have any chance at success, we need them on our side."

"Cassy's their governor, and I'm pretty sure the whole Confederation would follow her before they follow us."

"When I talk to her again via radio, I think I'll tell them to send back the ones who are willing to go and leave it at that. I'll let them know how much Doug strenuously objected to that, but that I supported their position. Tariffs are coming, but not until after the Constitution is ratified and not where it takes food off their kids' tables."

Eagan nodded. "That ought to keep them happy for the time being, and maybe they'll feel like they owe you another favor for backing their position. Plus, this will give them time to get used to the idea of paying tariffs again, just like the old days."

"Well, not quite like the old days," Taggart said. "It's not going to be as corrupt as the old system, at least not for another two hundred years."

"I don't know about that, sir, not with people like Doug still alive. It's good that we flushed the toilet on the old system, in a way, but I think we need to be vigilant against going back to the old ways."

Taggart could only nod. What else could he say? He agreed. "Summon Choony and Jaz for a meeting. Let them know it's about the trade agreement they're asking for, and give them a heads up on what's coming down from me later. Do your usual thing and subtly suggest to them that we'll need to get very favorable trade rates in the treaty they're asking for. One favor begets another."

Eagan left the room again, and Taggart frowned as he felt the onset of a headache. Running a government was strange and alien to him, and he didn't much like it. His thoughts drifted to the hypothetical upcoming election and how much he would enjoy being able to step down as president—if they could have peace for long enough to hold elections. "It is what it is, I guess," he said bitterly.

The only good point in all of that was the spread of the "New America idea." People for hundreds of miles in all directions were excited about the prospect, and about getting their chance to join up. Philadelphia and New York City were notable exceptions, of course, but they had more immediate problems to worry about. Life and death issues.

That was the reason Taggart had sent so many supplies to Philadelphia's insurgents. If he were being cynical, he mused, then it was also to tie up as many invader troops and resources as possible in fighting the city's growing insurgency. Keeping the two remaining East Coast enclaves in a state of continual native insurrection had prevented them from raiding too heavily into his own territory while he consolidated his hold and built New America's strength.

Maybe it was both, idealism and pragmatism.

Taggart smiled at that thought.

- 3 -

0900 HOURS - ZERO DAY +612

"I HAVE SOME new messages for you to send out," Mark said to the radioman on duty, who leaned back in his office chair with hands behind his head.

The radioman shrugged and sat up. "Let's see what you got."

Mark opened the folder and took out two sheets of paper. He handed them to the radioman and said, "These are for firebases in Louisiana. Orders from the Old Man himself."

The radioman took the papers and glanced them over, seemingly disinterested. He began typing furiously into his computer.

Mark knew that the way the system worked, the message was typed in and the system then delivered it to the intended firebase, using a series of relay towers. It would be encoded before sending, and only the intended recipient could decrypt it. In theory, anyway.

As he typed, the radioman grunted. "You're sure about these orders? Given what's going on down there, it seems kind of risky to send this many troops away east of Firebase Two. Any idea what's going on?"

Mark shook his head. "I think the General intends to throw our enemies off balance. Both orders are for troop movements, from what I understand, and I think it'll get the job done, with that many troops running around."

"Yeah, but it leaves the firebases themselves vulnerable. But who am I to question the General?"

Mark said, "Don't tell me you're one of those people who question him because of our losses in Pennsylvania? You know damn well that wasn't his fault, nor ours. Sometimes, in battle, things just happen. Like the military folks say, 'No plan survives contact with the enemy.'"

The radioman shrugged. "Well, for better or worse, the message has gone out to both bases."

"Thank you. I'll let the General know." Mark retrieved the supposed orders, then turned and walked out the door. He needed a walk, something to clear his mind and shake the fear that had washed over him all morning, ever since he had decided to go through with this plan.

The radioman had been right, of course. Taking so many troops out of the firebases, without even vehicle support anymore, would indeed leave the bases vulnerable. Mark hoped the insurgents were smart enough to take advantage of the small window of opportunity. And because Mark had received actual orders from the General's aide, any blowback would not fall on Mark himself. It didn't matter that he had altered the orders before giving them to the radioman because once General Houle questioned his aide's loyalty, the Commander-in-Chief's rising paranoia would take over.

Mark's nerves were shot. All he really wanted to do was go back to his suite and lie down for a while to let his stomach settle down. Unfortunately, he had to keep up appearances. He couldn't vary from his usual routine. So, instead of lying down, Mark went to the chow hall with his usual morning smile.

He found it difficult to eat scrambled eggs and waffles knowing that, if he were caught, he would likely be executed. There was simply no way he could sit back and let the General destroy what was left of America, however. Stopping a madman sometimes required risks, and it was a risk Mark was willing to take.

* * *

General Taggart heard a knock on the door and looked up from his paperwork. He straightened the papers he had been working on and set them neatly on his desk. "Come in."

The door swung open silently, and Taggart saw Choony and Jaz, responding to his summons. He found it easy to smile at them and had begun to think of them as friends. Unfortunately, today they were on the opposite side of an issue. "Thanks for coming. Have a seat, you two."

The Korean and the blonde-haired beauty smiled in return and padded across the carpet. They sat in the chairs set on the far side of Taggart's desk. Jaz said, "How's tricks, general?"

Taggart snorted. "You do have a way with words, Jaz. Unfortunately, this isn't a social call. You two and I have something important to discuss. It has come to my attention that the Confederation leader is refusing to return all of my troops. Is that so?"

Taggart saw his guests glance at each other. They suddenly looked like they felt quite awkward, and Taggart resisted the urge to smile. Of course, this was no big deal. He had already decided to let any troops stay who wished to. Orders or no, they would refuse to abandon their families, and Taggart knew there was no real way he could make them go—not without effectively declaring war on the Confederation, which was no option. Especially since, as far as he was concerned, he lacked the Constitutional authority to force them to return, despite the former president's declaration of Martial Law right after the EMPs had struck.

Jaz looked wary as she replied, "I'm sorry, sir, but I have been informed that your request is impractical at this time. It will take a while for Cassy to figure out who is willing to go and who's staying."

Taggart smiled. "Well then. I will have to insist that those who are willing to return come back in a timely fashion. Let's say, one month?"

Jaz nodded. "Sure. That seems like a totally reasonable request, but there is still the issue of the ones who don't want to go. What do you have in mind for them?"

"I suppose that depends a lot on how many do come back. Once they are here, I'll know how urgent it will be to get more of them to return. You know, there's always the tension up north in Scranton, what with all the skirmishes with the invaders up there. They've created sort of an Iron Curtain, and it's been hard to get my spies and scouts through the border. What little Intel we do have suggests they are preparing for something, and it makes me nervous that I don't know what. I need to have all my boys and girls back home so we can circle the wagons if the North Koreans come a callin'."

Choony said, "Yes, of course. We'll get as many to come back as we can within a month, but no guarantees on numbers. I guess we'll just have to go from there."

Taggart shrugged. "I do believe that's an issue we can resolve between us. No diplomatic incidents are needed. There's enough going on without us butting heads."

Jaz raised an eyebrow at that dropped hint, but then smiled and said, "I totally agree."

Taggart smiled. "Unfortunately, there's one more thing on my agenda for our meeting this morning."

Choony said, "I assume you mean the issue about the tariffs." His face was a mask, unreadable.

"Yes, that's the one. My secretary of state says tariffs are needed if we're to supply the protection merchants and caravans require. At the same time, the members of the Confederation seem unwilling to help pay for their own defense. What shall we do about that?"

Choony opened his mouth to reply, but Jaz beat him to it. She said, "We do pay for our own defense, stretching from our settlements all the way to your western border. I imagine you would keep your territory safe and free of bandits and invaders whether or not we were shuttling supplies back and forth. Look, trade is only just beginning to really get going. Tariffs are going to kill that trade between New America and the Confederation. That doesn't do anyone any good. You gotta see that, even if your pet bureaucrat Doug doesn't."

Taggart shrugged. "Doug is a real smart boy, and I believe he knows what he's talking about, which is why I made him my SecState. I can veto him, but I'd need a good reason. So, do you have one?"

Choony glanced at Jaz, then leveled his gaze at Taggart. "I believe my companion here just gave you one very good reason, which is that any tariff at this time will kill trade between our two regions. Open trade is vital to the recovery for both of us. I know you asked for a statement of findings regarding a Clan analysis of the effects of a trade tariff. But it doesn't take a data analyst to see that trade is too small and too unstable to start talking about making money off merchants' backs."

Jaz nodded, then added, "Not only that, tariffs are like theft. We deny your Constitutional authority to levy tariffs at this point. That may change when and if we ratify your proposed Constitution, but that won't be until, like, maybe this winter at the soonest. Any discussion about tariffs must be postponed until then."

Taggart frowned. He had expected this, of course. Unfortunately, Doug really had his mind set on establishing tariffs, and Taggart needed Doug for many reasons. Not just to settle the issues of interstate trade, but for the rebuilding process itself. The man was a genius, for a bureaucrat, and sometimes a bureaucrat was the one to hire to get things done at a governmental level. Especially when you had no experience in government yourself, which Taggart had discovered was entirely different from commanding men and women on the battlefield.

He said, "Very well, then. I see that your position is clear, and I can respect that. It puts me in a difficult situation, vis-à-vis Doug's priorities. Nonetheless, I believe I have strong grounds to delay the issue until at least after the winter gathering to discuss the Constitution. But you must understand, by doing this you place yourself somewhat in my debt. I'll expect that debt to be reconciled eventually. I'm no politician, so I'm just telling it to you straight."

"If we are talking straight," Jaz said, "then I have to say, I don't feel we owe you any favors by asking you to protect your own territory."

Taggart thought she made a good point. This was exactly why he hated playing politics. It could tarnish the greatest relationships—as well as good people—and that was the last thing he wanted. He decided to be honest. "I understand your point, and I don't like it either, but it's how things work in government."

Choony bowed his head slightly as if he understood.

"So, do we have a deal?" Taggart said, holding out his hand.

Choony got up and shook it. "Yes."

Taggart smiled. "Very well then. We have an agreement. I'll hold Doug off, and you'll let Cassy know where things stand."

About five minutes after they left his office, Taggart's aide entered and said, "Sir, Doug is here to see you. He seems rather... upset. He says he needs to speak to you immediately."

Taggart let out a frustrated breath. "Very well. Send him in."

As his aide left, Taggart steeled himself for a meeting with Doug. Talking to that bureaucrat was always very irritating, at the least.

Taggart couldn't wait for the elections.

* * *

Ethan sat on his horse's saddle uncomfortably and spent most of his time making sure his mount never sped up faster than a good trot. Over the last year, he had become much better at riding, but the others had spent far more time in the saddle than he had. He was pretty good by prewar standards, but barely adequate by today's.

His mission this afternoon was simple. Lititz had moved their directional Wi-Fi relay station, and now he had to readjust the last relay in the chain to restore a direct connection between the Clan and Lititz.

"How's the garden coming?" Ethan asked John Talbot, the rider next to him. John was his assistant for the task. "Did you ever get around to amending the soil with the lime the way you had wanted?" Ethan knew John had been struggling with his private garden, trying to get several herbs to grow in order to add them to the Clan's vast variety of herbs growing semi-naturally in the food forest.

John gently guided his horse around a large rock, then said, "Yeah, I sure did. It's too soon to tell, but I think I'm going to have good results. I already have a few little green shoots coming up. I know Cassy says they're not native to this region and won't last long, but since we have the seeds, I don't see why we shouldn't plant them."

Ethan chuckled. "Yeah, she's all about the perennials, especially, and whatever annuals will grow in this region year after year. Using up seeds that we could trade instead of growing is a tough sell."

John pointed up ahead. "Hey, I think I see the tower. Hopefully, we can get this done before dinner, and I won't have to eat field rations."

Ethan looked to where John had pointed, and it was indeed the tower they needed. A weird box-like assembly sat atop a tree, the upper portion removed. This allowed the box to sit up high where it could get a clear signal and avoided the need to set up a telephone pole way the hell out here. Boy, that would have been a real chore. They had used telephone poles where necessary, but a tree made a much more efficient option. "Maybe we can get back for evening chow. It depends on how long it takes to realign the box. How's your climbing?"

John frowned. "And here I thought you brought me for my good looks."

"Well, as handsome as you are, I still have to stay down here. Need to monitor the signal strength on both ends so we know when it's set up correctly. And only I know how to read these instruments."

John made a big show of grumbling about his fate when it came time to work, but he always hit his task with speed and intensity.

Life among the Clan was all about getting things done, no matter who was the best choice. They just had to suck it up and do it. Really, it was the reason the Clan was so successful. Frank made it a point to know the skills everyone possessed, and whenever a task came up, he'd make sure the best one for the job was chosen.

John scrambled up the tree, and Ethan heard the chink-chink of his spiked shoe attachments giving him purchase as he climbed. It took him a few minutes to get to the top, and then he called down, "I'm ready when you are, boss."

Ethan opened his laptop, one of the simple new Raspberry Pi computers he'd set up. It took only a minute to get the correct software loaded and honed in on both signals —the one from Lititz, and the one from Clanholme—and saw that the signal strength from Lititz was indeed at zero.

Over the next forty-five minutes, Ethan communicated by radio with his counterpart in Lititz, and between the two of them, they established a Wi-Fi connection to the box atop the tree. Still, signal strength was low, and Ethan decided more work was needed. John would be disappointed, he knew, but it was important to have a solid signal. He called up to John, "Lunchtime. Get your ass down here."

A couple minutes later, John joined him on the forest floor. He walked up to Ethan and said, "Well, I had hoped we'd get out of here faster, but it is what it is. Oh boy, field rations. It reminds me of an old Far Side cartoon, where a dog is standing at his dish, looking up all excited, and the caption says, 'Oh boy! Dog food, again!' You ever see that one?"

Ethan smiled. "Probably. I think I read them all. But I got an MRE and a pemmican bar. What about you?"

John shrugged. "I got an MRE and a peach. I'd rather have the pemmican bar, though. I'm super hungry."

Ethan raised one eyebrow as he looked at John. "You're crazy. I'd so rather have the peach."

"Shoot. I'll trade you."

Ethan nodded. "Here, take it," he said as he held out the pemmican bar.

John eagerly traded with him. "Thanks, man. I always knew you were a peach."

Ethan grinned. "Haha. Very funny. Enjoy your hard fat-and-powdered-meat bar."

"I will," John said, then he took a big bite.

They ate in silence for a little while, then John said, "So what do you think is wrong with the connection?"

Ethan finished chewing, then said, "I have no idea. Maybe there's a tree in the way, between us and Lititz. If we can't get it figured out soon, though, we're going to have to ride out and find the interference."

John groaned. "I sure hope not, because I'd hate to miss dinner—"

John stopped mid-sentence. Ethan looked over at the man and saw he wore a confused expression. Slowly, his face began to turn red.

"Are you choking?" Ethan cried.

John shook his head sharply, then grabbed his throat with both hands. His face continued to turn red, and his eyes started to bulge.

Ethan leaped to his feet and rushed to John's side. If he wasn't choking, then the only other option was an allergic reaction. Ethan reached into his pocket and pulled out an EpiPen, removed the cap, and plunged it into John's leg. Then he stood and took two steps back, waiting for the result. Mouth-to-mouth would be useless if John's air passages were completely closed off from an allergic reaction. It was the EpiPen or nothing.

Two minutes later, John sprawled on the forest floor, dead.

Ethan crouched, rolled the man over, and rested John's head in his lap. "Goddammit," he muttered. "That should've worked."

Then he saw a slight trickle of blood seeping from John's eyes. Ethan opened John's mouth and saw that there was blood in his mouth as well. What the hell could explain that?

Ethan bolted onto his horse and rode hard for Clanholme. When he arrived, his horse frothing and sweaty, he leaped off and left the horse to the stablehand.

He sprinted toward the complex, desperately looking for Lance Corporal Sturm. She had been a paramedic before joining the Marines.

After several minutes of searching and calling out her name, however, Ethan saw her running toward him.

"I heard you were looking for me. What's going on, Ethan?" Sturm asked, breathing heavily.

Ethan managed to say, "It's John Talbot. One of the new Clanners from out west. I think he's dead..."

"Where is he?"

"I'll show you."

Ethan rushed toward the stables, with Sturm following closely behind. They grabbed two new horses and rode fast out of Clanholme. Once at the site, Sturm vaulted from her saddle and scrambled toward John's body. By the time Ethan dismounted, she had her flashlight out and was shining it into John's eyes.

When Ethan caught up with her, Sturm asked, "What happened?"

"I don't know. I gave him my pemmican bar, and when he ate it, he looked like he was choking."

"Maybe it was a peanut allergy?"

Ethan shook his head. "I don't think so. I stuck him with an EpiPen. What about the blood in his eyes? I could guess that an allergy could blister and bleed where it touched his mouth and throat, but his eyes?"

Still crouching, Sturm looked up at Ethan. "Yeah, that doesn't seem very likely, does it?"

"Could he have had a medical condition that nobody knew about? He was pretty new to the Clan, after all."

"I suppose. But I don't think that's very likely. Did he eat the entire bar?"

Ethan glanced around, then saw the remains of the pemmican bar lying in the dirt. "Looks like he only ate about half of it. You think something was wrong with the bar?"

"I don't know," Sturm said, shaking her head. "But I think it's the most likely thing. I guess we need to take the bar in for testing. We'll know more then. In the meantime, I need to get a detail together to retrieve the body. He's one of us now, and deserves the regular funeral."

As Sturm gathered up the bar, Ethan stood staring at John's body. The way the man's eyes stared blankly up at the sky was unnerving. If something was wrong with the bar, then that could just as easily have been Ethan himself. Even as he stared, Ethan thought that perhaps he could see the blood on his face changing, coagulating. It shouldn't yet be coagulating. Something was definitely wrong.

Sturm rode off at full gallop, and Ethan gathered his equipment. It was hard to collect everything with the body lying there, seemingly staring at him. He would have to mess with restoring full signal strength between Clanholme and Lititz later and wasn't looking forward to it. Coming back out here would only remind him of John. For the moment, the weak signal would have to do. Ethan was done working on it for now.

Once he gathered his gear, Ethan packed it on the horse and mounted up. He flicked the reins, and the horse began walking home. He didn't feel like nudging it to go faster, but rather appreciated the long ride home. When he got there, he handed the reins to the stablehand without comment. He walked toward Cassy's house without returning anyone's greetings. He was in a daze, and only wanted to get back down into the safety of his bunker. Only there did he feel safe on a normal day, but this was no ordinary day.

An hour and a half later, one of the handheld radios on

his desk squawked. With a sigh, Ethan got up from the couch and went to the desk to look. He saw that Cassy's radio was blinking, so he clicked on the button and said, "This is Ethan. Say again?"

Cassy's voice came back. "Ethan, come on up. I have some news for you."

Ethan confirmed, then headed through the tunnel that led to Cassy's house. He came up through the stairwell entry and saw Cassy sitting on her living room couch. Her expression was somber, lacking its usual friendliness.

"Sturm ran some tests on that pemmican bar."

Ethan frowned and went to sit down on the recliner opposite the couch. If Cassy was calling him up there to tell him about the results, then they had to be bad. He braced himself, then nodded.

Cassy said, "Sturm crumbled up the pemmican bar and sprinkled it in some food she gave to a couple of rabbits. A couple minutes later, both rabbits were dead."

Ethan's jaw dropped. His mind raced—was someone trying to kill him, or just poison someone in the Clan at random? "Has she told Michael yet?"

Cassy nodded.

"And do they have any ideas?" Ethan said.

Cassy leaned forward and rested her elbows on her knees, steepling her fingers together. She stared at Ethan for a long moment, then said, "You packed that day bag the night before and left it in the gear area, I'm told."

"Right."

"For now, we can't tell whether you were the target or if it was random sabotage. Either way, I'm placing the Clan security forces on high alert, and I need you to be extra careful. If someone is after you in particular, we don't know who it is. I'd rather not give them another chance to take you out."

"I'd prefer they don't get another shot at me, too." Ethan looked up at the ceiling and let out a long breath. Who would be after him? Hard to say. The Clan had a lot of new faces over the last few months. They had accepted a number of refugees, replacing the Clan members who died during the war against the Mountain. They seemed to be integrating well, but any of them could be an agent of either the Empire or the Mountain. Or, they could just be a disgruntled Empire survivor. Ethan had no personal enemies that he knew of, but that didn't mean there wasn't one. Both the Clan and he were in danger now, whether they were after the Clan in general or him in particular.

Elbows still on her knees, Cassy let her hands relax, dangling between her legs. She gave Ethan a half-smile and said, "Don't worry too much, Ethan. Dark Ryder has survived too many clan raids online to be killed by something as ridiculous as a poisoned pemmican bar. Even so, I'm going to have your food tested by rabbits, or goats, or something before I let you eat it. And I'm doubling the guard on the food stores. Meanwhile, you should stay either in the bunker or my office building just outside of Clanholme. The new tunnel addition will let you go back and forth between the two unseen."

Well, this was a fine how-do-you-do. He preferred being in the bunker, but he did not favor being a prisoner in the bunker. "On the bright side, it gets me out of chores." He paused. "That was funnier in my head. Sorry."

Cassy shrugged and said, "Gallows humor is the best sort. What else can you do but laugh? It's better than crying."

Yeah. Better than crying. Not that he would do that. "Well, thanks for filling me in. I guess I'll be in the bunker if you need me," he said, chuckling. It was a forced laugh, though, and even to his own ears, it sounded flat and lifeless.

As Ethan stood, Cassy also stood and walked over to

him. She wrapped her arms around him and embraced him in a hug. "Don't worry, Ethan. I promise we'll get to the bottom of this."

And it couldn't happen too soon, Ethan thought as he headed toward the secret tunnel leading back to his bunker. He doubted he'd get sleep anytime soon.

It was going to be a long night.

- **4** -

1500 HOURS - ZERO DAY +612

"SIR, WE HAVE new activity to worry about," Eagan said as he stepped up to Taggart's desk and set a few sheets of paper down in front of him.

"What are these?" Taggart picked up the sheets of paper and saw that the headers on both sheets were from the Intel department.

Eagan shrugged. Usually, he would have a witty retort, but not today.

Taggart looked at the sheets and skimmed them, getting a sense of what they were about. The first one was a report of increasing violence between fishing boats that belonged to the invaders in North Pennsylvania and the fishing fleet of New America. "Why would they choose now to start picking a fight? The unofficial maritime border has held up just fine all this time, but now they want to pressure us? It doesn't make sense."

"Respectfully, sir, if the general had bothered to read his other Intel reports, he would have seen that our agents have been reporting a very poor fishing season up that way. Some of the spooks have a theory that survivors up in Nova Scotia are fishing them out. If the invaders are catching enough pressure from their north that they have to move south, that doesn't bode well for the peace."

Taggart harrumphed. "And if you had done your job and given me my daily briefing, as I've asked, then I wouldn't need to read all this stuff. I have plenty to do without having to do your job, shitbird."

Eagan grinned. "Sorry, sir. I shall endeavor to do better. Nothing gives me a sense of accomplishment like doing my job and yours, sir."

Taggart's sour face lit up. "Has Intel offered any suggestions as to what we can do about this fishing problem?"

Eagan nodded. "Yeah, they think we should throw some honest-to-goodness warships up that way. As you know, we've been working all winter to refit a couple of destroyers with old-school manual steering, which should make the squids happy. Your other reports, which I'm sure you also didn't read, say that we've worked out the kinks on the fleet. Which is to say, all three ships. Sure, nothing works on them except the guns and the rudders, but it's more than enough to deal with some fishing boats."

"As far as our spies report, the North Pennsylvania invaders don't have any warships."

"We lucked out because apparently, they had been ordered to harbors near New York City just prior to the invasion. They were out of commission after the counter-EMPs, and the invaders either didn't bother to scuttle them or didn't know where they'd been moved to. Either way, they all still work. Well, they still float."

"That is their basic mission, more or less," Taggart said. "Very well, then. Go ahead and order two boats up north. I want to keep at least one here, just in case we need it."

Eagan grinned and raised his eyebrow. Taggart had a

suspicion that maybe he should have read the other report before ordering some boats north. Eagan was never subtle.

"What now?" Taggart asked.

"The second report has to do with the Maryland invaders, sir. Ironic, huh? It seems they're beginning to put some pressure on the Confederation's southern border. Not only that, but it seems like they're being pushed back throughout Philadelphia. The Philly resistance has become suddenly much more effective over the last two months. Intel suspects they've finally been unified, or somewhat unified under a single leader."

"This could be a good opportunity for us, or it could become a major problem. It depends on what their new leader—if that's what's going on—decides to do in regards to their relations with New America."

Eagan shrugged and said, "We've been supplying them with arms and food for quite a while, so we should expect their loyalty, but you know how it is with rebels."

Taggart slowly nodded. "Nothing but a bunch of opportunists, usually."

Eagan said, "I guess it's a good thing that you didn't send all three boats up north. If Philly gets rambunctious, we may need it."

Taggart tapped one finger on his desk, thinking. Maybe they were viewing the problem the wrong way. "You know, Philly has all that good land just east of them on the peninsula. If they can get their shit together, they could be a perfect ally. Maybe even a new state within New America."

Eagan nodded. "I had thought the same thing. Maybe it would be a good idea to send a representative down there."

Taggart considered this new information. Yes, that would be a good idea, assuming their new leader was friendly. If he turned out to be just a glorified bandit, as so many resistance fighters had been, Taggart would be sending the representative into a hostile situation with no Intel. Sending an envoy couldn't be avoided, though.

"Yes, make it so," Taggart said. "And by the way, don't let our Clanner friends find out about this. The Confederation is entirely too good at this whole politics thing, so let's keep them out of it."

* * *

1900 HOURS - ZERO DAY +612

Down in the bunker, Ethan had just shut down his computer system when he heard a faint knock at the door. He spun in his office chair, a big grin on his face, expecting to see Amber. Instead, he saw Michael leaning against the doorway, arms crossed. "Oh sorry, I wasn't expecting you. Everything okay?"

Michael shook his head and heaved himself up from leaning on the doorframe. "Nope. Lucky for you, nothing's going on. I just thought you might like to come up and get some air, maybe join me for dinner."

Ethan tilted his head, frowning slightly. "Sure. I don't mean to look surprised, but you don't usually come down here, much less invite me up for dinner. You sure nothing's going on?"

Michael laughed out loud, then said, "Yes, I'm sure. It's just that, ever since the incident with the pemmican bar, you've been a hermit. It's not healthy for you to stay down here so much."

Ethan shrugged and said, "Perhaps. It might also be unhealthy for me to go up topside. You know what I mean?"

Michael turned his back to the doorframe and leaned against it once again, still looking at Ethan. "Sure, but you can't live your life in fear. Besides, we're not even sure that was an attempt on you. For all we know, it just got tainted with botulism. That happens sometimes, without refrigeration and all."

Ethan shook his head. There was no way that's what had happened. There were just too many coincidences. He also wondered why Michael suddenly found it so urgent to get him up topside. Or was that just his paranoia talking? Maybe Michael was right. Really, how long could he stay down there in the bunker? He had to go up sometime. "Well, I'll tell you what. If you go with me from here to the chow hall, I guess I'll take the chance. I'll just feel better having you with me."

Michael grinned and said, "This is coming from the guy who charged a machine gun nest before we ever got to Clanholme, the guy who saved all of us when we were pinned down."

"Charging that nest was just what it took for me to survive, along with everyone else. It's easy to be brave when you have no other choice."

Ethan saw Michael frown, but he quickly recovered. "Of course," Michael said, "I'll walk with you." Michael tossed his head to motion toward the entrance.

Ethan got up, straightened his tee shirt, and brushed off his trousers. "Okay, let's go. I was just thinking about getting some food anyway, and I could use the company. We haven't really talked much lately since we're all so busy."

The former Marine—now the Confederation general and Clanholme's defensive coordinator—stood straight and turned toward the door. Ethan wondered what had caught him off-guard.

They walked through the bunker together in an easy silence, and when they got to the ladder leading into Cassy's house, Michael motioned for Ethan to go first. A polite gesture.

Ethan smiled in thanks and climbed up, emerging in the

house from under the stairwell. The stairs were hinged and well-balanced, so when he pushed up from underneath, the whole assembly pivoted upward to allow them to exit the tunnel. "Do you know what's on the menu for tonight?" Ethan asked.

Michael glanced around, probably looking for Cassy, but no one was in the house. He shrugged. "I'm not sure. I know that a cow got caught up in barbed wire and ended up dying, so it's probably something to do with beef. It's the first cow we lost that way, but I still asked Dean to redneck-engineer a solution to make sure it doesn't happen again. He said it wasn't possible, but I figure he'll have an answer in a week."

Ethan nodded. If anyone could figure out an easy solution with the resources they had on hand, it would be Dean. The man was a genius with scraps. "I hope it's beef. I could use a steak," Ethan said.

Michael opened the front door and began to walk out, then held it open for Ethan. Together, they walked across "the courtyard," which was the open area between the house and the chow hall, and Ethan could already smell the mouthwatering aroma of cooking meat. They didn't often have beef, or at least, not steaks. It wasn't a very efficient way of serving up such a limited resource. Usually, meat went into the stew, sausages, and pemmican bars. Next year, they'd have many more cows and a lot more steaks.

On the way to the chow hall, they passed what Ethan assumed was a donkey. He couldn't tell for sure, being raised in a city. He knew what a cow looked like, but that was the extent of his animal husbandry skills. "When did we get a donkey?"

"What?"

"A donkey," Ethan repeated. "Don't you need a mule and a horse to make a donkey? I didn't know we had a mule."

Michael laughed and jabbed him in the arm with his

elbow. "No, you idiot. You need a horse and a donkey to make a mule. That one belongs to a visiting merchant, I think from the Free Republic."

"So is that one a mule or a—"

The mule's head exploded, showering Michael and Ethan with blood, brains, and bits of bone; a cloud of pink mist hung in the air. Ethan stopped and stared at the donkey as it toppled over, seemingly in slow-motion. Since when did donkeys have exploding heads? His mind couldn't make sense of what he was seeing.

Michael lunged at Ethan, tackling him around the waist. The big man's movements were so quick that Ethan had no time to react. It felt like he'd been hit by a truck, and he and Michael toppled to the ground.

Ethan heard a ringing in his ears, which he assumed was from the blow, but over the ringing, he could hear Michael's voice. It sounded faint and far away, but he could understand the words.

"Sniper! Get to cover, now!" Michael shouted. Although Michael's face was almost next to Ethan's, he still sounded distant.

Ethan scrambled to his hands and knees and scurried toward the first cover he saw—the chow hall, some 20 feet away.

He felt someone grab him by the shirt collar and his belt, heaving him to his feet like a ragdoll.

"Run, goddammit, to the house." Michael was half-dragging Ethan toward Cassy's house, which was actually the closest cover, Ethan realized through his fog of confusion.

Halfway there, his mind seemed to catch up suddenly, and he could have just kicked himself for trying to head to the chow hall. Apparently, his mind had been in Code Yellow, that space where you see things but you aren't thinking, aren't aware of your surroundings. Otherwise, he would have known to head toward Cassy's house, which was both closer and bulletproof. With each step, Ethan expected his own head to explode if there was a sniper. He and Michael were running across open ground. However, to his surprise, they both made it to Cassy's house, and Ethan slammed back-first against the wall, panting heavily.

"Thanks," Ethan said to Michael. The man had just saved his life. Again.

Michael didn't seem to be out of breath in spite of running and his obvious level of adrenaline. His head was in quick, constant motion, looking all around for the source of the bullet that had demolished the donkey. Or mule.

"Yeah, don't thank me yet. There's a sniper out there somewhere, and I suspect that was a fifty-caliber rifle round." Safe for the moment behind cover, Michael unclipped the small radio at his belt and clicked the button. "All units, all units, we're taking fire by the chow hall. Probably a fitty-cal. The only line of sight is southeast, all units scramble and engage. Eliminate any tangos found, and ask questions later. Better to receive a wrist slap than a bullet."

Ethan managed to catch his breath as he listened to the various units radio back to Michael their understanding. Then he said, "Still think that pemmican bar was random?"

"No," Michael said. "Someone's definitely trying to kill you."

- 5 -

0700 HOURS - ZERO DAY +613

CHOONY AND JAZ wandered in the early morning market, shopping for their day's food. There were many wagons set up throughout the Hackensack market space, impromptu vendor stalls hawking wares ranging from eggs to bullets, and Jaz often made a point to talk to as many of them as possible. They were the face of the Confederation, or at least of the Clan, and it was their responsibility to make sure relations stayed warm with these independent traders. Many of them became wandering merchants during the off-season, trading off the many wares they had taken in as payment during the spring agricultural season. It would be handy to have them stop by Clanholme.

Jaz stopped at one wagon that displayed myriad handcrafted jewelry. Necklaces, earrings, and bracelets dominated their inventory. However, it was a collection of bands that seemed to catch Jaz's eye. "Hey Choon," Jaz said, "look at this. It's tungsten, I think. Pretty much indestructible, just like us."

Choony looked at the bands Jaz was referring to. "It's

nice, but I don't think you can weld four of those into brass knuckles."

Jaz laughed. "Oh come on," she said, "don't you want to make an honest woman of me. Being a harlot upsets my Zen or Chi, or whatever it's called." She held up one of the black rings, each with a thin gold-inlaid line running around the circumference, analyzing it.

"You are already the most honest woman I know, and you're not a harlot."

"You know, tungsten is the hardest material used for jewelry," Jaz said, "so you may be on to something with the brass knuckles. I could wear four of them, one on each finger and then..." She glanced over his shoulder, and her face went rigid for a microsecond. He recognized the expression, having seen it often enough. Something had grabbed her attention and set off her warning alarms. It was exceedingly difficult not to turn around and see what she had looked at.

As she held the bands up as though to show them to Choony, she smiled and said, "I see two men standing at the wagon that sells pemmican bars and other durable foods, you know the one. They seem to have an unhealthy interest in us. One has a rifle, and I think I see a pistol under the other's coat."

Choony nodded and leaned forward, pretending to examine the rings. "Is their body language telling you they are up to no good? Perhaps they appear angry, or secretive?" Even here in eastern New America, there were many people with anti-Clan sentiments, mostly the refugees from the former Empire. It paid to be alert, especially if one wore the distinctive clanmark as he and Jaz did. Most Clanners did these days. Both he and Jaz had their clanmarks on display today, visible on their arms. The benefits outweighed the occasional setback they caused.

Still smiling, Jaz said, "No, they seem pretty open about it, actually. I'm not getting that threatening vibe. I don't think they'll start any trouble here in the middle of the New America capital. Hackensack seems well-policed, don't you think?"

Choony considered their situation. She was right about Hackensack being a fairly safe place, at least on the main path through the market, by modern standards. "Perhaps we should show our hands, let them see what cards we're holding. Let's go talk to them."

Jaz got a mischievous grin, then. She set the rings back down on the wagon counter and said, "After you, oh fearless leader."

He spun on his heels and walked directly toward the two men, who still stood at the wagon Jaz had pointed out. He kept his pace to what he thought would be neither aggressive nor timid. He crossed the open space between the two wagons, Jaz right behind him, and stopped about ten feet from the men.

Before he could say anything, Jaz beat him to it, saying, "Good morning, gentlemen. I see we have your attention, but I'm curious, is it my ass you're looking at, or our clanmarks?"

Choony tried hard not to frown. Of course, Jaz would begin the conversation like that, scandalous and aggressive like the woman herself. He glanced at the two men, but to his relief, they were smiling. At least they had taken Jaz's comments in the spirit she intended.

The shorter man wore his goatee in two long, woven braids like some sort of modern Viking, and was the first to speak. "Sorry to disappoint you, honey, but it was the tattoos."

Choony immediately thought of the trouble they'd had in Harrisburg due to their clanmarks and said, "I hope there is no problem."

Viking shook his head. "Naw. They're pretty cool. I'm always on the lookout for a cool new design. You can't see them under my overcoat, but I got full sleeves on both arms."

Choony cocked his head. Full sleeves? He got the impression that didn't mean what he thought it did.

Jaz seemed to understand, though, because she grinned. "Well, they're totally just for the Clan, but thanks. I dig them, too. So what are you two dudes doing in the market at this time of morning?"

The shorter man shrugged. "Same as you, I imagine. Getting breakfast." Then he paused, looking back and forth between Choony and Jaz's arms. "You know, at first, I thought your tattoos were identical, but up close I see they're a little different."

Choony took the opportunity to interject himself further into the conversation. "They are both very symbolic and personal. The crescent moon on top represents the scar our leader has running down her face. It's a symbol of adversity and triumph, and a copy of the one she used to highlight her scar."

As Choony paused, Jaz cut in saying, "Yeah, that's Cassy. She's pretty much a legend in those parts. And then the stuff below and around the crescent moon is done in the same style for every Clan member, but each one is different. Something personal for each Clanner."

The short man smiled and nodded. "Every tattoo should be unique and personal. So what do yours mean?" He glanced back and forth between Jaz and Choony.

"They are all done in Celtic knotwork style," Choony said, "with mine, if you look at it a little bit sideways like one of those find-the-sailboat pictures, you'll see that it's basically an abstract Buddha figure. I'm the Clan's token Buddhist."

"A Buddhist, you say?" Viking said. "I don't think I've ever met a Buddhist before."

"At least not in today's world," the short man said. He turned to Jaz. "So, what does yours mean?"

She replied, "Mine is a stylized Phoenix. The old one dies, but a new one rises even stronger than before."

The short man nodded slowly, as though weighing her words. "I imagine that's true. Then again, in a way, we are all like a phoenix since the EMPs."

"True," Jaz said. "So now that we offered some information about ourselves, what about you? Who are you guys?"

"Where are my manners?" the short man said. "Allow me to introduce myself. I'm Squirrel, and my friend here is Lance. We're traders from Philadelphia."

The larger man blatantly elbowed the shorter, who then hastily added, "I mean New Philadelphia. I was leaning toward Free Philly, but I was outvoted."

Choony glanced at Jaz and saw her glancing at him as well. That was brand-new news. He'd have to include that in his next report home. Given the rumors about the Maryland invaders mobilizing, that could be very good news indeed. He said, "How interesting. When did that happen? Clearly, that makes us natural allies."

The short man stuck his hands in his pockets, and Choony got the sense that his words may have rubbed the man the wrong way.

"You'd think so, right? But the Dude is keeping Philly's options open. The rumor mill says he is negotiating for trade with NewAm. Personally, I'd rather trade with your people, from everything I've heard about it, although you're the first two people I've met from the Confederation, much less the Clan."

Choony nodded slowly, the man's words echoing through his mind. Perhaps this was an opportunity. Cassy had given them the authority to negotiate in the name of the

Confederation, and Frank had done likewise for the Clan. This seemed like a once-in-a-lifetime opportunity. As his mind churned, Jaz bought some time by asking the shorter man, "So, like, who is this 'Dude'? Seems like a rather odd name."

Squirrel grinned wide at that, an apparently spontaneous, genuinely pleased expression. "May seem like an odd name, but he earned it. His real name's Nate Runke. Before the EMPs, he was the Neighborhood Watch captain for his neighborhood. During the Dying Time, he made hard choices and led us well, and as a result, only half of his people starved that first winter. A few other neighborhoods completely died out, between starvation and killing each other, but under the Dude's leadership, we stayed strong. He began raiding the invaders even in those early days, and with every raid, his people became better armed and equipped."

Lance, the other man, added, "Then, when a lot of the other bosses wanted to collaborate with the invaders, the Dude refused. He went so far as to send assassins after the ones doing the most collaborating with them. A lot of traitor commanders died gruesomely in those early days, and it motivated the rest to at least think twice before welcoming the 'vaders with open arms."

Jaz said, "Well, I can totally respect that. Your Dude sounds like a capable leader. I can see why you give him such loyalty, but if you are from New Philly, then what really brings you to New America's capital? Negotiating trade? Maybe a treaty?"

Squirrel chuckled. "You can't pick my brain that easily, miss. I applaud the effort, though. But whatever our main purpose for being here is, it would be easy to add something to our agenda. Who would we talk to if we wanted to deal with the Clan?"

Choony performed a bow. "May I present to you two of

Cassy's personal envoys. How do you two like the idea of meeting up for lunch?"

"Yeah," Jaz said. "We know a great place that's still serving real beer and whiskey from, like, before the war and everything. It'll be a lot hotter then, so I totally hope you're not offended by shorts and tanktops."

Lance was the first to agree, nodding his head with a wry grin on his face. "We'd both be delighted to meet you for lunch. There's a lot we need to talk about, and you just dress however you're comfortable."

"Fantastic," Choony said, putting as much enthusiasm into his voice as he could, "then we'll all meet back here about a quarter after noon?"

They shook hands all around, and then Choony and Jaz walked away.

"That's right, that's right, we bad. Who's the man? You the man," she said, jabbing a finger into Choony's ribs playfully.

"Ow, Jaz, that hurts," Choony said.

Jaz just laughed.

"But seriously, we should ask around about those two and try to learn as much as we can before the meeting. We might learn something important."

Jaz nodded. "You're right. You still the man," she said with a smirk.

Choony smiled and shook his head.

* * *

1145 HOURS - ZERO DAY +613

Jaz walked with Choony through the midday heat, heading toward the meeting spot they'd agreed upon with Squirrel and Lance. As they entered, she saw that the market was as busy as ever despite the rising temperature. It wasn't yet the hottest part of the day, but the market would remain busy no matter how hot it got.

"It's too bad nobody really knows these two," Jaz said.

Choony had to stop as a man crossed his path pushing a cart laden with a combination of fruit on one half and what looked like sun-dried fish on the other. She didn't notice right away. As she waited for Choony to catch up, she wrinkled her nose at the thought of eating sun-dried fish, and of having fish so close to all that fruit.

When Choony caught up, he said, "Then let's go over what we do know about them."

"Well, we know that they are two men from Philadelphia, claiming to represent those now in charge there," Jaz said. "And that's about it."

"Except that they have been here only since yesterday, and they've made a few deals in that time. That tends to support their story."

Jaz was about to reply with something totally witty, when Choony pointed up ahead and said, "There they are."

She looked where he pointed and saw Squirrel and Lance as they rummaged through a merchant's bin of spare parts. She had half-expected Lance to have dressed up for their lunch meeting, just as she had done, but as far as she could tell, he hadn't even done his hair. She hoped that wasn't a bad sign for the meeting to come. Either he didn't know how scruffy he looked, or he didn't care. If it was the latter, then it could be because he didn't expect anything to come from this lunch meeting.

They approached the two men, and Jaz put on her most winning smile as they came to a stop near them. She was trying to win them over with a bit of her womanly charm, hoping it would sway them in her favor. She placed her hands behind her back and stood on her tippie toes. For some reason, dudes always loved it when she did that.

Squirrel and Lance smiled as they turned, Lance smiling bigger at the sight of Jaz, while Squirrel reached out to shake Choony's hand. "I see you two made it. Jaz, you weren't kidding about how hot it would be. I see you dressed for the weather. I wish I'd been smart enough to do the same."

Lance nodded and, tearing his gaze from Jaz, also shook hands with Choony. "I hope you're right about that restaurant because I could use a real beer. I haven't had one in six months."

A slight gust of wind, smelling of dirt and fish, blew a lock of hair from behind her ear and into her face. She scrunched up her face and looked up, her eyes crossing as she tried to see the hair. She tucked it back out of the way and grinned at Lance.

Lance chuckled and then began to look around. "So, where is this place?"

Choony made a slight bow, a habit Jaz was now used to, and said, "It's about two blocks north. Shall we go?"

Squirrel nodded. "Lead the way."

They walked toward the restaurant and two blocks later, came to a cluster of buildings. The restaurant had no sign out front, other than the pre-war one that still hung outside proclaiming it to be Finnegan's Bar, 'purveyor of fine Irish whiskey.' Jaz knew that had nothing to do with what they served these days, nor was the owner named Finnegan.

"Here we are," Jaz said. "Real food and real beer."

Once inside, Jaz led the way between a few tables already occupied by people, their chatter filling the large, poorly-lit room. Near the back of the room, tucked away in a corner, she found a booth with benches on one side and two chairs on the other, a large table in the middle. It would easily seat them all and be far enough from where most of the patrons were congregated.

Lance pulled out one of the chairs and smiled at Jaz, offering her the seat. She gave him what she hoped was a coy smile and then sat in the offered chair, which Lance then scooted in for her.

"What a gentleman," she said.

Lance took the chair next to hers, while Choony and Squirrel sat on the bench opposite them.

They made small talk for several minutes as they looked over the handwritten menus which contained only a few options, such as various combinations of rice, beans, vegetables, and meat, which Jaz figured was either rat or dog. They also had beer—most likely a rebottled homebrew—as well as juice, which she knew Choony would order.

After a few minutes, an older woman stopped by the table and took their orders. After the woman left, they chatted easily back and forth about what things were like in their respective hometowns, how Philly was doing, and the various rumors they had each heard while in Hackensack. No one even addressed the issue of trade between Philadelphia and the Clan, for which Jaz was grateful. She preferred to have food on the table and a drink in her belly before beginning anything real. It gave her something to focus on if she felt uncomfortable, so it made a nice distraction.

Once the food and drinks arrived, Lance was the first to speak. "This looks really good," he said. "We have nothing like it in Philly. Hell, people are still lucky not to starve to death, there."

Choony nodded slowly and said, "That's terrible. In most places, the Dying Times are over. Isn't there a whole bunch of open land just east of the city?"

Squirrel replied, "Yeah, the 'Eastern Territory.'"

"Do you do any farming there?"

"Some. But so do the invaders who still remain in town."

Lance said, "Before, it was all controlled by the invaders.

We fought over control of the farming communes they put in place through slave labor. We've gained control of a lot of those communes, but with the disruptions of war, many necessary tasks have been left undone—"

"You're damn right they're going unfinished," Squirrel said, cutting Lance off. "Who has time to worry about weeds when the invaders are killing our children?"

Lance ignored Squirrel's little outburst and continued, "Things like transporting the food back to the city have also become a big problem since all of it has to be done by manpower alone. We don't even have any beasts of burden because they were all eaten over the winter or the year before that."

Squirrel let out a long, deep breath. "The elderly and the children, of course, were the first to die. They're still dying, mostly from starvation and disease. Without enough food, and with all the stress of living in a war zone, their immune systems just can't keep up. Kids are dying of diseases most people didn't even know still existed. Cholera. Typhoid. All preventable if we only had time to try to get the sanitation system working again."

There was an awkward moment of silence that stretched on and on. Squirrel and Lance seemed lost in thought, while Choony seemed at a loss for words.

Jaz took a sip of her beer. Finally, she interrupted the silence. "So you would say that starvation and disease is Philly's number one cause of death, right?"

"Yes, of course," Squirrel said.

"What if I told you the Clan has methods for dealing with such problems?"

Squirrel and Lance looked at each other for a brief moment. Then Squirrel said, "Let me just stop you right there so you understand that we are aware of our value to New America. We would make a perfect buffer state between the invaders in Maryland and your New America, would we not?"

Dammit, Jaz thought. These men were smarter than she had anticipated.

"That's true," Choony said, "But most are under the notion that since the Confederation has a governor and is technically part of New America, that we're not autonomous. Our function here is to negotiate for the Confederation— more specifically the Clan—not New America. Besides, Philadelphia's position as a buffer holds more value to New America than it would the Clan. Just hear us out first."

Squirrel leaned back in his seat and crossed his arms. "Fine, go on," he said, still seeming unconvinced.

Jaz continued where she left off, "We have the knowledge of new farming techniques that work in today's world. These techniques far surpass the old world ways."

Choony added, "If you try to farm the old way, the pre-war way, you'll burn your soil quickly. In a year, you'll have nothing but weeds."

Jaz cut in, "With our methods, you could not only feed your people, but it will also solve your sanitation and disease problem."

Lance seemed more than intrigued. He sat listening intently, leaning in. Jaz noted he hadn't even taken a bite of his food since the discussion turned to what the Clan had to offer. Finally, he broke his trance and said, "How?"

"Well," Jaz said, "I can't just be giving away, like, all our secrets, now can I? What I can offer is a trained consultant to come out and teach your people our methods." Jaz took a dramatic pause that she had mastered in the days of being a persuasive envoy. She traced the rim of her cup with her finger, then said, "Of course, such consulting would come at a price."

"Of course it would," Squirrel said, "but right now we

don't have enough supplies to go around. I don't see what we could even offer in return."

Choony said, "I guess it depends on how close of a friendship Philadelphia wants to have with the Confederation."

"I'm not even sure what that means," Squirrel said, eyeing both Choony and Jaz suspiciously.

Jaz smiled. "I think what my partner is trying to say is, like, perhaps we can set up a short-term loan—feed your people now until you start producing."

"No way," Squirrel said, "I have survived this new world long enough to know that everything comes with a hefty price. You basically said so yourself. Even an innocent loan comes with a mountain of interest."

"Squirrel, you misunderstand—"

"Darling, I don't think I do. You may have the wool pulled over my friend's eyes with your little daisy dukes, but it'll take a lot more than some skimpy outfit to dupe me."

Jaz's eyes went wide. She hadn't expected this reaction. She looked over at Choony and noticed his body language appeared to be calm and carefree, but she knew him well enough to see his telltale signs of stress.

"My understanding," Choony said, "is that you still have people who are hungry and dying. You won't find an offer like this anywhere else."

"Absolutely," Lance said with a smile, "but our leader will have to look at any offer's totality of circumstances before deciding which way to go, north or south."

Choony furrowed his brow. "South?"

"Oh, did I forget to mention," Squirrel said, unfolding his arms, "we're also negotiating with the Maryland invaders. My apologies."

Damn, these guys were really good, Jaz thought, excitement welling up in her chest.

Choony looked horrified. "Are you saying that your

leader is actually considering a deal with the very people who caused you all so much pain and loss?"

Lance shrugged. "Tough times call for tough measures."

"But why would you even consider talking to them?" Choony said.

"I think it's obvious," Lance said.

Choony and Jaz remained quiet. Jaz just couldn't see the obviousness or the benefits of being allies with the invaders.

Lance simply answered, "Loyalty."

"Loyalty?" Jaz asked.

Squirrel smiled condescendingly. "When we negotiate our official freedom and our border with the invaders—because no one wants a long, drawn-out war, especially over something as arbitrary as a border—then our loyalty and an alliance is a powerful bargaining chip."

"That totally sounds weak to me," Jaz said.

"If the only way to end the war for us is basically to swear fealty to them, like some medieval baron, then that's a powerful motivation to do it."

"Don't you think as Americans we should be resisting the invaders?" Jaz asked.

Squirrel stifled a chuckle. "Sweetheart, I hate to be the one to inform you, but there is no America anymore."

Sweetheart? Jaz thought. Now, this guy was just asking to be slugged. "I think you're wrong. There is an America. Travel anywhere around here, and you'll see it."

"If your people are so patriotic," Squirrel said, "then let me ask you something. The president of New America is an active duty soldier. Is that right?"

Jaz glared at Squirrel and held it as if not to back down. She had a feeling she knew where he was going with this, but she couldn't show any signs of weakness now.

Squirrel didn't wait long for her to answer. He leaned in close, almost in Jaz's face, and said, "Last time I checked, it was unconstitutional for an active duty military person to serve as president. For another, the only people who voted General Taggart into office were the very people relying on him directly for their food and protection." Squirrel leaned back. "That would make him... oh, what's the word," he said, snapping his fingers, "a warlord, not a president. So I wouldn't say either of us are saints of America."

Silence hung in the air for a moment as Jaz tried to collect her thoughts. She almost couldn't help but admire the guy. He had done his homework. But how the hell was she going to convince him to, at the very least, consider a deal with the Confederation?

Choony looked at Jaz and then diverted his gaze back to the two Philly envoys. "True," he said, "but did you know there is a new Constitution on the table being debated as we speak?"

Neither Squirrel nor Lance responded. Good, it was their turn to be silent. Jaz almost forgot about the constitution. Now, where was Choony going with this?

Choony continued, "It seems to me that you would benefit from being a part of those proceedings. Your concerns lie in that we might just take what we want from you and then leave you and your people, how you say, high and dry."

"What are you saying?" Lance said.

"What I am saying is that your leader could select someone, including himself, to be the governor of Philadelphia Territory."

Jaz wondered why she hadn't thought of that. Thank you, Choony. It was totally brilliant. Jaz said, "Ultimately, that would mean Philadelphia could ensure its needs get met and its concerns are addressed through this constitution."

Lance perked up. "That is definitely something to consider. We could recommend sending an envoy to

Clanholme to work on the agreement with your representatives there."

Squirrel interjected, "Hold up. What's the bottom line here? How would you expect us to pay the loan?"

"Obviously there are many details to work out," Choony said, "but I suppose a percentage of your agricultural production could be one way."

Squirrel was quick to reply, "That's if your allegedly superior agricultural methods begin to produce."

"Of course," Choony said.

"Though, either way," Lance said, "we don't make the decisions."

Squirrel nodded. "My partner here is right. Our leader does what he has to do in the here and now so we can survive long enough to even have long-term goals. His only focus is what is best for Philadelphia, whether that means an alliance with New America, the Clan, or Maryland. Our job is just to gather the information and send it back to him so he can make the final decisions."

Jaz and Choony both nodded in unison. They understood all too well the men's job description. Their leader, as ruthless as he may sound, was likely just as pragmatic as Cassy herself. How could they argue?

"Though," Lance said, "anything you can do to help us convince him that an alliance with the Clan or the Confederation is a good idea, we would sure appreciate." He grinned and gave a quick wink at Jaz.

Jaz knew that charm all too well. She used it all the time. In fact, she'd practically invented it, but the harm usually was in not playing along. She figured he wanted to sweeten the deal if at all possible. She understood and had a good idea of what she could offer to hook them.

Jaz smiled back at Lance and leaned forward, lowering her voice, "The Clan does have access to much more we can offer."

Lance leaned in, meeting her gaze. "Like what?"

"For starters, we could certainly spare a number of MilGrade weapons." She raised her eyebrows. "We've also figured out how to get cars running again. Boy, those trucks would be awfully helpful in your new farms, wouldn't they?"

Jaz saw a glimmer in both men's eyes. She continued, "I wonder whether the Maryland invaders are going to give you an armory and a fleet of working trucks."

Eyes big, Lance came out of their little huddle. "Well, I guess that could sway my leader's decision in your favor a bit. I need to jot this down in my report. Believe me, I would much rather be allies with Americans than with Koreans."

Jaz grinned. "I totally understand."

"Listen, here's how I see it," Squirrel said. "Sounds like the Confederation has plenty to offer in terms of a deal. I'll be honest in saying that I am interested in going over the finer details so my partner and I can write up a full report to send back to our leader. As I said before, he makes the final decision."

Jaz was elated. Hook, line, and sinker.

Lance nodded and pushed back his chair. "Sound like a plan to me." He turned to Jaz. "Well, perhaps the lovely Jaz and I could wander the market, and she can show me the sites. Squirrel and I are new here, after all, and all those details just aren't my forte."

Squirrel rolled his eyes as Lance got up.

"Shall we?" Lance asked Jaz.

Jaz didn't really want to show him around—she wanted to stick around during the overview of the smaller details. But she knew she should play along.

She rose from her chair and followed Lance to the door. She sensed this could actually be some sort of trick to separate Choony and herself but thought better of it. Lance was kind of a bozo, yet she couldn't help but respect both men. They were tough, smart, and reminded her of the good people who made up Clanholme.

As Jaz headed for the door just behind Lance, Squirrel said, "Jaz."

Jaz turned around. What, no 'darling' or 'sweetheart' this time? she thought.

Squirrel got up and approached her. "You're a good negotiator. Tougher than I expected. I respect that." He put out his hand to shake hers.

Yes, her intuition was right—these were respectable men. She smiled and gave him a firm handshake.

- **6** -

MARK ENTERED THE office and walked across the room, which had four desks with a computer on each, although only one seat was currently occupied. Behind one of the desks sat a woman in her thirties with long blonde hair.

"Janice," Mark said, reaching his hand out to shake hers.

Janice stopped typing and turned to face him. She smiled and shook Mark's hand firmly, making steady eye contact. "Hi, Mr. Bates. Nice to finally meet you in person."

"Please, call me Mark."

He dragged a nearby office chair over to her desk and sat down. He leaned back in his chair and smiled. His practiced eyes made him reasonably certain the information in the dossier had been correct. She had risen through the ranks on talent and drive—a woman he could respect.

Although she had spent her teen years in Colorado before joining the Army in Signals Intelligence, her family was from Louisiana. They were still down there if they were still among the living. She had reason to dislike General Houle's policies and tactics down there along the Gulf Coast. One of Mark's cell leaders had tagged her as a possible recruit.

"I have that report you asked for, Mark," Janice said. She reached down beside her desk and withdrew a folder, which she then slid across the desk toward him. "There were certain irregularities with the information request write up, but I guess at your rank, protocol is optional."

He nodded and slid the folder across the wooden desk, but didn't pick it up yet. Now was the time to get to know his latest potential recruit.

"So, you're originally from Louisiana?" he asked.

"Yeah," Janice said, her gaze shifting down and to her right. She stared blankly for a moment before continuing, "I have family there."

"Have you heard from them?"

Janice sat silently.

Mark continued, "Surely you've turned in a contact request form. I'm sure we have enough assets down there to make contact."

She said, "I imagine our troops down there have more important things to do than to look for one mid-level analyst's wayward family."

"Perhaps."

"Besides, Louisiana is a big place, and my family has always been hard to find. That was true even before the war."

Mark nodded. "I'm sure the troops will keep trying," he said, hoping to reassure her. The pain was written on her face, at least it was to anyone with the training Mark had. "On the other hand, some have said that Louisiana, in particular, is carrying more than their fair share of the burden in supporting our general's efforts to reunite the country."

Janice's eyes cut to Mark's, and that's when he knew he had her. So long as he didn't screw it up now, she'd make a fabulous asset.

"I'll let you in on a little secret," Mark continued. "You

already know I head up the civilian liaison department between Houle's military and the civilian contractors and residents, such as yourself."

"Yeah."

"What we don't advertise is that I'm also heading up a department for the intelligence services. Particularly the CIA, but indirectly, also the DIA. It can be rough, balancing the demands of the two jobs, particularly where loyalties conflict, but I find a way to navigate those rough waters."

"I see," Janice said. "That's... interesting. You know, I've been approached by the DIA to handle some analyst work for them. Specifically, handling the deciphering of data related to what's going on with the Midwest Republic."

Mark remembered seeing that detail in her dossier. They had approached her, and she had agreed to do the analyst work in her spare time. She had a lot of that, living in the bunker as a civilian. In fact, it was his own asset within that DIA sub-department that had alerted him to Janice's potential as an asset. If he recruited her, he'd have a safe chain of communications between himself and the DIA.

He said, "You know, that particular region has been a headache for the General for well over a year."

Janice nodded. "It's a mess there."

"Were you aware of the abortive invasion attempt?" Mark asked.

Janice shook her head and waited expectantly.

Mark continued, "Not only did we send what airpower we could spare, but we also diverted troops and especially vehicles from all over the controlled regions, sending them up there to fight. Houle's allies, the Midwest Republic, had gotten in over their heads messing with a small group called the Confederation, based in south-central Pennsylvania. Unfortunately for many of our brave men and women in uniform, the plan was poorly thought out, poorly supplied, and they went in with limited intelligence. The result, as you can imagine, was disastrous. We lost a lot of assets in that so-called war. That was a bit less than a year ago. More like six months."

"My God," Janice said. "How are we keeping control, then? We struggled to keep as much of civilization going as possible *before* that, but what about now? And where did we get the airpower?"

"Unfortunately, that was all the airpower we could get. We no longer have air superiority because of that decision."

"How on Earth did they manage that?"

"The method they used to defeat our airpower, vehicles, and ultimately our infantry forces is classified, but needless to say, it was very effective. We recovered less than ten percent of our original forces sent into the region."

"Wow. Ten percent?"

Mark nodded. "Now the regions we stripped forces from to support that war find themselves destabilized."

"That would explain the uptick in bandit and cannibal activity over the last few months."

"Yes," Mark replied, "pretty much our entire southern holdings are in turmoil, and our military personnel stationed in those regions are fatigued from being in a constant state of readiness due to the increased danger. Our losses are mounting, yet our leadership has, for whatever reason, declared their determination to hold every last inch of territory we previously controlled."

Janice looked suddenly wary. "You do know that in many of those regions, we only controlled the areas immediately around our prefab firebases in the first place, right?"

Bingo. Mark was fairly sure he'd found his 'in' with her at last. "Yes. And there are some who say—in private, of course —that we should pull back our borders so we can increase troop densities in the remaining controlled territory. But I'm curious to see what you think of all this."

Janice took a deep breath, but Mark suspected she was buying time to think of an answer.

Mark cleared his throat.

Janice hesitated a moment longer, then said, "Do you think perhaps the General isn't being given all the pertinent information?"

"What makes you say that?"

"I'm just trying to understand why he made the decisions he made. Of course, I'm not questioning his leadership—I want to make that clear."

Mark said, "You wouldn't be the first to do so. But some have said they feel it's equally likely that he did have all the available information and simply had an overall objective that's different from the rest of the people in the base."

"I see."

Mark shrugged. "People are entitled to their opinions, of course. My main concern, though, is the fact that your family is down there."

"Don't remind me."

"If they live, they are the ones dealing with the consequences. Actually, I wonder, is there anything I can do for you?"

"Why do you ask?"

"Given the personal recommendations I've received about you from people I trust, it seems the least I could do is offer to help in some way."

Now came the easy part—simply waiting for her to speak first. If she did, then odds were good she was internalizing what he'd said and was considering it.

After a long silence, Janice said, "If you're serious, Mr. Bates, I guess I would be really grateful if I could at least get some closure about my family. I'm not sure what you can do about it, though."

"I'm not sure how I can help, either, but I do know how to find out. I'll tell you what—write down their names, last known addresses, any other places they might be such as a vacation home, and their Social Security numbers. If you have photos of any of them, you should make copies."

"Okay."

"Then, during fourth shift, take the paper and any photos to the CIA's radio cubicle and ask for Tom Smith. Hand him what you have and say, 'Here's that weather report you asked for. The Navajos ought to like this.' "

"Got it."

"Do that, and they'll make sure we begin allocating whatever resources are available to go look for them."

Janice's eyes lit up, but she remained outwardly collected by giving a slight nod of appreciation.

"I make no promises," Mark continued, "and I'm sorry to say the odds aren't good, but at least it's something. Better than nothing. But if we do find them, any of them, I'll make sure they head this way on the next transport available."

"Thank you, Mr. Bates."

"It's the least I can do for someone on my team, right?"

Janice took a deep breath and nodded slowly, almost imperceptibly.

"Of course, there's no pressure," Mark said. "My team isn't about office politics or hostile takeovers of other people's staff silos. It's about getting things done—the things that need to get done, not just the things certain other people decide should be our priorities."

"Good."

"In return for doing what I can to help, I'm not asking you to do much. All I ask for now is that you just make sure I get a copy of anything you think I might be interested in. I leave that up to your judgment."

Janice turned to stare at her computer monitor, which

had gone black from entering sleep mode during their conversation. She paused, then said, "Actually, I do have something you might be interested in..."

Opening a desk drawer, she pulled out a manila folder and handed it to Mark. "Obviously, I didn't just give this to you, although I'm sure you have the security clearance. It's just that Chief Banez gave me specific instructions to deliver this to him directly, whenever it came in. I made a copy, of course. For the official file. Would you mind putting it in the department backup storage for me, when you get a chance?"

Mark rose from his chair. "Of course. Anything I can do to help," he said with a wink.

They made their polite farewells, then Mark headed for the door while Janice turned back to her computer, moving the mouse to take it out of sleep mode.

At the doorway, Mark stopped. He turned back to her and said, "It goes without saying that our efforts to find your family will go a lot smoother if I don't have to waste time explaining it to some petty bureau chief or other. Maybe you should just keep our conversation between us, okay?"

"Of course, Mr. Bates."

Then he walked out, closing the door behind him. Folders in hand, he strolled back toward his personal quarters, a bounce in his step. That particular analyst had chain-of-communications access to so much of what flowed to both CIA and DIA. If she was any good at being a spook, he was about to have an entirely new, independent source of information. Information was power—the power to get things done the right way, the power to mitigate the damage Houle had been doing, running amok.

And if Mark got really lucky, he'd find a way to get in touch with so-called President Taggart, halfway across the country in New America. But for now, that was only a pipe dream.

Of course, getting an asset within the CIA/DIA communications chain had been only a pipe dream as of an hour ago.

It was turning out to be a good day.

* * *

1900 HOURS - ZERO DAY +614

That evening, Mark sat in his private office, feet up on his desk while leaning back in the office chair. He had a tumbler of whiskey next to him on the desk and the file Janice had given him in his hands, open. As he read, he let out a low whistle. A few of the details were obviously in some sort of code, but he had learned enough of the standard-use code words around there to understand most of what he read. It appeared to be an ordinary directive from Houle himself, specifically instructing the head of the DIA to enact Operation Clean Sweep. In the document, the operation objective was referred to as "sweeping out the boiler room." A chill ran down Mark's spine, and he felt his heart pounding.

Operation Clean Sweep, he knew, was a set of orders for a hypothetical, what-if scenario, one of many contingency plans the military was so fond of creating. There were such orders to cover almost every eventuality, the idea being that with a plan in place, if that situation ever did come up, the powers that be could respond quickly. At worst, the existing plan could be rapidly revised for the specific factors of a situation, rather than having to create it from scratch.

These particular orders dealt with the possibility of a cabal of members of the Legislative Branch attempting a coup and how to quickly and quietly derail them and then deal with the traitors, all without stirring up the civilian populace.

The problem with that, and the thing that made Mark's heart thump hard in his chest, was that no such coup plot existed. Mark had access to most of the Intel files, and his position afforded him the opportunity to be spoon-fed the most important data coming through both CIA and DIA operating here at NORAD. If there was a coup even suspected by either of those agencies, he would likely know about it.

In other words, there was no way Houle would know about a burgeoning coup plot before the intelligence agencies did. Hell, they were the ones that briefed Houle.

"No way. Houle couldn't be that stupid... Could he?" Mark muttered under his breath. He reached to grab his glass and downed the whiskey in one slug. Then he poured himself another. If ever there was a day to have another double, this was it. If this was indeed going down, it would happen soon.

How could he stop it? The few dozen representatives who had made it to safety at NORAD, right before the EMPs fell, represented the last connection anyone had to the old America—the last, best hope of restoring the U.S. of A. Anyone who viewed them as enemies was by definition an enemy of the state.

That made General Houle an enemy of the state.

He sat for a moment in stunned silence, allowing that thought to sink in. Again, he asked himself how he could stop it. He brought his feet off the table and leaned forward to turn on his computer. When it booted up, he loaded his contacts list. Not the publicly available one that sat on his hard drive, but the hidden and encrypted one disguised as a graphics image. He let it decode and then pulled it up to go through the list of names. Could he trust anyone on this list? At any other time, the answer would have been a resounding yes, but with Houle engaging in what was probably treason,

Mark wouldn't be so foolish as to make his move alone and without support. Powerful people within the base must have given Houle their backing or that old man would never be brave enough to pursue so rash a course of action.

No, the only way to save America's last representatives would be to notify them of the threat they were facing directly. Once they were aware of the plot against them, they could circle the wagons. They could reach out to the people they trusted, many of whom were very influential. In fact, if it came down to it, a lot of the people on Houle's side would probably flip on him if they received a direct command from all the legislators themselves. It was a lot easier to commit treason when the people you were about to screw over weren't looking you in the eye and giving you a direct counter-order.

The best one to start with, he decided, would be the Texas congressman. To Mark's knowledge, Congressman Randall was just about the most popular person on the base and had the support of almost all the other legislators. He also had the support of many mid-level military officers on base and chaired several of the committees that interacted with Houle behind closed doors on a daily basis. He would probably be America's next president if an election could ever be arranged in this lifetime.

"Yes. I'll go to Randall and make him see the truth. He has to believe me. He just has to."

Mark stood and shuffled the papers back into the manila folder, then tucked it under his arm as he walked toward the door. He glanced both ways as he entered the hallway, but saw no one. He turned right and headed toward Randall's quarters, which were at the far side of the base and up one level. Randall was a smart man, Mark figured, so he could be made to listen to reason and see the truth.

As Mark walked down the hall, an Army officer came

around the corner and nearly collided with him. Mark's first thought was that the man was there to arrest him, but logic quickly caught up and he realized that, if he were to be arrested, it wouldn't be handled by a lone officer. No, it would have been done by a small group of enlisted men who could be counted on for their loyalty.

The officer's insignia showed he was a major, and his uniform and hair were both in perfect order. To Mark, he looked like an ideal rear-echelon commander, but probably not much of a soldier. That made him dangerous—he would be loyal to Houle for his position, rather than relying on his experience and talent.

The major eyed Mark up and down, clearly evaluating what he saw and just as clearly found Mark wanting. "Watch where you're going, Mr. Bates," he said, his lips curled back. "Assaulting an officer here is a federal crime, no matter your position, civilian."

Mark's gaze shifted from the officer's eyes to the floor, and he muttered, "My apologies, sir. I didn't see you there."

The major's eyes narrowed. After a pause, he turned his head a little to look at Mark sideways. "And where are you going in such a hurry?" His gaze cut to the file in Mark's hand. "Surely you're not doing paperwork and running reports back and forth at this time of night."

Mark stood frozen, struggling not to let his eyes widened as he stared at the officer, but he couldn't think of what to say. His mind raced and he tried to force himself to say something, anything, just to stop standing there, staring like an idiot. "I... I am..."

There was a brief pause, then the major began to laugh, his head tilted back, the sound loud and harsh. It was a throaty laugh. "Oh God, you should see your face. Come on, Bates, you wouldn't be stupid enough to try anything rash. You need to lighten up. If you stay so uptight, it's going to give you a heart attack."

Mark's mind immediately seized on the opportunity to give the major a little misdirection. "Oh damn, sir. You got me good, I have to give you credit." Mark forced a little chuckle. "You know, you military guys scare the crap out of us civilians. Hell, most of us are just glad you're on our side." He gave the major a huge grin.

The officer clapped Mark on the shoulder and then walked onward, chuckling as he went, and Mark was left standing in the middle of the hallway, trying to control his shaking. That was damn close.

He realized that he was too shaken up now to try to convince someone as perceptive as Randall that Houle was a traitor. Mark would have to be at his best for that, and he was probably not at his best.

He spun on his heels and walked back the way he had come, passed his office, went around the corner, and entered his suite. When he got inside, the lights were off and he didn't hear any movement. His wife must've been out talking to one of the other socially important women. That was how she spent most of her days, actually. For once, he was glad not to have any company when he got home. He needed a minute to regain control of himself and get himself back in gear.

He went to the refrigerator and grabbed a beer, half of his daily ration. The less important civilians didn't get any. He flopped down on the couch, shoved his shoes off, and put his feet up on the coffee table. He let out a sigh as he felt his feet breathing after spending all day in shoes. They weren't the most comfortable things, those dress shoes.

He flipped open the file and skimmed through it again, hoping that maybe he would get more out of it, but no such luck. All the coded phrases he didn't already know stubbornly refused to reveal their meaning to him.

As he kept reading, on page two, he noticed something odd. The second word written, "exacerbate," was misspelled. Where there should have been an X, they had typed Z. That was surprising, because there weren't usually such noticeable typos in these sorts of official coded communiqués.

He wondered who had written it, so he flipped over to the first page to see whether the transcriber was noted in the footer. Again, no such luck. That wasn't surprising because, by leaving out the transcriber's name, if the orders became public knowledge, no one would know who to subpoena. Or grab and torture, depending on who benefited.

Then he noticed something else unusual. On the first page, the second word was "offices," as in, the offices of General Houle, but the word was misspelled. Where the second letter F should've been, there was instead a lowercase L.

In the back of his mind, Mark felt a tingle of alarm. Something wasn't right with this.

- 7 -

0600 HOURS - ZERO DAY +615

JUST SHORT OF the hill crest, Jwa Dae Geon dismounted from his horse and crept forward until he had a good view of the village below. Just as his scouts had reported, the tightly clustered domes with their encircling walls were organized in a very specific pattern. Five domes per cluster; five such clusters were likewise arranged in the same pattern, and the assembly had its own, larger wall. The pattern continued from there with five of these bigger clusters neatly arranged the same, with yet another wall surrounding it.

As he had suspected, this must surely be a Clan village—one of the many Clanholds. Intel estimated the super-cluster of domes could house as many as five hundred people, but scouts had only counted two hundred and fifty people. It turned out that many of the buildings were used for other purposes, such as storage, work areas, and even indoor kitchens, though the central outdoor kitchen was large enough to feed a small army.

From Jwa's point of view, the arrangement presented a terrible challenge to his mission. Reports from earlier battles said those domes couldn't be breached by mere bullets, nor even by the light mortars an earlier army had tried to use against the Clan. He suspected these dome dwellings were somehow built out of sandbags, beneath their adobe exteriors, though he couldn't imagine how they could have been constructed.

To add to the challenge, the concentric rings of walls made any direct assault difficult. He remembered hearing from some disgraced soldiers of the New York cantonment, who had straggled their way south, that assaulting these Clan clusters was like trying to navigate a labyrinth. The people who dwelled there knew every twist, turn, nook, and cranny. It put any assault at a severe disadvantage, especially since the damn Americans had launched EMPs over U.S. soil a second time last year, purely out of spite, just to make the Great Liberation more difficult. That had come as a terrible surprise, and it had worked.

Well, their feeble and spiteful actions may have made the Mission more difficult and delayed the outcome, but the final resolution was inevitable. The Great Leader's plan could not be stopped; it was simply the evolution of mankind, the next great leap in civilization. The dying carcass of capitalism would resist its final demise, but it couldn't stop it. They could only make its death take longer. Capitalism's time was done, it just didn't know it yet.

Jwa backed down the hill toward his waiting men, then approached his *Taewi*, or Captain as the Americans would call him. Jwa quickly told his captain and his fellow sergeants about the situation on the other side of the hill. The residents were already awake and working at their chores, and it seemed that even the children carried a pistol. Anyone in their mid-teens and older carried rifles. However, the residents were scattered all over the village rather than clustered together, and many were out in the fields to the north and west of the village, not near its formidable defenses.

The *Taewi*'s Intel reports suggested the villagers would gather for breakfast in about two hours, but until then, they were more vulnerable. There was no way the residents could organize an effective resistance or organize a response if the Koreans launched a surprise attack at this time of the day. Which, of course, was why the captain had chosen this time to attack.

He felt his pulse begin to speed up as he anticipated starting the assault and resuming the Great Mission. His only regret about the new offensive was that the higher-ups had decided to begin the campaign with a barrage of raids all along the Confederation's southern border. He would have preferred a courageous and righteous full attack to conquer this feeble 'Clan' outright.

He was confident, however, that his betters had more information than he did, and were wiser. Otherwise, they wouldn't be his superiors. He didn't know what the other two companies and the command platoon would be doing during the assault, but he didn't need to know. He trusted his commanders. They had kept him alive this long, after all. Jwa took pride in the fact that he had never second-guessed his commanding officers, and was quick to tell complaining soldiers that they didn't need to know every detail in order to identify their places within the great machine.

Jwa was handed his orders and learned that his platoon was to flank the hill and assault from the southeast, a coordinated attack from several directions, involving the entire company. The captain spent the next ten minutes organizing each squad, getting them into perfect place. Perhaps his captain was secretly a Buddhist, Jwa mused, because he always paid great attention to patterns and alignment when arranging his troops. Jwa had once asked why he did so, and he had only replied that, "Harmony in formation brings harmony in the hearts of men. Only this way can we all have harmony with the Great Leader's will."

Jwa's company received its orders to move out, and they marched around the hill's base, moving stealthily toward their launching point. Then it was a matter of waiting, waiting to hear the glorious whistle blast that would sound the assault's beginning. That was always the most difficult part of any mission, for him. Certainly combat was frightening, but once he was in it, adrenaline took over. Adrenaline and training made the fear of battle easier. No amount of training could make the waiting easy.

Ten minutes later, four short, sharp blasts from his captain's whistle resounded, bouncing off the hill much like bullets soon would be. It was the moment Jwa had been waiting for, the removal of his leash. He screamed his battle cry, and it was taken up by all his men. As one, they charged forward, surging around the base of the hill and sprinting toward the village. Within moments, he could hear the glorious sound of many AK rifles firing.

Up ahead, people in the village began to drop, and he could only imagine with joy the surprised looks on their faces as they died without knowing why or even how. Many fell before they even reacted to show they knew they were under attack.

His unit reached the compound's outer wall and slid to a halt in the shelter it provided. He did a quick head count and was beyond pleased to see he had lost no men on the approach, yet. That would change, probably, but he urged them on regardless. They wasted no time before going up and over the wall, surging into the very heart of the enemy's village. Jwa grinned the entire time, and he felt certain that victory would soon be theirs. It was just too one-sided to end any other way.

The killing wouldn't begin in earnest, he knew, until the battle had been won—then they would deliver their message to the Confederation with bullets, not diplomats.

Today was a glorious day.

* * *

0800 HOURS - ZERO DAY +615

Hasa Jwa Dae Geon went down his line of men, examining each in turn. His four Korean brothers, of course, were squared away with all the right gear, in all the right places. His eight ISNA soldiers... less so. The dirty savages, with their unruly facial hair and their disgusting hygiene, couldn't be trusted to carry their ammunition where it was supposed to be. Some had even discarded their ammo pouch to carry their magazines in their cargo pockets.

Jwa turned to his translator, an Arab, and explained what was wrong with the man's uniform and gear, then dragged his translator down the line to explain to each of the other soldiers what was wrong with their gear. It took fifteen minutes, a completely stupid waste of time that was totally avoidable if they were only smart enough to follow simple directions. How many times, over the past almost two years, had he explained this to them? He was sure they did it only to annoy him. Sand-eaters biting their thumbs at their betters.

Once he was sure his men were finally in order, he put his black whistle to his lips and blew two long blasts to let his *Taewi* know his platoon was in order. Then came the return whistle, alerting the whole unit that they were about to move out.

Jwa ordered his men to turn right-face, and they were on the march moments later.

To Jwa, it was a beautiful sight—his platoon, just one of ten in the battalion strung all along the road, heading north again. It was finally time to begin the Great Mission again. He had absolute faith that the swine Americans living in the feeble Confederation would soon know the glory and honor of dying in service to the People, though misguided. They would be easily defeated; everyone knew that, as his superior officers so often told him.

The North Koreans, of course, would be at the top of the resulting food chain. After all, someone had to be in charge.

* * *

1100 HOURS - ZERO DAY +617

Cassy stood inside her office, looking out the window to where dozens of people had gathered. They weren't shouting, but the mood did look ugly. She recognized many of them as high-ranking leaders of various Clanholds. "They ought to be yelling at you, Frank, not sending you in here as their representative."

Frank shrugged. "Trust me, they have yelled at me. But it is what it is. I'd be lying if I said I didn't feel the same as they did."

"Don't they all answer to you? They are your subordinates, after all."

"Yeah, but the Clan answers to the Confederation. And this is one of those things."

Cassy turned away from the window to face him. "What do they want me to do, tie all those soldiers up and refuse to let them leave?"

Frank slowly shook his head, his lips pursed and eyes narrowed. "You and I both know these people outside are important, Cassy. I rely on them to carry out my instructions, to be good leaders of their various Clanholds. It's important to work with them."

"But they're not our soldiers, they're Taggart's. He's the one they owe their allegiance to."

"The truth is, they are the Clan. Ever since you brought them in and set up all those new Clanholds, it has made the Clan into something more than just Clanholme itself."

Dammit if Frank wasn't right. Of course, he was right— she just didn't want to deal with this problem. As far as she was concerned, they were Frank's responsibility. "So tell me again exactly what it is they would like me to do. Could you send your top five figures?"

Frank began to pace, and said, "Look, they need to be reassured."

"Reassured about what?"

"How many of our most remote southern holdings were raided, Cassy? Half a dozen? One of them was almost finished, ready to become a new Clanhold. We've lost four hundred people or more and tons of supplies, half from just that one holding that got razed to the ground."

"We can't expect anything else from the invaders."

"Worse yet, while we know it was the 'vaders, we don't know why they chose now to attack. I thought things were going well enough with them, and some members of the Confederation had even begun to trade with them."

Cassy nodded. It was true that even the Clan had begun trading with the invaders in Maryland, often through intermediary merchants, but a few traded directly. It looked like the Maryland invaders were there to stay, after all, and they had things the Clan needed. And needed things the Clan had. "I don't know why they're attacking us now any more than you do. They haven't sent any messengers. We sent an envoy, but she hasn't yet had time to get there and back."

Frank frowned. "So we don't know what's going on?"

"No, but it's your job to keep these people out there calm. We can't panic now, not when the enemy is acting up just when New America is demanding its troops back."

"Listen, Cassy. Many of those loaner troops married into the Clan. They don't want to leave any more than we want them to."

Cassy hesitated, then said, "Well, the only thing I can tell you with certainty is that I'm not going to force any soldiers back to New America. Those who wish to stay are welcome to."

Frank nodded and said, "Well, that's a good start. I can tell this to our people, and many of them will calm down. But we still need a long-term plan."

"Look, I've already put every member of the Confederation on high alert. I've sent out requests to have them shift as many units as they can to the south, to support the Clan against any future attacks. I've sent word to all of Taggart's soldiers, spread throughout the Confederation, that New America wants them to come home, and that if any of them consider the Confederation to be that home, then they are welcome to stay. I've even made sure they wouldn't be considered traitors in New America, thanks to Jaz and Choony."

Frank raised one eyebrow at her and said, "Damn, Cassy, that's all you really had to say. I imagine most of Taggart's troops will decide to stay. As long as we can start defending ourselves against the Maryland 'vaders, and winning sometimes, then all the Clanhold leaders will settle down."

"And hopefully, so will you," Cassy said. She forced an easy smile on her face.

"I'll try. But you know, all of this makes me wonder why Taggart chose now to call his troops back. Our reports from Jaz and Choony suggest New America might be getting some pressure from the 'vaders in northern Pennsylvania, and of course, there's the chaos in Philly."

Cassy shrugged. "No one knows what's going on there. If

the Maryland invaders won in Philadelphia, they might now be putting pressure on Taggart from the south. That's a lot of pressure coming from north and south alike."

"It would explain why he wants his troops back."

Cassy paused as an idea struck her. They needed more Intel. "That's just conjecture. We need to get eyes on the situation. So... maybe you should send Joe Ellings to Philly. He's got family there, right?"

For a brief moment, Frank's face flashed with surprise. Clearly, he hadn't considered that option before. "Yeah, and Joe is charming as hell with that thick, farm-hick accent and easy smile of his, so if anyone can get into Philly alive and then get out again, it would be him. I'll make the arrangements."

Cassy shifted her gaze to the window, looking outside again. The crowd hadn't inched any closer to her office building, which was a good thing. It meant they weren't likely to start any real trouble. She didn't think they'd harm her or anyone else, but they were pissed and scared—much like she felt—so who knew for sure? She kept her eye on them.

She didn't relish the idea of sending Joe off into unknown territory, and usually, she would have sent Jaz and Choony, but she did have confidence in his capabilities. Plus, 'Jazoony' were stuck in Hackensack, doing something just as important.

"All right, Frank, is there anything else I can do for you?"

Frank took a deep breath, letting it out slowly. "No, that's everything. I guess I'd better get back out there before the natives get restless."

"Yeah, I don't like a crowd outside my office."

"They'll be glad to hear you aren't forcing the soldiers to leave while we're getting raided again. Maybe while Joe is on his mission, he'll hear something about what's going on with the 'vaders down there."

"Hopefully."

She patted him on his back as he walked out her door, leaving her alone in the office. She spared a couple of seconds to watch as he approached the crowd and began to talk to them, and could see from their body language that the tension was draining from them.

Satisfied they weren't going to lynch him—or her, for that matter—she went back to her desk and looked forlornly at the stack of paperwork she had to get through by day's end. Tomorrow, there'd be an entirely new stack—she could mostly thank Ethan and Michael for the reinvention of paperwork.

As she hunched over her desk to whip up a reply to a Lititz request for nails and bolts, she heard the crowd outside dispersing. Before diving into her work, she said a little prayer for Joe's safety. It would be a dangerous journey to Philly, and he would need it.

- 8 -

1600 HOURS - ZERO DAY +617

NATE STOOD IN the truck bed, elbows on the roof. All around him, the neighborhood was a bustle of activity. His fighters were still going door to door, rounding up the last of the 'vaders in that area, but almost everything on that street had been cleared. For the moment, the risk from snipers was minimal, and he took the time to enjoy the rarity of relative peace and quiet. He even managed to slouch, looking oh-so-relaxed. Even when things had looked grim in earlier battles, he always made it a point for his troops to see him looking confident. It was a morale booster.

Half a block away, in the parking lot of what used to be a big-box store, whatever enemy survivors had surrendered were being rounded up. Of course, his own people wanted to kill them, but Nate had given orders to spare the ones who surrendered. He had to think about the long game, not just what would feel good right now. If he wanted to negotiate favorable terms with the Maryland invaders later, he had to give a little to get a little.

As far as he was concerned, such forward thinking was the reason he was in charge. It had made him the most successful resistance commander, by far. Over the last few months, since his troops had begun the offensive in earnest, all the other resistance leaders had fallen in line to join him, one by one. Everyone wanted to be on the winning team. Hell, just before this latest offensive, the other commanders had sworn their personal allegiance to him.

All was going according to plan, and it was a glorious sight.

Standing next to the truck and leaning against the bed, his "associate" Robert, bodyguard and lead enforcer, looked as bored as Nate felt. Robert said, "You aren't really going to spare all those 'vader prisoners, are you? I don't know about you, but I'd really like to get a piece of them. A little bit of payback for what they done to my family. A lot of people's families."

Nate ignored him. He'd already taken the time to explain to Robert what his plans were, more than once. Robert was smart, in a cunning sort of way, but he lacked forethought. It made him a great bodyguard and a poor strategist.

When Nate didn't answer, Robert spat on the ground and walked away. Nate watched him as he left toward the supply train. Maybe the big lug needed something to eat. He always seemed hungry. How Robert could eat at a time like this, Nate didn't know. His own stomach was in turmoil, and he wouldn't have kept anything down even if he tried.

A soldier ran toward him, stopping ten feet away, and almost saluted. At his raised eyebrow, the soldier stopped himself. He had a rule: no saluting out in the open because it made him a tempting target for any nearby snipers. "Don't be shy, son," Nate said, putting on a warm smile. "What do you have for me?"

The soldier, a young man of perhaps nineteen, nodded and replied, "Sir, we have the neighborhood ninety-five percent contained. Estimates are about twenty prisoners so far, and we expect no more than five or six more if they keep to their average so far. I was told to let you know there is a bit of a mob gathering outside of the POW area."

Nate frowned. No one had better even think about disobeying his orders, or he would have them strung up. And that was no euphemism. "Let the ranking officer on site know that I'm on my way. I'll handle it myself since he seems incapable."

As the rebel ran off toward the POW area, Nate turned toward another nearby soldier and said, "Go find Robert. Tell him I need him right away, and to meet me at the POW area."

When she nodded and ran off, Nate vaulted out of the truck bed, landing nimbly on his feet, and then briskly walked toward the prisoner area. Damn it all; this wasn't what he wanted to be doing right now. He was tired, just like the others, and rank should have its privileges. Instead, it had only more responsibilities. He hoped that would change once peace came again.

Well, someone had to be in charge, and he had turned out to be the best choice. The proof was in the pudding, as the saying went, and Philly was almost free now because of his leadership. It was the only reason the other commanders had fallen into step behind him.

* * *

1700 HOURS - ZERO DAY +620

Nate sat in the parlor, a tumbler of whiskey in hand. For this meeting, he wore his old Neighborhood Watch commander's uniform: khaki pants and a black polo shirt embroidered with the neighborhood watch logo on one breast and the word 'Commander' on the other.

He wore it with pride. Although it had been only a minor honor before the war, in the nearly two years since then, he had used his role to save the people in his neighborhood. Unlike the ones surrounding his, only half of the people under his command had died during that first terrible winter, at the start of the Dying Times.

Across from him, sitting in the recliner, was an envoy from the Maryland-based invaders. Nate guessed the man had been chosen because of his skill in English and his demeanor, which was far less abrasive than most of the gooks. He appreciated the man's ready smile, but he would never make the mistake of trusting it. The envoy's eyes reminded him of the cold, unyielding stare of a pit viper.

"Commander," the gook said, "thank you for receiving me. It's important that we maintain an open line of communication, despite our differences these past couple of years."

Differences. Ha. That was one way to put it. Another way might be 'crushing, grueling oppression.' Nate merely nodded, saying nothing.

The envoy, whose name was Jwa, continued, "Allow me to ask you a question. We struggled continually with the gangsters throughout the city. Our spies found that you had no such problems in your territory, and as your occupied territory grew, you alleviated those problems in the newly controlled areas, as well. What's your secret?"

It was a harmless question, Nate thought, so he could see no harm in answering it. "Early on, we captured a high-ranking gang member, offered him enough food to survive the winter if he would join up and help us deal with our gang problems. He brought as many of his gang members as he could convince to join us. A few were hanged, and the rest fell in line."

Jwa nodded, and Nate almost shivered at the sensation

of being set up for a lethal strike. "Did you not have people starving over that first winter?"

There it was. He was fishing for information, hoping to learn the secrets of how he had done so well when others had struggled and died. "Yes, we lost a lot of people. And keeping that one gangbanger and a handful of his gang alive meant that several of my own people starved to death over the winter."

"A tough choice. I wonder how your people would feel about that now, if they knew."

Nate eyed Jwa warily. "I've been open about it, even at the time. The question really should be about how many of my people were spared from gang raids and having their food stolen, because of my decision. I was the Watch commander, and it was my job to keep my neighborhood safe. Sometimes, the greater good requires an exercise of will to make decisions that others aren't strong enough to make for themselves."

"Interesting."

"I've seen plenty of my people starve—people that would still be alive today if we had killed the gangbanger. I carry that burden, but that's the burden of leadership."

Jwa nodded vigorously. "Yes, this is something I can understand. I, too, have sentenced a soldier to die in a hopeless mission in order to save the others. It requires a great leader to make hard choices. The ignorant people they lead would never have made that choice for themselves, and more would be dead because of it. When the people align their will to their leader's, that's when great things are truly accomplished, as you have discovered. My respect for you grows. Now you see the strength and promise of the Korean way."

Nate couldn't be sure, but he thought Jwa's words had the ring of truth to them, but he was still the enemy. Nate changed the subject when it came to the Korean superiority, though—they had lost, after all. "As the leader of these people, it's my will that the remaining invader forces leave Philadelphia. I'll agree to a cease-fire period of one week. If you're still here, we'll renew our offensive. I would much rather you and I come to an understanding, but if your leaders insist on being the immovable object, then I must be the unstoppable force."

Jwa then leaned forward, resting his elbows on his knees so he could gaze at Nate more directly. He said, "Your spies have surely discovered by now that we're gathering much of our army in Maryland's northern area. Most of this force gathers a mere day or two away from here. While I admire your strength and courage, I ask you this: What is to prevent us from simply rolling over Philadelphia once again? It would be easy to take over what we have lost here, using only the force we've already assembled."

Nate's lip curled up into a half-smile, and he chuckled. "Yes, I've heard those reports. I also know that half of them are Americans. You're rebuilding your army the old tribal way, by pressing those you've conquered into military service. But how hard do you think they'll fight against their fellow Americans? Especially when their brothers fight harder than they do. We protect our homes, while they fight to ease their burden."

"That may be true, yet the result would be the same. You would not be able to resist such a force."

Slowly, Nate nodded. Jwa was right, but that wasn't the entire story. "Winning a battle isn't the same thing as winning the war. Yes, you might very well be able to retake this city, but that would change nothing. The result would be the same. The only difference would be the number of people who must die before we take back our freedom."

Jwa shrugged. He said, "There's a simple alternative, of

course. We could simply kill everyone who resists, even if that meant depopulating the city. Total warfare and the complete slaughter of your followers remains a solution we could choose."

"Be that as it may," Nate replied, "my people would find their freedom in the end. Whether we are freed in victory or in death, your choice is only in how many of your own people you lose before we find one freedom or the other. We'll take a lot of you with us, and then what? A useless, dead city and a weakened army are all you'll have."

Jwa glanced away and stared into space, letting out a long, deep breath. His frustration was written on his face. It was the first spontaneous emotion Nate had seen from the envoy, but he tried not to show his pleasure at rattling that calm, confident demeanor.

At last, Jwa said, "After reading the dossier and psych profiles our intelligence agents have built up on you, I believe you. To be honest, I was sent in mostly to see whether the analysis was wrong. I don't think it is."

"What did it say?"

"You're cold and calculating, well-loved by your people, and your results show you're a capable insurrection leader. I think you have the will and determination to do exactly as you have suggested, grinding your own people into dirt, preferring death to surrender. As a North Korean soldier, I am well-indoctrinated into our own Great Leader's similar struggle during what you call the Korean War. I know how powerful the will to win or die truly can be."

Nate was a little surprised they had a dossier on him, or even knew who he was. How they had built a psychological profile on him, he couldn't even guess, but he knew nothing about the field.

He said, "Where does that leave us? I suspect that mighty army you're gathering isn't intended for us. If it was, you would have already rolled over us. No... I think you're gathering that army for some other reason. I also don't think your new army is quite as strong as you pretend."

Jwa was unreadable. "Whether or not that's true, if we allowed you to remain alive and free, it certainly concerns us to have your hostile force gathered so close to our own territory. I would hate to see your people get in the way of our other goals in this region."

Nate laughed. "My word of honor is meaningless to you, so I'll put it to you in a different way. I'm going to spend at least the next two years rebuilding my own little group of survivors here in Philadelphia. We have more to do than time to do it in. I don't think it's in our best interest to interfere with whatever else you've got going on, so long as it's going on somewhere else. You know what I'm saying?"

Jwa nodded. "I do. You're saying that we must come to some sort of agreement, or you'll continue to be a thorn in our side. Eventually, we would have to deal with you. If I'm right about the kind of person you are, you'd rather keep fighting than agree to unfavorable terms. You've chosen an all-or-nothing path, for you and your followers."

"That's exactly right, my man. I want peace, and I'm tired of fighting. But I'm not so tired that I'll agree to a bad deal. I'd rather just keep fighting. If you want to avoid that, we can work out the details later."

Elbows still on his knees, Jwa steepled his fingers in front of his face and gazed intently at Nate. "Very well. I will recommend to my superiors that we accept your terms, at least regarding a division of territories. I have no wish to kill everyone in the city because it would hinder our other efforts as you have so wisely guessed."

Nate suppressed a grin. Victory was almost at hand. He could practically taste it. "What's the catch?"

Jwa shrugged and said, "If my superiors end up agreeing

to your terms, as I will recommend, then your victory will come at a cost. It won't be a clean break. I sincerely hope we can eventually work out a cost we both can live with."

Nate stood and said, "Very well. If your leaders take your suggestion, we'll leave the rest for other people to negotiate. But keep in mind, if I don't like the treaty you end up proposing, we'll keep fighting. Remember, this is an all-or-nothing deal."

Jwa followed Nate's lead and stood as well. "It will be in my report, of course."

"In the meantime," Nate said, "my friend Robert here will see you to the door. I'll make sure you get a decent supper before you leave, if you wish."

"Very well. I thank you for your hospitality, but I believe I will leave the city immediately." Jwa walked toward the door, but then stopped and turned around. He stood looking at Nate for all of three seconds before saying, "You have been a worthy opponent. You're nothing like what I've come to expect from Americans. If they had more people like you, perhaps the world would not be in the condition it's in now, and we wouldn't be here."

Then Jwa turned around again and walked out the door.

Nate heard the door close, and a few seconds later, Robert came back in and sat in the other recliner—not the one Jwa had been sitting in, Nate noticed—and slowly shook his head. "Do you really think we can trust these bastards?" he asked.

Nate gave him a wide grin. "Of course not. There's no way we can trust those snakes, but we have to negotiate if we want to end this."

"Gotcha."

"I don't know about you, Robert, but I'd like to get on with the business of living. We still have to organize our farming in the Eastern Territories, restore some services like water, and organize some way to distribute food and supplies among us. We only have so many supplies left, and we have to figure out who's going to get them. I know the Dying Time is over, but we will lose more people if we can't get food from the farms into the city fast enough."

An idea struck him, and he paused for a moment to work it out in his mind. Then he said, "You know, it seems to me that the Confederation or New America must have some supplies nearby. Lord knows they have people pretty close to here, and they have to feed those people somehow."

Robert stared at him, apparently not comprehending. "But do we really want to start a new war? This one isn't even over yet."

Nate shook his head, smirking. "You dumbass. Don't you realize, we've got more enemy uniforms than we know what to do with?"

"Wait. You want us to strip the uniforms off of our dead enemies' bodies?"

"Precisely."

"And wear their uniforms? That's really fucked up, man."

"Might be, but the Confederation and New America are already at war with the invaders. Think about it. We could do a little 'scrounging,' and they wouldn't know the difference. We wouldn't be getting more Americans killed. We would just take what we need, and—"

Robert cut in, "And that would keep us from having a new war on our hands. That's brilliant."

Nate nodded. "We have a lot of mouths to feed, and harvest isn't coming any sooner just because we need it to."

"New America has more than enough food and supplies, anyway."

"You know, Robert, you're not as much of a dumbass as you look."

Robert laughed and flipped Nate his middle finger, then

went and got his own tumbler of whiskey. "No shit, I'm not stupid. I figured out a long time ago that if I ride on your coattails, I get to have good whiskey."

"Only because I let you, you big lump. But stick with me, and the sky's the limit. I'm going to be the king of Philly, man. That day is coming real soon."

* * *

Joe Ellings reined in his horse, slowing to a mere canter. Ahead, the outskirts of Philly rose into view marking the end of his journey. He hadn't wanted to go on the mission, but he reckoned Cassy had made the right choice in sending him. Most of the other folks would have gotten themselves caught long before they got here. Even with his skills, there were a couple of times when it had been a close thing. For some reason, it seemed the Maryland invaders were really being lots more active all along the border, proving Cassy's worries were the Gospel truth. They really were up to something.

Joe smiled. He had made it through, and Philly stretched out before him. Now he had to get in without being shot by 'vaders, who would likely confuse him for them boys and girls in the resistance. Once he was in, he had to somehow find their boss and jaw out a deal. That would be the hard part, on account of folks in the cities had a hard time getting along with his talking, but he reckoned he could make do. Yes sir, old Joe would get that job done, even if city folks didn't know how to talk right, with that stupid accent they all had.

After another minute spent enjoying the view, Joe spurred his horse forward, heading down toward a huge greenbelt along the city's northwest edge. For the next hour, he and his mount wound in and out through the trees, using dead reckoning to keep his course. Most of the city itself lay to the southeast; he'd have to go through the suburb before he got to the city. But as sure as possums play dead, whatever resistance movement was in town would likely be in the main city, not in the 'burbs. He had no way of knowing whether the resistance had kicked the invaders out yet, or been defeated. He'd find out what the situation was after he got there.

"Well, I'll just have to talk to whoever's there. Let's just hope it's the good guys, right, Rusty?" he asked his horse, patting her on the neck.

He soon found a freeway onramp and decided that might be a whole bunch safer than going through the ramshackle neighborhood he had been riding through. He hadn't seen any movement yet, which was both good and bad. On the one hand, no people meant less danger for himself. On the other hand, of course, it meant all those people were likely dead. Or taken away—everyone had heard the rumors about slave camps from them 'vaders in New York City, but he figured it couldn't only happen in New York. 'Vaders was 'vaders, right? Probably happened here, too.

Whoever was in charge in Philly, Joe hoped they'd let him get a quick shower, because he felt dirtier than ol' uncle Jim used to smell. He decided to camp out, then take the onramp first thing in the morning. He'd hopefully be wasting hot water in a shower by noon.

- **9** -

0500 HOURS - ZERO DAY +621

HASA JWA DAE Geon crested the low hill and stopped pedaling, then dismounted, and his unit followed suit. While looking at the ground before each step, in case of a booby-trap, Jwa cautiously approached the pole. He had noticed it about a half-mile away, a single pole with a box on top, which stood in stark contrast to the surrounding wide-open terrain. His second had felt it was a waste of time to investigate, but Jwa wasn't so sure, so he had told his second they weren't leaving until they checked it out.

The pole itself was about forty feet tall and ramrod straight. Up close, he could see that it was made of wood. It looked like it had once been a telephone pole, but instead of a T-assembly at the top, there now stood only a single wooden box about the size of a person's head.

After he investigated the ground surrounding the pole, Jwa was reasonably certain there were no booby-traps. Only then did he motion his translator to step forward. "Please have one of our ISNA brothers climb the pole and investigate what is in the box on top. Instruct him not to touch it, only to observe and then return."

His Arab translator nodded and approached the ISNA troops. A few seconds later, one of them stepped out from among his brethren and approached the pole. He was small and wiry, perfect for climbing it. Jwa watched the small man scurry up the pole like a monkey, hardly even slowing down as he got higher and higher.

Jwa was impressed. He could never have gotten to the top of that thing, at least not without some rope, so when the man came back down ten minutes later, Jwa gave him a slight bow as a sign of respect. The savage grinned, for Jwa's approval was a rare thing, especially to his ignorant, barbaric ISNA troops. Jwa wished his entire unit were Korean, but the Great Leader had decided in his wisdom that an alliance was the best way to proceed. Jwa had long ago aligned his will to his leader's, but he still wished he didn't have to deal with them.

"Well," Jwa said to his translator, putting his fists on his hips. "Ask him what was up there."

The translator gave him one curt nod and then spoke in his native gibberish language to the climber. Their conversation seemed to go on for quite some time before the translator turned back to Jwa. "*Hasa*, the box contains some sort of electronic device."

Jwa felt his irritation grow. What use was an old, burnt out electronics device? "Very well. Make note of the coordinates for our report and prepare to move out."

The translator gave a slight bow. He said, "Sir, he reports the device is active."

"How so?"

"There are several blinking lights."

"What else did he say?"

"The device itself resembles a small, flat box, and he says there is a solar panel on top of its container."

"Interesting."

"There is more, sir. He said that there is also a long tube, which he believes to be plastic, fully wrapped with tinfoil. The tube extends several inches beyond the container."

Jwa raised an eyebrow. That was indeed interesting. What could such a device be? If it was active, it was obviously erected after the EMPs, and that probably made it important.

"Kim," he called, and one of his Korean privates stepped forward.

"Yes, how may I serve you?"

Jwa pointed at the pole, then looked back at him. "Our ISNA brother says there is an active electronic device at the top of the pole, inside that container. You were an electronics expert before the Americans launched their EMPs, is that correct?"

The man fidgeted, shifting from foot to foot, uncomfortable under Jwa's gaze, earning him a disappointed look. Hastily, he said, "Yes. Such skills are no longer in demand, but they are at your disposal as the Great Leader wills it."

Jwa nodded. It had been an appropriate response. "Take some rope and climb that pole, then examine the device. Find out all that you can, and when you return, I expect a full report. What is the device? Can it be salvaged, or can we make some other use of it? Ask yourself these things when you see it, and then come back."

Private Kim bowed, then set about finding the team's rope. He tied a makeshift loop that went around the pole and his own body, and despite turning a slightly paler shade when he stood at the pole's base and looked up, he hesitated only a moment before beginning his climb. After he reached the top, he was up there for about five minutes before he began his descent. Once he was back on the ground, red-faced and breathing heavily, he let the rope fall to the dirt and approached Jwa, saluting.

When Jwa returned his salute, he said, "Sir, I am pleased to report that the device is a wireless router. There is a battery in the back of the box with wires leading to a solar panel on top. I believe that the tinfoil tube is being used to harness the signal and direct it somewhere else with pinpoint accuracy."

"To what purpose?" Jwa couldn't think how having a router in the middle of nowhere made any sense at all.

"Sir, I think it relays the signal from another such pole standing far away in the opposite direction. The sand-eater did not report this, but I found another tube that extended out the back of the container, but ending flush with the back panel. They cut a hole in the back, precisely the same diameter as the tube, and because it doesn't stick out, we couldn't see it from the ground. The mujahid should have reported it."

Jwa was stunned. He barely remembered to give the slight bow to dismiss Private Kim while his own thoughts raced. Someone in the region had a wireless network and computers, still up and operating. That was indeed interesting, and his commanders would find the intelligence valuable. Perhaps they would even praise his ancestors when he delivered the news.

It most likely belonged to the Clan, given the area, which meant those foolish Americans somehow had *working* computers. Jwa had no doubt that his superiors would definitely restructure their priorities in the region, once they heard of this.

Barely able to contain his excitement, he turned to his troops and said, "Mount up. We are immediately returning to base by the most direct way. Engage no enemy units while en route, do you understand? The intelligence we carry is worth far more than a few more dead enemy soldiers."

In less than a minute, the unit had mounted and was

cruising downhill. Jwa rode near the front, and he pretended not to notice the Arabs grumbling behind him. He couldn't understand what they were saying, but he assumed it had to do with missing breakfast. They were a most undisciplined lot.

* * *

1300 HOURS - ZERO DAY +621

As two assistants carefully laid out an exquisite service set and fine China on the antique mahogany coffee table, as well as a carafe of coffee, Taggart shook the envoy's hand with a faint smile. Mr. Lee's handshake had been firm, and his gaze direct, giving Taggart the impression of a confident, capable young man. His hair was well trimmed, his face entirely clean shaven. His eyes sparkled with intelligence and alertness, seeming to catch every movement, every nuance. Taggart knew he would have to be careful with this one.

Taggart motioned toward the two lavish couches, which faced each other from across the coffee table.

Mr. Lee nodded, then gave Taggart a slight bow, which Taggart knew indicated the man considered them to be equals. He wasn't sure how he felt about that, but it only added to his impression of the man's confidence.

After straightening up again, Mr. Lee walked to the couches and raised an eyebrow. When Taggart nodded, he sat and looked up toward Taggart's server. "Coffee, please. Two sugars, no cream." As Taggart sat down opposite him, Mr. Lee turned his attention back to the task at hand. "President Taggart, I thank you for taking time out of your busy day to see me. We have much to discuss."

Taggart gazed at his opponent. His English was excellent, although he still maintained a slight Korean accent. "Of course, Mr. Lee. New America understands the difficult situation we both find ourselves in. While animosity remains, many issues still require a resolution. But in the meantime, we can avoid further conflict as long as we maintain open communications."

Mr. Lee looked at Taggart as if studying him. "I truly hope that it's possible for us to resolve our differences. I hope that the issue I came to speak with you about will not lead to bloodshed. I must tell you that my leaders are adamant about the issue at hand."

Taggart resisted the urge to clench his jaw. He kept his composure as he spoke. "Well then, I find myself curious as to the issue you're here to discuss."

"Very well, sir," Lee said. He took a slow sip of his coffee and set the cup gently on the table. "I must begin by asking if the Confederation is a de facto part of New America."

Taggart felt alarm bells going off in his mind. He would have expected Lee to insist the Confederation was *not* a part of New America, leaving open the option of attacking them without automatically going to war with him. "They have recently become so, yes, although they remain semi-autonomous."

The corners of Lee's lips twitched upward slightly, and he appeared bemused. "My report will show that you acknowledge the Confederation as a member state of New America, of which you are both president and commander-in-chief."

Taggart gave a curt nod. "Yes."

"I am sure you are also aware that the Confederation recently fought against the Midwest Republic—also known as the Empire—and their allies from the American general Houle since my intelligence Intel says you allocated many troops to be deployed under Confederation command, and that those troops fought during that war."

Taggart wasn't sure where the envoy was going with all of this. Politics was not his forte. He had only been thrust into this role out of necessity. "Yes, I was aware of that war and the troops I stationed within the Confederation to participate in that fight."

"Good. Though, there was a development during the conflict that you may be unaware of."

"Is that so? Do enlighten me."

"Toward the tail end of that war, the Confederation's chancellor sent envoys north to speak with my leaders in the Northern Cantonment."

Taggart felt his heart beating a little faster. No part of this could bode well for him. Was Cassy capable of falling in league with one enemy to beat another? Then he almost laughed; of course, she was! She was tough and pragmatic. She'd do anything to keep her people safe. Taggart couldn't honestly tell himself he'd have done any differently. Furthermore, he hadn't known they called themselves the Northern Cantonment until just now. This was disconcerting because it meant his intelligence in that region wasn't as good as he had imagined.

Lee continued, "As it turns out, the political situation between the Confederation and the many refugees from the Free Republic, fleeing east, had become rather complicated. Part of the solution to their problem was to offer those refugees weapons, ammunition, and supplies so that they could return to the Free Public and engage the army with guerrilla warfare tactics."

He had known this already, although the news had come through his spies and representatives. "Right. They would also be offered land and membership in the Clan when the war ended, if they would fight in the meantime."

"Of course. So you'll understand that where I come from, regional commanders are not allowed to negotiate separate treaties, but I understand that you will run your territory as you see fit, which is the right of every warlord."

Taggart smiled. Of course the North Koreans would think in terms of warlords and lesser commanders. "It was hardly a separate treaty. They negotiated with refugees, not another country, and the result was supposed to be a large force of immigrants who would become citizens of the Confederation later."

"I believe you are misinformed. You seem to be under the impression that they didn't negotiate a treaty with another country. In fact, as I mentioned, they had sent envoys to the Northern Cantonment to do precisely that."

Intellectually, Taggart understood the envoy was playing games. He had little patience for such nonsense. It was time for Mr. Lee to get to the point. "And just what sort of treaty did they ask for? It seems unlikely that they'd reach out to you under any circumstances, much less for help in a war that didn't involve you."

"Indeed. That was also what we thought, but it turns out that we—and you—were wrong about that. It seems they gave the refugees more supplies than they could afford to part with, and so they would not have had enough to support themselves throughout the long winter."

"I would hate to continue this discussion under assumptions, Mr. Lee. So tell me, what was the nature of the agreement?"

A faint smile reached Mr. Lee's lips. "They requested many wagons full of supplies, particularly food. They made the argument that it would cost us less in both the short term and in the long run to support them now, helping them to fight General Houle, rather than allowing Houle to win a foothold in the region. They pointed out that if that happened, the Northern Cantonment would then have to fight him directly. The argument made much sense, so we agreed to meet their request."

"So they asked you for supplies to help them fight their war against General Houle, and you agreed? It seems to me that you wouldn't likely give them tons of supplies and food out of the goodness of your hearts."

"It made long-term sense."

"No one gives away what they have today for a promise of something tomorrow, not anymore," Taggart said with a polite smile.

Inside, he seethed. He had trusted the Clan and had viewed them as his most stable and reliable allies, yet now they were making deals with the enemy, if Lee's word could be trusted. He dreaded finding out what the cost would be for the Clan, and he had the sinking suspicion that Mr. Lee wouldn't be here unless his cantonment wanted something from him, as well.

Lee frowned, leaning back and placing his hand on his chest. "You wound me, sir. Even North Koreans are capable of making wise decisions motivated by self-interest."

"So what does all this have to do with New America?"

"They made it clear that the Confederation was a state within New America. They asserted that their debt would be met regardless of the outcome of that war. There was no specific date by which full repayment was demanded, which left it open for us to decide."

Taggart said, "I question the authority of the Confederation to make binding treaties in the name of New America, plus I won't be bound by a treaty I haven't seen."

"I have a copy of it here." Lee reached into his suit coat inner pocket and withdrew a sheet of paper, which he unfolded and then set on the coffee table. "As you will see, the repayment date isn't listed. It only says that repayment will be made at a future date agreeable to the Northern Cantonment."

Taggart read through the document once carefully, and to his dismay found that Mr. Lee's position was indeed supported by the treaty, which had been signed by two Confederation envoys in the presence of several witnesses. Damn. But he wasn't going to admit to anything. Not yet. He couldn't let Lee win that easily.

Taggart looked up at Mr. Lee and raised his eyebrows. "This still means nothing to New America. Sounds like you need to take this up with the Confederation, not me."

"Since a member-state of New America was engaged in a war for its survival," Lee said, "it can be reasonably assumed that New America has a vested interest in the well-being of that state, and therefore would support any steps it took to secure its survival."

Taggart hated being painted into a corner. The only reason he didn't immediately dismiss the idea of assuming that debt was that the supplies had probably made the difference between life and death to the Confederation, and therefore the Clan. As the governor of the Confederation and his secretary of agriculture, Cassy's loss would have been a tremendous blow. The loss of the Confederation would also have left Houle with a strong beachhead from which to threaten the rest of New America.

Taggart glanced back at the document. "It says in this treaty that the specific items requested and their quantities are to be listed in an addendum. I don't see that here."

"Of course," Lee said, reaching into his pocket a second time and pulling out another folded document. "Here is the addendum, signed and countersigned by the Confederation envoys and witnesses."

Taggart clenched his jaw and reached for the paper, unfolding it.

Lee continued, "As you can see, it's a significant quantity. It wasn't easy to gather everything they requested and deliver it, especially not in such a short order, but time was of the essence. I don't know why they didn't come to you for this. Perhaps you lacked the supplies they needed?"

Taggart stared at Lee, unblinking. He probably still lacked so many supplies, but if Lee became convinced of that, then they'd be at war in a week, if not less.

"In any case," Lee continued, "we would rather have the Confederation on our border than General Houle, especially if we have bought some peace from them by doing so."

At last, Taggart said, "So what is it that you're asking?"

"Now that spring is here, and you have begun harvesting the early crops and planting more, the Northern Cantonment is asking for those supplies back. The Confederation obviously cannot repay this debt, given that they are still rebuilding from the damage done during the war."

Taggart took a deep breath. The first war debt of post-America, and it had fallen on his lap. There was no way he could repay such a sizable debt right now nor could he really afford renewed hostilities with the Northern Cantonment. Not when things were so up in the air with the Maryland invaders, not to mention the situation in Philadelphia. The only option, then, was to buy time.

"Mr. Lee, I thank you for bringing this to my attention. I'm sure you're a busy man, too. That being said, I can't just commit to repaying this until I've had a chance to study its effects on New America."

"Of course. How much time will you need?"

"Well, I need to gather data on our stockpiles, our transportation capabilities, and other relevant details. I require, let's say, three months to gather this information. Only then will I be able to tell you whether New America can honor the Confederation's debt."

Lee's face became a rigid, iron mask. "That isn't acceptable, Mr. President. I've been advised that we have no issue with waiting for the results of your study, but no more than one month."

"And if that's not possible, or if we find we're unable to meet your request?"

"If one month isn't acceptable, or if your answer is no, then the Northern Cantonment will have to consider alternative means of ensuring this debt is settled."

Taggart felt trapped. If he blatantly said no, then he risked open conflict with the invaders to his north just as things were heating up to his south. But he wasn't going to promise anything either. "As the President of New America, I am officially telling you that we acknowledge your position, and we find that one month is at least enough time for us to gather preliminary information, and to contact the Clan and Confederation leadership to obtain more details about the treaty and your interaction with their envoys."

At this point, Taggart hoped that Lee would accept the possibility of a resolution rather than choosing to go to war. At best, he hoped to avoid escalating border tensions, but avoiding more open warfare would be good enough.

"Very well," Lee said as he stood. Taggart rose to his feet as well. "I will return in thirty days, though, I sincerely hope for all our sakes that you will have completed your studies and can commit to fixing this. It's in everyone's best interests."

Taggart nodded and shook Lee's hand, then escorted him to the door and closed it behind the departing envoy. As Taggart returned to the couch and sat, he called out for Eagan—he needed a stiff drink. When Eagan came out of the side office, Taggart said, "Whiskey, please. I assume you heard all of that?"

Eagan wandered to the bar and poured a tumbler. "How could I not listen in? Far too interesting to respect your privacy, sir."

"Of course you were eavesdropping, why do I even ask?"

Eagan handed him the glass. "I'll immediately put out word to gather the information you need, so you can at least make an informed decision."

Taggart let out a long, deep sigh. "So... Jaz and Choony. You think they were involved?"

Eagan moved to the other side of the table and sat in the chair recently vacated by Lee, and leaned forward. "There's no way they knew about this Confederation deal with the 'vaders. If they had, they would have brought it up by now. I mean, they've been here all winter, right? I suspect they were just out of the loop."

Taggart nodded. That made sense, especially since those two had been running around the countryside acting as Clan envoys since long before the war against the Mountain. "I tend to agree. Let's not mention this to them until we hear back from the Clan. Which reminds me, I need you to send someone out to Clanholme to get their side of the story."

Eagan pulled out a pen and notepad and wrote a quick note to himself. "Well, at least we have a month to figure this all out. Hopefully, that's enough time to deal with our situation to the south."

Taggart furrowed his brow. "Yeah, and maybe we can figure out why the southern invaders are putting so much pressure on our border. I had thought the situation was stable, not only because winter made it impractical to keep the war going, but because we've expanded far enough south now so that we have a stable border with them. I'd like to keep it that way, and hopefully add Philadelphia to the list of people we have a stable border with."

Eagan frowned and said, "I thought we were trying to get them to join New America? I mean, I understand they're dragging their heels, but I'm still hopeful. They should prefer an alliance with us to one with the people they're fighting against, even now."

Taggart shrugged. "Perhaps. But it seems to me that, in this new day and age, people are more pragmatic than they are patriotic. They'll do what's best for themselves, and I can't say I blame them. That's all anyone can do these days if they want to stay alive." Taggart downed his whiskey in one gulp. "Stupid people don't survive anymore."

- **10** -

1400 HOURS - ZERO DAY +621

NATE RUNKE STOOD within the command post and stared at the huge, laminated map, spread out on the table, covered in grease-pen notes and symbols. In the distance, he heard a continual barrage of light mortar fire, the result of his own huge push to fabricate those oh-so-effective weapons of war.

When he ordered their production, some of the other commanders had given him a lot of pushback. They had argued that those resources could be better used elsewhere, but he was The Dude, now. This was his show, and he made the rules.

He didn't particularly enjoy being in charge, but he was certain that he was the most effective choice for the position. History had proven him right. His forces had taken over, his strategies had pushed the enemy back, and his leadership had liberated Philadelphia. Given his successes compared to theirs, he hadn't hesitated to ignore his fellow commanders' advice when they pushed hard to put resources elsewhere. He had continued diverting resources into mortar production, and now they were seeing the results. As with every other issue so far, he had been right about the mortars.

Now, on the day of the largest push against the invaders so far, message runners had been coming in and out of his headquarters all afternoon delivering good news. Everywhere, the enemy was falling back. Nate's forces had secured access to the lightly forested area southwest of the city—the last bastion of enemy resistance—and were fighting their way to completely outflank the enemy. They had nowhere to hide, now. They weren't safe anywhere, and he had no intention of letting them catch their breath.

There was no frontline anymore, Nate thought with a grin. Instead, his troops were becoming fully interpenetrated with the enemies. He felt confident that by dinnertime, the war would be over—at least for Philly.

Two hours later, just as Nate had suspected, an enemy envoy was dragged into his command post. Nate saw he had been stripped to his skivvies and sported several fresh bruises on his chest and face. Clearly, his guards had gotten over-enthusiastic with their questioning. Nate felt slightly surprised that it didn't bother him. The last two years of slavery and war had changed him, as it had changed everyone.

He turned to face the envoy, who had been shoved roughly to his knees on the floor, and waited. The now-prisoner spent a couple of seconds getting himself adjusted on his knees, regaining his balance, then looked up at Nate and met his gaze directly. He was clearly Korean, and he bowed his head for a moment before saying, "I have been instructed to deliver a message to the one who is called Nate Runke, commander of the rebel forces."

Nate stared the envoy in the eyes for several seconds, then began to walk slowly around him clockwise, his pace slow, and his eyes roved every inch of the man. Not only was he gaining the measure of the envoy, he was also using an old psychological trick he had once seen on a TV episode, where standing behind someone created a position of power and caused the other party to feel a lot of anxiety. Hopefully, it would put the guy off balance and establish dominance.

It took Nate about twenty seconds to finish his circuit around the envoy, ending where he had started. He met the man's gaze again, then slowly nodded. "I am Commander Nate Runke. I assume you're here to negotiate your unconditional surrender. For your sake, I hope so."

The envoy bowed again, saying, "Yes, sir, I am. The rightful commander of the city of Philadelphia, a holding of the Eastern Cantonment, has determined that his situation is untenable. Although we could cause you great harm and many losses before the last of us fell in battle, the end is now inevitable. He would like to know your terms."

Nate laughed out loud, but it was forced. Just a little bit of theater. "Well, it's good that your leader can see the plain, simple truth. He has lost. Philadelphia is mine. The only question now is whether he and what's left of his soldiers die before I complete my victory."

The envoy clenched his jaw, but nodded. He didn't respond, apparently content to let Nate lead the conversation now that his purpose had been stated.

"My terms are simple. All remaining invasion forces in and around the city must leave immediately. They will not bring their weapons or ammunition, and they will not bring their food or other supplies. Their equipment and gear will also remain. They will be allowed to leave with the clothes they wear and personal effects, nothing else. If your commander meets these conditions, then I'll agree to a seventy-two hour cease fire."

The envoy didn't flinch or break eye contact. "What must we do with the materials we leave behind?"

"Your forces will gather them into a single, convenient location and leave them there before you march south forever. My observers will be everywhere, and if any are harmed, I will kill two of you for each of mine who are injured. I'll kill one of your officers for each of my men who is killed. And in the end, I will kill every last one of you bastards who remains after the seventy-two-hour cease fire ends. Those are my terms, and if they are not met, then you'll die."

The envoy bowed low and brought his forehead almost to the floor. From that position, he said, "It is well. The rightful commander of Philadelphia agrees to your terms. And by the way, he has instructed me to tell you that you have his word of honor that we will comply."

Nate took one long step forward, then snapped his right foot forward, smashing it into the man's jaw. The envoy flopped over, grabbing his face and crying out in pain. Nate said, "Your commander has no honor. My guns will make sure he keeps his word far more effectively than his so-called honor. Now go. And if you are not all out of my city in three days, not only will I exterminate your forces who remain, we will chase the rest of your bloodied lot and ride you into the ground, sparing none." He waved his hand at the envoy dismissively, and his two guards grabbed the man roughly by each arm to drag him limp and dazed out of the command center.

Nate smiled, hoping it took the man a few minutes to regain his footing after a blow like that. It felt good. Part of him wished they had refused to leave so he could enjoy the feeling of killing more of the bastards. Sadly, life had put him in a leadership position; he had to put aside his own desires for the welfare of his people. Also, he had other plans to occupy his time for the next few days.

* * *

0800 HOURS - ZERO DAY +625

Nate stood in the copse of trees, and his command staff surrounded him. His HQ consisted of several pavilion tents set up in a clearing, with his personal tent set dead-center. Nearby, he had two desks with old-fashioned typewriters on them, each manned. That would be how orders were relayed if the rudimentary flag system he had created proved inadequate. In that case, he had a dozen runners standing by to carry typed orders to his subordinate commanders, who would then relay down the chain as needed.

The problem with that method was that it could take five minutes or more for his orders to go into effect, assuming they didn't ask for clarification and there were no interruptions. The flags were much faster, but the distance he could deliver orders with them was pretty limited. He made a mental note to work on a more complex semaphore system for the future.

Beyond the trees, in the vast fields surrounding the Gap, he had three of his sub-commanders and their units arrayed in a semicircle south of the town. For this mission, all the soldiers had shaven, there were only men in the frontline units, and he had ordered black face paint on every soldier. They wore stolen North Korean uniforms.

The Gap was the newest Clanhold, from what he had learned, and was still being reconstructed. That meant tons of supplies lying around, most importantly food. It was all sitting deliciously in a warehouse on the south side of town. Today's raid had one objective: seize as much food as they could and escape without revealing their true identity. He wanted the North Koreans to take the blame for this.

In the distance, he heard the first shots being fired. Two of his sub-commanders were running interference, engaging the town's defenders and trying to hold them in place or push them back. The third commander and his unit would raid the warehouse itself and escape on foot to the wagon train parked nearby. For this mission, he was using fully half of his total troop strength and all of his wagons and mules. Most of those had only just been taken from the North Koreans when they left the city.

It had been a grueling fast-march from Philadelphia, and his troops were still tired. They would soon be even more tired because after the battle, they would have to fast-march back home using a roundabout route to complete the deception.

His was a simple plan, and with any luck, the defenders would blame the 'vaders. Everyone knew the Koreans were pressing Americans into service down in Maryland, so even if they saw a few of his American soldiers, the ruse should still hold.

Nate's heart beat a little faster as he thought of all the food they would seize, enough to keep his troops fed until the fall harvest. A few people from the Confederation might end up starving, but Nate was a realist. Right now, Philly had more people than food. He could either let his own people starve or take it from those better able to absorb the losses. It had been an easy decision.

One of his flag messengers ran into his HQ and saluted him. He said, "Commanders One and Two are in place and report they're ready to begin the operation. Commander Three can now move in."

Nate patted the man on the shoulder with enthusiasm. "Excellent. Go flag the third commander and advise him to begin. Tonight, we all eat well."

As the messenger ran out, Nate turned back to his maps. They were being continually updated by his staff, who based changes on reports from messengers and scouts with binoculars. It was slow and tedious, but these days, it was the best he could do. He was fairly certain his preparations and troops would be enough.

He grinned. He, Nate Runke, was now supreme commander of the Philadelphia Free City, and he was about to lead his people into having enough food for the summer.

As he looked at the map, Nate's mind danced with visions of new ranks, new uniforms, new ways of running the government. He decided that not everything about this postwar world was a bad thing.

* * *

1400 HOURS - ZERO DAY +628

Mark Bates swiped his key card and entered his suite, and was immediately bombarded by his seven-year-old son, Junior. He gave the boy a big hug and ruffled his hair, smiling.

Lucy came out of the kitchen, and on seeing him, her expression changed from one of wariness to one of joy. Mark never came home early; his days were too busy for that, so he had surprised his family.

Lucy said, "You scared me half to death. What are you doing home so early?" She walked up and wrapped her arms around his waist, leaning her head against his chest.

Mark rested his cheek on her head, enjoying the way her hair smelled. For some reason, it had been one of the things he liked most about her since they had first met. "I had a department meeting today, but it fell through. I decided to bring my work home so I could see you guys. Besides, if anyone needs me, I've got my cell phone."

Lucy disentangled herself from her husband and took a step back to look at him. "We had lunch a while ago, but I can make you something."

Mark nodded and smiled at his wife. "That would be fantastic. I didn't get a chance to grab lunch today." He didn't tell her that he missed lunch because he had been busy finding alternate copies of the report Janice had given him days ago.

As Lucy wandered back into the kitchen and Junior went back to playing video games on the suite's single TV, Mark sat down on the couch and set his briefcase on the coffee table. He popped it open and pulled out a single manila envelope. For a moment, he eyed it warily. Three copies of the report, all from different sources within the chain, meant for different divisions. He hadn't examined them yet, and he had actually been putting it off. He was a little afraid of what he might find.

Lucy came back out carrying a plate and a glass of juice, which she set down on the coffee table. "I've got to go to the PX and run a few more errands. Could you watch Junior while I'm out?"

Mark nodded. Of course he would. He didn't get enough time with the boy as it was. A few minutes later, Lucy left to run her errands, leaving Mark alone with Junior. He opened his envelope and pulled out the three sheets of paper. At first glance, the other two copies were the same as the one Janice had given him. He went carefully, line by line, first checking the headers and footers before moving on to the main body.

Mark read through each copy carefully, circling any subtle variations on his original with different colored pens.

Twenty minutes later, when he was finished, he looked at the original report, now littered with blue, red, and black marks. None of the circles overlapped. This clearly ruled out a simple typo. No, he now had clear confirmation that the Intel spooks had laid out a honey trap.

Which meant that if he had sent Janice's report out and any were discovered by the counterintel people, he would have revealed that there was a leak. After that, they would have gone through the chain of possession, starting at the top and working their way down. Eventually, they would have found the leak. If that happened, the best possible outcome would be that he lost a valuable source. Far more likely, Mark's asset would have given up his name under "questioning," and then he and the asset would both be dead.

His mind raced, trying to decide whether they suspected him or one of his assets, or whether they were just casting out a counterintelligence net simply to see if they caught anything.

Either way, there was a crucial piece of the puzzle he was missing and only one person who knew it—Janice.

Taking a deep breath, he slid the papers back into the envelope, then secured it in his briefcase. All he could do now while he waited for Lucy to return was finish his lunch, spend time with his son, and forget about all the ways this could go wrong.

* * *

The market area was a chaotic maze of stalls and wagons, pavilions and simple tables, all set up to display people's wares. The Hoboken security forces kept a broad stretch open in a single line running from one end of the market to the other, wide enough for four wagons, but other than that, it was left up to the merchants to arrange themselves.

The result reminded Jaz of something out of an Arabian Nights movie. Merchants were selling all kinds of food on the main drag, but it was often overpriced. They had to pay more for those spaces, and they passed that on to their customers. It was sort of like a convenience tax. Jaz wanted the fresher stuff, at a better price, but it took a lot of time to wander through the maze to find those.

She carried a basket on her left arm, keeping her right hand free in case she needed to reach for her weapon. After all, Hoboken was a bit like a frontier town, still. Wild and woolly.

After winding her way through ever-narrower ad hoc alleys, she found a covered wagon way in the back that had a pull-out table built on the side, on which were arranged all sorts of kimchi jars. Different sizes, different vegetables, and it looked like some were made with vinegar and others the old-fashioned way with just salt and spices.

Choony could never get enough kimchi, and Jaz too became addicted to the stuff. Something about the way it was fermented always made her feel better after eating it for a few days, so when she found it, she always bought it. She stepped up to the table and began looking through the jars.

The merchant was a heavyset older woman, though she looked Hispanic, not Asian. She said, "I see you have an eye for quality. You'll find nothing but the best, here. Can I help you find something in particular?"

Jaz smiled and said, "Yes, my... boyfriend, I guess, grew up eating kimchi, and now I love it too. He likes the stuff that's made the old-fashioned way, and I want to surprise him for dinner. What would you recommend?" She knew she was inviting the merchant to offer her most expensive wares, but she had learned that these were often the best-tasting ones. Also, with some haggling, these more distant merchants would usually throw in some of the smaller jars of stuff that wasn't selling well. They certainly made a nice snack.

The woman smiled, the many creases that formed around her eyes suggesting she did so often. It was a warm and friendly smile. "You know, the ones they put out on display are mostly for the locals, most of whom don't really know good kimchi. The best stuff is in the back. Give me a moment while I pull some out for you." Jaz nodded, and the merchant went to the back of her wagon and climbed inside.

Jaz could hear her rummaging around. She occupied herself by examining the many smaller bottles on the table as the woman rummaged about when something hard jammed into her ribs and her head spun around by reflex. She found that there was a man standing next to her, and he looked familiar. It took a moment, but then she recognized his scheming blue eyes and the baby face that was nothing more than a facade. A wave of fear washed over her as her subconscious alerted her to danger. It was Jack, the creep from the party at Clanholme before the war against the Mountain.

As Jaz's eyes grew wide, Jack grinned. "I see you remember me, but of course, how could you forget?"

She felt a flash of rage and turned to face him, the better to yell at him. Then she felt something hard against her abdomen. She looked down to find that Jack held a pistol to her. Her jaw dropped.

Jack said, "That's right, I'm in charge here. You and I need to have a talk. Let's walk—go that way," he said and pointed to his left, toward the market maze's farthest edge. Beyond that lay a deserted part of the city, not yet reclaimed.

When Jaz didn't move, his eyes narrowed and he pushed the barrel into her belly even harder. "If you don't want to die right here in the street, I'd suggest you get moving."

Jaz had been momentarily paralyzed with fear, but now her mind began to race. There was no one around except a few merchants, and none of them were looking at Jack and her. The nearest merchant was still inside her covered wagon. Jaz could scream, but she felt pretty confident Jack would kill her if she did. Not only that, he might also shoot whoever came to help her. She couldn't have that on her conscience, but this guy was weak. She could deal with him later, when there weren't any other potential victims around. She nodded once curtly, then headed toward the edge of the market.

A couple of minutes later, they were out of the market and well into the deserted part of town. It had been mostly small warehouses and light construction before the war, and most of those buildings still stood.

They reached an intersection and Jack said, "Turn left."

Silently, she obeyed. They walked many blocks before he told her to stop. He pointed toward a door that had been left slightly ajar.

"Go in there," he said, "and keep walking until you're in the center of the room."

Stiff-legged with fear, she walked through the dark portal and knew she was making a bad decision. But what else could she do with a gun pointed at her? She couldn't spin around and kill him. She couldn't go for her gun. If she tried to do either, he'd just pull the trigger. She figured it'd be best to bide her time until the asshole slipped up.

When she got through the doorway, she saw that the warehouse had been arranged like a large studio apartment. On the far wall was a California King bed set, and all the other features of a real house spread out from there. To the bed's right, in the back corner, Jack had used room dividers to set up a separate area. From the disgusting odor, which she could smell even from the middle of the room, that would be the bathroom. Probably using a bucket toilet, and not even smart enough to add sawdust. Super.

She heard the door close behind them and the distinctive click of the lock being secured.

Jack said, "Home sweet home, darling."

She was really getting tired of men calling her "darling."

Jack motioned to the dirty mattress that was supported by a sturdy-looking frame, maybe solid steel, and was bolted to the cement floor. "Do me a favor and move over to the bed."

She didn't want to go near the disgusting thing, but she didn't want to die either. She stood frozen, unable to make herself walk to the bed.

"Jaz, I really don't want to hurt you. I really want us to get along, so it would be a shame if I had to mess you up. Now be a good girl and go to the bed. Lie down on your belly and put your hands behind your back."

Oh, hell no. She tried to think of something fast, but nothing was coming to her.

"I'll count to three, and if you're not on that bed, I'm going to shoot you in the knee."

Stiffly, she nodded and sauntered toward the bed. Her eyes darted all around the room looking for something to save her, some way of getting out of this situation. Maybe she'd be able to shoot him when he wasn't looking. Did he know she had a gun? He hadn't looked, yet. She reached the bed and stood at the end, staring at it. Then she felt a rough shove from behind, and when her knees hit the bed, she toppled onto the mattress face first. Gross.

Jaz felt Jack's weight on top of her as he wrenched her arms behind her, one at a time, and she let out a grunt. When both arms were behind her back, she felt cold metal on her left wrist and the ratchet of handcuffs closing, followed quickly by the same on her right. Now she was cuffed with her hands behind her back, almost completely helpless. She said, "Despite what you may think, chicks totally don't dig this sort of thing. You want me to like you, don't you?"

He laughed aloud, still sitting on top of her and said, "You don't like me? That's a shame because I know what you want. Little skanks like you, always asking for the 'Big D' and then acting all surprised when dudes want to give it to you." Jack brought his lips close to her ear and whispered, "I've been watching you. Last week, in the market, you dressed the same way you did back at Clanholme. You obviously need a real man. We both know your gook boyfriend can't get the job done. That's what ol' Jack here is for."

"You do know that only lonely, pathetic freaks refer to themselves in the third person, right?" Jaz said. She shouldn't be surprised, having dealt with men like him before—they always blamed their insecurities on how she chose to dress. Only this time, she wasn't going to put up with it. Not without a fight.

Jack sat up, moving away from her ear and clicking his tongue. "So unfortunate, Jaz, that even in the new world people still stereotype others."

Jack moved to the head of the bed, his gun never wavering as he pointed it at her. From behind the headboard, he reached down to grab something. She heard the distinctive *clink, clink* of a chain rubbing against metal.

Sure as hell, when Jack stood up straight again, she saw he held a chain in his hand. "But I won't hold it against you, darling. Since you are a guest in my house, I suppose my job, as a host, should be to show you a good time." With a pistol in one hand and chain in the other, Jack moved until he stood directly next to her as she lay cuffed on top of the bed. He pointed the gun at her temple, "So, let's try to play nice, shall we?"

Then he climbed onto the bed and sat on her back. She felt her shoulders strain as his weight pushed her down into the mattress, and she bit her lip to fight from crying out. She was totally not giving the guy the satisfaction.

He moved the chain over the back of her neck, then brought it around the front. As he reached under her neck, she had the brief urge to bite down on his arm. Maybe she could tear a chunk out of him. But of course, if she did that, he would just pull the trigger, and she would be dead.

She felt the chain being wrapped around her neck and heard the metallic sound of a padlock being secured.

Jack climbed off her back, and she breathed deeply to catch her breath again. Then she felt a tug on her hip—Jack took her pistol. He must have felt it while he was straddling her. Then he undid the handcuffs around her wrists. "Sit up. Hold your hands out in front of you, wrists together."

Jaz did as she was told. She soon found her wrists cuffed again, but this pair of cuffs had a much longer chain connecting the two sides. Jack then padlocked that chain to the first one. In effect, Jaz could use her hands, but not very well.

He grinned at her and said, "There. Now, I suggest you behave yourself, and this will go a lot easier for you."

She resisted the urge to spit on him. Her mind reeled, not quite believing this was actually happening to her. Jack had to leave sometime, if only to get food, and maybe she could scream then... draw some attention, get rescued. Of course, this was an abandoned part of town, and the building had once been a warehouse. She could see the distinct pattern of brickwork all throughout the walls, meaning they were thick and solid. They were made of cinder block and would be all but soundproof from the outside.

She looked at Jack and saw him looking back. His expression was one she had seen many times before when she was younger. It was a look that promised bad things to come.

Well, she had learned how to survive all those other times, and she could survive this.

Eventually, she would have her opportunity. And when she did, Jack would die.

* * *

In her office building, just outside of Clanholme, Cassy sat in her swivel chair at the desk, looking at her monitor. Six other faces stared back at her, members of the Confederation. Over the last few months, Ethan had managed to set up a haphazard videoconferencing system, but it only worked at a certain time every day—after lunch and before dinner—because it relied on satellite uplinks. Apparently, the "bird" was only overhead at that time.

Cassy had called the impromptu meeting today to discuss what she felt was a growing threat. "Thank you all for being available on such short notice. I'm sure you'll all agree, we face a threat worth your time."

On-screen, Frank nodded. "Thank you, Chancellor. I appreciate that the Confederation takes this threat seriously."

The Liz Town leader, Carl Woburn, frowned. Cassy had felt pity for him since the very first video conference, a couple of months after the Mountain War. He had looked so haggard compared to the vibrant man she'd first met as the Liz Town envoy. The rumors said that he had lost his one true love during that war, and ever since then, he hadn't been taking care of himself. Apparently, he rarely ate or slept, and his face showed it. Cassy could see none of the vitality that had once oozed from his every pore.

"My apologies, Cassandra," Carl said, unenthusiastically, "but I fail to see how this is a Confederation-wide problem. So you've had a few raids from the south, lost a few people. Liz town dealt with that and more during the entire first year after the EMPs, but I don't recall everyone coming to our rescue, or even offering to help. You were all just glad to have us as a buffer against the Harrisburg raiders. You only stepped in during the endgame."

The Lititz rep shook his head, and his eyes flashed with anger. "That's bullshit, and you know it. We all sent supplies we couldn't afford, trying to help you deal with the Harrisburg and Hershey raiders, and we couldn't send troops because there weren't enough fighters to go around. You may remember, we all had our own problems back then. Hell, Brickerville almost got conquered twice and Ephrata lost a tenth of its people defending the rest of the Confederation. We all did what we could, and faced our many threats together."

On the screen, Carl pursed his lips and shook his head, but didn't reply.

Cassy seized on the opportunity Lititz had provided her. "That's right, we all dealt with the threats we faced. We all helped each other as best we could, whether that was with supplies or troops. We also all faced local problems alone. Liz Town wasn't unique in that."

The Lebanon rep spoke with vigor, saying, "And I daresay Clanholme and Lebanon were the two that did the most for the Confederation. Or have you forgotten how, during that first year, Clanholme provided enough grains for all of us to save most of our remaining people? Most of us would have died without the Clan's help."

Cassy kept her voice even and replied, "We were happy to give that help, then as now, because we were allies. The Confederation is in no way meaningless."

The Ephrata rep slapped her palm against her desk, startling Cassy. "Please don't ever suggest you did more than us, Cassy. We all face problems even now, so I wonder... why is the Confederation chancellor pushing so hard for us all to intervene in a Clan problem?"

Cassy put on a relaxed, casual smile. "I understand your concerns, Ephrata. I think you know as well as everyone else here just how tirelessly I work on behalf of every member of the Confederation. Whether it's to relieve a problem facing one member or to head off a threat to all of us, it's the

Confederation chancellor's job to help coordinate a response to those issues, and that's what I'm doing here. But I don't think this is only a Clan issue. We may be facing a threat that endangers the entire Confederation."

Frank blurted, "When the Maryland invaders get done with the Clan, where do you think they'll go next? The Confederation is a juicy plum, these days, compared to just about everywhere else we know of. It's why we maintain such a strong military. But the Maryland invaders have thrown us a wildcard—they've pressed thousands of Americans into service. They're even wearing North Korean uniforms, as we learned when they raided our supply depot at the Clanhold at the Gap. That changes the game entirely. What was once a nuisance, with raids every couple of months on a small scale, has become a major threat. They aren't raiding us with a company anymore, but with battalions. Maybe more."

Liz Town said, "We haven't seen any evidence of that. We have only your word, based on the reports of your own citizens, that Americans were involved in the Gap raid. Did they collect any enemy bodies? Are we to believe they killed no attackers? I don't think so. If the raid was small enough that no enemy bodies were found, it couldn't have been that large."

Cassy looked directly at her Raspberry Pi-based webcam, her gaze steady. "The residents made it very clear that the enemy attacked in a highly coordinated fashion. They knew exactly what they were going for, pinned the defenders down while they took it, then left. They brought their dead and wounded with them. I ask you, if there was only a company, how did they steal so many supplies? The Gap had a huge wagon train. What the raid took sets us back months."

Carl let out an audible sigh, looking irritated, and replied, "Very well. I'll go with whatever the Confederation says. Liz Town has always been a strong Confed supporter.

Now, if you'll excuse me, I have more important things to do than talk about your conspiracy theories. Let me know what everyone decides."

The Liz Town feed went abruptly dark. Cassy shook her head and wondered just what the hell had happened to Carl. He wasn't the same man after the Mountain War. "Well then. Lititz, Ephrata, Lebanon, Brickerville. I ask you to take this threat seriously. Send us two battle cars each so we can increase our patrols. We can at least see when they're coming, and hopefully, have enough time to respond. Make no mistake—they are coming. The Clan is only the first in line, and Lititz or Ephrata are going to be next."

The Lebanon rep shook his head slowly. Cassy thought he looked sad or perhaps disappointed. He said, "I'm sorry, Cassy. We really would love to help you, but we've got our own problems at the moment."

"Like what?"

"Well, the Northern Cantonment is putting pressure on New America, and if they come to blows, then Lebanon will quickly find itself on the front lines. I know that's only a maybe, at this point, but I believe the threat from the Maryland invaders is also just a maybe. All you have right now are a handful of raids and some lost supplies. I think the Confederation leaders will all agree that more evidence is needed before we divert our resources into what could just be a wild goose chase."

Cassy looked at the other leaders and saw them nodding unconsciously. So, whatever they decided, they agreed with Lebanon. It was damn frustrating. "I completely understand your position. I disagree, and others may as well. I think we need to get in front of this threat before it becomes an overwhelming challenge. I propose that each member of the Confederation send two battle cars, as I said, and one company of infantry to be placed under the Clan leader's command until such a time as the threat has been diverted or more troops are needed. All in favor, raise your hands."

Of course, Frank raised his hand. Lebanon kept his hand down. Lititz, the most likely next in line if Clanholme fell, raised her hand. Cassy looked to the Ephrata and Brickerville reps. It would be up to them. In her head, she counted to three, fervently praying for one of them to raise their hand. If one did, the other probably would also.

No one else raised their hand. Cassy realized she had been holding her breath, and let it out all at once, making a whooshing noise into her microphone. It was done; no help for Clanholme would be coming from the others. She heard Frank curse and log off.

Cassy struggled to put a smile on her face and figured they saw right through it, but politics were politics, and the smile was expected from the Confederation chancellor. After all, the Confederation had spoken.

"Thank you all for making time to come and sit in on this Confederation emergency meeting. I thank you for taking time to vote, as well, and I respect your decisions. I know that each of you voted your conscience, in the best interests of the Confederation as you saw it. I will let you know as more information comes in so that you can each decide individually if you wish to send assistance to Clanholme."

The Ephrata rep smiled back and said, "Of course, Cassy. I understand how urgent you feel this is, and I'm sorry to have to disagree. Until we are at war or more proof of their intentions can be shown, we'll have to sit this one out, but if either of those things happens, call another vote. The Confederation stands together."

The Lebanon rep added, "Strength through unity." Lititz, Brickerville, and Ephrata knocked on their desks in support. Reluctantly, Cassy did, too.

Then she made her formal farewells and ended the

meeting. She put her elbows on her desk and rested her face in her hands, then shook her head. This couldn't be happening. They had to know what was coming. Had Cassy ever led them astray before?

For a moment, she truly missed the old days when she could dictate what happened. It was a faster, easier process getting everyone to toe the line and get together to face any given threat. Now, she had to rule by consent, and that had been her own damn choice. In the long run, of course, the Confederation would be better off for that, but when a threat like this first loomed its head, it was proving to make a rapid response all but impossible.

Dammit. She had to find Frank. They had to think of something.

- 11 -

1900 HOURS - ZERO DAY +628

CASSY FOUND FRANK sitting at his favorite getaway spot, a log bench the Clan had set up on the far side of the eastern retaining pond. It was set amidst a variety of pretty plants, most of which had multiple functions. In that instance, however, they had been chosen more for their scent and their beauty than for their medicinal or food value. Frank often went there when the burdens of leadership were heavy on his mind. She sat down next to him, then said nothing for several minutes before he finally spoke up. "I know you tried to get them to do the smart thing."

Cassy said, "You can lead a horse to water... when this thing blows up on us, they'll rush to our rescue. It's not that they don't want to help, they just don't see the immediate danger."

Frank took a deep breath and let it out slowly. "I only hope it's not too late by then. I know that we're all tired of fighting. Tired of facing a new threat every damn day. We've had peace for a few months now, and they're enjoying it."

"I can't really blame them for that," Cassy said. "I'm tired of fighting, too, but that doesn't mean I'm just going to shut my eyes to every new danger and hope it goes away."

Frank nodded. "Well, I'm not just going to wait for the hammer to drop. The Clan is going to put together a force to try to nip this in the bud. If we can hit them hard, before they're ready to fully invade, then we might be able to delay their attack or even derail it completely."

"I worry that the other members of the Confederation might view that as aggression on your part. Some may not be willing to support you in a war that, from their viewpoint, you started."

He sat up and spat into the dirt. "To hell with them. The Clan has dealt with attackers alone before, without their help. We can do it again. And if the Confederation means anything, then once we're really at war, they'll join the effort."

Cassy was quiet for a moment. What could she say to that? He had a point. A worry crossed her mind that the Confederation might break up, each member joining New America independently. In that case, the Clan would stand alone. She knew Frank had no intention of joining New America until the new constitution was signed. She hoped the other leaders would see reason before that happened.

* * *

Mark Bates stood in the hallway, facing the door. He glanced both ways then knocked, feeling the cool surface against his knuckles. He waited a few seconds but heard nothing.

He knocked again quickly.

A moment later, he heard footsteps coming to the door and Janice's voice from the other side.

"Hold on. I'm coming."

Mark only had to wait a couple seconds before there was a pause of silence, then the jingle of a couple locks before the steel door opened to reveal Janice, hair wet, wrapped in a large towel. Her eyebrows were scrunched together in confusion. "Mr. Bates? Is everything okay?"

"Yeah, I just have to ask you something."

"Okay," she said, motioning for him to come in.

He quickly stepped inside, and Janice closed the door behind him.

"Give me a second," she said. "I'll go get dressed."

She walked to the far corner of the apartment and stopped near her bed. Janice took out some clothes and carried them into the nearby bathroom. While she was dressing, Mark glanced around her studio apartment and noticed the sparse decor. A minimalist perhaps, he mused. Or maybe she was simply more focused on her work than collecting whatever things were available in this new world.

Once dressed, Janice walked out of the bathroom and back into the so-called living room. She wore a pair of shorts made from cut-off sweatpants and a gray tank top.

"What's going on, Mr. Bates?"

"It's about that file I 'found' in your office. Can you tell me where you got it? Who gave it to you?"

"I got it from the department head, of course. He said he got it through his CIA liaison."

"Harry Emerson?"

"Yes, he comes by regularly to talk to the department head. Why? What is this about?"

"Harry Emerson," Mark said slowly to himself, his gaze shifting away from Janice. He took a deep breath as he digested this new information.

"Are you okay?"

Mark looked back at Janice. "What?"

"You look pale. Is it—"

"I'm fine. Thanks, Janice." Mark turned toward the door. "Listen, I gotta go."

Mark stepped toward the door and heard Janice call from behind him. "Wait."

But Mark was already out the door, rushing along the hallway to return to his quarters. He had a lot of thinking to do about what Emerson's involvement with all three trap documents meant, and how to adjust his tactics.

It was going to be another long night.

* * *

Choony sat on his living room floor, legs crossed and hands resting on his knees. His eyes were closed, but he was far from asleep. Jaz had not returned yet, and she should have been back two hours ago. He hadn't wanted to separate in the first place, but their duties in Hackensack sometimes sent them in different directions, and that day had been one of those times.

After he finished a string of brief meetings with various merchants, politicians, and some suppliers with whom he and Jaz had been negotiating on behalf of the Clan, he had rushed home only to find that Jaz wasn't back yet. He had assumed she was simply out shopping, but as the wall clock's hour hand continued to sweep forward, he grew increasingly concerned.

Worrying about Jaz wouldn't make her get home any faster, he reminded himself as he went through a series of chants that were used to calm turbulent minds. It wasn't working nearly as well as he had hoped.

Now, it was nearly 8 o'clock, and his mind bounced back and forth between being angry at Jaz and being frightened for her welfare. Neither of those emotions would help her nor bring her home faster, but he couldn't help it. With a heavy sigh, he gave up on meditating and climbed to his feet.

He grabbed his jacket and headed out through the door,

but when he put his hand on the doorknob, he paused. Maybe he should leave a note... He searched and found a pen and paper, then wrote a note for Jaz—if she got back before he did, he wanted her to know where he went. That done, Choony left the house. He locked the door behind him, then went down his walkway and out onto the sidewalk.

Ten minutes later, he found himself at the hotel where Squirrel and Lance had said they were staying. He got the room number from the front desk, then knocked on their door.

Squirrel answered it. On seeing Choony, he smiled and said, "Hello there, buddy. Did you forget something?"

Choony shook his head. "No. Listen, have you seen Jaz? She went to the market but hasn't come home yet. I thought she might have stopped by to socialize a bit." Choony realized he was speaking too fast, his fear threatening to overwhelm him, so he took a deep breath and let it out slowly. He felt his pulse begin to slow a bit.

Squirrel's smile faded in an instant. "No, I haven't seen her since our lunch meeting. When was she supposed to be back?"

Lance came up to the door, standing behind Squirrel, and nodded at Choony in greeting. "Don't just stand there, Squirrel. Invite a guest in."

Squirrel stepped aside and motioned for Choony to come in. "My apologies. Please, come in. So when did you last see her?"

Squirrel closed the door behind him. Choony glanced around the hotel room, but there was nothing unusual about it. Nothing was out of order, and he thought their body language said they were being honest. "I saw her at lunch, but then I had to go to a bunch of meetings. She went to the market to get dinner while I was doing that."

"What time was that?" Lance asked.

"That was at fourteen hundred hours. I got back to our house at about seventeen hundred hours, I think. I've been at home waiting for her ever since then."

"Maybe she got distracted when she was wandering around the market by herself?"

"I thought of that. But she would never be this late."

As Choony spoke, Squirrel and Lance listened quietly, their expressions growing more concerned. By the end, Lance was shaking his head. Squirrel rubbed his chin and seemed to be deep in thought for a moment, then he looked back at Choony and said, "All right. We have a very attractive young woman who was out shopping by herself, now missing. Hackensack may be the New America capital, but it's still a rough place."

Lance shrugged. "Like just about every city is. Anything could've happened. You don't know it's bad, yet." Then he took a step forward. "Obviously, Squirrel and I are going to have to join you in looking for her. I suggest we each take a different section of the market to search through and meet up every half hour at that one merchant's stall selling copper pipes."

Choony nodded. "Thanks. I won't forget this. Just leave a message with Roy, the owner, saying what time you checked in."

Squirrel nodded in agreement as he put his hand on Choony's shoulder and looked him in the eyes. "Let's all agree to come get the rest of us, if any of us find her before we move in. We don't know what we're dealing with."

Choony's eyes dropped to the floor, and he clenched his jaw at the thought of something happening to Jaz.

Lance put his hand on Choony's other shoulder, then squeezed reassuringly. "You know, the odds are good that when we get back, she'll be at your house waiting for you, or she'll have come here looking for you. She's probably fine, just got lost checking out jewelry or something. Or in her case, maybe a collection of Misfits tee shirts."

Choony realized they were trying to cheer him up, so he gave them a polite smile. After all, he really was thankful that they were going to help him find her. "Okay. If we find nothing, though, I'm going to have to let the local defense forces know. I don't know what they'll do, but what option do I have?"

Squirrel said, "Of course you will. That way, they can keep an eye out for her on their patrols."

Lance added, "If all else fails, I know a few people here in town, trackers—you might call them bounty hunters—who can help for the right price." He gave Choony a smile.

Choony nodded. That was a fantastic idea and one that he had not thought of himself. "Okay, grab your coats and let's go."

The three headed out from the hotel and walked toward the market, where the real search would begin.

* * *

Ethan sat in front of his computer, closing down yet another game from his library. It had been weeks since he left the bunker and he was more bored than he ever remembered being before. He reached up and scratched his chin, then rubbed his hand across his cheeks, realizing he hadn't shaved since his last brush with death.

After the first week down there, he had stopped showering. What was the point? He wasn't going topside, after all. His last human contact had been with Amber, though she had stopped coming down to visit him after their argument. She somehow knew he was hiding something from her. She had always been adamant about being transparent, and here he was, keeping a secret and spiraling deeper and deeper into depression. Part of him thought she should just go on with her life without him because as soon as he stuck his head up out of the bunker, he figured whoever was trying to kill him would get the job done at last. The two failed attempts had convinced him that whoever was out there gunning for him wouldn't stop.

He leaned back in his chair, hands behind his head, and grew more frustrated as he thought about his situation. If he left the bunker, he died; if he stayed in the bunker, he wasn't really living. Eventually, he would get so tired of this that he would go topside anyway, damn the torpedoes. At some point, he would simply stop giving a shit.

His computer beeped loudly, causing him to jump in surprise. He looked at the monitor and saw the old green monochrome chat box, a utility the 20s had remotely installed on his system to communicate with him way back when this had all started. He hadn't heard from Watcher One in a long time, or so it felt.

With a sigh, he leaned forward and clicked the tiny square to bring the chat box to full-screen mode. The green box grew to take up his entire monitor, and as expected, the chat room occupants listed at the top included only Watcher One and himself. Goddammit.

> **Watcher1** >> *Hello Dark Ryder. A little birdie told me you were still "kicking it real" with the Clan. I was disappointed to see that you didn't retire.*

Ethan immediately noticed that Watcher One was chatting in real English. Something wasn't quite right. Though it was unsettling, Ethan responded in kind.

> **Dark Ryder** >> *Yeah, early retirement seemed pointless, what with the general trying to take out the*

Confederation anyway. Instead, I stuck around to kick him in the nuts. Figure of speech, but you know what I mean.

Watcher1 >> *I understand completely. I'm sure my actions over the last two years have been somewhat confusing, but let's not talk about that. You should know that it isn't Gen. Houle who's trying to kill you now. You can blame Maryland for that.*

Dark Ryder >> *Maryland... Why would they target me, specifically? Besides, they're putting tons of pressure on us right now. I don't think they would be concerned with just little old me.*

Watcher1 >> *The Mountain has passed certain information to the Maryland invaders' leader. Some of it was even true, but all of it was meant to inspire them to break the status quo. It worked, it seems, because now they got their finger in your Kool-Aid.*

Ethan looked at the ceiling and spat curses. Goddammit... No doubt Watcher One had been instrumental in arranging communication between Houle and Maryland, too. As far as Ethan could tell, Watcher remained in Virginia somewhere, well within the Maryland invaders' sphere of influence.

Dark Ryder >> *So why are they targeting me, specifically? I'm tired of beating around the bush. Let's just lay it out there. Why does Maryland want me dead any more than some other Clanner?*

Watcher1 >> *As far as I can tell, it's just a favor to*

Houle in return for the information he sent them. They seem awfully buddy-buddy for the self-declared American president and an invading warlord. But what do I know?

Dark Ryder >> *So how did you find out about all this? Kind of makes me wonder. And what's in it for you?*

Watcher1 >> *Let's be real. I know about it because I'm the one who sent the information to Maryland for the 20s and forwarded your information to them at the 20s' directions. I do work for them, after all. As long as we're being honest, I should let you know that the 20s ordered me to try to kill you any way I can. I figure you deserve to know what's coming at you, and why. I don't look forward to it, but it is what it is. I've enjoyed our games.*

Dark Ryder >> *If you're so keen to kill me, why tell me you're coming? I imagine your 20s masters won't be happy with that.*

Watcher1 >> *Oh, this chat utility uses P2P and tunneling. My watchers aren't watching at the moment, so this is just between us. I've respected you since even before I recruited you to the 20s, before all this crap began.*

Dark Ryder >> *Good to know. Thanks for the heads-up. I don't know what games you're playing, but I assume you have a reason for playing them. So, what would you do if I decided not to sit around here and just wait to die? What if I decided I should* *entertain myself in my final days by taking you out with me? Not that I hate you, or anything, but mostly for something to do before I die. Plus, turnabout is fair play.*

Watcher1 >> *You are welcome to try. Who knows, maybe I deserve it. I certainly feel like I do. Still, I'm not going to just wait for you to come. Let's do this! Let's entertain ourselves with some good old-fashioned spy-versus-spy shenanigans. Whoops, my babysitter is waking up. Bye-bye.*

>>*Connection terminated*<<

Ethan stared at the monitor, dumbfounded. Did that really just happen? It was seriously disconcerting to see Watcher One chatting in real English instead of "leet-speak" the entire time. It made the whole conversation feel somewhat ominous. But what was he going to do about all of that? Then, an idea struck him. He grinned and padded softly to the shower. He needed to be presentable when he went topside tomorrow.

If he didn't die before he started playing his game with Watcher One, he would at least entertain himself before he went, and remove a thorn from the Clan's side.

- 12 -

0600 HOURS - ZERO DAY +630

CASSY AWOKE TO gentle shaking. She cracked her eyelids open and found herself squinting at the window; it was still dark out. She turned to look at whoever had woken her, and saw Michael looking down on her as he sat at the edge of her bed. "What... is something happening?" She could barely make her tongue form the words.

In the dim light, she saw Michael smile, but even through her sleep fog, she knew him well enough to see that he was tense.

"Hey, I just wanted to let you know that the increased scouts you authorized are working."

Cassy rubbed her eyes and felt little scratchy bits of sleep sand fall away. "I need to know this now?" she said.

"One of the scout teams radioed in. The Maryland invaders have a battalion of troops, split into three separate companies, advancing through the open area east of Clanholme. Their direction of travel suggests they're headed toward Lititz."

"What's in Lititz worth raiding?" Cassy said. It was too early for this.

"We don't know whether that's their target or if they'll just stumble across it, but they'll be there within an hour. I'm keeping all the Clan troops here. But we have enough Confederation forces to engage them, so that means the Confederation chancellor needs to make a decision."

Cassy let out a huff. Why had he awoken her for this? Of course they should intercept the Maryland raiding party. But then she froze, as a thought struck her. What if the Confederation force didn't move to intercept? Lititz surely had enough troops to hold off a battalion, but more importantly, a raid on Lititz would alert everyone in the Confederation that the Maryland invaders weren't just a Clan problem. Interesting. Of course, if they found out she hadn't sent troops when she could have, the result would be pretty catastrophic.

Cassy looked Michael in the eyes and said, "Who else knows about this?"

"No one but me, you, and half a dozen scouts. It was a Clan battle car patrolling the frontier area who first noticed the raiders."

Quietly, she said, "I think it's best if we keep that between us. I think for the good of everyone, sometimes it's best to let things happen on their own. They would leave Clanholme to fend for itself, so let's remind them what it feels like to stand alone."

Michael nodded. "Of course. Understood."

Cassy felt her brain coming back on line. "See if you can direct that scout unit to some other area, far from Lititz, and then keep them the hell out of Clanholme. Maybe there's a long-range recon thing you could put them on that might distract them for, say, another week?"

Michael stood and brushed his shirt and trousers straight with his palms. "Of course. I have the perfect assignment for them. After all, the Confederation's southwest territory needs patrolling, too. I'll handle the arrangements."

Michael then headed for the stairs down to Cassy's living room. At the archway that led to the stairwell landing, he turned and looked at Cassy once again. "I know this isn't an easy choice for you, but for what it's worth, I think you made the right decision."

* * *

Ethan stood behind the pavilion that covered the Clan's outdoor kitchen and waited. The morning breakfast line was beginning to form, and as new people joined the line, he scanned each person's face while he waited. He had to wait about a half hour before he caught sight of Amber and her daughter, Kaitlyn, getting in line.

For some reason, he felt rather nervous. Probably because he hadn't been topside in far too long, he told himself. He calmed his nerves by straightening his shirt, double checking that his belt buckle was in the right place, and general fidgeting. It gave him a good opportunity to catch his breath and try to calm down. Based on his conversation with Watcher One, he had good reason to believe he had a window of opportunity to leave his bunker. They would come for him, but not today. How many assets and resources had they already wasted, trying to kill him? No, the next attempt would be well organized, and final.

As Amber got closer to the serving stations, Ethan stepped out from behind the pavilion and walked up to her. She didn't see him at first, but when he was a couple feet away, he coughed once hoping to get her attention.

She turned by reflex, and when her eyes met his, there was a brief moment of confusion before her face lit into a smile. He gave her a broad smile back and patted Kaitlyn on the head.

Amber said, "The troll emerges from its cave."

Ethan shrugged and tried to look nonchalant. "I was missing you."

"I missed you."

He smiled. "I needed to see you again."

They both remained quiet. Ethan didn't know what else to say. He knew she was upset with him and knew perfectly well he'd have to answer for his behavior lately, as she wasn't the docile doormat type. He wished he had told her about the assassination attempts. Now, for the first time in a long time, he was nervous to talk to Amber.

As the chow line advanced, they reached the serving stations. Each took a plastic tray salvaged from nearby fast-food joints and received their morning helping of the Clan's simple but hearty chow.

Finally, Kaitlyn broke the tension. She smiled up at him and said, "Hugs." She lifted her arms in the universal symbol for kids wanting to be picked up.

He chuckled and crouched down, then scooped her up in his right arm. His left hand was occupied with holding a tray precariously. "And how is my favorite little girl, today? I missed you." He gave her a deliberate smile.

"Good," she said as she wrapped her arms around his neck and buried her face in his shoulder.

Amber, carrying two trays, smiled at the spontaneous display of affection. "Well, I see somebody missed you."

After they got their food served, he followed Amber to an empty table and set his tray down, then managed to sit while setting Kaitlyn on his lap, in one fluid movement. Amber slid her daughter's tray across the table, placing it next to Ethan's, and Kaitlyn began to squirm on his lap trying to get at the food.

Ethan chuckled. It was amazing how much he had missed this. Some small part of him felt it would be better to die than to live the rest of his life in a dingy cave separated from his two best girls. He sat, enjoying their company, breathing the fresh air and seeing the vibrant signs of life all around him as the Clan came together to enjoy their communal meal. They may kill him soon, but he was going to actually live, in the meantime. Really live.

Amber poked at her eggs quietly for a moment as Ethan interacted happily with Kaitlyn, just watching the two of them together. At last, she said, "So, you want to tell me why you've been hiding out down there?"

Ethan glanced at her and saw she wore no smile. He looked down at Kaitlyn sitting on his lap. "How 'bout you go say 'good morning' to Uncle Michael? He looks like he could use some company."

Before Kaitlyn could respond, Amber said, "No, Kaitlyn, stay here." Amber looked at Ethan. "Kaitlyn has a right to know why you've been hiding yourself away and not talking with us like a family."

Ethan sighed. "The truth is..." he started. He looked down at Kaitlyn again and decided to cup his hands over Kaitlyn's ears.

Amber rolled her eyes but didn't say anything.

"The truth is, someone's trying to kill me."

Amber's eyes went wide. "What? Are you sure?"

"They've tried twice already, the first time killing the wrong person, the second time killing a hapless donkey. And they're still after me." Ethan took his hands from Kaitlyn's ears.

Unblinking, and not taking her eyes off of Ethan's, Amber said, "Kaitlyn, honey, um... why don't you go say 'good morning' to your Uncle Michael."

Kaitlyn slid off Ethan's lap, and he handed the tray of food to her. She carried her tray off toward where Michael was sitting. Once she was out of earshot, Amber said,

"Dammit, Ethan. You didn't think you could trust me with that?"

Ethan looked down, cheeks flushing warm with shame. "I didn't want you to stop coming around. But you did anyway. I know you're not the kind of person who can abide that sort of behavior. I want you to know that I'm sorry. I really regret it, and I regret missing this time with you and Kaitlyn."

When he finished, she replied, "So, what changed your mind?"

"About what?"

"I mean, here you are braving the great outdoors with all the risks that it entails. What changed between yesterday and today?"

Ethan looked her in the eyes for a moment as he tried to decide how honest to be. In the end, though, he decided honesty was the best policy. If he was going to die soon, she deserves to know how and why. He slowly nodded his head as he came to his decision. He said, "I was finally contacted by Watcher One through the old green chat box. He let me know that General Houle is gunning for me. He also said he disagrees with that decision, and while he understood the 'games' he and I played before, there was no purpose to it now."

"What does that matter? He's still after you, I imagine. Who cares if it makes him feel bad?"

"He said he'd had orders to communicate with the Maryland invaders and to provide them with information that would help them attack the Confederation."

"You're ignoring my question..."

"It seems one of Houle's agents is there with him in his Virginia bunker, so he had little choice but to comply."

"And that would make you less dead because... why?"

"I don't know. It's just that this is what precipitated all

this nonsense with the southern invaders. So now, Watcher One and I are engaged in a friendly and deadly game of spy-versus-spy. I think I failed to understand him earlier, back during the last few wars we've had with our neighbors, but maybe I understand him a little better now. And no, that changes nothing."

She raised her eyebrows and took a deep breath, held it for a moment, then let it out slowly. "Oh my God, Ethan. That's... that's quite a story. It seems that Houle is an even bigger prick than we thought. Someone needs to do something about that guy."

What could Ethan say? He totally agreed that Houle could use a bullet to the cranium. Of course, seeing the need and somehow getting into NORAD undetected, 1500 miles away, were two different things. "Well, we can't do anything unless he trips over his own feet. I wish we could be more proactive, but we can't get to his mountain bunker complex. I hate being on defense, but for now, it is what it is."

"Well, I think we should play it safe and you should stay in the bunker. You really shouldn't be out here, Ethan. I'll come by tonight with dinner. I know you haven't had a real meal in over three weeks."

Ethan smiled. He had missed Amber's company, sure, but he had also missed real food. Yes, his decision to come up topside was looking more and more like he'd made a good choice. He nodded. "Thanks, Amber."

* * *

Jaz rose slowly out of sleep, feeling Choony's hands gently stroke her hair. She smiled and wiggled her hips a bit, snuggling into the bed. She cracked her eyelids and squinted against the morning light streaming in through the many skylights.

Wait a minute... their house didn't have skylights. A feeling of vertigo shot through her as her sleep-fogged mind tried to make sense of it, and she spun her head to look over her shoulder.

It wasn't Choony sitting on the bed next to her. Who was that guy?

Her situation came flooding back to her in an instant. *Jack.* She scrambled away from him, but caught up in her blanket, she rolled off the bed and landed on her side. The hard cement floor didn't yield a bit, and fire shot through her hip and shoulder. Despite the pain, she frantically scrambled to her feet, but as she moved, her rattling chain reminded her that she was bound, neck and wrists, to the bed. She could only get so far away from the monster.

"Don't touch me," she screamed, feeling her heart pounding in her chest.

Jack laughed at the display.

Jaz felt loose fabric brushing against her and looked down. Her mouth opened into an "O" shape in her surprise; she was dressed in what looked like a royal-blue toga. She tried to remember when she might have put the thing on, but the last thing she recalled was eating din—

She realized she must have been dosed with something, the "date rape drug" more than likely, and a wave of revulsion washed over her. She imagined that freak undressing her, staring at her, licking his lips, and putting her in this glorified sheet. What else had he done?

Her gaze slid over the toga-thing from shoulder to hemline, the part she could see. It fell only to her upper thigh. The waistline was tied tightly to hug her body, and from the waist down, it was slit on both sides to reveal more of her hips and legs.

"You fucking freak! What did you do to me? Why do I look like a Greek pinup?" Her face flushed red, and she imagined snapping his neck with her legs.

"Oh don't be like that, Jaz," Jack said, getting up and walking toward her. "If you truly didn't want men to adore you for your amazingly hot body, you wouldn't have shown off so much of it."

"Is that the reason you're doing this, Jack? Because you think I dress like a whore?"

Jack chuckled. "Jaz, Jaz, Jaz," he said, shaking his head. "Did you quickly forget how you done me wrong that night we were together?"

Jaz could never forget. It was Blackout Night at Clanholme, where they were commemorating the one-year anniversary of the EMP, when Jack struck up a bizarre conversation with her when she was away from the crowds, walking alone. Jack had grabbed her, and she knew by the look in his eyes, he was going to have his way with her whether she liked it or not. Luckily, Choony found them and was able to defuse the situation and get her away from him safely. Afterward, she'd learned he was on probation as a new member of the Clan, and when Choony told Frank about the situation with Jaz, he was exiled from Clanholme, left to fend for himself.

Now Choony wasn't here. No one from the Clan was. She'd have to get out of the situation herself.

"I get that you're angry about getting kicked out of Clanholme, but when the Clan finds out you kidnapped me, they're going to hunt you down and kill you with their bare hands."

Jack crept closer. "Oh, but it's much more than that. You think I'm doing this alone?" he said with a smile. "The foreplay is just for me."

Jaz's mind reeled. If it wasn't completely personal and he wasn't alone, then he had to be working for someone.

"Who are you working for?"

"I wouldn't worry your pretty, little mind over it. Just relax, and we'll have a good time."

Jaz was far from relaxed. This meant that her kidnapping was much more than she had initially thought. She wondered how long he would keep her before she found out who else was behind this. Or would she ever find out? The only hope she had was that he would slip up, make one small mistake, but then there were the chains. There was no way she could get out of them. She'd have to play along. Gain his trust.

"You know," Jaz said, her voice quiet. The chains from her wrist rattled slightly as she reached out to touch him. "I'm, like, tired of playing coy. I know what you want..."

Jack grabbed her hair, pulling her head back. Jaz let out a yelp. He leaned his face into hers. "You think I am stupid or something?"

"No, no," Jaz said.

"I like my women to beg."

Just then, the door opened, and a man came through with some bottles. Jack, still with a fistful of Jaz's hair, pulled her toward the bed and released her. She toppled on top of the mattress. Shit. Another man.

"Hey, found a few more bottles of liquor stashed in a drawer a couple of buildings down."

"You hear that, Jaz?" Jack winked at her. "We are going to have our own party tonight."

Fuck.

The man with the bottles set them down on a table by the door and looked at Jaz. "Oh, you weren't kidding, Jack. She is a hot, little kitten."

Jaz looked at the man. She didn't recognize him. He was a little tall, but just looked big in every way. Corn-fed, as they say. His jeans were loose and frayed, and his blue tee shirt had old grease stains and what looked like little moth holes here and there. His eyes were mean, brown and dull—when they could be seen from under his shaggy brown lump of hair. He wore a permanent vapid smile, as though everything people said was a joke he didn't want to admit not getting. The lights were on, but no one was home.

Jack turned to Jaz, gazing at her up and down. "She sure is, Chump." A chill ran down Jaz's spine. She felt violated, like he was fondling her with his eyes. "Hand me that bottle of vodka, would ya," Jack said, not tearing his eyes from Jaz.

Chump handed him a clear bottle. Jack opened it and took a swig.

"Your turn," Jack said holding the bottle out to Jaz.

Jaz shook her head. No way did she want to drink with this psychopath. If anything, she'd need a clear head.

"C'mon, it'll relax you," Jack said.

Jaz just stared at him. She wasn't going to give in. There had been too many times in her life she had to deal with assholes like him, and she was tired of being afraid, feeling trapped and helpless. She wasn't going to give in anymore or play their game. She would tell him what he really was to his face—a pathetic loser who preys on women because he was a pussy of a man. And if he wanted to hit her, fine, he'd hit her, and it would prove her point.

But before she could act, Jack leaped on top of her. She struggled against him but he was on her hand, and with the other hand bound to it, she couldn't fight him. He grabbed her face, squeezing her cheeks together, jamming the mouth of the bottle into hers. The alcohol burned her throat as she choked, and she felt more burning through her nostrils as it leaked through her nose. Jack rose and laughed.

"You fucking bastard," she said after a fit of coughing. Her face flushed with rage. "You know what you are? A pathetic loser." Jaz got up. "You're weak, Jack. Why else would you beat and prey on women? You even had to chain me." Jaz put out her hands to show him the cuffs on her wrists. "Unchain me, Jack," she said, her eyes squinting, "or are you too afraid?"

Jack clicked his tongue. "First declining drinks, and now calling your host names? You shouldn't be so rude, Jaz." Jack reached out and stroked Jaz's hair, and she pulled away. "I think it's time you learned your place, kitten." He took another long swig and grinned. Keeping his eyes glued to Jaz, he said, "Chump, grab me another bottle. It's time to get this party started."

* * *

Taggart stood to welcome the envoy as he came in and extended his hand. He shook it with a firm grip, then motioned toward a chair. The envoy sat, and Taggart followed suit, opposite him.

"Mr. Lee, thank you for meeting with me on such short notice. I thought you'd want to know right away."

The young man presented a welcoming smile and said, "Of course. I would assume this means you've gone over your paperwork and considered our requirements?"

Taggart nodded as he placed his hands on his desk. He drummed his fingers on a manila folder and looked intently at Lee. He was a bit uncertain about how his news would be received, given that it was bad news—from the invader point of view. New America could hardly afford a war in the north right now, not when the southern invaders were acting up. It reminded him of an old book he had read on military strategy, before the Industrial Revolution. Back then, without cars and trucks, most warfare occurred during what was called 'campaigning season,' that time between spring and autumn when roads were dry enough and food plentiful enough to accommodate an army on the move.

"We have reviewed it," Taggart said. "It is a lot of information, and we had to send for updates on much of it before we could analyze the data."

Mr. Lee leaned back in his chair and casually crossed his right leg, ankle resting on his left knee. "Of course. I know it was an unusual request, although I'm surprised you didn't have that information already at hand. In the Northern Cantonment, we receive regular reports from each district, and each district commander receives regular reports from the areas under their control. Before we get into your decision, I would just like you to know that your staff has treated me well, and I have found my accommodations to be most adequate. Pleasant, even."

Taggart flashed a brief smile, nodding. "Thank you. Frankly, while I would love nothing more than to shoot you where you sit, we understand that the Northern Cantonment isn't going anywhere. Not anytime soon. Since you're here to stay, at least for the foreseeable future, I afforded you every courtesy due to a visiting foreign dignitary. I'm a soldier, but I'm also a realist."

Taggart envisioned himself plunging his boot knife into Lee's eye. Every damn invader deserved that much and more, but while that would have felt extremely gratifying, killing one enemy underling wouldn't have helped the people who relied on him for their safety. Not yet.

"Indeed," Lee said. "Now that we have the pleasantries out of the way, I'd be delighted to hear what you called me in to discuss."

Taggart reached for the folder on his desk and handed it to Lee. "This is our official analysis, not including anything vital to national security, of course. It's a bit complex, with a lot of numbers and equations, but that's the source data we used in making our decision."

Lee took the offered folder and tucked it between his leg

and the chair's arm, then looked at Taggart expectantly.

Taggart continued, "Unfortunately, we're unable to accommodate your request. First, there's the obvious issue that your deal was between the Northern Cantonment and the Confederation, not New America. More importantly, however, is the second factor. Our analysis shows that we simply are unable to spare so many supplies. It is not our intention to antagonize you or your government. We have managed to leave each other alone since the stalemate after the Second Battle of Scranton, and we've both benefited from the brief, relatively peaceful time since then."

Lee's face shifted subtly, once vaguely welcoming but now stone-cold, unreadable. Taggart resisted the urge to shift in his seat. He reminded himself yet again that a two-front war, if both enemies should turn to open conflict, would be hard to maintain for the still-recovering New America.

Lee was silent for several seconds, his gaze unwavering. At last, he said, "I must say, I'm deeply disappointed. I had hoped we would come to some sort of arrangement. I suppose that this means my leaders will choose to take the issue up with the Confederation directly. It would be preferable for New America to review that situation as a purely regional conflict, rather than allowing the tensions— and any related conflicts—to affect your relations with us."

Nodding slowly, Taggart said, "I do understand your position. While that's a reasonable request, you should know that the Confederation is a New America member-state. Along with that status, there come certain responsibilities on the part of New America as a whole."

Lee folded his hands in his lap and looked up at the ceiling. With his eyes locked onto the ceiling panels, he replied, "I understand your position. I've been authorized to grant you a delay of one month. In that time, it's our hope that you will remind the Confederation of their obligation under the terms of the agreement we made with them."

"You can rest assured I'll be talking to them directly about this."

"Perhaps they could even negotiate a payment plan, rather than the lump sum we first agreed to. The Northern Cantonment wants to be reasonable. Everyone has their challenges these days, but as I'm sure you can imagine, we faced a winter of hardship in order to send off those supplies to the Confederation. Without our supplies, General Houle would almost have certainly won that war, yet we stepped in to assist them. We helped them out of enlightened self-interest, but that changes nothing."

As he spoke, Taggart sat quietly, patiently listening. He found himself nodding in agreement. He realized that he would probably do the same, feel the same, if he was in their situation. Nonetheless, he had an obligation to protect the Confederation, just as he would any other state within New America.

He let out a long breath and said, "We'll definitely speak with their envoys. They have representatives here in Hackensack who are authorized to negotiate on behalf of the Confederation in general, and even more so for the Clan in particular. I'll break this down for them, and if we can't find a good resolution through the envoys, I'll communicate directly with the governor of the Confederation, sending an envoy and put pressure on them."

"I am glad to hear that. It will look better for you in my report, that way."

"That said, I would like two months rather than one."

Lee exhaled sharply through his nose, lips pursed in frustration. "I'm not authorized to give you two months. I'll send a message to my leadership to ask for an extension, but I don't think they'll grant it. So please, operate under the assumption that you will only have one month. After that, the situation will change dramatically, even though it's not what any of us want."

"What do you mean by 'change dramatically'? We want to avoid a military conflict, no matter how heated the economic debate."

Mr. Lee shrugged. "We don't want a military conflict, either. Nonetheless, it will be what it will be. We view economics and troops as being both tools of war. It's not up to me to decide the Northern Cantonment response—that's up to you first and my leaders second."

"It would be a shame to have to fight again." Taggart eyed Lee warily.

"I want you to know I like you, Mr. President. New America has been reasonable to me during my stay here, and I see a profound sense of duty from your people, much different from what our agents observed before the war."

Taggart shrugged, but he couldn't argue with that. America had shed its fat, just as its citizens had. "It seems that those who have survived were the ones who understood hard work and the strength of people working together. If this conflict should escalate into a military conflict, even a low-intensity one, I want you to know that it isn't personal."

Lee smiled wanly. "I, too, would rather we get along well. I wish you the best of luck in getting the Confederation to meet their obligations."

With that, both men stood, and Taggart shook the young man's hand. His grip was as firm as ever, and they exchanged a smile. They were both faking friendliness, Taggart figured, but it was his political obligation to be polite here. He showed Lee to the door and closed it quietly behind him as he left.

When Taggart got back to his desk, he pulled out his favorite whiskey in the world—Wild Turkey. "Eagan, get in here. I know you're listening."

The back door to his office opened, and Eagan stepped in. He didn't wear his usual smile.

Taggart said, "So, I guess that bothered you as much as it did me. It seems that a conflict might be unavoidable."

"Yes, sir. I've seen the numbers from the Confederation's output, current and forecasted. There's no way they can meet more than half of this obligation, and that's assuming they don't have to waste a bunch of resources in a pointless conflict with the other invaders."

Taggart rubbed his chin. "Take a note. I want to send a message to the Southern Cantonment leaders to ask for a diplomatic resolution to whatever issues caused them to be so aggressive lately. Between you and me, if we can get one or the other, north or south, to step back from conflict... well, then we should be able to beat either one of them, individually."

Eagan nodded. "True. And if we can get the southern invaders to stop putting so much pressure on the Confederation, then they'll be in a better position to repay their debt to the Northern Cantonment. As distasteful as it is, it's in everyone's best interest if it goes down that way."

Taggart was quiet for a moment as an idea struck him, and he worked it through in his mind. It just might work, he decided, and snapped his fingers. "Eagan, one more thing. I want you to put your mind toward how we can get the new leaders of Philadelphia to join us, maybe even putting some pressure of their own on Maryland."

"If we can keep the Maryland invaders focused on Philly, they won't be able to divert so many resources into attacking the Confederation."

Taggart nodded. "And it'll be easier to supply one group, Philly, than to feed the entire damn Confederation. I think if we can get Philadelphia to back us, then we can resolve all the rest of these issues piecemeal."

Eagan grinned. "You're getting the hang of this civilian leadership thing, sir. If you ever have kids, you'll be a force to be reckoned with on the local PTA."

"God, Eagan. Just start talking to Philadelphia and see what we can arrange."

Eagan wandered out to the doorway, giving Taggart a sloppy salute on his way. The door closed softly behind him.

Taggart leaned back in his chair, thinking about the problem. It was a pretty shady situation all around, but there was still a reasonable hope that he could navigate these waters without smashing into the reef. Nobody wanted a war, especially not him. Not right now, anyway.

- **13** -

0600 HOURS - ZERO DAY +634

ETHAN RUBBED HIS tired eyes and gently closed the laptop. He hadn't slept much during the past few days as he worked diligently to pinpoint Watcher One's bunker location in Virginia. He'd had to code a new database, into which he had imported every IP address his nemesis had ever been tracked through, and GPS coordinates for each of those relays and servers. To these, he added GPS coordinates embedded in various satellite photos he had previously taken of likely spots for the bunker. Then, he had programmed a new application to narrow the field, trying to get a fix on its exact location.

Although he hadn't reduced the best options to a single location, he had gotten it down to a number he could count on one hand, all within a twenty-mile radius within rural north Virginia. Twenty square miles was an unimaginably large area to search for something as hard to find as a bunker entrance, but that number was a bit misleading because within that area, there were only three likely spots. If he could get someone out there, perhaps one of Michael's recon units, they could check each location with their own eyes.

Once they had the actual GPS coordinates, then he only had to decide how to eliminate the threat.

A couple days ago, when he had brought up the idea of raiding Watcher One's bunker, Michael had thought it was a good idea. The only problem, he had said, was that he would need a much smaller list of potential targets. No one had time to be gone for a year while searching, and every extra day they spent wandering around the countryside was another chance to be discovered by the invader security forces.

Also, Michael hadn't said so outright, but he had hinted that he wouldn't be willing to leave the Confederation bare of any capable military commander, not with the Maryland invaders pushing on their southern border.

In the back of his mind, Ethan had also been churning through a list of possible candidates to temporarily step up to the plate and handle Michael's position while he was gone. Because, he had to face it, no one he had ever met was better at warfare than Michael.

At least he had one of those problems solved, now. With only three possible locations, all within a day's march of one another, they could probably find the bunker fairly quickly if they could avoid discovery during their wanderings.

He checked the clock and saw it blinking 6:00 a.m. Their little local power grid often flickered, and the clock wasn't on the same uninterruptible power supply, or UPS, system that all the computers were connected to. About once each month, he had to readjust the time to get it close enough to actual time. He had long since switched to a system based on the sun so that when the clock read noon, it was always Solar noon. Without trains and planes to schedule, time zones no longer made sense.

He made a pot of weak coffee. Just as it beeped its finished brew cycle, there was a knock on the bunker door.

He grumbled as he walked to the hatch and opened it. There was Michael, right on time.

"So what's the good news, my friend?" Michael asked, smiling warmly.

Ethan grunted and, as he rubbed his eyes again, opened the door wide for Michael to come in. "The good news is, I made a pot of coffee to celebrate."

"Celebrate what?"

"I've narrowed the target list down to just three places, all pretty close together in rural northern Virginia."

Ethan closed and locked the door after Michael entered, a precaution he took every time he entered the bunker now. Then he led the way into the living room. He waved at the couch for Michael to sit, then went to get two cups of coffee. He added fresh cream—always on hand, now, and way better than the store-bought stuff had once been—and some honey for his own cup. He handed Michael the unsweetened cup and sat in the recliner on the coffee table's opposite side.

Michael thanked him for the coffee and then said, "So tell me about the terrain. Is it in the western mountains or the flatter lands below?"

"Unfortunately, it's high up in the foothills. Not quite in the mountains, but still plenty rough terrain."

Michael shrugged. "Rough terrain is no problem, although it slows us down. It also helps us stay undetected, so I'm okay with that. I'm sure they chose that location because it was far away from the settled areas, or as far away as you can get anywhere east of the Mississippi."

Ethan had thought of that factor, too, but he still didn't relish the idea of marching over hill and dale. It would be great if he only had to walk downhill, both ways. Ha.

He was about to make a witty comeback to that effect when his standby laptop woke up from rest mode, and a second later, his HAM radio squawked.

"You expecting HAMnet traffic?" Michael asked, looking at the laptop screen, where a window had popped up.

"Nope." Ethan stood and walked to the small secondary desk on which he'd set the laptop up. He rested both hands on the chair's backrest and leaned forward to read the screen. There was indeed an incoming file on HAMnet. "Good guess. There's a file coming in, but I'm not sure yet who sent it."

HAMnet file transfers were painfully slow, but this one finished in only a few seconds. A glance told him it was a simple .txt file, and the header read 'Jazoony.' He double-clicked the text file to open it and saw that it was only two paragraphs of unencoded text.

```
Ethan,

This is to let you know that Jaz disappeared
while shopping three days ago. I have recruited
as many resources as I can to help me search for
her, but despite my best efforts, we haven't
found anything yet.

Please let me know if you hear anything on the
Intel side that might give you a clue as to who
is behind it. I wanted to let you know so that
you could look into it, if possible, and also so
you can plug that into your Intel analyses.

Your friend,

Choony
```

He stared at the monitor wide-eyed and shouted, "Holy shit. Michael, come look at this."

Michael set his cup on the table and came over, then

looked over Ethan's shoulder and read the note. A second later, he let out a long, low whistle. "Goddammit... you know very well it's the Maryland invaders. Their agents must've recognized her Clanmarks and grabbed her."

Ethan grit his teeth. His mind flooded with images of the most terrible things they might be doing to her. "Do you think she's still alive if it was the Koreans?"

Michael nodded emphatically. "Absolutely. They'll want to take their time in questioning her, so as long as she is strong enough not to give them everything they want right away, they have a good reason to keep her alive. You and I both know she's a strong bird."

Ethan shook his head, trying to clear his mind of the images. He didn't want to think about what they could be doing to her anymore.

Michael put his hand on Ethan's shoulder, glanced over to make eye contact, and said, "This changes everything, you know. I was resistant of the idea of wandering into Virginia on what could just be a wild goose chase, but I suspect that the only way agents of the Maryland invaders in Hoboken would know about the Clanmarks is through Intel provided by Watcher One. Even if not, he's probably also doing a lot to coordinate their raids on our southern border. I think it just became a strategic priority to remove him as a threat. We need somebody who can take over my role and lead our defenses while I'm gone."

Ethan took a deep breath and tried to think of someone who might be both qualified and willing. Michael had led the Clan's defenses long before he became the Confederation general. The most willing people were probably Clanners, but the most capable would be elsewhere. "I think there was another major who came with that battalion Taggart loaned us for the war last year. If I'm not mistaken, he was one of the ones who stayed behind when Taggart recalled everyone willing to go. I think he's in Lebanon. Does that sound right?"

Michael nodded and said, "Yes. A major did come with them, and he had a lot of experience fighting in New York City under Taggart. But he moved in with Ephrata, not Lebanon. I think he took over that city's defenses, so he won't be willing or able to leave that post. What about Carl?"

Ethan frowned, but stopped to give the suggestion serious consideration. Carl had always been cruelly efficient, but since losing Sunshine, he'd become somewhat sadistic when confronting Liz Town's enemies. That sort of savage, pragmatic approach was exactly what the Confederation would need in Michael's absence. It was simply what it took to fight in low-intensity, low-density attrition warfare of the sort Liz Town excelled at.

"That's not a bad idea, if he'll do it. I'll reach out to him and see. It might take a day or two. In the meantime, you should start to get your unit ready. I have to go with you into Virginia, of course, so plan for that."

Michael frowned, but quickly recovered. "Sorry Ethan, but you just don't have the necessary military experience needed for this type of mission."

Ethan could hardly argue with that. Still, he knew he would need to go in order for the mission to succeed. "Unless you plan on carrying five hundred pounds of explosives with you, or half the plastique in the Confederation, you're going to need me to hack through his defenses and get us access to the bunker."

Michael shook his head. "No, not necessarily. If we can find the bunker's vent tubes, we can just cover those or smoke them out. He'll open the door for us or die, and either of those solves our problem."

A vision of Watcher One running out from the bunker, chased by smoke, made Ethan smile. Still, that was a lot to bet on one outcome. "Maybe, but that's putting all your eggs in one basket. If you don't find the vents, then you won't be able to smoke them out. I'm the only one around who could hack through their access systems. And I'm the only one who can access the satellite and get us a bird's-eye view of the area as we move through it, which we'll need to stay ahead of any incoming threats. Our best way of overcoming Maryland's defenses is by avoiding them."

Michael raised his eyebrows and nodded. "Affirmative. You have a valid point. All right, you reach out to Carl, and I'll get a team and equipment together. Plan on being out there for quite a while, so you'll need to give refresher training to your radio and computer monitor."

Ethan grinned. "Computer monitors are notoriously slow learners."

Michael laughed, his eyes lighting up. He always did seem to enjoy a bit of back-and-forth. Maybe that was just more common as part of being a Marine. He said, "You know what I mean. The guy who watches the systems while you're asleep."

"I'll reach out, then, and train up my guy while you handle the rest."

Michael turned to leave, but when he got to the door, he stopped and said over his shoulder, "You do realize that if Carl is unwilling, I'm not going to be able to leave. I can't jeopardize the Clan and the Confederation to save one person, even if it is Jaz."

Ethan could only nod. It was the simple, harsh truth, no matter how much he disliked it.

* * *

Joe Ellings wandered in the "green zone" in downtown Philly. The new top dog in town, Nate Runke, hadn't been able to make time to meet with him. Joe reckoned it wasn't personal, and he could well imagine how busy the man must be after taking over that huge city from them Maryland 'vaders.

He'd been cooling his heels in town ever since, waiting to get a summons, and had found it easy as pie to earn his keep in the meantime just by showing their farming folks how to do the stuff Cassy did at Clanholme. "Theories and practices in Permaculture," Cassy had called it, but Joe just called it God's way of doin' it. After all, there were farms before ol' John Deere came along. You only had to be willing to get your shoes a mite dirty.

That morning, he was out in the fields with the leader of one of the nearest communes, checking out its workers and showing them how to dig swales and make berms on a hill to keep the soil where it belonged and keep the water in the dirt instead of runnin' away with the dirt.

At first, it had been slower than molasses teaching them all, because they didn't understand how digging ditches could help with all that. Then they'd wanted to argue about why he told them to plant ground covers on the fresh-turned dirt. He had helped teach enough new Clanners that shutting down them argumentative types was practically second nature by now. Easy as pie.

Currently, he was teaching them on how to use an A-frame level, with a tube full of water, to help them reckon where to dig so that the swale would stay on contour.

A second shadow joined his own, and he turned his head enough to see who had come up behind him. He stayed tense and alert but maintained his calm, relaxed appearance. It turned out the shadow's owner was a teenage boy, but Joe didn't recognize him. Maybe he wasn't one of the workers from this commune.

"Can I help you?" he asked the newcomer.

"Yes, sir. The Dude sent me to deliver a message to you. He wants to meet with you in one hour, and sends his apologies for the delay."

Joe nodded and shot the boy a smile. "Hot damn! I appreciate you. Tell 'em I'll be there come hell or high water."

When the boy ran off, Joe turned to the commune workers and shrugged. "Sorry, folks. I gotta go. If you feel like you have this measuring contours down pat, then by all means, get 'er done. You got my sketch to show where to dig 'em. But if y'all don't think you can do it just perfect, then find something else to do until I get back. I'm sure there's plenty that needs doing around here."

He left the commune on horseback and headed toward the house he had been squatting in. The house they had loaned him, he corrected, which meant he wasn't no squatter.

He needed to get washed up before he met with the Dude, and the house had running water, just cold as hell. For some reason, he felt a bit excited to meet the Dude, and for once he didn't mind the cold shower.

He got to City Hall, where the Dude had set up his HQ and residence, a full fifteen minutes before he was due. He checked in with the receptionist, then sat in a chair that made his butt hurt something fierce, and waited. He had to wait another twenty minutes, during which time nobody strolled in or out of the office.

When the wall clock showed five minutes past his appointment time, right on the nose as the minute hand swept past the number twelve, the receptionist looked up at him and said, "The Dude will see you now."

He fought the urge to chuckle. It was just so clearly a game, like one of them power-plays out of an Office Politics for Dummies book or somethin', it was hard not to laugh. He thanked the receptionist and was extra sure to call her ma'am so she'd remember him next time. When he got to the office door she had pointed out, he knocked lightly three times.

Ten seconds later—another stupid, pointless wait—a man's voice from inside hollered for him to enter. Joe let out a sigh, fixed a smile on his face, then went inside and closed the door behind him. He couldn't help but glance around looking for that Office Politics for Dummies book, but didn't see anything of the sort. He did see that it was pretty clear the Dude hadn't changed a thing since taking over that office from the old mayor. He even still had the mayor's family photos on the walls, along with his old awards and certificates. This dude—or rather *The Dude*—was a bit of a joke, Joe figured, and it was fairly disappointing.

The man behind the desk stood and said, "Mr. Wellings, thank you for coming. I'm sorry I was a bit late, but you know, duty calls. I'm Nate Runke, leader of Free Philadelphia. It's a pleasure to meet you."

Joe was caught off guard that the Dude introduced himself by his given name. He'd expected to hear his nickname. Then again, maybe Cartoon Boy didn't think "the Dude" reflected the dignity of his new office, as Cassy might have said it. As far as Joe was concerned, Dude had about as much dignity as Elmer Fudd. Who the heck kept other people's family photos on the walls?

"Thanks for taking time to jaw with me, Mr. Mayor. I know you're busy and all, what with them transitions going on since you took over. Congratulations on that, by the way." Joe smiled, stepped forward, and extended his hand across the desk.

Nate shook his hand. "We all have our burdens. Please, have a seat." Nate sat back down in his big old chair, which looked more like a throne than an office chair, and waited for

Joe to sit.

"Thank you," Joe said as he plopped down in the offered chair. "I suppose you want to know why the Clan sent me here."

Nate shook his head. "Not really. I'm the new top dog, so it figures everyone in the neighborhood would send another dog to sniff around and get to know each other. Actually, I was more surprised at how long it took the Clan to send someone."

Joe bit his tongue. He almost said what he thought, which wouldn't have been good. Not suitable for diplomacy anyway, though it might've been funny. "Oh, I've been here for a little while, now. I figure your staff just prioritizes what's going on and who you gotta meet. A man in your position, well, I reckon he's got more responsibilities than time. I'm just glad I finally made it to the top of the list." He favored Nate with a grin, even if he had to fake it.

Nate leaned back in his chair, gazing at him and obviously sizing him up. That was good, as far as Joe was concerned. He could trust a direct man more than some fop.

"I'm told you've been making the most of your time since you arrived, teaching my people some new kind of farming. It's the way the Clan does things, am I right?"

"Right as rain, mister. A fella's gotta eat, and I figured I'd make the most my time, like you said. It's not why I'm here in Philadelphia, though."

Nate put his hands behind his head. Given the way he was leaning back, it seemed like he was looking at Joe through drooping eyelids. "Well, it doesn't take a genius to figure out why you're here, but why don't you go ahead and tell me in your own words. I hate operating from assumptions."

Joe's left eyebrow twitched once. Maybe this guy wasn't the yahoo he seemed like. Actually, how could he be? He had pretty much single-handedly sent packing all those 'vaders who had the run of Philadelphia almost since the war began. Oh ho, Joe thought, so it was an act. He decided not to take anything Nate said for granted.

"Sure, I'll tell it true. The Confederation ought to keep things civil with you and your people, after all, and they want me to make sure you know to keep an open mind if New America sends an envoy. And the Clan, as the southernmost part of the Confed, wants to keep a neighborly relationship with Philadelphia. That's you, mister."

Nate smiled, a good-natured expression. "Of course, of course. That's pretty much what I thought you would say, but here we are in my office, talking for the first time, and I don't really know what you want. Just some vague crap about being neighborly." Nate paused then inhaled deeply. "Let's try a different approach. If you had some sort of mutual agreement written down on paper, ready for me to sign, what would that paper say?"

Joe reached up and scratched his head just above his right ear. It was a bit of a delaying tactic while he gathered his thoughts. A moment later, he said, "The Confederation, the Clan, me—we all want to have a strong friend to our south. From where I sit, it looks like you got three choices. You can get friendly with the people to your north, or with the people to your south, or you can take your chances by trying to stand alone. Everything else boils down to one of those three choices, as far as I can reckon. But my momma always did say I was an idiot, so maybe you see something else?"

Nate took his hands from behind his head and sat up again. He smiled, but faintly shook his head. "That's fairly observant, but there's a problem with your logic. As you know, we only recently pushed the invaders out of the great city of Philadelphia. That's still a sore spot for their leaders and their soldiers alike. They might enjoy trying to get a little payback, don't you think?"

"Yeah, but—"

Nate cut him off, "And I know you must be aware that the Southern Cantonment has been building up their forces along their northern border. Maybe they will send those troops to deal with me, maybe they want to deal with you. It could even be both if they get enough fighters together. As long as they're gathered so close to us, if I were to publicly ally with the Confederation, I'd be inviting another invasion. We only just got rid of the last occupation."

Joe tried again. "If you joined the Confederation or New America, we could—"

"Uh huh, and would either one of you go to the mat for people you don't know? People who didn't help you get through the Dying Time?"

"Damn straight we would. Maybe we couldn't free you, but we can sure as hell work to keep you free."

"And what help could you send, since both of you have other problems to deal with like the Northern Cantonment? The information I get says the invaders up north are rattling their sabers against New America and the Confederation. It seems like if I join you, there wouldn't be much you could do to help me given that you must first and foremost defend your own territories."

Joe's jaw dropped. Maybe this dude really was a yahoo. Couldn't he see that the Confederation and New America had been kicking invader ass for the last two years? Joining the 'vaders would only make an enemy of the Confederation and New America.

He said carefully, "Maybe, sir, but it seems to me that if you join the 'vaders, that pretty much gives you the same problem, just only on the flip side of that coin."

Nate cocked his head and said, "And you think my

problems will be smaller if I join you instead of the Maryland invaders?"

Joe weighed his words carefully. He had a nagging feeling that his answer might decide things one way or another, that they had reached a key moment in their conversation. "I think... you're going to have challenges no matter which way you go, just like the rest of us, but it seems to me that those challenges will be easier, their weight bearing down later, if you support Americans and not the 'vaders. To them, you'd never be anything more than a pawn, a resource waiting to get plundered again whenever they reckon it's convenient. And if there's one thing I've learned since the war began, it's this... no one stands for long on their own. It takes a community, a support network of people rooting for each other because we're all Americans, and we all have what my buddy Ethan calls 'enlightened self-interest.' You're a smart man, mister. You gotta see the truth in them words."

Nate folded his hands in his lap and sat still, looking at Joe. The clock on the wall ticked by, seconds melting away with only the ticking noise to mark their passing.

Joe counted twenty of them ticks before Nate got around to answering.

"I do believe I see a third path, one that prevents me from having to pick sides and suffer the accompanying war. You see, Philadelphia lies between the two biggest fighters on our block. If I join one side or the other, all that fighting will probably be done right here in my front yard. My people have suffered too long and fought too hard to merely walk right back into a war. You give me options in A, B, and C. I'm going with D, none of the above."

As he spoke, Joe racked his brain trying to figure out what another option might be, but he came up blank. "I'm sorry, sir, but I just can't figure that fourth option. I'd sure appreciate it if you filled me in. Maybe I can offer some advice, or figure out a way to take advantage of it, if I'm being honest."

Nate nodded and smiled. "No surprises there. We all just do what we can to take care of our own, and hopefully help some others out in the process those times when we can. This isn't one of those times, not for Philadelphia. I've thought seriously about this for many days, and I've come to the one resolution that protects my people... so long as I can pull it off."

Joe cocked his head to the side without thinking about it. He waited a couple seconds, and when Nate didn't continue, his curiosity got the better of him. "I'd surely appreciate it if you shared that fix with me. I didn't figure on a fourth option, so now you got my curiosity up."

Nate chuckled. He leaned forward, resting his elbows on the desk and his chin on his hands as he looked at Joe. "The thing is, I don't need to pick a side. I think I'm just as valuable to all of you—invaders, New America, and Confederation—if I simply don't pick the other side. If I just do me, I think everyone would leave me alone purely so they don't drive me into the open arms of their enemies. My job is to protect Philadelphia and its people, not New America. Not the Clan. And definitely not the invaders."

Joe forced himself to smile. It would have been nice if the Dude had told him this when he first arrived, rather than making him cool his heels waiting for this meeting. Then he felt a slight tickle at the back of his scalp, a growing wariness. He couldn't quite put his finger on why, but something didn't sit right, not after that last thought.

Still smiling, he said, "I can respect your choice to protect your people first, but I think—and this is just my own opinion, not as a representative of the Confederation—your people would be better served getting in on the ground floor of a growing, strong New America. The goodwill that would create will last a generation."

"Perhaps, but my people can't eat goodwill. They can't defend themselves with it, either."

"It would put you in a good way to take on the boss role in this region. After we beat them Maryland 'vaders back, assuming it comes to war, someone's got to control that territory for New America. I think a body as smart as you could do darn well in that situation. Or so I reckon."

Nate smiled at him, nodding. "That's very astute of you, Joe, but I think by walking the middle line, my people are going to be in a good position to control this region regardless of who wins out there. Whether that's New America or the invaders, we represent a pretty juicy plum. I won't take sides until it's clear who's going to win, and then I'm going to jump in on their side. Or, after the fighting has gone on for a while, if it's still a close-run thing then I can jump in to help the underdogs, and that works out even better for me."

Joe couldn't believe what he was hearing. For some reason, he had thought they would be chomping at the bit to join New America. After all, they had been enslaved by the Maryland invaders. Why wouldn't they want a bit of payback? Well, Nate had explained why; he was an opportunist, nothing more. Not a patriot, he stood for his own and no one else, and that was just not the way things were done in New America. And definitely not how they were done in the Confederation.

"I'm sorry, Dude, but I'm having a hard time believing you could really come at it that way. Those people enslaved you, but you talk about making deals with them? I don't know. I guess I had just thought you would be more... American." He tried to smile again, the diplomatic thing to do, but just couldn't bring himself to do it.

Nate said, "I see your point. The problem with that is, America turned its back on us during the invasion. They fought for New York, they helped you folks out near Lancaster, but they left Philadelphia to suffer under the invader's heel. You and I are here talking about the future of free Philadelphia, not because of any help from you and your masters but because I stepped forward and took the reins. A lot of people believed in me, fought, and died. But because of that sacrifice, which was one I was willing to make for my people's sake, now we're free. And now that the fighting is over, *now* you want to talk about helping us? No, I think you're here to talk about us helping you, not the other way around."

Joe's sense of foreboding grew, and he anxiously glanced at the door to reassure himself of where it was. Just in case he had to hightail it out of there in a hurry.

Nate said, "Nervous about something? I promise you, the door is still there. However, whether or not you get to use it is up to me. You're right to be nervous."

Joe's eyes narrowed at the Philadelphia leader. Damn it, he'd betrayed himself with his damn fidgeting. Had Nate just threatened him? It darn sure felt like it. "Well, how's about I go and put together one of them propositions that Cassy's always talking about. We'll put together some real numbers and show you why it's in your best interest to join us. I'll ride back to Clanholme, put that together, and be back in a week. I think I can show you why I figure our interests and yours are about the same."

Nate's face took on a sad expression, one of regret, but Joe thought it looked pretty insincere. Nate said, "You see, that's going to be a problem. I need you here to keep showing my people how to do that permaculture thing you folks do."

"You telling me I can't leave?" No damn way... this guy was crazy. He had to get out, but how?

"Like I said, I do what's in the best interest of my people. If you stay and spend some time teaching us about your methods like you have been, I'll definitely consider that to be real help from your people, and it might well impact my decision as to which way Philadelphia will go—invaders or New America."

"Making me a slave ain't going to earn you brownie points."

"Yes, but that is why you're here, right? To convince me to join your side? Stay here as the Confederation's official ambassador, help us with learning how to farm sustainably without tractors and pesticides and fertilizers, and it will go a long way toward proving your point. What do you say, Joe? Can I count on you? Can the Confederation count on you?"

Through sheer effort of will, Joe forced himself to smile. He didn't think he had much choice in the matter, but if he could make the Dude think he wanted to be there, they'd likely keep his leash not quite so tight. It was clear that Philadelphia was going to pick its side, and it didn't much matter what he thought of it.

The problem was that Nate's side needed the permaculture knowledge Joe had. Since Philly wasn't going to join New America right now, the Dude couldn't rightly ask for consultants, which only left Joe as their source of that information. He'd been right to feel paranoid.

"Of course, Dude. Anything I can do to help our cause. But it figures that I'll need some more long-term accommodations and plenty of supplies if I'm gonna be here for a while. As long as I'm here helping Philadelphia, I don't see how that'll be too much of a problem, though, will it?"

Nate stood and put his left hand on the desk, leaning forward to extend his right hand. "Of course, Joe. I'll put you up in some decent accommodations and make sure you have what you need. Shall we shake on it?"

Joe could only nod and stand to shake Nate's hand. He was pretty sure he would be staying in Philadelphia whether he agreed or not, so it was time to play nice. "Yes, you got yourself a deal, mister."

The next few minutes were terrifying as he tried to negotiate the best possible deal for himself. The longer the leash they gave him, the better his chances of getting out of there, getting back to Cassy to let them all know what he found out. Play along. Be a good old boy. Get home alive.

When Joe finally was told he could leave the Dude's office, he found half a dozen rough-looking people standing around the lobby, and they stood as he opened the door. His heart sank as he realized he'd been right. He said, "So, I guess you're gonna escort me to my new house? I surely appreciate it."

He smiled at his captors, burning their faces into his memory.

* * *

Carl looked around his house, the Speaker of Liz Town's opulent manor, and bared his teeth in a savage snarl. His staff kept it immaculate, and that pissed him off; it no longer bore any resemblance to what was going on inside of him, a mirror's reversed image of the raging storm of desperation that, behind closed doors, had virtually consumed him ever since Sunshine had died. She was the only woman he had come to truly love, and her death at the hands of the Empire and the Mountain troops, during that last desperate defense against their invading troops, had shattered whatever soul he had left. As far as he was concerned, he had been a damaged man before falling in love with her, but she had healed him. Now that she was gone, he was far worse off than he had been before she came along.

A fifth of Jameson's Irish Whiskey in one hand and a pack of cigarettes in the other, he climbed the stairs to the only sanctuary in his entire miserable damned house. Once he got to the top, he padded down the hallway and stopped at the door at the end of the hall. The door to her room. The room he had set up for her in the desperate hope she might someday be found alive.

Her body had never been found, and he had since given up hope of ever finding her. He went inside and closed the door behind him, then kicked aside cans and bottles as he made his way to sit in the luxurious leather recliner in one corner. The rest of the room was perfectly kept, but that recliner was his sanctuary. It was as close as he could get to Sunshine now, and it was where he dwelled on what he had gained and lost in that war.

He no longer truly cared about the Confederation, nor even about Liz Town, really, and spent his days just going through the motions. Signing whatever his assistants put in front of him, making the decisions his cabinet suggested. They were all highly skilled, and he trusted them, so why bother? Let them run that shitty town if they cared to.

He had hoped that taking over the leadership position from Mary Ann, so she could focus again on leading her own Band, would take his mind off his loss. It hadn't.

He uncapped the bottle and took a long swig, enjoying the burning feeling washing down his throat. The pain felt good. He had already finished off the last part of another bottle of whiskey, but wasn't yet drunk enough to suppress his feelings. All he wanted in life these days was just to be numb.

There was a knock at the door. Carl yelled, "Go the hell away. Whatever it is, put it on my desk. I'll get to it in the morning."

A woman's voice on the other side of the door replied,

"Alpha, you have a phone call from Ethan in Clanholme. He says it's important, but that he can wait until morning if you wish."

Carl grit his teeth. Yeah, Ethan was his friend and knew better than to call him at this time of night. Unless it was important... Screw it, his dawning buzz was already killed thanks to the interruption, so he might as well get it over with. Then he wouldn't have to deal with it the next day. "Very well. I'll take the call. Enter."

Carl had one assistant in the house at night, and tonight it was a woman whose name he couldn't remember. Linda? Lisa? It didn't really matter.

Linda or Lisa opened the door and brought him the cell phone. Ethan had found a carton of the things buried in a galvanized trash can on some farm they had reclaimed. The phones still worked. Although there was no cell reception, with the improved Wi-Fi connection that the major Confederation leaders had access to now thanks to Ethan, the phones had a new app installed. It was something Ethan had coded, somewhat like VoIP but for a Wi-Fi network. Call quality was dubious, but it was quicker than the usual messaging system everyone still used. The phones were for emergencies and vital secure communications.

He snatched the phone from her hand and waved at her dismissively. She kept her face neutral, to her credit, and left the room. He said, "Ethan. What's going on?"

The voice on the other end crackled, but he recognized it. "Hey man. I'm glad I caught you. I know you're busy during the day, and I didn't want to bother you while you were dealing with official business."

"So what's up?"

Ethan said, "You know we're getting a lot of pressure from the Maryland invaders, right? So far, the Clan has handled it just fine, but it seems to be escalating. Our Intel says this is a precursor to a larger conflict."

Carl leaned back against the recliner headrest and closed his eyes. "Okay, but what has that got to do with me?"

"So, just as all of this is happening, our envoys to New America go missing. Or at least Jaz has. We think operatives from the Maryland invaders snatched her to disrupt the alliance. Special ops stuff. I have a pretty good idea of who is coordinating all of that, and a rough idea of where they are. You know that Michael is the best special ops guy in the Confederation, and we have a plan for him and his team, plus me, to head down south to try to disrupt that. If we can take out that enemy asset, their communications will be disrupted. And on a personal note, that asset is coordinating some sort of revenge trip by General Houle, trying to take me out. I need to take him out first."

Carl was buzzed enough that his brain was a bit foggy, but he pretty much followed the logic. "So you want me to take over Michael's responsibilities for the Confederation, is that it?"

There was a pause on the other end. Then Ethan said, "Yeah, man. You'd be helping the Confederation deal with this growing threat, but you might also be saving my life since this guy is trying to kill me. It would also be a favor to the Clan. Plus, we have to get Jaz back."

"Ethan, you know I have responsibilities here. I'm the Speaker, and dealing with that bullshit takes up most of my day. I really want to help, but Michael took the job as General of the Confederation. We all have our cross to bear."

There was a long pause. He had begun to think Ethan terminated the call, until he said, "I get that, man. I really do. But you aren't down here; you don't see what's going on. I'm about ninety percent sure war is coming to the Confederation. All of us, not just the Clan. If we can take out this asset hiding in Virginia, it's going to go a long way toward leveling the playing field when that war comes. You may be Liz Town's speaker, but you Lizzies are part of the Confederation. It's going to affect you personally if you try to hide from this one."

In the back of his mind, Carl knew what Ethan said was very likely true. He also knew he didn't really give a damn. He was just going through the motions of life, and the idea of taking on more responsibility wasn't high on his list of priorities. "I got my own problems, Ethan. You're going to have to deal with this yourself. That's your job in the Confederation, right? Intel and special ops planning?"

"Carl, listen to me. Just hand off your role as Speaker. You and I both know you don't want to do it anyway."

"Ethan, stop acting like you know me. You know nothing."

"Oh, yeah?" Ethan said. "How 'bout you get out of the damn recliner in Sunshine's room and do something instead of drowning your sorrows in a bottle of whiskey and smokes. I'm giving you that chance. Don't you want a little payback?"

"Payback? What do you mean?"

On the other end, Ethan let out a sigh into the phone and then said, "The guy Michael and I are going after is the guy who coordinated the airstrikes. I'm pretty sure he's personally responsible for what happened in Harrisburg. If you step up and take over for Michael, you're giving us the best shot we got at taking the bastard out with extreme prejudice."

Carl felt a jolt shoot up his spine, like electricity, and his heart beat faster for the first time since the latest war. "Screw taking over for Michael. Let me come with you."

"No, man. This guy is really good. I don't put favorable odds on our success, but it's the only chance we got. If you want this guy dead, Michael is your best chance. Do you want revenge, or do you want to die heroically?"

"I need to find this guy."

"I know, but we have to do it this way in order for that to happen. I promise you, Carl, if we can take him alive, I'll dump him right at your feet."

Carl's knuckles popped as he clenched the phone. "I'm going with you. End of story."

"No, Carl, you're—"

"Take it or leave it."

"So you want to die heroically then..."

"I never said that... I want revenge, but I want to do it my way. What don't you get about that?"

Ethan was silent for a moment.

Carl continued, "Listen, Ethan. I'm not going to run in circles with you. Call me when you have a real plan."

And with that, Carl ended the call to return to his bottle of whiskey. His mind spun at all the possibilities of how he could seek revenge for Sunshine's death, with or without Ethan's help.

- **14** -

0600 HOURS - ZERO DAY +635

CHOONY HAD BEEN spending most of his time wandering the city. He hadn't yet found Jaz, but in his heart, he was certain she was still alive.

Squirrel and Lance had done quite a lot to help with the search in the first few days, but they had their own responsibilities. The town guards had done a fairly systematic search of the most likely areas where she might be found, but once that had turned up empty, they had to return to their regular duties.

For the last several days, Choony had been searching on his own. Now, with his meeting over, he could get back to doing what he did all day, every day—searching for Jaz. He had a city map and had been conducting his search methodically. He investigated one house at a time, one building at a time, exhausting every structure on one block before moving onto the next. When he completed searching a block, he scratched it off on his map with an X.

Today, he was tackling a block that had been in the commercial and industrial area, largely consisting of workshops and small warehouses. He spent most of his time focused on residential areas, figuring that houses would be a better place to keep her—he felt strongly that someone had kidnapped her—but he believed in being thorough, and he would spend the rest of his life searching if he had to. He had time.

The first commercial building he had entered looked like it had been an auto body shop before the war. Since then, almost everything in it had been stripped out for salvage, and now the interior was simply dark and foreboding. He started with the office area, breaking in with practiced ease. Papers were strewn about everywhere, but there was nowhere to hide a person. He examined every wall, every square meter of the floor, looking for something that might indicate a trapdoor or hidden passage, but he never found any.

Today had so far been no different, and the office was exactly what it appeared to be: uncomplicated and ransacked. He turned to the door leading into the auto bays area and steeled himself to go through. He always had to brace himself before doing this, because he never knew what would lay on the other side. He only checked the office areas first because it allowed him to gain entry much more quietly, but the warehouse proper was always where he figured Jaz's prison would be if she was in the warehouse district at all.

He let out a deep breath, reached for the door, and then strode through. As always, he felt a split-second of intense excitement, a hope that he would find her on the other side, but just like every other time, his spike of anticipation was followed by a crash of disappointment. Just as he had suspected, the bay was empty. The gas cylinders were gone, the power tools were nowhere to be found, the fluids had been taken for other uses. It was empty, and it had been for a long time.

He fought back the tears for a minute, then his Buddhist nature took over. He grew calm, accepting the fact that Jaz wasn't here. Standing around crying would not find her. Only searching could ever hope to reunite him with his love.

Without a word, he turned around and walked out of the building the same way he had come in. On to the next building.

* * *

Mark Bates sat at his desk, stealing a glance at his watch. At 10 a.m. sharp, which was in about a minute, he was to meet Janice's friend, Charlie. She had assured him that Charlie was both trustworthy and patriotic. Not patriotic in the photo-op sense of General Houle's cronies, but in the true sense—he wanted America back, the real America. Not this warped shadow it had become under Houle. Even better, Janice said she had dirt on this Charlie guy, so he would never flip.

He looked at his watch again and saw the second's hand sweep upward toward the twelve. As the second's hand hit the top and began another tick to the right, there was a knock on the door. He smiled—he appreciated punctuality. He went to the door and opened it.

Standing at the door was a nondescript-looking gentleman wearing a simple, navy-blue suit. His eyes were light brown, and his hair well-trimmed.

Mark said, "Charlie? Thank you for coming. Please come in." He stood aside and held the door open.

"Thanks for meeting me," Charlie said, his voice a surprisingly deep baritone that seemed out of place coming from him. He was of average height and build, but his voice had a deep resonance.

Mark closed the door behind him and then motioned toward the couch. "Have a seat, please."

Charlie sat on the couch, and Mark sat across from him,

adjusting himself to be more comfortable. Mark said, "When Janice told me about you, I had a feeling we could be friends. She tells me that you and I share a similar definition of patriotism."

Charlie's expression was friendly and nonchalant, but Mark tried to observe every detail of the man's face, noting every change. For a brief moment, Mark saw that he looked pleased, but he quickly covered it up.

"I hope so. I know we're under Martial Law, but military rule in America seems somehow not right, no matter the circumstances. Sure, the invaders are still here, but they're everywhere. We need to be bringing the rest of the country together, reforming the ties that once bound us together into a country, not trying to extract resources from them like some sort of colonial power."

Mark felt two simultaneous strong emotions. On the one hand, his heart leaped for joy hearing those words, because they echoed his own thoughts. He wasn't sure what his end goal was, yet, but he knew he would need like-minded people to achieve it. On the other hand, however, it was exactly what he wanted to hear. If Charlie was a plant, someone from counterintel, then it was just the sort of thing he would say.

Mark said, "You know, that's apparently Houle's goal as well. That's what the propaganda tells us. I may not be comfortable with the path he's choosing to restore America, but I bet if you ask ten people how to solve this problem, you will get ten different answers."

Charlie paused and eyed Mark warily. Then he said, "Do you honestly believe that? About Houle wanting to restore America? If he did, he would have already started with the territory he controls now. Supposedly, Houle already controls America's heartland, at least a third of the country. Definitely enough territory to hold some sort of elections and get a new president in office. As it stands now, nobody elected Houle. He's the Commander-in-Chief because he says so, not because he's authorized to be."

Mark raised one eyebrow and stared intently at the man. Being so open about what Houle would consider treason, well, it was either foolish or entrapment. The thought suddenly occurred to Mark that maybe he wore a wire. It certainly was something that counterintel would do and had the resources for. And yet, maybe the fact that Janice had recommended him made Charlie more open and comfortable than he would be otherwise. It was possible the man was only trying to make an impression.

Unable to read any dishonesty in Charlie's face, Mark stifled a sigh. He gave Charlie a faint smile and said, "You seem rather certain of your position on the matter. You do know that the rest of the country doesn't have radio communications, right? It might not be practical to hold an election yet."

The corners of Charlie's mouth turned down and his lips pursed. He looked rather disappointed. "Perhaps, but I know that our troops are scattered throughout those regions, safe in their little bases, and they all have radios. It wouldn't be hard to communicate the results of local elections back in. At the very least, he could get new governors and new congressmen and so on, and at least put back the trappings of checks and balances if he wanted to, even if electing a new president had to wait."

"It's admirable, but how would you collect those results? I'm not saying I disagree, but I see challenges in making it legitimate." Mark eyed him, gauging his reaction.

"If you really believe what you just said, then I think I will just thank you for your time and call it a day."

"I understand, Charlie. I appreciate you coming down."

They shook hands, and both men stood. Mark walked him to the door. As the door shut behind Charlie, Mark took a deep breath, letting it out slowly. His mind was racing. This guy could be just what he needed—a fanatic, and not too bright. He decided he was going to let Charlie leave under the impression the meeting hadn't gone well, and then he would only deal with the man indirectly. Janice could be Charlie's handler, and he would get no dirt on his own hands. It wasn't quite what he had hoped for, but an asset was an asset. He would use the tools available the best he could.

He felt a little guilty at his decision to turn Charlie into a peon instead of a partner, but it was just a simple fact that if Mark were caught, he didn't think there was any chance of getting rid of Houle. That goal had to come before his own squeamishness, even before ethics. He was pretty certain that his ethics wouldn't matter one damn bit if Houle ended up taking over the show permanently.

* * *

1400 HOURS - ZERO DAY +635

Back in the Hoboken market area, Choony sat eating a late lunch. He didn't have the heart to eat at his and Jaz's favorite restaurant, the one that served real meat, so he had just grabbed a plate from a random food cart vendor in the market's heart. He looked down at his plate as he sat at the table by the cart, and he saw that his meal consisted mostly of potatoes, chopped and fried, with some green vegetables, thin-cut carrots, and what was probably bits of rat meat.

A mug of weak ale sat next to his plate. Even the weak stuff was far safer than the water because nothing that could harm a person would grow in beer. Heck, every big house or block of houses now had its own microbrewery, or so it seemed. He had read about the role of beer in medieval times and found it amusing that it had come back into fashion. No one wanted to drink water, for good reason. He gulped the room temperature beer, grimacing.

He picked up his spork, a titanium camping model he carried everywhere with him, and leaned over his plate to take a bite. Bent over, eyes fixed on his food, he felt his hat fly off his head but didn't feel any wind. Startled, he looked around frantically and saw a man in a long coat, hunched over, about twenty feet away from him and blending into the crowd. Odd. Why would anyone want to knock his hat off? He was wearing a long sleeve shirt, so even his clanmark wasn't visible.

He turned to face the opposite direction to find his hat, but saw a folded piece of paper tucked under his plate's right edge. What on Earth? He got up and fetched his hat, a straw "islander" variety, and put it back on as he returned to his seat. He picked up the paper and unfolded it, finding a handwritten note. He quickly scanned it, but it had only one short line: *1701 Lincoln Ave*. The rest of the paper was blank. It was just that one address.

He looked around surreptitiously, trying to see whether he could find anyone looking at him suspiciously. It was hard to tell in the crowded market, but he didn't think anyone was watching him. He tucked the paper into his breast pocket in his cargo vest, then took his time finishing his meal. The address was on the far side of Hoboken, and he didn't want to get caught out in the wildlands—as they called the uncontrolled areas back in Liz Town—after dark.

He ruled out using a bike as that would make him too much of a target. No, he would have to prepare for a long walk at first light the next morning.

Plate empty, he chugged the last of his warm beer and rushed back to his house to gather his gear.

* * *

"Eagan!"

Taggart's sidekick stuck his head through the doorway. "Yeah?"

Taggart's eyes widened. "I'm the president for God's sake, Eagan. Show some respect."

Eagan stood ramrod straight and saluted. "Sir, yes, sir."

Leaning back in his office chair, Taggart shook his head. "Listen, Eagan. I cleared off my list today and was wondering if you and Priscilla would like to come over for dinner. Maybe she can cook that stuff I like so much. Oh, what's it called?"

"*Asopao*." He cocked his head to the side, smirking. "You'd think after she made that for you three or four times, you might remember the name."

Taggart nodded. He had a point, after all. "I could remember it if they named it something easy, like 'cheeseburger.' You should tell her to have them rename their national dish."

Eagan shrugged. "Actually, her national dish is—"

Taggart's office door swung open and the post's officer of the day marched in. His uniform was always crisp, his hair perfect, and he was mostly only good for delivering reports. Taggart couldn't remember his name, offhand. He marched into the office, stopping crisply at a perfect seventy-two inches from the desk, and saluted with a snap.

Taggart resisted the urge to roll his eyes. He spared a moment to thank God for the real soldiers in his army because if all he had were clones of this guy, they would never have made it out of New York City. Irritated, Taggart gave a pitiful excuse for a return salute and said, "Yes, yes. What is it?"

The officer of the day cut his salute, then stepped forward with a manila envelope and set it on Taggart's desk. "Sir. A new Intel report has come in. This captain thought the general would want to see it right away. Sir."

Taggart stared at the young man, but still, he didn't leave. Taggart took a deep breath and remembered that he had to dismiss the guy. "Very well. Carry on."

After the officer gave another crisp salute, followed by a perfect about-face, Taggart watched his back as he marched out and closed the door behind him.

"Well. That's one outstanding soldier, boss."

"Maybe for a barracks soldier, but I doubt he's any good in a fight." Taggart stared at the folder. The seconds ticked by.

Finally, Eagan said, "Oh for crying out loud. Just ask me to read it."

"Good idea," Taggart said.

Eagan walked to the desk and picked up the folder with a melodramatic sigh. Then he read whatever was inside, his eyes skimming back and forth across the page. He closed the folder and set it on Taggart's desk.

"Well? What's it say?"

"It seems our field scouts have found out what happened to our supply depot north of Philadelphia. We thought maybe it was the people now running the city, but it seems that the American 'recruits' within the Southern Cantonment army have been spotted carrying gear and wearing uniforms that match what was taken from the depot."

Taggart felt the beginnings of a headache. That couldn't have waited until he checked his inbox? What did the officer of the day want him to do, go and get the gear back himself? "Does it say anything else?"

Eagan shrugged. "Nope, that's it. Would you like me to deliver this to the Intel analysts?" Eagan tossed his head toward the folder.

Taggart nodded. They would be the ones to advise him as to the strategic implications of the raid. He really disliked that officer of the day... "Hey, can you talk with whoever does the scheduling, while you're out there, and make sure to transfer that guy? He'd be a perfect liaison for that douche bag, Doug Holloway. My Secretary of State would appreciate that officer's supreme ass-kissing skills."

The clock struck 1700 hours, 5:00 p.m. Taggart let out a short whistle and felt the tension draining from his body. He figured now was as good a time as any to go home. Besides, Wild Turkey was waiting for him. "So, are you and Priscilla coming over in a bit? Preferably with some dinner?"

If Eagan declined, it would be just as well; he liked their company, but he also wanted some quiet time. He didn't get enough of that, not since he'd taken over the whole region. To think, he had once been a mere sergeant... he missed those days.

- **15** -

0615 HOURS - ZERO DAY +636

CHOONY PULLED ON his backpack, as he had every day before, to search for Jaz. Unlike the previous days, however, today's journey had a destination. Would he find Jaz at that address? Or would it be something else entirely? It was more likely someone who wanted to meet with him in his role as envoy to the Confederation, he thought. And yet, they hadn't listed a specific time. It was that fact that gave him the most hope, and the most cause to worry.

Also worrisome was the location. If he remembered correctly, the address would put him close to the Bergen Mall. Not only was that an awful neighborhood from what the various scroungers who came in to trade at the market Center had said, but it also meant he would have to travel on foot through Maywood, and that was something he did not look forward to. It was much safer during the daytime than at night, but "much safer" was a relative term. It would be a foot journey of two or three miles outside the safety of Taggart's Hackensack capital, in their version of Liz Town's wildlands. People still lived out there, but they weren't civilized. They were the ones too stubborn or crazy to leave, but too cunning and smart to have perished during the Dying Times.

Most of them were usually safe enough if one simply left them alone, but they often suffered from mental illnesses and could be unstable. Of the rest, however, some were simply evil. There were still cannibals in Maywood. They often raided travelers, making off with everything their victims possessed, including the bodies.

He patted his pocket once again, reassuring himself that his pocket was full of loose bullets. Although he refused to carry a weapon he would never use—unless Jaz's life was in danger, he had learned to his own dismay—the bullets still made excellent currency. Lightweight and highly valued, if he got into any trouble out there in the wildlands, he could use the bullets to trade for his freedom. At least, he hoped that he could, but he wasted no time worrying about what would happen if he couldn't. There was no point in worrying about the things he couldn't change.

In his backpack, Jaz's gun rested at the top. He thought perhaps she might need it when he found her.

He locked his door behind him and headed north from his house. In minutes, he found himself winding his way through the market area, which had a moderate level of activity even at this early hour of the morning. Many of the stalls were still setting up, the area still pretty chaotic, bearing little resemblance to the orderly rows of stalls that would be on display later in the day after the market opened.

He was startled by a wagon speeding by, pulled by two horses. If he hadn't seen it coming at the last second, he probably would have been hit, and resisted the urge to yell at the driver. He dusted himself off and continued onward.

As he reached the far end of the market, he turned back and looked behind him. He would be going far into the wildlands that day, and it was always possible that he wouldn't be coming back. He wanted to see it one last time, just in case.

And then he froze. In the distance, he saw a small wagon driven by a young man with a familiar face. It looked like Jack, the young man who had immigrated to Clanholme but was kicked out when Choony had told Frank about the incident between him and Jaz. The face was only visible for a split-second, and at that distance, he couldn't be sure that it had been Jack. He shook his head to clear his thoughts, but couldn't get rid of his sense of foreboding. If that had indeed been Jack, did he have something to do with Jaz's disappearance? Or perhaps he was merely imagining things. With a sigh, he turned back around and continued northward.

As Choony left behind the Taggart-controlled part of Hackensack, his surroundings went from run down but maintained to a great state of disrepair. Trash littered the streets, windows were broken everywhere, and several of the buildings had burned down over the past two years. It looked like nobody had been there in a century, but Choony knew that people did still live in these wildlands.

He kept alert, eyes darting everywhere to look for any movement. Every twenty steps or so, he abruptly turned and looked behind him, hoping not to see anyone following him. So far, his luck had held out; he saw no one.

It took him a half an hour to walk to the edge of the Maywood neighborhood, a journey that should've only taken ten to fifteen minutes. The need to stop and look around, and to take a route that wasn't quite so obvious—turning left, then right, then left—made his journey take longer than it should have. Still, it was better to be safe than sorry.

Maywood looked worse than he had thought it would. When he and Jaz had gone exploring and scrounging, they rarely went that far, and never into Maywood. All the scouts reported that it was dangerous, so he had avoided it for Jaz's sake. Today, however, he had to get through that neighborhood to get to his destination, as the address was on the other side.

Choony had only gone a block when, from the corner of his eye, he caught movement. His head snapped to the right, reflexively looking, and he cursed himself. If anyone was watching him, they would know he was aware of their presence now. Dammit. His cover was blown anyway, so he stared, waiting for the movement to show itself again.

After a minute, he was satisfied there was nothing there. At least, that's what he told himself. In reality, his heart began to beat faster, and in his mind, he chanted a Buddhist mantra meant to calm himself and strengthen his resolve. It worked, and within seconds he was on his way again. Even so, his senses were heightened, even more alert than before.

He traveled west along Anderson, keeping two blocks between himself and the nature preserve that lay to the north. Jaz had told him that an area like that was a perfect place for the residents who still survived in the area to congregate. He had no desire to meet people, not when some of them might want to eat him, and the best case scenario was that they would chase him off. When he saw a street sign showing that West Anderson was turning into Park Avenue, he knew he was only a block or two away from Maywood Avenue. Crossing that street would likely be the most dangerous part of this journey. It was miles long and straight, so anyone looking in his direction would be sure to see him from a far distance while he would be unlikely to see them. He recited his mantra again, steeling himself. He had to cross it, and if he was seen, there was nothing he could do about it. There was no point in worrying about it—he could not change his fate.

By the time Maywood Avenue came into view, he had

reconciled himself to his fate, whatever it might be. After he had crossed and was back in the relative safety of winding residential streets, he felt rather silly for his earlier concern. It didn't seem that anyone had seen him, no one was chasing him, and he berated himself for his earlier fear. Fear was a pointless emotion.

And then he heard a scuffing noise behind him, as of shoes on pavement. Calmly, he turned around to face whatever or whoever was behind him. He had good reason to feel silly for the second time in five minutes because the source of the noise he'd heard behind him was no threat. It was only a dog, and it was pretty much the cutest thing he had ever seen. It stood only about a foot high but had the build, long hair, and distinctive markings of a Husky. It would definitely be the smallest Husky he had ever seen. It made his heart leap to see such a cute creature, but the terrible condition of its fur coat offset his joy. The long hair was knotted and bedraggled, and its paws were covered in mud up to its tiny little knees.

As Choony turned around, the dog stopped too. It turned so that its left side faced Choony, and it lowered its head to the ground, nose on the pavement. Its tightly-curled tail uncurled slightly, and Choony thought that it must be the equivalent of having its tail between its legs.

"Hello, little fellow. Where did you come from?"

The dog stood back up to its full height, all one foot of it, and responded with a small, quiet bark. It looked like it was smiling, and Choony smiled back.

He reached into his pocket, where he kept a pemmican bar to nibble on as he walked. He pulled it out and unwrapped it, peeling the wax paper back, then broke off a large piece. He broke that into two parts and put one part in his mouth. As he chewed, he made a yummy noise, then set the other part on the ground and took two steps back. "Are you hungry, fella? It's okay, I got a piece for you, too." He made a *tsk tsk* noise, trying to summon the dog.

The dog raised its nose into the air, catching the scent of pemmican—dried meat and rendered fat, mostly—and again made the small yip of a bark. It took one hesitating step toward him, but then stopped. It made a tiny whimper noise.

"You needn't be afraid of me, doggie. I'm the last thing you need to be afraid of. Are you hungry? Yum Yum. Go ahead." Then he took another two steps back and crouched down, making himself appear smaller.

The dog inched its way toward the chunk of pemmican that lay on the pavement, one hesitating step after another, until it drew close to the morsel. It grabbed the pemmican between its teeth, then raced away several paces, stopping when it got about ten feet away. Then it turned back to face him, lay down on the pavement, and set the pemmican between its paws. It nibbled at it, tearing small chunks off and devouring them.

It took very little time for it to finish eating the treat he'd given it. Then it bounced up to its feet and spun in a circle, prancing. It looked at him and barked again, this time slightly louder. Its earlier barks had been the dog equivalent of a whisper, he thought, bemused.

"You're very welcome, little guy," he responded with a grin. "I take it you're hungry. I have some more. Here you go," he said as he set the remainder of his pemmican bar on the pavement. Then he backed away, but only a couple of paces. Then he crouched down again and tsk'ed at the dog.

Choony's new friend rose up onto its hind legs prancing again, then ran to the pemmican. This time, instead of taking the food and running away, it lay down where he had left the bar. It nibbled at the bar as it lay between its paws, but its eyes never left Choony.

"Well, little dog, you're lucky I don't plan to be out here

very long. I could spare a pemmican bar. Enjoy your tasty treat. Take care." Choony turned around and continued onward.

Half a block later, he turned around to check his six, as Michael would have said, and saw the small dog following him. Even from a hundred feet away, it looked almost exactly like a tiny Husky. When their eyes met, the dog barked once. Its head was held high, and Choony thought it seemed happy. He turned around again and continued onward, shaking his head. He tried to focus on his surroundings, tried not to think about the dog, but it was hard. Just knowing the thing was following him made it a bit of a distraction.

When he was a little over halfway down the block, he came across a large tan-colored, three-story building. A white sign with black lettering hung from the building, only one end still attached; the other end hung nearly to the ground. The sign read, "Maywood Police Department." It might once have been, but now it was a shell. Perhaps it had been the victim of rioting in the weeks following the first EMPs. The entire bottom floor was blackened from fire, soot rising up the outside wall from every window and empty doorway. All the windows had been smashed or blown out in the fire, and much of the building had been vandalized with crude graffiti since then, including its east wing with its accompanying Fire Department sign.

His eyes hung on one particular item, where someone had spray-painted with Navy-blue spraypaint, "Give food or be food 607 M-TOWN CCREW." It certainly hadn't been tagged recently, Choony figured, because much of the paint had faded away or even peeled off. What was left looked as sad and neglected as the rest of the neighborhood.

He also noticed several large brown stains on the cement in front of the building, and he gave one curt nod. He recognized the old bloodstains for what they were and felt a deep somberness wash over him and through him as he imagined what happened in this neighborhood during those first chaotic, terrifying weeks and months.

The vandalism was obviously gang-related, but he still couldn't help but wonder what had happened to whoever had painted it. Was he dead now? Had he found his way into Taggart's territory and rewritten the course of his life? Or perhaps he had been among those unfortunates that General Ree had once rounded up and enslaved. If so, he could still be alive somewhere, liberated by Taggart. He could just as easily have been among the many thousands Ree had lined up and shot as Taggart's army had overtaken them.

As Choony stood staring at the wall, lost in sad thoughts, he felt something touch his right leg and looked down. The same small long-haired little cute dog sat by his right foot, looking up at him. When Choony's eyes met its, it let out another small bark as if to say, "Hello. You aren't alone, and some of us made it."

Choony grinned. Of course it couldn't talk, and he realized he was projecting his own thoughts onto it. Still, at least the dog seemed happy now. He wondered why it had followed him, but just as quickly realized it probably wanted more food. His grin widened, and he reached into his pocket for another pemmican bar; he always carried two in his cargo pockets to munch on as he walked.

As he pulled the bar out and began to unwrap it, the wax paper crinkling loudly in the unearthly silence of the dead city, the dog sat up on its hind legs, and Choony could have sworn it was grinning. "Fine, you little beggar. But this is the last one, okay?"

He broke the bar into four pieces and set them on the cement in front of his new canine friend. Cautiously, he reached down as the dog gnawed upon the bar, and scratched it behind its ears. He kind of expected it to snap at him, given that it was eating, but instead, it ignored him and just continued eating.

A man's voice behind him said loudly, "Well, ain't that just cute."

Choony spun around, being careful to keep his hands away from his sides and visible.

The dog sprinted away into the underbrush, startled, but it had taken the last piece of pemmican with it, Choony noted.

Choony saw a raggedy man wearing torn, dirty clothes, and he looked like he hadn't shaven in a month. With so many dead around, not to mention the stores full of clothes that no one took because they couldn't eat jeans, there was no reason for the man to be wearing such clothes. Unless, perhaps, he was one of the crazy ones, the dangerous people who had become unhinged over the last two years, unable to deal with this terrible new reality.

Choony said, "Yes, it was a rather cute dog, wasn't it? Just a stray."

The man brushed long, dirty locks of hair out of his eyes, tucking them behind his ear. "Yeah, I've seen him around. He did a lot better for himself than most of the people who used to live here." Then he eyed Choony from head to foot.

Choony didn't think the man looked predatory, which was a relief because all alone in the open, he was pretty vulnerable. He put on a disarming smile, or at least he hoped it was, and replied, "The dog probably eats rats. There's lots of those around. I'm Choony, what's your name?" He had seen on TV that the survivors always tried to establish a personal connection with their kidnappers in order to hopefully make them more human in the badguy's eyes. He hoped it worked with homeless people, too.

"They used to call me Andy," the man said without a smile. He made no move to approach Choony. "Well, I'm pleased to meet you, Choony. That's a weird name, by the way. I guess I was sort of hoping that any man with enough food to spare for a stray dog might have something for me, too."

Choony paused to look the man in the eyes, gauging his expression. He didn't seem hostile, wasn't making any aggressive body language, but Choony knew that could change in an instant. That was especially true if the man was unhinged, as he suspected, but even those with minds that had snapped didn't deserve to starve. He happened to have three days of food in his backpack, as always. "Actually, I do, but you'll have to pay for it."

The corners of Andy's mouth moved down, and his left eye twitched once, faintly. "I think it's pretty obvious I don't have anything to trade," he said, his voice dropping an octave.

Choony nodded and forced a smile on his face as he replied, "That's okay. I had more in mind that you could pay for it by giving me some company as I have breakfast. Assuming you're okay breaking bread with a stranger."

Andy threw his head back and laughed, then looked at Choony again with a grin. It was kind of a pleasant, easy-going smile, Choony thought.

Andy said, "If your currency is my time, well, I got plenty of that. I'm a rich man when it comes to free time. Why don't you follow me, and I'll take you someplace where it's safe to eat. We really shouldn't be standing out here in the open like this, especially not here at the police station."

"Not safe? It doesn't look like there are many cops on duty right now. I don't think they're giving tickets for loitering."

Andy snorted and said, "The cops around here didn't do much of that even before everything went to shit. Unless you were homeless, which I was not at the time, in which case they were happy to do their job. The part of the job where they beat the shit out of homeless people."

Choony shrugged and said, "Hopefully they got to see what that felt like when everything went to hell. Karma is a very real thing, you know. Lead on, and I'll be happy to follow. I hope you like pemmican because that's what I've got."

Andy walked across the street, aiming between two large houses on the far side. He waved to Choony to follow. Over his shoulder, he said, "I don't know what that is, Mr. Choony, but if you're sharing, then I'm not complaining. I tried to eat that dog, but it never lets me get close. It sure seemed to like you, though."

Choony followed in silence. He certainly couldn't judge the man for trying to eat a dog—he had eaten worse, back during the Dying Time—but couldn't think of anything to say in response.

When they got across the street, Andy angled so that they went between the two houses, just as Choony had suspected. There were no fences, there, and they found themselves in a large, open area. It had once been the backyards of four houses, unfenced between them, but with an eight-foot tall fence around the conjoined yards.

In the far left corner, Choony saw a tent stashed among the growing shrubs and brambles that had overtaken that area, easily defeating the lawn that had once grown there. He smiled; Cassy would have had a long monologue about the evils of yards and something about permaculture, no doubt. Another quick glance all around showed they were alone.

"Why don't you just make camp in one of these houses? They all seem vacant, right? It seems like a house would be a better choice."

Andy smiled at him, the way a parent might smile at a child asking ridiculous questions, and explained, "You'd be wrong if you thought that. There are little bands of scavengers and raiders wandering around Maywood. The scavengers aren't above slitting a throat for some free gear, and the raiders would do it just for fun. They stick to the houses, though, and you can't see my tent from any of these buildings. It's hard to see from the side yard we came through, too, so I'm kind of surprised you spotted it."

There was a picnic table on the back patio of the house to his left, which he led Choony to, then motioned him to have a seat.

Choony unslung his backpack and set it on the table, then sat down. He unzipped one of the pockets and took out two pemmican bars, handing one to Andy, and unwrapped his own, even though he wasn't really hungry. It would be rude not to break bread with Andy since he had agreed to, and he didn't know if the man might snap if he didn't eat also. No one could ever tell what might set off the unhinged ones.

Andy sat at the table and stared at the pemmican bars like... well, like a starving man looking at food. When Choony slid one of the bars toward him, he snatched it up and almost frantically unwrapped it, then devoured the whole bar in three bites. He barely paused long enough to chew.

Choony said, "At least someone likes these things. Our leader taught us how to make them, but I never did like them. Not even when we were starving. The only reason I eat them now is that they are easy to carry and don't ever seem to go bad."

Andy licked the wax paper from his bar and, apparently surprised, his eyes flicked up to meet Choony's gaze. "What do you mean, they don't go bad? Everything goes bad, eventually. How old are these bars, anyway?"

Choony shrugged. He had always thought the same thing, but had taken the risk because he had been starving, just like everyone else at Clanholme during that first winter. "Maybe a month. A pemmican bar is meat that we dehydrate until it's crispy-dry, then we crush it until it turns into a powder. We mix that with nuts, maybe some raisins, and the rendered animal fat. You have to use the kind of fat that turns solid when it's cool, not the buttery kind. Then you wrap a bit in wax paper or a big leaf—it doesn't matter which —and it'll keep almost forever. I guess the Native Americans used to eat it, and my leader picked up that knowledge somewhere. I'm sure glad she did, even though they taste pretty bad."

Andy laughed, but Choony saw that he kept glancing at the backpack. He decided to give Andy another, so he reached into his pack and took out two more bars, which he slid across the table.

Andy's eyes sparkled. Judging by his appearance, Choony figured this pretty much was a feast for the guy. Andy grabbed them eagerly and began eating the next bar.

After Andy had gotten halfway through his second bar, Choony said, "What can you tell me about the area between here and the mall? That's the direction I'm going, and I'd hate to be surprised by something nasty."

Andy let out a sharp breath through his nose and said, "No, man, you can't go that way. That whole area belongs to a group that called themselves the Crew. You know, like from that spray-paint you were looking at. The Crew has owned that mall since about two weeks after the power went out."

Choony shook his head and said, "That doesn't really concern me. It's where I need to go, so if you know anything, I'd appreciate you sharing it with me."

"Okay, well, it's your funeral," Andy said. "What's so important that you're braving probable death, mister? And do you have anyone back in town you want me to pass a message to? You know, like a will."

"No, nothing like that. I have to go in there to search for my friend, Jaz. Well, she's more than a friend. She's my soulmate. I know that may sound stupid, but I'm a Buddhist. I believe everyone has a soulmate."

Andy raised an eyebrow and said, "I've known a couple of Buddhists, back in the day. They were more interested in sitting cross-legged than helping anyone."

"There is more than one kind of Buddhism. You're referring to a stereotype of Southern Buddhism, which focuses entirely on inner enlightenment, ignoring the world around them. I was raised in the traditions of Northern Buddhism, which believes there can be no inner enlightenment as long as there is pain in the world. We seek to help the world, in order to help ourselves. But to help the world, it's necessary to have a deep inner knowledge. That's why we meditate."

Andy rubbed the back of his neck, looking slightly uncomfortable. "I apologize. I didn't know that."

"It's quite all right, friend," Choony said with a polite smile.

"So, are you going someplace in particular, Choony? Maybe I'll pop by if I get the chance. See how you're doing."

Choony nodded. Then he reached into his pocket and withdrew one of his last two pemmican bars. "Thank you, but there's no need for that. I don't think I'll be out there too long, so here. Have another pemmican bar. I'll keep one for myself, and you can have the rest."

The man eagerly took the food when offered. He gave Choony a queer look, staring at him for several seconds before he finally said, "I have a couple of tips for you. Might help you stay safe."

Choony nodded. "I would sure be obliged," he said.

"Here, hold out your right hand, like this." Andy extended his right hand, with his pinky and ring finger bent to touch his palm, other two fingers extended, thumb straight up.

"Like a finger pistol?"

Andy grinned and said, "Yeah, exactly. When you do that, anyone in the Crew will reach out with their hand to shake your hand like that. What you gotta do is hook your bent fingers into their bent fingers, and use your other two fingers to tap their wrist lightly two times. That's like, their secret handshake. Or something. Don't ask how I learned that, but it seems to work. If they don't just shoot you first."

Choony smiled. That actually was useful information, and this man had no obligation to share it with him. It only went to reaffirm his belief that not everyone in the world was evil, given a chance to do right. "Thank you very much. If I make it out of here, when I get back to town I swear to you that I will gather up some supplies, whatever I can afford, and bring them out here for you. It's the least I can do, after all."

Andy nodded slowly, his expression pensive. "You know, I actually believe you'll do that. Most people say they'll do things, but then they don't. I just get a sense about you, like you're a man of your word. Well, best of luck. It was a pleasure to meet you, Choony."

Choony opened his mouth to respond, but Andy already rose from the table, striding away in the opposite direction. He was walking as though he had someplace to be. Maybe he was late for an important business meeting, Choony mused with a smile, then adjusted his backpack on his shoulders, getting more comfortable. He left the open area and headed deeper into Maywood.

- 16 -

0700 HOURS - ZERO DAY +636

AS THE DAWNING light rose above the horizon, Jwa waited patiently for the order to attack. It had taken days of moving at night to avoid detection deep in Confederation territory. Striking with complete surprise was of the utmost importance, as their force would be vastly outnumbered. If the defenders were allowed the chance to prepare themselves to defend against the upcoming attack, Jwa's unit and all the others would likely be eliminated.

Thanks to their leader's policy of pressing Americans into his military units, they had been able to maneuver through the territory quite easily—several of them were familiar with the terrain and the locations of Confed settlements that dotted the landscape. The Clan, in particular, had dotted their territory with their Clanholds, which were essentially small fortifications. The Clan's strategy had been so effective that the raiding unit, of which Jwa's squad was a part, had been forced to go around. That lengthened the journey and increased the odds of being detected, but their American conscripts had been effective. Fortunately, the scout/snipers had also done a good job of killing anyone who might have seen them traveling, so the units passed undetected.

Jwa took advantage of the few free moments before the battle to inspect his men and ensure their gear was secured and working properly. His squad for the raid consisted of six ISNA fighters and four Korean soldiers. He counted himself lucky to still have the same interpreter he had been assigned previously because his ISNA translator was one of the few Arab soldiers he had any respect for. It frustrated Jwa to know that the majority of his squad were ISNA, but at least he hadn't been assigned any of the American conscripts. Those poor bastards were certain to meet their ancestors soon after the fighting started because Americans made terrible soldiers. He'd been told that back home, and he hadn't seen anything about the conscripts to improve his opinion of their fighting ability.

After conducting his fourth inspection, satisfied that all of his men were in good order, Jwa had nothing to do but wait for the whistles that would launch the attack. He and his men were facedown in the dirt about a hundred yards from Ephrata's walls. The residents had spent most of their efforts to reinforce the north and east walls, presumably the direction from which previous attackers had come. Jwa's commander, however, had been smart enough to recon the walls and planned this raid to come from their south, where the walls were more poorly defended, making it easier to get over.

Just as the sun fully breached the eastern horizon, Jwa heard faint whistle blasts traveling all up and down the line. His heart leaped for joy—it was time to do something. He much preferred battle to the tedium of waiting.

"Rise, men—and charge!" Jwa shouted. He scrambled to his feet along with his men, and they rushed toward the southeast corner of the southern wall. Once over the wall, they would raid northward along the east wall, then shift west to strike at the enemy's storage areas. This would put the sun at his back, shining right in the eyes of any defenders alert enough to see them coming.

As he sprinted toward the wall, surrounded by his men, Jwa grinned. When they reached the rubble wall, he and his men breached it just as they had practiced. Half the soldiers interlaced their fingers, creating a stirrup to launch the other half up and over. Those men then hung over the edge to pull the first half up. In no more than twenty seconds, Jwa's whole unit was over the wall and in the town. To his left and right, other squads did the same. So far, so good... no shots had been fired, yet.

Jwa put the other units out of mind, focusing only on his own mission. "Advance by twos to the blue building north," he said.

His unit moved by leaps and bounds, one half advancing while the other half covered them; the process then repeated itself. After three bounds, the first men arrived at the building and stood with their backs to the outside wall, covering every direction with their rifles while Jwa and the rest of the unit sprinted toward the building.

During the briefings, many of the other squad leaders and even some of the platoon leaders had ferociously argued in favor of clearing every building as they advanced to avoid leaving any enemies to their rear.

Thankfully, the battalion commander was wiser than the fools and knew that doing so would slow everyone down tremendously. They couldn't afford to allow the defenders to regroup. Their only hope of success was to get in, cause havoc and confusion, and then grab what they could before vanishing over the wall once again.

Not far behind where Jwa and his unit had been down in the dirt, they had stashed enough bicycles for the whole unit to escape on, and if they could get a few miles away before any serious opposition began pursuing them on horseback, they'd be able to outdistance the horses. It was a solid plan, if risky.

His back against the wall, Jwa glanced to his left to ensure his interpreter was still with him. He said loudly enough to be heard by everyone, "Advance west by twos to the machine shop across the street."

Next to him, his interpreter babbled in Arabic, and then the unit moved out. Half sprinted across the street, while the other half kept their weapons at the ready and pointed in all directions.

The first half made it safely across the street, took up position, and then Jwa and the other half of his unit charged across the street. Their objective was two blocks west, a large covered parking lot that Intel said contained many crates of supplies. The whole battalion was converging on that point, approaching from many different directions. Jwa suspected the firefight would begin soon, at least for some of the units, but it would only add to the general sense of chaos, preventing the defenders from knowing their objective and rallying effectively.

His unit repeated the cycle several times, advancing slowly down the block, then the next. When they were still a block away from the covered supply depot, one of his Korean soldiers sprinted back from the front, stopping in front of him; he reported that they had seen six guards with rifles, two posted near the gate in the fence surrounding the depot and four wandering the interior.

Jwa nodded. That was two more guards than he had expected. "Two men on each of the interior guards, and on my mark, fire."

The interpreter nodded his understanding and went to pass the word among the ISNA soldiers, while Jwa himself passed the word to his Koreans.

The seconds ticked by as they got into position, the Koreans first in place, of course. He really didn't think of the ISNA men as soldiers, but rather as scruffy fighters. Bullet catchers. Barely better than untrained villagers with guns, and that was only because his commander had wisely insisted on giving them some additional training. It was frustrating to have them in his unit because they were always hesitant to obey the orders of a Korean superior. That was the reason every unit's interpreter was also its second-in-command, in fact—it was the only way to get the sand-eaters to obey quickly.

Just as his troops were finally all in position and almost ready to fire, the Americans within the depot disappeared from view as they dropped to the ground all at once. Jwa felt a moment of surprise, stunned, but a faint whistling noise broke him free of his indecision—the sounds of mortar fire.

"Take cover," he shouted and dropped to his knees, placing his helmeted forehead on the ground and covering his face with his arms.

Half a second later, his world shook violently. A concussive shockwave washed over him, then he glanced around to get a grip on his tactical situation. The building to his left, across the street, had been struck by a mortar and now debris rained over him and his men. Smoke and flames billowed up from the shattered building as bits of rubble fell, some large enough that he was sure he'd have welts.

Then he heard another explosion, and another. All around him, the entire area east of the supply depot was being hammered with mortar fire. He quickly noticed, however, that it was not accurate fire. The Americans were simply bombarding the entire area. How could they have enough rounds to waste like that? Intel hadn't reported such a stockpile, dammit.

It dawned on him that, with such a volume of mortar fire and such poor accuracy, it must be a simple screen. A "rolling thunder" of fire sweeping forward from the depot's perimeter. There was no other explanation but that the mortar fire was intended to disrupt and slow the attackers while the Americans brought up reinforcements.

How had they known about the raiders? There was no way. His unit's scouts had shot every person they came across out in the open, empty lands they had traveled through to get here, so no one could have alerted the defenders. In the old days, with electronic communications, he would have expected this and planned around it, but those didn't exist anymore. Certainly neither he nor his commander had taken such communications devices into account. After all, nothing electronic still survived. Had they missed an enemy scout? Maybe the garrison had been warned, if the Korean scouts/snipers had missed one. It was the only explanation.

Jwa came to a quick decision. As the Americans said, no plan ever survived contact with the enemy. His ancestors would not approve of him wasting the lives of his men or himself.

He reached up, grabbed the whistle that hung around his neck, and blew three short, sharp blasts. It was the signal to retreat.

His interpreter grabbed him by his shirt front and spun him around, then put his face inches away from Jwa's. He growled, "Why do we retreat? We must attack! We need the supplies, and you have your orders. We must obey."

Jwa was acutely aware that his Korean soldiers were outnumbered by the ISNA fighters with them. His indignation at being handled by a subordinate—much less a filthy sand-eater—began to rise, and he felt his cheeks flush. With one deft movement, he drew his dagger from his belt and plunged it into his interpreter's chest. The knife slid easily between two ribs. The interpreter had a look of surprise and anger on his face as he slid away to the side, pulling Jwa's knife with him, and he collapsed to the ground. He lay with his eyes open, unmoving.

It was time to go. In Korean, Jwa shouted, "Disengage and pull back!" He used his arm to motion his soldiers back, and they rushed toward him from among their ISNA companions.

He and his four Koreans sprinted east, retracing their steps—he knew the path they'd taken was probably just as empty as it had been on their approach.

He heard the sound of an AK-47 firing two shots from far behind him, and a Korean private running next to him grunted and flew forward, landing face first on the pavement. Jwa saw blood spreading across his back between his shoulders.

He turned back around and continued sprinting. "Go, go," he shouted. He would probably be executed when he got back to his unit commander, but he hoped at least to save his troops, whom he would exonerate of any responsibility. His ancestors would understand his sacrifice.

Behind them, more mortar shells landed, exploding all over the neighborhood. Jwa and three other Koreans ran for their lives.

* * *

Choony trudged through the desolate streets of Maywood. He kept alert for any movement, any sign of people, but so far, he had seen nothing except empty streets lined by vacant houses with blank window frames. The neighborhood was a ghost town for as far as he could see. His journey to the address he had been given could have taken only another fifteen minutes or so, but he made it a point to wind his way back and forth, shifting direction every block as he continued his journey generally northward. He could make sure that he wasn't being followed, that way.

He had begun to feel somewhat silly and was debating whether he should simply make a beeline for the address, rather than taking so many precautions, when he glanced down the street to his right at an intersection and saw, in the distance, a figure on a bicycle.

He immediately thought of the man he'd seen at the market who looked like Jack, but he shook his head. That must only have been someone who looked a lot like Jack. He grabbed his backpack straps and adjusted the weight on his back, then continued onward, moving more quickly. He was definitely not going to take the direct route, not right after seeing his first living person since leaving Andy's company many blocks ago.

At the next intersection, he glanced right again. He saw the figure on the bicycle again, but this time closer. Close enough to be fairly confident that the rider was male. He reassured himself that it might still be a coincidence to have seen him twice, and continued on his way.

At the end of the block, he turned right. The man on the bicycle rode slowly across the intersection, perpendicular to Choony's new direction. At the next intersection, Choony glanced again, and that time, the man on the bike was traveling parallel to him and was still closer. He was now maybe five blocks away.

Choony's heart beat faster. There was no way it could be a coincidence. He glanced to his left, looking for a way out or a place to hide, but his heart skipped a beat when he saw another man on another bike, about the same distance away. There were two of them, one to either side.

"Damn." He kept walking northward. It was all he could do, now.

Midway down the block, he saw an open gate leading to a large backyard, and he ducked through it. When he got to the back fence, he climbed over it and then climbed over the side fence into the yard next door. He crossed it, going around a rusty children's swing set, then jumped over the next side fence, too. He continued like that until he reached the last house on the block, then peered over the fence and looked up and down the street. He didn't see either bicycle, so he took a deep breath to calm his nerves. He ducked down and slowly counted to ten as he evened out his breathing.

Choony stood again and peered over the fence. Damn— he saw both bike riders two blocks down the road, to his right. They had stopped, talking to one another. He quickly ducked down, then went to the house's side gate. Thankfully, it wasn't locked, and he had no problem opening it. Hopefully, the two men around the corner wouldn't see him. He took three quick, deep breaths and then sprinted across the street and then through another side gate. He kept running, crossing that backyard as well, and hopped the back fence into another backyard. When he reached that side gate, he found it ajar and poked his head out to look up and down the street, which ran north to south. His two followers should now be three blocks east of him if they hadn't moved out.

He stepped out onto the sidewalk, then put his head down and sprinted across the intersection, heading north. When he got across the street, he kept running down the block, continuing north.

Panting, he got to the last house on the block and then ducked into its side yard, crouched behind a shrub, and waited. If the men on bikes had seen him, they should be riding by any time now. As he waited, he counted from one to one hundred, allowing his pulse to calm again while he caught his breath.

Seventy-five... Seventy-six...

The shadow of a man appeared on the ground in front of him, and his heart leaped as he realized that somebody was standing behind him, between him and the easterly sun. He didn't waste a heartbeat before he shot to his feet and sprinted out of the side yard. He ran across the street, then turned to head north again.

As he ran across the next intersection, he glanced behind him and saw the same man who looked like Jack, right behind him, knees and fists pumping as he bolted after Choony.

Choony turned forward and redoubled his efforts. A block went by, then another. He glanced behind him and saw Jack still behind him, but he had closed the distance a little.

His chest ached, and his legs burned, so he cleared his mind of everything but the need to take one rhythmic step after another. He allowed himself to get lost, hypnotized by the even repetition of his feet pounding on the cement. Two more blocks went by, then a third.

When he reached the next intersection, although his legs were in agony and he was sucking for air like a fish out of water, he didn't slow. He kept going, sprinting. Everything was silent except for the sounds of his pursuer's foot strikes and his own.

Choony kept running, crossing the next intersection. Halfway across, he felt a massive weight strike him on his left side. It sent him flying through the air like some toy kicked by a petulant child. His mind reeled, confused, trying to catch up to what was happening, but he was too dazed to make sense of what he saw. Why was he looking at the ground? Why was he looking at the sky? Why was he looking at the ground again? The ground rose up to meet him, and by sheer reflex, Choony flung his arms in front of his face as he crashed into the pavement.

He tumbled and rolled, a human tumbleweed, until he came to rest on his backpack beneath him. He urged his body to move, but it just wouldn't respond. He could only lay there stunned, staring up at the sky. It was over, he realized. Whoever had been chasing him wasn't chasing anymore. Now they had him, and he'd never find Jaz...

He wondered how badly he was injured because he couldn't feel a damn thing. Couldn't move anything. Even his fingers just wouldn't respond to his commands. His dazed mind told him he was dead and awaiting transference. He felt... serene. Not frightened, as he should. He had done his best, he knew, and dying in the attempt to rescue someone would grow his Karma. He would die increased. Perhaps reincarnation would take his Karma to someone who wouldn't have to struggle quite as much as he had in this life.

At least, those were his thoughts. After several seconds, however, he realized he wasn't dead yet. How sad. The first part to obey his commands were his eyes. He glanced around as best he could. As he looked up from his back, a face appeared into view from his right, hovering over him. It was definitely Jack's. Then, from the other side, another face slid into view. He didn't recognize that one.

Jack opened his mouth and began to speak, his words sounding very far away. "Well, if it isn't the mighty Choony. I see you got my message."

The other man said, "Yeah, Jack. Looks like he got it alright." He grinned down at Choony, his brown hair and freckled face contorted into a sneer that looked very much at home on the young man's face like it was simply an extension of his inner self, displayed for the world to see. "You was right, where ever Jaz was, this fuckin' guy would be."

To Choony, the words were barely understandable. He was still too much in a daze to focus, but he caught most of it.

Especially when they mentioned Jaz's name. "Jaz...?"

Jack chuckled and moved in closer to Choony. "She's my bitch, now." His foot shot forward, connecting with Choony's ribs.

As pain exploded in his side, bursting through the dazed numbness, Choony tried to roll over but couldn't; he tried to move one of his hands, but it merely flopped over onto his chest, completely uncoordinated.

The younger man said, "I think you broke him, dude. He didn't even flinch. Is he dying?"

Choony looked up at the two faces that leaned over him, the known and the unknown, burning their images into his mind.

Jack smacked the younger man upside his head and said, "Don't be stupid, Chump. It's not like we shot him, just knocked the sense out of him when you smashed him with your bike." He smiled. "Though, I have to admit, it's not as much fun as playing with Jaz."

Choony felt pain shoot into his side. He curled up reflexively covering his stomach with his arms and whimpered in pain. He forced the anger away. It would only cloud his mind, and he suspected he would need all the clarity he could muster if he wanted to survive long enough to rescue Jaz, assuming that would even be possible. If they beat him to death here in the middle of the street, he wouldn't get the chance.

Chump grunted, then kicked Choony in the back.

Choony cried out and rolled onto his back, arching from the pain so that only his buttocks and the back of his head actually touched the ground. Through the agony that spread down his spine to his very toes, he heard the two men laughing.

The world was full of such men, and it was only Choony's misfortune to be caught by them this time. He hoped that if they were going to kill him, they would do it quickly. He preferred not to feel a lot of pain before moving on in the great cycle of life, though he knew the world was made of pain.

Jack bent down and grabbed Choony by the neck with one hand, and with the other, he grabbed Choony's arm. "Help me get this prick up."

The younger man did as he was told, but laughed out loud. "You said 'help you get this prick up,' dude. Need some Viagra, old man?"

Jack didn't respond, and Choony found himself yanked painfully to his feet. He still swayed a bit, but the two held him up. He didn't struggle or try to get away. There was no way he could escape, so he simply accepted what was. He was captured, and they would do what they wanted with him. He did offer up a prayer to Buddha that, if Jack and his crony, Chump, were going to kill him, he'd have the chance to see Jaz one last time, but that was the extent of his resistance.

Chump stripped Choony's backpack off, then wrenched his arms behind him. He felt a zip tie binding his hands behind his back.

Jack grabbed a handful of his jacket and wrenched hard enough to spin him around so that he faced the asshole, who looked at him for a couple of seconds with an irritating smirk on his face. Then, in a blur, Jack's fist whipped out and connected with his left eye. There was a wet *plop* noise when the fist struck, then pain exploded inside his head. He staggered back, but from behind, Chump grabbed him under the arms and held him up.

Jack said, "That was for being an asshole and cock-blocking me back in Clanholme." Jack gave Choony another hard kick. "And that's for getting me exiled. And what I do to you later will just be purely for my pleasure." Choony's vision was blurred, but he could still make out the wide grin on Jack's face looking down at him.

The two grabbed Choony by his jacket and arms, and shoved him hard, forcing him to walk between them. They walked through Maywood like that, Jack whistling aloud like he had not a care in the world.

* * *

Jwa and his three Korean companions turned left at the next intersection, sprinting down the block, then doglegging to the right. This took them out of the line of fire from the ISNA troops they had left behind, assuming any of them had survived the mortar fire. He didn't waste any energy on speaking—they simply ran toward the wall, and kept running.

It seemed like they had run for hours by the time they got to the low rubble east wall of Ephrata. He wasted no time giving orders, but simply got in the position to launch one of his men up onto the wall, his fingers interlaced and waiting to receive a foot. The others followed his example, and it took only a couple of seconds to get two of them up on the wall. They reached down and pulled Jwa and the other Korean up, and then all four dropped down to the open ground beyond the wall.

He turned south and ran, no longer sprinting but settling into a quick, measured pace he could keep up for miles. If they were being actively pursued before he could get to the bikes, they would likely be caught whether he sprinted or kept up a sustainable pace, but it wouldn't do them any good to be exhausted after a couple hundred yards. They still had some ways to go before they got to the bikes.

After a lot more running, during which time he had been unable to resist the urge to look over his shoulder time and time again, looking for pursuit, they reached the bikes. Before leaving, they had strapped their backpacks to small frames that had been fabricated to make long-distance travel on the bikes a lot easier. Jwa grabbed his bike, the one with his own custom saddlebag arrangement, picked it up, and pedaled south. Another glance over his shoulder told him that his three men were right behind him.

It had only been a few minutes of hard riding when Jwa heard the report of a rifle. He glanced back yet again, but this time, he saw what he had been fearing all along—half a dozen or more people on horseback riding hell-bent for leather, as the American cowboys said. Two more shots rang out from among the mounted pursuers, but they again missed. Thankfully.

Jwa put his head down and pedaled for his life. Every so often, another shot would ring out, but so far they had all missed. They had traveled at least another couple of miles by the time he risked another look back; their pursuers were gaining ground on him. He really had no hope of escape because the cavalry would outpace his bicycles in the short term. It was only after an extended pursuit, half a day or more, that the bikes would again take the lead. He didn't think they had that kind of time.

One of the two men to his right shouted, "We will never make it. It has been an honor to serve with you, my leader."

Jwa wasn't certain he had the breath to respond. He was sucking air, couldn't get enough of it, and his legs burned like they were on fire. His three Korean companions were all excellent soldiers, loyal to the Plan, and had served with distinction so far. They were all going to die, and they were his responsibility. The Arabs had been, too, though he cared less about those animals.

It dawned on him, then, that although he couldn't have saved his ISNA brothers, even if they hadn't turned traitorous under fire due to their reckless fanaticism, he just might still be able to do something to save his brethren. Better to lose one irreplaceable Korean soldier for the cause than to lose all four. He shouted, "Turn left one-five degrees... aim for the rocky outcropping. When we get there, keep riding. I will stay behind so you all can make it home. The honor has been mine."

"But, sir—"

"Save your breath. Just do it." Jwa redoubled his efforts. Another look over his shoulder showed him the cavalry was bearing down on them. Soon, their random potshots would start finding their targets.

The large rock outcropping loomed ahead of them, rising up from the field seemingly at random. It was about thirty feet tall, made of large boulders jutting from the earth. All around it, the field was flat in every direction. From there, he might be able to hold off the cavalry for at least a little while. Long enough for his men to escape, and for him to do his duty.

Just before the line of Korean cyclists drew parallel to the outcropping, one of the men shouted, "You honor your ancestors." The other two shouted a hurrah in agreement.

The line of bikes curved around so that the outcropping stood between them and their pursuers' rifles, and his men kept riding for their lives, obeying his final orders.

Jwa, however, veered sharply left and dumped his bike at the foot of the hill. He unslung his rifle and scrambled up the outcropping until he reached the top. He flopped onto his belly, nearly knocking the wind out of himself, and drew aim. He drew in one deep breath, began to exhale, and halfway through letting it out, he held his breath long enough to gently squeeze the trigger. His AK-47 bucked, and one of the pursuing riders fell from his horse.

The others scattered and rode for cover. He had time to

snap-fire one more round at one of their horses, lacking time to aim at the smaller targets riding them, and the horse fell. It skidded to a halt in the dirt, kicking up a cloud of dust, and its rider scrambled for cover behind a bush. Jwa cursed, lacking time to aim for another shot to drop the briefly-exposed man.

Two tufts of dirt and gravel flew up into his face from two feet in front of Jwa, and he ducked down as more shots were fired. He counted to three, then rose up long enough to snap off a shot, but he didn't have time to aim. He remembered where his pursuers were and had to rely on his reflexes to try to aim in someone's direction in order to fire off a burst. Then he dropped down, and just in time, too, as more ricochets fell around him.

Jwa smiled. His men would escape, and his ancestors would be proud of him. He would likely join them soon. An incongruous thought streaked through his mind, looking forward to sitting by his grandfather's side again and listening to one of his old tales of legend. Jwa had loved those stories, growing up.

He rose up long enough to snap off another burst of fire, immediately ducking down again to avoid the inevitable return fire. His heart raced as he made peace with the idea that he was about to die.

* * *

By the time they had crossed through the Maywood neighborhood, Choony sported two new bruises over his cheek and jaw and a limp from where Jack had kicked him in his thigh one time, after Choony had fallen. His shoulder hurt, too, since they had yanked him roughly back to his feet by his arms, still bound behind his back with a ziptie.

Eventually, they came to a street—*the* street, according

to the sign—and he saw that the nearby addresses were in the 1900s. They turned down that street, and ten minutes later came to a small warehouse. Address: 1701. Choony felt his heartbeat accelerate at the thought that perhaps Jaz was within.

Just outside the door, Jack stopped and spun Choony to face him again. "Your eyes are all dilated, dude. I can *see* your adrenaline pumping. You know what's inside, don't you?"

Choony didn't answer. He figured it was a rhetorical question.

Jack shrugged. "You don't need to answer. I can see it in your eyes." Jack grinned in his face, as malevolent an expression as Choony had ever seen.

Chump threw open the door, and Choony saw an office on the other side. Jack shoved him firmly through the doorway and in the sudden darkness inside, it took a moment for his eyes to adjust. It must've taken them a moment as well, because they both simply stood beside him in the dark, not moving except to get a firmer grip on his jacket.

About ten seconds later, from behind him, Jack's voice said, "All she needed was the touch of a real man to open her up. You should hear the way she goes nuts when I'm giving it to her. Straight porn-star status."

Chump said with a grin, "She's always talking about how you got that short little Chinese cock."

Jack's hand lashed out in a blur, smacking the other man upside his head. "Not Chinese, dumbass. He's Korean. There's all different kinds of slant-eyes," Jack said. He then looked at Choony and said, "I apologize for my friend's racist remarks, but you gotta admit, you all do kinda look the same."

Choony felt rising anger, but quickly allowed it to pass.

Not only did he refuse to give them the satisfaction of displaying his impotent rage, but anger would also not solve his problem. Nothing he could do right now would save him, so his best option was to follow the Buddha's teachings and simply accept his circumstances. After all, not accepting them would change nothing, it would only disturb his own harmony and darken his Karma.

His two captors stared at him for what seemed like a couple of minutes, but was probably only a few seconds, obviously expecting a reaction from him. He simply looked back, passively. No, he must wait patiently for the right opportunity.

Jack rolled his eyes and said, "This guy is so damn stupid, he don't even know when he's being insulted."

Chump laughed and said, "Maybe, but I bet he reacts to what you got planned. I don't figure he can ignore that, eh?"

Jack barked out a laugh, then walked toward the door leading to the warehouse bay, dragging Choony behind him. As the doorway loomed closer, Choony's heartbeat sped up. On the other side of that doorway, he would surely see Jaz. He hoped she wasn't completely damaged or, at the very least, he hoped she was still alive.

* * *

The sound of the front door closing woke Jaz with a start. Her heart raced, palms sweaty, before she was alert enough to comprehend what had woken her. The jackal and his pet hyena must have returned.

Once she realized it had been the door, she rushed to cover herself with the blanket as she plopped back down on the dirty mattress, pretending to be asleep. It was difficult because she totally felt the urgent need to gasp for more air. As her heart continued to race, adrenaline pumped. Then she heard Jack laughing, and her blood ran cold. He only laughed when he was hurting her, or thinking about doing it. Like, relishing the thought. Jack was evil.

As they came through the doorway from the office, Jaz cracked one eye.

Choony. He was with them!

She nearly gasped, nearly clamped her hand over her mouth, but they would see or hear that. It took all her willpower to stay silent and still. Every little part of her wanted to jump up and rush to him, but she wouldn't dare. She imagined what she might look like, bruised from head to toe. She couldn't let Choony see her like that. It would crush him, and if he flinched away from her in any way, that would destroy what little soul she had left. She couldn't avoid it forever, but please, God, just a little longer, she begged. She wanted time enough to build up her resolve. She only hoped she could show herself to him on *her* timeline, not Jack's.

"...that lump of fine ass on the bed over there, that's your boo," Jack was saying, his voice carrying to her from across the warehouse bay. "She don't look as good as she did the last time you saw her, I bet. She has more miles on her now, you know?"

Through the tiny gap she'd left between the blanket over her head and the pillow beneath it, she saw Choony turn his head to stare at her, but he didn't move. He didn't cry out. Thank God, because if he had freaked out, those two assholes would have fallen on him like sharks on chum.

Choony said, "Whatever you have done to her, you also do to yourselves. Your Karma is stained, Jack. You dishonor your ancestors."

No, no, no... was he *trying* to get himself killed?

Jack laughed—a high-pitched, crazed laugh that sent shivers down her spine—then replied, "My parents dishonored themselves, shithead. They made me what I am, so whatever I've done to that hot piece of ass, well, that just stains my parents' Karma. Loophole, bitch!"

He tossed his head toward Jaz's covered, apparently-sleeping form, and his little crony nodded and headed toward her bed. She braced herself for whatever they had in store for her. It was never good, and now with a captive audience, it would surely be the worst yet.

"Let's see what's behind door number one," Jack said, rubbing his hands together as if bracing himself for the big reveal.

* * *

Choony stood passively as Chump walked toward Jaz. He could do nothing to stop this, and struggling would only give Jack pleasure. He resolved himself to simply await his fate or his first opportunity to save Jaz, whichever came first.

Chump strode to the bed. He paused and said, "Wakey, wakey." With a sudden burst of movement, he ripped the blanket off with the enthusiasm of a child on Christmas morning, revealing Jaz, nude except for the cuffs around her wrists and the collar padlocked around her neck. Those bindings were all chained to a larger single chain that ran somewhere under the bed, coils of it visible on the concrete floor.

And she looked terrible. His heart broke to see her. Her once-beautiful, lustrous hair was matted and dull, and something like dried blood had crusted clumps of it to the left side of her face. Half of her body was covered in the fading yellows and grays of healing bruises, large enough to see even from his distance. The bruises on her inner upper thighs were fresh, as was the bruise under her left eye.

Chump grabbed her by the hair and yanked the sleeping woman to her feet. She cried out in pain and surprise, complying frantically with his shouted order to get the hell up. As she struggled to ease the pain of her hair being pulled, she saw Choony and locked eyes with him, but he saw no sign of recognition in those eyes. There was no light in them. She looked like a zombie.

Beside him, Jack chuckled. "You like my artwork, Choony? Chump and I had a couple little blue party pills, and your woman here was the party favor."

Choony refused to react. He could do nothing about what had happened to Jaz, but if he got the opportunity to make things right, he wouldn't hesitate. He decided that, although he wouldn't go out of his way to kill Jack, he wouldn't hesitate to if he got the chance and saw hope he could capitalize on it to let Jaz escape. The stain to his Karma would be offset by the goodness restored to the world with Jack's killing.

After a couple seconds, Jack shrugged and said, "No comment, eh? I bet you didn't know she was such a slut. Hey, Chump, come tie the gook to a chair, yeah? I've always wanted an audience."

Choony felt his stomach churn, but not from fear of the rope Chump used to bind him to a metal office chair. He kept his eyes locked on Jaz the whole time, willing her to take strength and Chi from him. He was here for her, and he wouldn't look away no matter how it hurt to see what he suspected Jack was about to do. Choony would let her see his eyes and the love they contained so that she might lose herself in his gaze instead of in what was to come.

- **17** -

DOWN IN THE bunker, Cassy sat at Ethan's computer desk, looking at the monitor. It was still blank, the black screen's slightly off-hue its only sign of being turned on. Frustrated, she turned to Ethan sitting next to her and frowned. "You said they wanted to talk to me, but where are they? Is it a technical glitch?"

Ethan shook his head as she drummed her fingers on his desk impatiently. "No, sorry. I got an urgent query about a report I had sent, with a message that only said they had to talk to you about a top priority. Then I came and got you so you could respond right away, and when we got back, they weren't on the monitor anymore. I've got it set to auto ping them for a call response every three minutes."

Cassy took a sip of hot apple cider infused with hazelnuts. Since almost all the coffee was gone now, it had become the Clan's favored morning drink. The infused cider took a bit of getting used to, but she had forced herself to learn to like it. If that's what everyone else drank, then it was what she had to drink, too. Still, it would've been nice to have some real coffee down there in the bunker, where the rest of the Clan couldn't see.

A couple of minutes later, an icon appeared on the monitor that looked a lot like an old-style telephone. Ethan muttered, "Here they are." Without getting up, he reached across her to tap on one of the keyboard's function keys, and the chat window expanded to full-screen mode.

She saw a tired, ragged-looking man on the other end. It was Tony all right, the new Ephrata leader, but in the months since he had taken over he seemed to have aged several years. She gave him a cheerful smile and said, "Good morning. You look as handsome as ever."

The man in the monitor chuckled. He said, "Always the flatterer, Cassy."

Her smile faded a bit, and she said, "What's going on?"

At her comment, he grimaced. She felt her stomach lurch. That expression couldn't bode well. He replied, "Well, I appreciate that. In fact, that's why I asked to speak to you like this, securely and in private."

Cassy stared at the screen, waiting for him to say something more. He obviously had a point and was taking a long time to get to it.

After a few seconds, Tony coughed, looking physically uncomfortable. He was pale enough that even through the video conference screen, he looked ill. At last, he said, "The thing is, we've been getting hit by the 'vaders a lot, lately. We think they're from the Northern Cantonment, groups of raiders penetrating the empty area east of us in order to hit us from the south and southeast where our walls are thinnest. It has happened enough in the last few weeks that everything here has been brought more or less to a standstill. I'm really glad most of our planting was already in because it's not even safe out in our fields. It's like our own little Bosnia situation."

She shook her head, fairly sure he had the wrong Intel.

"Actually, our scouts tell us the raider groups have been coming from the Maryland invaders. They're raiding deep into Confed territory and focusing on Ephrata, although we don't know why."

He shrugged back at her. "I don't know about that, but it could be true. It doesn't really matter, though. Wherever they come from, we need Confed support. We need battle cars, cavalry, you name it. We need to be able to keep our work parties safe outside our walls while they tend our remaining crops, you know? If we don't get backup from you and the Confederation, we're not going to be able to help out in other areas, which we hear are also heating up."

Dammit. This was what she had been afraid of. While it pissed her off that a key member of the Confederation was telling her they couldn't meet their duties, couldn't loan troops to fight the Maryland invaders, she also understood their position. The Clan had been in that position before, after all.

Biting her tongue, she said, "I understand the gravity of your situation. But we need those contingents of troops that Ephrata has promised to the Confederation. We need them so we can fight off the southern invaders. Once we fight them off, the situation gets easier for you and we can divert other troops to you. You know that, right? Holing up and circling the wagons isn't in your best interest."

Tony shook his head again. He looked up at the ceiling and took a deep breath, audible even through the webcam connection. "It's not going to happen, Cassy. I don't think you understand how bad it is here. Just this morning, we got hit by a full company of raiders, Korean and ISNA both. They got through our walls."

"How bad did it get?" she asked, imagining the worst. No, the worst would have been if Ephrata got overran, but obviously they hadn't.

"They almost raided one of our main supply depots, and they would have blown it up afterward if we hadn't had a scout report back through one of those handheld Raspberry Pi short range radios that Ethan hooked up. Thank God we had all our mortar batteries supplied with coordinates to deal with an attack from that direction since so many of the raids have been coming from there. We pretty much wiped them out, although we lost a lot of buildings that could've been useful down the road. We only lost a couple of people, and we decimated that company, but they'll be back. They were part of a battalion."

"I don't see the problem then, Tony. The raiders were wiped out, more or less, and they aren't going to send another battalion at you unless we go to actual war with the invaders again."

He pinched the bridge of his nose. "I don't like having to tell you this, but I have to order our troops to stay here in town. We need to be ready for the next raid because I promise you, it's coming."

Cassy's eyes went wide. She had known about the raids, but not about the extent of them, nor about how close the raid this morning had come to destroying much of Ephrata's supply stockpiles.

She scrambled frantically for a solution. There had to be a way to alleviate the pressure on Ephrata and still be in a position to defend against the Maryland invaders, where the real raiders had been coming from as far as her intelligence sources could tell.

Then an idea struck her. Clan scouts were continually reporting on the movements of a growing army from Maryland, a huge force comprised mostly of American citizens pressed into service, the rest mostly ISNA fighters. Only a few of the raiders were actually Korean. What if, instead of hitting them hard before they got deep into

Confederation territory like she had planned, she just let the next company of raiders slide through Confederation defenses?

They would march on Ephrata again, which Maryland had apparently decided was the easiest, weakest link in the Confederation. Then the Clan and other Confed forces could sweep around behind the raiders as they engaged Ephrata. They could hammer the attackers on the anvil of those town walls. If she could arrange for allies' forces to demolish the attackers, Ephrata would have to realize that their raids were indeed coming from Maryland and not from up north. It would prove that the Confederation stood strongest when it stood together.

Plus, by eliminating so many enemies at once, before the full war began, it would free up Ephrata defenders for other operations that were just as important... which was maybe even more important, in the long run. After all, the Confederation had to get that southern border under control before the war, or they would all be overrun.

She looked directly at the webcam and put a grimace on her face, nodded curtly, and said, "Of course. I understand completely. You're in a rough situation, and you're just not able to help us deal with this other threat at the moment. You keep the invaders off our backs, and we'll keep your flank protected. We'll get through this as we always do, right? Together."

He nodded and smiled, though his expression looked more grim than happy. "Thanks for understanding, and I'm sorry we won't be able to meet our obligations." He gave the camera a haphazard salute, then the screen went blank as he disconnected the call.

From behind, she heard Ethan let out a low whistle. He said, "I'm kind of surprised at you, Cassy. We really need those troops."

She spun around in the swivel office chair, coming to a stop facing Ethan. She let out a deep breath, then nodded once. "I hear what you're saying, Ethan, but I have a better plan. You know that we aren't likely to withstand a full assault by Maryland without Ephrata's support. We need to take the pressure off them to get that support, and the best way to do that is to use them as bait."

Ethan looked confused for a moment, then his eyes lit up with understanding. "Oh hello! You're going to let them get attacked and then have the Confederation swoop in like the cavalry, saving the day. Did I guess right?"

She shrugged, smiling with her most innocent expression plastered on her face, and he burst out laughing.

Now, she would just have to convince Michael.

* * *

Mark came to a stop in front of the nondescript door, his footsteps continuing to echo down the long, barren corridor. He took a moment to catch his breath and prepare himself mentally, then knocked lightly on the door. A man's voice from inside hollered out for him to enter, so he opened the door and stepped through, closing it behind him.

The office was Spartan, almost completely unadorned save for a massive bookshelf that consumed every inch of one entire wall. Half of the shelves were stuffed full of binders, unlabeled, and the rest were full of various bits of equipment: radios, fax machines, and still other devices he didn't recognize at all.

On the other side of the huge office desk, Harry Emerson sat in his office chair, leaning to one side lazily, his eyes roaming over Mark from head to toe. Harry's gaze always seemed to be searching, looking for information and always seeming to shine with disapproval. Mark hated dealing with the CIA's liaison, but it was part of his job. He was, after all, the civilian liaison representing the many civilians ensconced in NORAD.

Harry motioned toward a simple chair on the opposite side of his desk and said, "Mark, it's great to see you again. Grab a seat. We have a few things to discuss."

Mark smiled, a well-practiced expression, but he sure didn't feel it. Harry was a shark, and Mark knew it. Any conversation with him was dangerous, even if he was your friend. He was most definitely not Mark's friend.

Mark crossed the office and sat in the offered chair. He tried desperately not to fidget under Harry's intense, unblinking gaze.

Harry, shark extraordinaire.

Mark said, "I'm not sure why you called me here today, but it's always a pleasure meeting with you."

"I know you don't mean it, but that's okay. You and I are both professionals. When we have a job to do, we simply do it. Even when dealing with people we like, even with those who may not like us either. Such is the way of politics, eh?"

Mark nodded. There wasn't much he could say to that since all of it was true. "As much as we may not like it, you're right. Politics is part of the job. So are our meetings, for that matter, but I was a little surprised to receive your invitation to meet here." Of course, it had been an 'invitation' in name only, but since declining such a meeting would likely be fatal, professionally if not physically, it was hardly a request.

Harry smiled. He crossed his right leg over his left thigh, forming a figure-four, and interlaced his fingers on his belly as he leaned back in the chair again. He made a clicking noise with his tongue, acknowledging Mark's comment. "Of course I appreciate your coming," he said. "I need to pick your brain for a minute, and I know you're familiar with the situation in Louisiana with several of our bases being raided somewhat regularly. What else is going on in Louisiana, do you think?"

A shiver ran up Mark's spine. What did Harry know? Mark had taken great pains to hide his messages to the troops in Louisiana, regarding the search for Janice's family, but it was still possible that Harry had discovered it. If so, what would he make of it? Obviously, he didn't know what to make of it or Mark would be dead already. He still might end up that way if he wasn't careful...

He said, "What do I think? Well, I'm surprised that you're looking to work with my department on something like that, but I'm glad to hear it. We civilians owe our lives to you folks in the Agency and our military leadership. We don't forget that, never fear. Anything I know, you only have to ask. I'm kind of excited to be helping, actually."

If his situation weren't so dire, he would have smiled. He had delivered that line masterfully. The only thing that remained was to see whether Harry bought it. By itself, putting in an order to search for a bunker resident's family wasn't unusual, but those orders had to come from the CIA or the DIA, not from the civilians like Mark no matter who he knew. Harry was smart enough and paranoid enough to wonder what it meant, and would eventually figure it out if Mark slipped up.

Harry sat looking at Mark for a long moment, his face frozen in a neutral half-smile. At last, he said, "Good. It relieves me to hear that. So, if you're familiar with the situation in Louisiana, what do you know about the troops in our firebases searching for surviving relatives of people here in the bunker?"

It was a bit of an effort of will for Mark not to fidget with his hands. He was an old hat at this sort of thing, however, and kept his face carefully friendly. "I know there's a form our people can fill out and submit. On approval by the military chain of command, our troops in those regions will make at least some effort to locate those people. Usually, they go to any last known address provided on the form, and sometimes following up on any clues left behind if the residents moved on and left a note. I know that seven out of ten people out there died in the last couple years, but from what I gather, the success rate at finding surviving relatives is more like one in ten. Probably because there was so much chaos and dislocation during the post-EMP population adjustment phase."

Harry nodded slowly, his eyes never leaving Mark's. "Good to hear. So, I need a favor of you. Some help you can provide. The short version is that I need your department to pass out new survivor location request forms to all the civilians here on base. This new, modified version of the form has a simple checkbox for those who have no known family members in the regions we control. As of tomorrow, the old forms will no longer be in use, and the CIA is trying to build a database of all family members who might live in the controlled territories."

Dammit. Mark struggled to keep his expression neutral, to mask his sudden fear, but that new system would mean that the search request forms he had slipped in would no longer be valid. Since he would have to deliver a new form to everyone, including Janice, she would know that nothing was being done anymore to find her family unless she filled out the new form correctly, which she would do enthusiastically. That would remove much of his leverage with her.

"Of course, Harry. My department reports to yours and the military chain of command. If you can have someone deliver the forms I need to have distributed, I'll make sure it gets done quickly."

Harry's eyes were still locked on Mark, unwavering. It was a little creepy. "Thanks. I know I can count on you. You are, after all, one of the few truly professional people I have under me, outside the analyst group. I have another meeting in five minutes, but I'll be sure to get those forms to you today. Please make sure the completed forms you get back are delivered to us daily so we can stagger sending them out to our field units." He then leaned forward and grabbed a sheet of paper on his desk and began reading it.

It was obvious that Mark was dismissed. He left the office without another word, quietly closing the door behind him. Once he was out in the dull gray corridor again, he let out a long, slow breath, allowing some of his tension to flow away. This might be really bad for him, he realized. When he had put through Janice's search request, bypassing the chain of command, he had fudged her name so that if the communication had been intercepted, it couldn't be traced back to her, and eventually to him. With new forms going out, one expected from every person, any halfway-decent CIA analyst—not to mention the DIA computers—could cross-reference the names of those family members with the new form, and so discover her real name. From there, it would only be a hop, skip, and a jump before they realized how it must have been able to slip through the cracks the first time.

He stood up straight and adjusted his tie, then strode purposefully toward his own home. If there were any cameras on him, he didn't want them to see him behaving in any way unusual. By the time he got to his own suite, he was sweating from anxiety. Now he'd need a shower and a change of clothes before moving on to his next scheduled meeting.

* * *

Jwa staggered, one foot after the other, his hands bound behind his back and a rope tied around his neck with the other end tied to the pommel of one of the horse saddles. The

Confederation pursuers had bound his head to stop the bleeding—while he was still unconscious from the bullet that had grazed his head, mercifully—but the bandages were haphazard. They covered his left eye, and the resulting lack of depth perception made it hard to walk across the uneven ground. Each time he fell, they stopped their horses and allowed him to get back on his feet.

He was grateful they hadn't simply killed him, nor had they even dragged him by that rope when he fell. They hadn't spoken to him directly, perhaps assuming he didn't understand English, but nothing they said in earshot had led him to believe they were going to kill him immediately. They were going to deliver him to their leaders and leave the decision to them.

At least this group of Americans understood the proper role of soldiers, even if they didn't show any sign of truly appreciating the sheer joy that came from knowing their place within the chain of command. Part of him would rather have been killed by that bullet that had knocked him unconscious, yet the weaker part of him was happy to be alive. He cursed his weakness. Surely the Great Leader would have wanted him to sacrifice himself rather than allow capture, but his body had betrayed his purpose by falling unconscious when he'd been struck.

The only saving grace was that, from what he overheard, his sacrifice allowed his other three men, his loyal troops, to escape their pursuers. Those men were his Korean brothers and his responsibility. At least he had succeeded in that duty.

Ahead, he saw the familiar-looking walls of Ephrata rising in the distance, the same walls he had climbed over twice before, today. This time, of course, he wouldn't be climbing back over. They would merely march him right through the gate, a victory prize and trophy of war. A spectacle.

Jwa spat on the ground at the thought, then focused on preparing himself mentally for the rough "questioning" that no doubt lay ahead.

* * *

Cassy looked up as her front door opened, and Michael walked inside. He came over to the couch opposite her, facing where she sat in the recliner, and made himself comfortable. She set down the paperwork she had been working on and said, "It's been a while since you had any time to come see me. I was starting to think you were avoiding me."

Between the storm clouds brewing to the north and the south, Cassy knew he'd been spending every day crisscrossing the Confederation to ensure the army was prepared, as well-supplied as possible, and ready at a moment's notice.

"So Ephrata is positive the latest raiders came from the Southern Cantonment," Michael said. "They seem to be catching on, up there."

"How'd they come to that conclusion?"

"The surprise raid this morning—a full battalion successfully got inside their walls before the battle started."

"Right. I heard about that."

"Ephrata reports that they think only three escaped, all Korean. They also captured one Korean who I am told wears the rank insignia of a sergeant. The rest were slaughtered to the last man."

Cassy paused to consider the ramifications. She knew the town of Ephrata was even more adamant now about their decision not to contribute troops to the Confederation, feeling the need to protect themselves first. Not that she could blame them. The problem was, she needed Ephrata's numbers placed under Michael's command where they could do some good. Whether the Confederation defenders could hold off the full weight of an assault from the Maryland invaders remained to be seen. It would be dicey without those additional troops. She thought back to her plan with Ethan and tried to figure out how to use that to resolve this new problem. First, she had to get Michael to see the danger of *not* doing something like she had planned.

She let out a long, frustrated breath. "So much for whatever little headway we had made in getting them to contribute troops. What do you think are the odds that we can hold off an attack if Maryland throws everything they have at us? Can the Confederation hold?"

Michael broke eye contact, looking down, and his silence spoke volumes.

Slowly, as though thinking to herself, she said, "What if their reluctance to send troops stems not from shortsightedness, not from cowardice, but from some other more pragmatic reason? We've never known them to be so shortsighted in the past. It's gotta be something internal, some sort of political thing. It's the only reason I can think of that would make them tuck their nuts away and hide."

Michael clenched his jaw and gave her a slight nod, remaining silent.

"So then, we have to get them involved," Cassy said. "In the long run, we need that to have the best chance of winning. But if the problem really is their internal politics, which we know little about, what can we do to shake them up?"

Michael reached up and rubbed his chin with his thumb and index finger. He looked a little bit like a supervillain contemplating his next plan to conquer the world. He said, "You're right. The problem must be his opposition making it difficult for him to divert troops away in the face of being raided regularly."

Cassy frowned. "I think what we need to do is help our friends in Ephrata get some sort of decisive victory. Something really big and noteworthy, or at least something we can spin that way."

"That's what you did before the war, right? Public relations?"

She felt the corners of her mouth turn up in a faint smile. She hadn't thought about that life in a long time, almost like it had happened to someone else entirely. "Yes, in Marketing. I intend to make much ado about nothing, given the opportunity. A real PR victory, even if it's really only a small victory strategically. It just has to look great for us to spin it."

Michael stood and began to pace her tiny living room.

It made her a little anxious to see him pace like that, but she didn't interrupt his thoughts. She and Ethan had come up with a plan already, but she worried Michael might not like it. She had to present it the right way, or get him to think it was his idea.

He said, "The option that comes to mind would be for us to divert some of the forces we're gathering. Instead of preparing to receive a full assault from the 'vaders, a smaller force can hold it together down south for a limited time."

She nodded, grasping the basic idea. "And what do we do with the troops we pull out? If only we could get Ephrata to see the value of working together."

He stopped pacing then, his eyes looking distant as he thought through the problem. "We know that Ephrata is getting raided from both the north and south, right?"

"Right."

"What if you manage to convince our friend there to shove some of his outlying units east and west, making it appear that they're weak militarily in the area facing the Northern Cantonment? If we could lure either side into an attempt at another heavy raid on the town itself, then the diverted Ephrata troops could move back into place, encircling the attackers. That's where the other Confederation units would come into play."

Cassy suppressed a smile. "It wouldn't take the invaders long to figure out they had an apparent window of opportunity." She felt her excitement growing and stood from her chair without realizing it. She pounded her right fist into her left hand and said, "How amazing would that be? Trap them, then hammer them with Confed troops. Not only would we demolish what could be a fairly sizable enemy unit, it would happen right at Ephrata's very walls. The residents couldn't help but notice that battle."

"And with a victory like that, due to the Confederation's help no less. It might give our Grand Mayor friend just the ammo he needs to push through a change of policy. Then we'd have access to all of Ephrata's resources, and yet with those walls, they could leave a much smaller force to protect just the town itself—"

"—and the rest of them could march south with us to deal with the bigger problem," Cassy interrupted.

Michael ran his palm over his close-cropped hair, then sat back down. "I do believe we have a plan."

* * *

1100 HOURS - ZERO DAY +637

Jwa had spent the last day confined in a bedroom. The bars on the inside of the windows, the heavy steel fire door, and the cinder block walls had ensured he couldn't leave. The Americans had put a bag over his head as they marched him through the town anyway, so even if he escaped, his only option would have been to simply walk in one direction until he eventually found himself at the city walls. He had no idea which part of town he was in and would be just as likely to walk into a nest of soldiers as he was to avoid detection long enough to reach a town wall.

He had spent some time yesterday trying to figure out which way to go if he got the chance to escape, but he was locked in solid. It had proven to be just a frustrating exercise in futility. Perhaps he might eventually be able to chip away at the cinder blocks enough to remove the bars over the windows, and thereby escape, but that would take much more time than he figured he had left on this Earth. The room he was in was fairly large, too, and even had a working bathroom in it. He wasn't quite sure how they managed that without power. And the bed was comfortable, as was the couch that lined much of one wall.

For whatever reason, they had not yet begun to torture him. He knew that sort of questioning would commence at any moment, of course, since that was standard military procedure for prisoners where he was from, but in the meantime, they had been treating him well enough.

They had even fed him, which was rather surprising. Both times, four soldiers had been present, three with rifles ready. He had no chance to escape through them, and so he had complied with their instructions.

The problem was that, in following their instructions, he had accidentally given away the fact that he understood English. He still refused to talk, still pretended not to understand, but they had merely smirked and spoke to him in regular, conversational English. They were even polite.

It actually bothered him that they had not yet begun to torture him. It meant they had something else in mind, probably something more gruesome. He wasn't afraid of dying, nor was he afraid of their questioning techniques, but the idea kept running through his mind that the Americans planned to publicly execute him. For whatever reason, the idea of being the subject of a gruesome spectacle for public amusement rattled him to his core. That idea did cause some fear. He had never been a POW, so he had never experienced those feelings before.

As he continued to obsess on that hypothetical fear, he paced back and forth across the length of the room, moving from wall to wall and then back again. They probably were watching him, but he couldn't help pacing, regardless.

As he thought more and more of a hypothetical scene in which he was publicly beheaded, just as the ISNA fighters did when punishing one of their own for a capital crime, his heart rate sped up. His vision narrowed as adrenaline flowed through him.

At last, he couldn't take it anymore. With his jaw clenched and breathing deeply to catch his breath, he stormed up to the steel door and began banging on it with his fists.

He kept banging for several minutes, and his fists began to hurt. He switched to pounding on the door with his palms, and it made no less noise than his fists had. If this kept up for much longer, he thought, perhaps he might lose his mind. As iron-willed as he was on the battlefield, as fearless as he might be in the face of the enemy, this confinement was something altogether different. His training had not prepared him for anything like this.

After several minutes, he heard an answering bang from the other side of the door, three hard knocks, and he stopped his tantrum. A man's voice on the other side said, "Settle down in there, prisoner. If you keep that up, I'm going to 'accidentally' drop your lunch before it gets to you, got it? Understanding the Engrish?"

Jwa heard the undisguised irritation in the man's voice, but he was pretty irritated, too, at having been spoken to in that way. He had a split-second realization that being talked down to was infinitely preferable to torture. Really, it was the unknown, the question of when the torture would begin, that had made him so aggravated and riled up. He suddenly knew that he wasn't truly angry, but afraid. The anger was a secondary emotion, and if he was a true Korean soldier at all, then he must have more discipline over himself. More control. Even if he had no control over his situation, he could still comport himself well as long as he yet lived.

From the other side of the door, he heard the soldier chuckle, and then the clacking of boots on the floor as the other man walked away, leaving Jwa alone with his thoughts once again.

- **18** -

1000 HOURS - ZERO DAY +638

ETHAN SAT AT his desk down in the bunker, absorbed in his video games. He had brought several flash drives, loaded with some ISO files, digital copies of his favorite games. His truly favorite ones, of course, no longer worked since the host servers were down and there was no one left to play with, anyway. The era of MMO games was long since over. He pressed the button to unleash missiles at the pirate spaceship attacking him on an interstellar trade route, and he was rewarded with a satisfying fireball and the fantastic sounds of explosions in space. Totally unrealistic, but a lot of fun.

A soft ping to his left grabbed his attention. He turned to look at the three monitors he had set up, each of which displayed images from four separate cameras scattered around Clanholme. His heart skipped a beat when he realized the motion alarm had come from the camera that covered the hidden entrance to the bunker, disguised as a shrubbery in the vast field between Clanholme and the southern food forest. Very few people knew about that entrance, and none of them had any reason to be using it right now. The image was too grainy and distant, he couldn't get a good look at the figure, but he got the impression it was a male. With the poor camera resolution, he couldn't even be certain of that, but at least he then knew that some person was there.

He carefully made sure his game was properly saved, then shut down the program and grabbed a handheld radio. "Charlie Two to Oscar One, come in."

After a brief pause, the voice responded, slightly static. "Oscar One here. Go ahead."

As Ethan looked at the monitor, he saw the figure walk in a circle around the concealing shrub that was the only defense set up at that entrance. The figure occasionally reached out to touch the shrub, but Ethan couldn't be sure what the person was doing. He clicked the button and said, "Possible intruder sighted in sector Sam Three. You are Code Two on intercept."

The voice on the other end said, "Charlie Two, acknowledged. Code Two intercept at sector Sam Three, affirmative. Oscar One out."

Ethan opened his desk drawer and pulled out his pistol, a simple 9mm semi-auto, and double-checked his magazine. Seeing it was full, he racked the slide to load a round from the magazine into the chamber.

Then he glanced back at the monitor and saw that the figure was reaching deep into the shrub, its arm buried up to its shoulder. Then one of the two lightbulbs over his desk flicked on, indicating that the secondary entrance had been released. On the monitor, he saw the figure slide the shrub to one side. It was a cleverly disguised planter, really, built on rails. If the clasp was undone, the whole affair simply slid to one side, allowing access to the ladder that led down to the escape tunnel.

Ethan cursed under his breath. Where the hell were the

on-duty guards? On the monitor, he saw the figure enter the vertical tube, climbing down the ladder. He closed the hatch, sliding the shrubbery back over. Ethan cursed again. None of the guards knew that the backup escape tunnel even existed... only the Council knew.

He pressed the button on his handheld radio and said, "Charlie Two to Oscar One. Belay my last order. Redirect responding guards to location Bravo One, Code Three. Out."

Without waiting for a response, he turned his radio off. The figure would be emerging from the tunnel in moments, and he didn't want the squawk of a radio response to alert them.

With his pistol at low-ready, Ethan exited the small office area. The figure would be coming down the tunnel that opened up into the barracks bay, so he maneuvered through the living room module and took up a position behind the small kitchen counter that extended from the bunker wall. This gave him a little bit of cover and good concealment. He crouched down low and took aim at the doorway that led from the living room into the barracks. Whoever had broken into the bunker would have to pass through that doorway to get to him.

He realized he hadn't unlocked the hatch to the main tunnel, the tunnel his backup would be coming through. They could eventually get the access code from someone who knew it, but that would take time. That was the one thing he didn't have. Or he could go and unlock it, but to do so, he would have to turn his back to that doorway and leave the relative protection of the kitchen counter. His scalp tingled as his heart raced faster. This had been a huge screw-up. He only hoped he lived long enough to learn his lesson.

As the seconds ticked by, each seeming practically eternal, he felt his fear rising. He thought back to the battles he had been involved in, latching onto those to give him courage. Before the war, he had been just a gaming geek and a conspiracy theorist, not to mention a rich dotcom sellout. His very first firefight had been alongside the Clan, well before they ever got on the road from his old bunker.

His second had been during their westward journey from his bunker to Clanholme when he and Jed had assaulted an invader machine gun nest. They had cleared that out with grenades, but Jed died during that assault. Ethan rolled those memories around in his mind, drawing strength from them. He could handle this. This wasn't his first rodeo.

He heard a noise from within the barracks bay, a metal-on-metal clang that echoed throughout the bunker. Nervously, he adjusted his grip on his pistol and tried to hold it steady, aiming at the doorway.

He caught a glimpse of motion and fired off a quick double-tap, but he was certain that he had missed. His target had just been moving too fast and had caught him by surprise, even though he had been waiting for precisely that.

A man dressed all in black darted diagonally through the doorway, entering the living room bay and firing a burst from a fully automatic pistol, or perhaps it was an Uzi.

Sheer reflex caused Ethan to duck down behind the counter. He counted to two, then leaned forward to bring his pistol out from behind the counter and fired another two rounds.

Seven left.

He immediately ducked back, just as another burst of incoming fire blew away the wooden edge of the cabinet he hid behind, which held up the countertop. Cabinets were clearly not intended to stop bullets.

Ethan heard another metallic sound, like bouncing—*ting, ting, ting*—and saw a small cylinder skitter across the floor, passing him by. He looked at it, wondering what the hell it was, until horror flooded him as he realized it was a grenade. Up close, the sleek black metal object looked every bit as menacing as he had imagined in his dreams. Dreams where he had been tormented with reliving the memory of the people in the machine gun nest... people whom he himself had devastated with a grenade. Along with Jed.

Ethan's reflexes took over, and he shifted on the balls of his feet to lunge away from the grenade, his mind screaming that he was about to die. He never made it to the other side of the counter, not that it would have stopped a grenade from five feet away; it went off, and he found himself struck with a force like a fly on a windshield. The explosion's light and noise overwhelmed his senses completely.

For a second, he thought he was dead. For another second, he thought he must be lying on the floor bleeding out. Then he realized that he didn't feel the agonizing pain one must feel if caught in a grenade blast. He couldn't open his eyes, and in his ears, it sounded like the deafening roar of a train. He could neither see nor hear, but he was alive. Still blind, he rolled over onto his stomach and pushed himself up with his hands, then got his feet underneath him. He fell over again, his balance completely destroyed. In the back of his mind, he remembered reading that severe trauma to the ears would ruin a person's sense of balance.

He paused for a moment on his hands and knees. He realized that his pistol was no longer in his hand and had no idea where it had gone. Slowly, wobbling, he rose to his feet with his hands stretched out to aid his balance. Every time he felt the beat of his heart, he expected to feel his attacker's bullets ripping into him.

Instead, he felt a cloth abruptly pressed over his mouth and nose. His attacker had slid one arm around his neck and was holding something over his face with the other. Ethan struggled with the strength given by life-and-death adrenaline surging through his body, but after being hit by the flash-bang, he was no match for the man who held him from behind.

Lightheadedness struck him, and the bright light he saw even through his tightly closed eyes grew black around the edges, the darkness crawling toward the center, obliterating the bright after-light that had been all he could see. The lightheadedness increased as the blackness met in the middle so that all he saw was darkness, and he felt like his brain was spinning in his skull. Then, the blackness overcame him.

* * *

The first thing Ethan became aware of was the feel of dirt and rocks beneath him, pressing into his muscles and his spine. The ringing in his ears was now faint, and over it, he could hear what sounded like voices. They might as well have been very far away, or underwater. Just a garbled murmur. He willed himself to open his eyes, and to his surprise, he saw blue sky. Nothing but the vast, blue sky. He still had spots in his vision from the flash-bang, but he could see again. He wondered how long it had been since the grenade went off, and then marveled at why he would be thinking of such a thing when his life was so obviously in danger. And why was he still alive, anyway? He moved his head to look around, the muscles sore and aching at the slightest movement.

All around him were Clan guardsmen, and his eyes went wide. He felt a flood of both relief and confusion.

One of the guardsmen knelt next to him, and Ethan locked eyes with him. His mouth was moving, but all that came out was the same murmuring noise. Ethan narrowed his eyes as he concentrated on trying to hear and understand what the man was saying. Slowly, the ringing faded and the garbled voice became more clear.

"...okay, sir? Can you hear me?"

As Ethan's awareness grew, he realized the man had one hand resting lightly on his shoulder. He said, "What happened and where am I?" He couldn't really hear himself speak, so he tried again and repeated himself, but stopped when the guardsmen flinched and looked away. He realized he must be yelling. He tried a third time, this time trying to whisper. He couldn't be sure he had succeeded, or that any noise had come out at all. It could've gone either way.

The man grinned and patted Ethan's shoulder. Very faintly, Ethan heard him say, "Thank God you're all right. You don't need to scream, though, I'm right here. Are you injured?"

Ethan wasn't sure whether he was or not. His senses were dulled, still suffering the effects of the grenade and what he could only assume had been chloroform on the cloth. That was the only thing that made sense of all of this. And if it was chloroform, then he had been unconscious for at least fifteen minutes. Probably longer.

He sat up, drawing his knees up toward his chest and wrapping his arms around them for support as he looked around. He saw that they were merely ten feet from the hidden bunker entrance, which now lay open and exposed. Great, so all these guardsmen now knew where the hidden access was. He would have to make sure to swear them to secrecy.

Ignoring the guardsman's question, and still dazed, Ethan checked over himself for wounds, looking at each arm, his chest, his legs. He saw no blood, and all his parts were right where they were supposed to be. How strange.

Then he noticed another person lying down a dozen feet or so to his right, dressed head-to-toe in black BDUs with a black shemagh wrapped around his face and neck. He was also lying in a pool of blood, a large bullet hole in his BDU top. It dawned on Ethan that this must be his attacker.

As his senses continued to clear, Ethan looked back at the guardsman who knelt next to him and said, "What happened, here?"

The guardsmen said, "We got the order to rush to this sector, and we saw that shrub move. Then this guy popped his head out and somehow managed to drag you up that ladder in there in a fireman's carry. It wasn't an easy shot with you in the line of target, but we took our chances."

Ethan felt shaky, the after-effects of adrenaline rush, trauma, and chloroform. "I appreciate you not shooting me," Ethan said, trying to smile. "Radio in and put the compound on high alert, then pass along my orders to the OOD to send everyone out searching to find where this guy was taking me. He must have a vehicle or a horse nearby, or there may be others. I want everything cleared, out to one mile from the compound."

The guardsman saluted, then rose to his feet and walked a short distance away as he pulled out his radio. Ethan turned to the nearest guardsman and glanced him up and down. Yes, the man was large enough. "Help me stagger my ass back to HQ, will you? I need to talk to Frank."

* * *

0745 HOURS - ZERO DAY +640

Jaz awoke with a start, but stayed motionless. Her stomach ached from where she had passed out with her toga yanked up around her waist. She kept her eyes closed until her mind cleared a bit. She felt something in the bed with her, and a flood of nightmare images from only a few hours earlier nearly overwhelmed her; she bit her bottom lip to keep silent as a wave of nausea passed.

As she waited for the sleep fog to clear, she realized that whatever was in bed with her wasn't moving. She heard a faint snoring, and her heart dropped. Jack.

Cracking one eye open, she saw he was passed out beside her on the bed, lying on his stomach.

Jaz glanced around—Chump was gone. She knew he must have left to go scrounging, though she wasn't sure when he would be back. He could return at any moment.

The thought made her heart race.

Jaz took a deep breath in an attempt to calm down. She had to think clearly.

Then a thought hit her—the keys. Jack always kept her padlocks keys in his pocket, or at least that's what she remembered. She struggled to remember which pocket he kept them in, if at all. Unsure either way, she decided to start with the pocket closest to her. There was only one way to find out.

Jaz froze, steeling herself for what she had to do.

She took another long breath and let it out slowly. It was time to swallow her fear and remember who she was—a survivor.

Briefly, she thought about using her chain around his neck to strangle him, but in her current condition and bound, she doubted she could outfight him when he awoke. Drunk or not, he would certainly wake up when she began to squeeze his neck, and then he would use his strength to his advantage. She had no doubt that would be the end of Choony, and probably herself as well.

No, going for the keys was the best idea.

She counted to three, then used her right hand to press her other wrist deeper into the mattress, angling to get her left hand into his pocket. Inch by inch, she slid her hand in.

She had her fingers half into his pocket, her tender skin

scraping against the rough denim. Just a little more...

He grunted.

Jaz froze, and her breath grew shallow. Her eyes darted toward his, half-expecting them to be wide open in one of his horrid stares. But they were still closed, for now.

His body started to roll, and when she pulled her hand reflexively, she realized it was stuck. She knew if she didn't act fast, she'd be pinned under the sonuvabitch.

Jaz clenched her jaw and felt the fabric burn against the top of her hand as she yanked her hand out. In the next moment, he rolled from his stomach onto his left side.

She exhaled slowly, realizing that she'd been holding her breath. Now it was even more clear to her than ever—one wrong move, and it would be over.

He muttered something indecipherable.

Her heart pounded, and her mind reeled. She had almost been caught, and now the keys were under his hip. There was no way she could get them out from under—

He wiggled a bit, raising his right knee up, and she heard a jingling from his exposed right pocket. The keys hadn't been in his left pocket after all.

She made herself take deep, even breaths as she tried to calm her speeding heart, then braced herself to try again.

For long minutes, she stared at him, watching his face for any twitching that could give away the fact that he was awake, that he was testing her. Then she observed his chest rising and falling. When his breath was slow and rhythmic, she was convinced he was really asleep and readied her nerves to try again.

She rose up slightly, positioning herself in a precarious position as she loomed over his body. Any wrong move and she would fall on top of him.

That time, getting her hand in was even harder. The pocket opening was on top instead of flush with the mattress, and the keys' weight pulled on it and caused it to bulge outward slightly, though there was barely enough space for her hands to squeeze in as she tried to maintain her balance.

She slid her fingers in a fraction of an inch further and felt the tip of one of the keys—cold hard freedom was now within reach. She tried to grasp the key between her pointer and middle fingers in an effort to pull the entire key ring out, but couldn't get a good grip. So close, yet so far...

Jack murmured and let out a long, putrid exhalation. Jaz gasped at the stench, even more motivated to escape.

Jaz held her breath and waited, expecting him to open his eyes any moment. Time seemed to stand still as the milliseconds crawled by. She let out her breath slowly, praying that he would doze just a little longer.

Focusing on keeping her body steady, she slid her fingers further into his pocket.

Finally, she was able to hook her index finger into the key ring. She paused, took a deep breath, and slowly withdrew the keys, just far enough to where she could get her entire hand around them.

She had just about pulled them out completely when Jack shifted, and the keys jingled softly.

Her eyes went wide.

This was it—she would surely be caught.

She grasped them quickly to mute them.

She couldn't mess this up—freedom was so close, she could almost taste it. Her muscles shook from the effort of holding herself up one-armed and off-balance, but she waited there until he was back to his rhythmic breathing before she unfroze and resumed. Slowly, she managed to pull the keys the rest of the way out without making another sound.

Her hands trembled as she slid the smallest key into the lock at her wrists. The lock opened with a slight *plink* noise.

Finally able to separate her hands, she rushed to unlock the padlock at each wrist, removing the cuffs entirely. The final lock was the one around her neck, larger than the others. Jack had almost a dozen keys on his ring, but she found the right key on the third try, trying to keep the keys silent as she worked on freeing herself.

Finally, she was free of those damn chains.

Jaz's spirit surged with a fierce joy, but she reminded herself that she wasn't free yet. She had to get off the bed without waking Jack. She slid toward the end of the bed as slowly as she could, trying desperately not to shake the mattress or touch her passed out bedmate. It felt like it took forever, like she was moving at a snail's pace, but she was soon on her feet.

She glanced at Jack to make sure he was still asleep, then padded softly to Choony. He was unconscious, and he had a thin layer of sweat. She felt his forehead. He didn't react, but his skin felt like fire under her hand. They had bound his feet together beneath the chair, so she went around to the back.

Looking down, she saw that his wrists weren't bound. Instead, his elbows were tied together behind his back, around the chair back. He was also bound around his arms, keeping him securely fastened to the chair, as were his ankles. Another rope led from his bound ankles to the rope between his elbows, which was why his feet were forced up under the chair.

There was no way he could run. He was too messed up— practically helpless. Maybe she should leave him and go get help? No, if Jack woke up or if Chump returned, which were both good possibilities, Choony would surely be killed. But if she brought him with her, he would slow her escape. It would make them easier to catch.

Those were her only two choices: bring him or leave him.

Well, she sure as hell wasn't going to leave him. He had

sacrificed so much for her. He was the only man she had ever truly loved, and she wasn't going to leave him to die. Screw it, she would untie him and take her chances.

To one side of his chair was a small metal table like the ones she saw on old TV hospital shows. On it were a few knives, clamps, pruning shears, and a pipe cutter. She walked around the chair to the tray and picked up a knife. It felt kind of heavy in her hand for being as small as it was, larger than a pocket knife but smaller than a combat knife. She checked the edge with her thumb and decided it was sharp enough.

Jaz turned back to Choony, deciding to cut off the rope coils around his chest first. She tried to ignore the blood that was already on the knife. Choony's blood.

As she leaned over him and began to cut the ropes, her mind raced trying to think of ways to get him out of there in his condition. She wasn't sure she could carry him, not in her current condition—

A strong hand grabbed the back of her toga and yanked her aside. The force flung her backward and she lost her balance, landing hard on the cement floor. The impact knocked the blade from her hand, and it skittered across the floor. The knife finally came to a stop when it ran into a pair of boots.

Shit.

Jaz looked up and saw Jack staring down at her. He looked strangely relaxed. Maybe even a bit amused as he bent down and picked up the knife.

"Going somewhere, sweetheart?"

She scrambled to her feet and took a step back, but felt the bed behind her. She had nowhere to go. She shouted, "Go to hell!"

"I like a girl with fire." Jack grinned and took a step toward her, holding the knife in front of him. "Though, you disappoint me, love. I wanted to see if you would go through with it—the whole trying to escape thing—and you did. Can't trust a bitch, I guess. But I have to say, it's good to see you have some spine left in you, which means more fun for me."

He took another step toward her, holding the knife out in front of him. He thrust the tip at her, and she saw light glint off its razor-edged blade. She took a step backward and felt the bed behind her. He crept closer toward her.

Her adrenaline spiked when he stopped a little less than an arm's length in front of her. He brought the tip of the blade up to her breasts.

Jack chuckled. "You think you had it bad before, bitch? Wait until I—"

There was a loud, metallic bang outside to her left. It sounded like somebody had punched the corrugated metal siding. Startled, Jack turned his head to look.

Jaz didn't.

She brought her fist back and, with her entire weight behind it, gave a forceful blow to the side of his jaw.

Jack staggered backward, dropping the knife. It skidded across the floor, and Jaz lunged after it. She took only two steps toward the knife before she felt a surge of pain travel along the back of her scalp. Jack had grabbed a fistful of her hair, and the floor disappeared under her feet. The next thing she knew, she was being hurled into the air and felt a moment of weightlessness. Her side slammed down on the cement floor, her hip hot with a fiery pain that rushed to her knees.

Before regaining her senses, Jack was already upon her, grabbing her throat and lifting her to her feet. She struggled as the blood swelled in her face, and she began to gasp for air. He rammed her into the wall, still clutching her neck, now with both hands.

"You're going to pay for that," Jack said, teeth clenched.

His face was puffy and red with rage. She could still smell the rancid alcohol on his breath as he spoke.

She brought her hands up to pry his fingers off her neck, but when that didn't work, she instead beat his arms with her fists.

Nothing seemed to break his iron grip.

She could feel the oxygen draining from her lungs.

This couldn't be the last moments of her life. Her last sight couldn't be this asshole. No way.

She felt his legs straddling her right knee as he held her up against the wall. She didn't have much room to make a powerful blow, but it was worth a try.

She brought her knee up as forcefully as she could, making contact with his groin.

Jack huffed, releasing Jaz almost immediately. His face was scrunched up in agony as he leaned forward slightly.

Now was her chance.

"Freeze, fucker!" an unknown voice shouted from over by the door.

Again, Jack turned his head, but only for a split second.

It was enough. When he turned his head away, Jaz put both hands together as though swinging a bat, and with a strength born of desperation, she swung her two-handed fist at him. She felt it connect with the side of his face, knocking him away from her.

Jack landed face down. In a heartbeat, he scrambled forward and up to his feet, and kept running. He was leaning far forward, and almost fell once, but then regained his footing and just kept going. He jumped up onto a low table, then dove through the open window on the shop's back wall.

A second later, he was gone.

Jaz looked to see who the newcomer might be, and to her surprise found half a dozen men and women coming in through the office door into the shop. Their clothes were ragged, but they were all armed and had the hard, direct gaze of people who had lived through a lot.

The man in front, who carried himself like a leader, said, "You okay, miss?"

"Yeah, thank you."

"I see you managed to keep my friend over there from getting himself killed." He tossed his head toward where Choony still sat, tied up.

"Friend?"

The man nodded, but said nothing as he stepped toward Choony's limp body.

- **19** -

CASSY CLICKED THE transmit button to perform a radio check. Michael's voice came through loud and clear. Then Ethan, back at Clanholme, confirmed both their radios were coming through as well. He was coordinating communications during the battle.

To her right sat Amber—her randomly chosen passenger. She remained silent, probably deep in thought.

In the distance, the Clan's scouts were reporting on the enemy's movements. Just as the earlier reports had said, it was a large unit, perhaps two battalions. Most of them were Americans who had been pressed into service, and of the rest, all but a few were ISNA fighters.

Cassy sat inside what she thought of as the cockpit of a Clan battle car, one of a dozen ready for the coming battle. Their fires were stoked, but the engines were off until it was time. It conserved wood, yet the cars had to be kept ready to go at a moment's notice, which meant leaving the gasifier lit so that they could move out immediately when needed.

Michael, however, was sitting this battle out and leading from a proper command post. Radios and runners would handle unit movements.

Her radio squawked again, and she recognized a scout's voice. "Confirmed, two battalions with small arms and two small mortar trains. They appear to be led by Korean officers, who are the only ones in uniform. All the rest are on foot. Over."

Michael responded, "Roger that. We can presume the supply train with their horses is hidden nearby. September One, circle around and backtrack along the enemy's likely path of advance. If we can find that supply train, we can hit it hard."

Then it was back to the usual radio chatter as Michael conducted status checks of each unit commander. The Clan had about six hundred soldiers present, not including the battle cars. The goal wasn't to defeat the invaders in a head-on fight, but to let them "fully engage the town defenders," as Michael had put it, then sweep in and smack them in the rear.

In the distance, over the eerie silence surrounding her in the battle car detachment, Cassy heard the *pop-pop* of small arms fire. It seemed the latest battle for Ephrata was beginning.

She felt the first tingling of excitement begin in her stomach. She had been in enough battles that, although it was always scary, the way she felt during and after a battle was the sort of high that some people would spend a lifetime chasing.

After her first life-or-death combat, she had spent weeks wondering whether that feeling made her a bad person. People naturally avoided violence and combat, right? One quick talk with Michael had squared her away in that regard, and she learned it was just human nature. Sure, peaceful resolution was the first choice, but if it took a fight to survive, there was nothing wrong with the euphoria she felt after combat.

She would be giddy all the next day, she knew. Sunlight would look brighter, birds would chirp prettier, food would taste the best it ever had—until the next battle. If she survived, that is. She had also been in enough combat to have decided that, when it was her time to go, it was her time. There was nothing she could do to change it, so she didn't worry about it.

Cassy drummed her fingers on the steering wheel, impatiently waiting for the battle to begin.

* * *

While Barry waited for the command to advance, he grew increasingly listless. His mind wandered everywhere. He wondered how his wife and two-year-old son were doing back at the Taj Mahal—the name of the Clanhold he'd commanded ever since the Clan first took mercy on a ragtag band of Indian refugees from Adamsville.

Frank, who led the Clan as a whole, hadn't asked for the Taj Mahal to send troops. These days, the Clan had more than enough soldiers for a midsize battle like this one. But Barry had always made certain to volunteer some troops for every engagement, and his people had developed sort of a ceremony to wish a safe return to the departing warriors, a ceremony that focused on thanks to the Clan for allowing a hungry band of strangers to settle in their territory near the beginning of the Dying Times.

The Taj Mahal had become the favored settlement for arriving Indians throughout the Confederation, along with other dark-complexion immigrants like Persians, so long as they were willing to give lip service to the Hindu religion. That was mostly for political reasons and hardly enforced, though, at least not under his leadership.

He was proud that the Taj Mahal was arguably the most

loyal, most enthusiastic Clanhold.

He ignored the increasing sounds of gunfire echoing from far away. The Clan wouldn't encircle the invaders until after they had begun their full offensive against the Ephrata defenders.

During battles, Barry turned ice-cold, feeling neither fear nor anger, becoming only a cold and calculating machine. After the battle, however, he knew he would explode with energy, feeling a weird happiness. It would be a damn good night for his wife, too, he grinned.

He decided to burn up more of his time spent waiting by rechecking his troops' weapons and gear, shouting encouragement, and doing everything else he was responsible for as a leader, even though he only brought fifty troops. Most of the other Clanholds only sent a single platoon, and only Clanholme itself had brought more.

By all the gods, he mused, waiting for the fight to begin was the worst part of any battle.

* * *

Captain Mueller had been watching the battle progress for the last two hours. He glanced around at the forty men and women under him and felt the weight of his responsibilities. In a way, he missed the staff sergeant rank he'd held when he first met the Clan. Only he and a few other Marines had survived their hellish trek away from their training base after hordes of hungry civilians had overrun it. He hadn't gotten along with the Clan leader at the time, Cassy, or their security manager, who was now the general for all Confederation forces. But nowadays, he and Michael got along famously. Which was a good thing, too, because he'd be leaving soon with Michael on his secret mission, whatever it was.

He shook his head to clear his mind. This battle was what mattered right now, and his role in it would begin shortly. He turned to Sturm, one of the Marines he'd left the base with and now his right-hand man—or woman in this case. She was a capable soldier, maybe even better than he himself, but she'd probably never rise above the rank of lieutenant. She was just better as his XO than as a leader, if he was honest with himself. That was too bad because he would've liked to have her combat skills out there at the front of the fighting rather than in the rear with him. Of course, in the Clan as in the Marines, everyone fought unless they were unfortunate enough to be at the field HQ with Michael. Those poor, sorry bastards never got to kill invaders themselves.

"Lieutenant, when did we receive the last report from Ethan?" Mueller asked.

"Ten mikes. He told us to be ready to move out within the next half hour, no solid TOD on that."

Mueller nodded. In a fight like this, it was impossible to plan to the minute when they would be ordered to move out. Frankly, he was tired of waiting and itched to get into the fight. Not because he enjoyed fighting, of course, but because it was preferable to this damnable waiting. Unless someone had experienced that a couple times, they'd never understand how he was feeling at that moment.

He turned to Sturm. "What's the latest from the company scouts?"

Sturm picked up a sheet of paper with handwritten notes on it, and her eyes flicked back and forth as she skimmed it. "OpFor hit Ephrata beginning at the southeast corner and stretching westward. Estimated enemy force, eight hundred. Defending forces along the wall were not immediately overrun as the scouts had predicted, and they transitioned units from all over town to reinforce the point of engagement. For the last two hours, the enemy has been able to press toward the wall taking only light casualties, but Michael says they'll finally get onto the wall within the next fifteen mikes."

"Good."

Sturm continued, "Once the enemy is up on those walls, fighting the defenders at short range or hand to hand, they won't be able to disengage without taking massive losses. If they try, our battle cars will run them down, and that's even assuming they can breach our infantry lines."

Mueller rubbed his face with both hands. She was right, of course. "The enemy will most likely be forced to increase op tempo in a desperate bid to secure the wall for themselves so that they can hold us off while they raid Ephrata's interior supply dumps. They might be able to hold us off indefinitely, that way."

Sturm shook her head. "Yes sir, but we're not going to let that happen. If we hit them all along their line as hard as we can, while they're still pinned in place and before they can maneuver to respond with a rearguard, we're going to decimate them."

The radio squawked, and both Mueller and Sturm turned to look at it, waiting to see if it was for them. "September One, Charlie two."

Scouts to Ethan. So, not for them. He kept an ear out for the conversation anyway. It was good to keep updated on what was going on around him, but it also helped to pass the time.

"Go for Charlie Two."

"OpFor supply train has been located," the voice said, followed by a string of coordinates that might be a couple miles southeast of Ephrata, he figured without looking. Logical. "Sir, I estimate that its size is not consistent with a simple supply train. We think we found an FBO to support the invasion later. Defenses are minimal, and it appears to be still under construction. They're using earthbags. Request permission to engage."

"September One, affirmative. Engage at will. Take what you can and deny the rest to the enemy. Hit hard and fast, but if you can't overwhelm defenses, exfiltrate immediately, and we will begin barrage. I don't need you locked up out there; we need you mobile."

"Aye aye. September One out."

Mueller grinned. The Clan had seized some functional artillery a year ago, and Ethan had jury-rigged the electronics to make it effective again. Ammo was priceless, but better to deny the enemy a mountain of supplies than to see it slip away to be used again later. If the depot was close enough and it came down to artillery, he might even be able to see the explosions from where he was. At least, he hoped he would, because Arty made for lovely fireworks.

* * *

Barry sat with a telescope and watched the battle, his frustration at having to stand by growing each minute.

The invaders were split into two groups. One group of six hundred had been grinding away at the town's south wall for quite a while. The other two hundred or so were mounted and had arrived from the southeast not long ago. They'd been probing other parts of the wall ever since they arrived, keeping highly mobile and forcing the defenders to try to protect everything at once. It kept Ephrata from applying overwhelming force against the largest OpFor to their south.

He saw a group of invaders approach the wall with boxes, the rest of their unit pouring covering fire at the top to pin down the defenders. They did it just long enough for the squad to place the boxes along the base of the rubble wall.

Then the defenders mowed the squad down, but it was too late. The boxes were already in place.

He counted under his breath. When he got to seven, four massive fireballs went up, engulfing the wall in flames. When the blast faded, he saw people atop the wall on fire, running around, and about a third of the attackers charged the wall while the rest covered them with suppressive fire. In a minute, the enemy had a foothold atop the wall.

Someone nearby said, "Looks like it'll be our turn any minute. Who wants to pray with me?"

Barry left them to their prayers. It bolstered their resolve. Vishnu was the day's favored deity, he noted. Who better than the Protector against the forces of destruction? Since the Dying Times, Vishnu had gained a lot of popularity. He understood why, but he prayed quietly to Kartikeya, instead. He didn't need protection; he needed to kill his enemies before they killed him. Kartikeya fit him better.

When he heard them finish their prayer, he said, "Alright, brothers and sisters. Gear up, and check each other out. I don't want to hear anyone left their spare mags in the rear, got it? Get ready to show them what a real Hindu can do against these demons."

A cheer went up, and he smiled again. Soon, he'd live or he'd die, but at least the damn waiting would be over.

* * *

The radio crackled, jolting Cassy out of her daydreaming. "Charlie One," Ethan's voice echoed hollowly, "begin. You know the plan."

She confirmed, then shouted out, "Gentlemen, start your engines." Finally. Her pulse raced. Somewhere to her north, the Clan infantry was beginning to move out, too. The battlecars would clear their path and take out the two mortar teams, then rampage through the main enemy lines on their way to hunt down the enemy cavalry team.

Clan infantry would head east and then north, enveloping the invaders and pressing them hard toward the wall. Few would escape, and the Clan infantry wouldn't have to worry about enemy mortars barraging them from behind. Plus the enemy formations would be disrupted from the battlecars plowing through them.

All around, she heard the car engines roar to life, fed by nothing more than wood. She loved the battlecars. In less than a minute, just as they had trained, they moved out together in a row and swept in a gentle arc to the east, where the enemy mortar teams were emplaced. The Clan had a surprise of their own for them—each car had a single, fabricated mortar strapped to the hood, activated by a lever the passenger controlled. A simple welded crosshair showed where the impact would be, with concentric rings showing scatter at different speeds.

"Speed twenty," she shouted to Amber. She had to shout out her speed so that Amber would know which crosshair and ring to use. On the roof was another Clanner she didn't personally know, handling the light machine gun on the roof, standing up from the back seat.

"ETA, sixty seconds."

Ahead, she saw occasional flashes of light. The invaders' mortar crews were pumping rounds into the city itself now that the walls were partly overrun. "Speed thirty and holding."

To her left and right, she saw the other cars spread out in a line. Within a couple seconds of each other, all twelve cars entered the range band together and fired their single-shot mortars. Cassy's car jerked hard at the recoil, but the reinforced shocks handled it without breaking a strut, or whatever cars did.

A glance told her Amber was on her M4 after firing the mortar. It was mounted on a spindle welded to the car's frame, giving a 90-degree field of fire ahead and to the right. Half the cars had them mounted on the left, with the passenger in the rear.

Two hundred yards ahead, two blast clusters marked where mortars were landing, and huge secondary blasts a moment later engulfed the mortars and everything around them. Cassy worried she might drive into it, but the fireballs receded as the miniature mushroom clouds rose into the air. "Take that," she muttered.

On her lapel mic, a short range radio tying the cars together, she gave the order to veer left. The row of cars turned ninety degrees to become a column, and then the rear half angled to pull up on the left. It created two rows of six cars, with M4s covering both sides. They would plow through the enemy gathered around the town's south wall like a nail punching through plywood, emerging on the far side and continuing on to engage the cavalry. That was where her real battle would be.

* * *

Barry and his two platoons had been charging east for a couple of minutes when the radio squawked to turn left. The two parallel columns stopped, rotated left, then advanced in two rows. He was breathing heavily, but these days, everyone alive was in good shape from the daily routine of surviving. They'd be at full effectiveness when they reached the enemy's formations.

His units ran right through the formations, mowing them down, and continued toward the enemy's main body. He'd only seen one or two of his own men and women fall, back there, which wasn't bad.

He crested a low rise in the gently rolling terrain and saw the fierce battle up ahead. Cassy and her battlecars were just emerging on the far side after smashing through them, and the invaders were scattered like ants. Perfect.

A whistle blew, and he dove to the ground on his belly, using the butt of his rifle to slow his fall enough that it hurt, but wouldn't injure. Then he and the rest began pouring on a steady, rhythmic fire. He ran the mantra through his head: Breathe in. Exhale. Hold. Fire once. Finish breathing out. Repeat the cycle.

Rows of enemy soldiers fell to the surprise attack; they were definitely not in the best positioning to receive fire from a new direction. Barry put a fighter in his sights—American conscript, it looked like—and pulled. *Bang.* Down she went. The woman next to Barry had dropped the man next to his own target.

They kept firing.

From the enemy mob, there was a commotion just to the left. He glanced over and his eyes went wide. A huge mob of fighters in jeans and tee shirts charged straight for his part of the Clan line. He could see movement behind the mob, too, and reasoned that those would be the more disciplined ISNA fighters bringing up the rear, using the Americans as a meat shield.

He realized at least a quarter of the invader force was charging. Maybe a hundred in all. Enough to overrun him if he didn't get real serious, real fast. He shouted at the top of his lungs, "Burst fire, burst fire! Fire for effect." He flicked the selector switch on his AK from single fire to auto, and began tapping out short bursts, three or four rounds at a time.

To either side, he heard shrill whistles, calling out "Reinforce left," and "reinforce right," which told him reinforcements were on the way. He just had to hold the line until they arrived. He glanced to the enemy's right at another sudden change in movement, and saw another cluster of enemy troops just like the one coming at him, charging a little farther east down Clan lines. He hoped that didn't mean no reinforcements from that side.

When the dozens of enemy men and women charging him were two hundred yards away, however, huge orange blossoms of flame began sprouting among them, sending bodies and flaming people flying in all directions. The Clan mortars! They must have shifted fire from the enemy at the wall's base to the oncoming units. *Boom. Boom.* It was a beautiful sight.

It also wasn't enough. Many broke through, closing the distance to a point where mortar fire had to stop or risk hitting Clanners. Barry shouted, "Grenades!" The four fighters under him who happened to have scavenged a grenade or two stepped up and threw them into the path of the oncoming invader force, and he heard screams of pain as more people died.

A round went *ping!* off his Kevlar helmet, and he reflexively ducked. The enemy fire was becoming more intense. Still, only a couple dozen enemies, mostly ISNA, had made it that far. Barry fired at full auto into the oncoming Arab soldiers and then heard the *click, click* of an empty magazine. It took him half a second to realize he was out of ammo, and another half to realize he didn't have time to reload. "Fall back," he shouted over the din, and ran down the back side of the slight hill he'd fired from—straight through the second line of Taj Mahal fighters, freshly loaded. They tore into the enemy coming up over the hill while he dropped down behind them and started to reload. He finished just as the second line was emptying their magazines. Coincidentally, the ISNA fighters stopped shooting at that time as well, reloading.

Barry got his fresh magazine in first, and sprinted forward, firing and screaming. Others all around him followed his example, and in seconds, they'd overrun the last of the enemy sortie. He blew his whistle, four short and two long blasts, code for enemy neutralized. In the distance, Clan mortar fire began dropping again at the base of the wall.

The battle was almost over. He had survived once again. He thanked all the gods, even some who weren't his own, for bringing him through it alive again.

Briefly, he wondered where the enemy cavalry had gone. He hadn't seen them in quite a while.

* * *

Once the battlecars were out of sight from the main battle, Cassy ordered the unit to halt while half reloaded their mortars and the other half covered the perimeter. Then they switched off. With the unit fully reloaded, they pulled out again. The cavalry had to be around somewhere, and they couldn't outrun battlecars. Not without a much bigger head start. "Okay!" she shouted, "wedge formation. Circle Ephrata and keep your eyes out for the cavalry. Let's go kill some invaders."

The Clanners whooped and hollered, and then the roar of engines drowned it out. They headed north, keeping the eastern wall on their left side. They followed the wall as it curved gently to the left and soon found themselves north of town with no sign of the enemy cavalry. There was nothing to do but to keep going, and so they did. When they'd circled to the west of town, she still had no sign of them.

She was beginning to wonder if the cavalry had fled. Or maybe they had somehow fought their way into Ephrata, and she had missed the breach in the wall. She decided to make another circle around the town and drove onward.

As they came around to the more southerly side of town again, her little handheld radio buzzed. "Charlie One, be advised I see a mounted unit ahead, near the wall, heading southeast. Looks like the cavalry heading back toward the battle."

In response, Cassy stepped on the gas, and her car surged forward. The alert must've been from one of the outlying cars which, being farther from the wall, could see ahead better. Her heart began to speed up, anticipating another charge. She was fully in battle mode and had been for quite some time. It was liberating, in a way.

That feeling—that battle joy—would've marked her as a social deviant three years ago, but now it was practically normal. Only the strong survived. It had taken the end of the world for her to lose that baggage, which "civilization" had given her. People weren't supposed to enjoy killing, but what they didn't know back then, or at least most of them didn't, was that killing in battle wasn't the same thing psychologically as looking them in the eye and doing the same thing to a neighbor.

Her thoughts were interrupted as she saw the cavalry coming around the wall at last. They were stretched out in a long column, sweeping around the wall toward the battle. She wasn't sure the cavalry could change the outcome since it wasn't like they were charging with lances—they would have to fire from horseback or dismount—but two hundred enemy soldiers smashing into the Clan's left flank all at once would definitely cost a lot of lives. She had to stop them, and time was running out.

Into her handheld radio, adrenaline pumping through her, she screamed, "Fire all mortars," and grinned savagely as her car jerked wildly from the recoil.

To her left and right, she heard the *thump, thump* of mortar fire going down range. Seconds later, giant flowers of fire and shrapnel and blood erupted all along the cavalry's line. People and horses flew through the air, and she briefly worried some of them might land on the cars further back in her unit's V-formation. Then she remembered they were all armored, and the worry turned into a grin.

When she got within twenty yards of the surviving cavalry, which continued to bear down on the infantry battle up ahead, she stepped on the gas pedal and pushed it all the way down. The engine roared like a dragon, and her battle car surged forward again, pressing her into the seat. Every gun in her formation opened up, concentrating heavy automatic fire at the cavalry's backside. More horses and people fell, chewed up by a hail of bullets.

There was a deafening thump from beneath her car, and the whole vehicle rose into the air far enough for the shock absorbers to fully extend. She could hear them click as they hit their maximum extension, so she knew she had gone up at least a couple of feet. She had probably run over a horse, and spared a moment to thank Dean Jepson for figuring out how to give the battle cars solid tires.

As she smashed into the cavalry line, some tried to split away from her deadly cattle prow. Her car pierced their lines like a hot knife through butter. She didn't look back, but she already knew what that scene would look like behind her—as the cavalry had veered left and right away from her car, all they had done was swerve into the path of the cars behind her in the flying wedge formation.

Amber's victory calls rose above the roar of the engine and the guns, and Cassy's face twisted into a snarl of savage joy. Then she had a chance to look at the battlefield ahead. The fight for the wall, too, was all but over. All that remained was the mop up.

Atop the walls, lined with the Ephrata defenders, she saw them standing with their fists in the air and screaming in victory down at the dying invaders. Whatever the town's leaders felt about meeting their obligations to the Confederation that helped protect them, she suspected the townspeople themselves wouldn't forget this Confederation victory anytime soon. This had probably saved hundreds of lives and secured the town's help with the general war effort for at least the next five years.

"A real PR coup," she muttered. They had saved the Confederation. Or at least, they had given it a fighting chance.

- **20** -

SLOWLY, CHOONY BECAME aware of voices. No doubt Jack and Chump had returned. He was dead, though, so it mattered little to him. He simply lay there where they had left his body, enjoying the fact that he felt very little pain for the first time in... he had no way of knowing how long, actually. A day? A week?

He became aware of an odd sensation, something gently rubbing his hair, as something else rested tenderly on his upper arm. He wondered if he was perhaps being devoured. It occurred to him that people didn't often get to watch themselves be devoured, so he turned his head to the left, the side on which he felt the touch, and opened his eyes. He saw Jaz sitting beside him on the bed, leaning over him and smiling. His heart cracked, realizing this meant she was obviously dead, too, and had joined him in whatever afterlife this was.

"Dammit, not you too," he said, looking at Jaz's spirit.

Jaz's expression shifted from tenderness to one of confusion. She cocked her head to the side a little and said, "Choon, you're safe. Do you understand me? Can you hear me?"

Choony shook his head and closed his eyes. He really didn't want to see the ghost of his beloved Jaz, a painful reminder of his own failure. He was too ragged, mentally, to pray or meditate to regain his serenity. At the moment, he was in chaos, and he simply let that be his truth for the moment. Now that he was dead, he had an eternity to restore his harmony and be a good Buddhist. Maybe after rebirth, even, because he didn't much feel like being serene at this very moment.

He said, "Why do you torment me, spirit?" This was completely unfair, and he still had no interest in having serenity about the fact. His mind felt like he was slogging through thick mud.

Jaz's voice said, "Choony, I don't know what you're talking about. What spirit?"

A pause.

"What the hell is wrong with him?"

Another voice, a man's, said, "He's got one hell of a fever. Feel how hot he is. He's probably delusional."

Jaz's voice replied, "Get a wet rag or something. We have to cool him down."

The male voice, which sounded somehow familiar now, grunted. "That's not gonna cut it, sweetie. Look at these cuts... they're all infected. I wouldn't be surprised if he has some internal bleeding, too. And where they tore his cheek, I'm pretty sure that's infected. He needs antibiotics."

That sounded entirely too mundane and logical for spirits of the dead. That wasn't the conversation spirits would have. He slowly opened his eyes. He still saw Jaz, now fully dressed, standing over him beside a demon. Only the demon looked different, now—its wings resembled a backpack, and its hideous face seemed now to be somehow artificial, like a mask. No, a helmet.

It dawned on Choony that he was looking at an ordinary

person. A familiar-looking one, at that. He tried to place the name to the face, and then it dawned on him. It was the transient he had met and fed on his way to search for Jaz. "Andy?" he asked, incredulous.

Andy nodded and grinned. "Yeah, it's me."

"How did you...?"

"One of my friends saw two suspicious guys coming and going from this place. We came to grab their shit and go..."

As the fog in Choony's mind cleared, he noticed how much of Andy's gear was splashed with red paint. He looked around the room and saw another half-dozen men and women, all similarly attired. Fear shot up his spine as he drew the obvious conclusion. "You're not going to eat us, are you?" Choony was too tired to be truly terrified anymore, and his voice was calm and even because of it.

Andy grinned again, this time with a mischievous twinkle in his eyes. He nodded and showed no sign of shame. "I see you noticed that about us, huh? Yeah, we do that on occasion, but not to you. You know why?"

Beside him, Jaz let out a tiny squeak of alarm, and from the corner of his eye, Choony noticed her looking all around. Probably looking for a weapon or a way out.

Choony said, "Because I'm such a nice guy?" He forced a smile on his face. It would be just his luck to be rescued, only to become someone's dinner.

Andy shrugged and said, "Yes, actually. You gave me way more than you had to. You didn't have to give me anything, really, but you gave me a lot more than I would have given you if our roles had been reversed. Giving food, that's not something you see every day, not anymore. Anyway, we don't eat people when we don't have to. And Korean barbeque gives me gas."

Choony squinted to get a better look at Andy's face. The guy still showed no sign of being ashamed of his cannibal status. Choony pursed his lips for a moment, and then said, "So how many of you are living out here in the wildlands?"

Choony wiggled his fingers and toes, testing them. The movement caused him intense, shooting pain, not just where he was missing digits. That was a good sign, considering how long he had been bound—he might have suffered some cellular death in his hands and feet from how tightly he had been tied up, but apparently not. That was fortunate, but he still felt like roadkill from the fever they'd mentioned and his injuries.

Andy said, "We have made arrangements with some of the homesteaders within about ten miles of here. We can't just take too much food from them, or they'll starve, and that would be a waste of both a resource and the meat on their bones. They give us what they can spare in exchange for being left alone."

"Sounds like a good deal."

"Yeah. And we supplement with any meat we can catch, of whatever variety. Whatever it takes to stay free, and out from under the thumb of New America."

"I see."

"We all got no interest in being told what to do by that Taggart. We've spent two years without big government, and we like it that way. I guess freedom isn't free, and the cost is other people's lives on occasion."

Choony could only nod. He was too weak and dazed to argue the point, nor did he really feel like picking a fight with his rescuer. Especially a rescuer who was still capable of butchering him and Jaz for a tasty snack. After a moment's pause, he said, "I would say you should just go start some farms."

"You gotta understand, this is solid New America territory. That's not the way to stay free."

"You know you won't be able to stay here forever, right?

Hoboken's population is growing, and fast."

Andy let out a sharp breath and frowned. "Yeah, but our options are pretty limited. I figure we'll stay alive and free as long as we can, then fight for our homes and hope they spare our kids."

Jaz said, "How many kids?"

"Twenty-five, maybe thirty, all told." Andy scratched his cheek as he seemed to be mentally counting.

Jaz covered her mouth with her hand in shock. "I'll see what we can do to help you people, once we're back and safe."

Andy nodded.

"You have my word, too," Choony said. "But what about the two jackals who did this to us? Did they escape?"

Andy looked at Jaz, then turned his gaze to Choony and winked. "One got away, and we haven't spotted the other, but don't worry about them. They're not your problem now."

One of the other Road Warrior-looking fighters, searching through unattached cabinets that had been laid out in one corner of the warehouse, shouted, "Sweet! Hey Andy, take a look at this."

Over his shoulder, Andy hollered back, "What do you got?"

"Cases of MREs and canned food. A whole stockpile. Some funny looking paperwork, too."

Andy disappeared from Choony's view for a minute, and Choony briefly closed his eyes.

When Andy came back, he had paperwork in his hands. "This doesn't mean anything to us, but you two might find it really useful." He handed the papers to Jaz.

She skimmed through the papers and as she did so, her eyebrows rose. She looked at Choony and said, "You aren't going to believe this. Our little friend Jack has been a very bad boy."

From the papers, she pulled out a black-and-white glossy photo.

"What's that?" Choony asked.

Jaz held the photo up in front of his face. It showed him and Jaz in the marketplace, standing among other people. Both of their faces had been circled in a red marker.

Choony stared at the photo in shock until Jaz pulled it away and set it down. She turned her attention to one of the sheets of paper, studying it closely.

"Looks like this was typed up on a typewriter."

"What does it say?"

"It's a message from someone called 'Killjoy,' with details of hiring Jack to tell them everything he knows about Clanholme and instructions to capture you and me. Pretty specific orders, too."

"Wow. What about that other page?"

"It's basically a commendation for a job well done, and states that because of the information Jack provided, they had all the tactical intelligence they needed to 'ensure mission success in the next stage of the Great Plan.'"

"Great Plan? Do you think...?" Choony's voice trailed off as his mind spun.

Jaz said, "There's a series of four coordinates here, detailing latitude and longitude."

Jaz read the coordinates aloud to Choony. He couldn't be sure, but the numbers were close together, and he thought they were all from a nearby area, no more than a few days' ride from the coordinates he remembered for Hoboken.

Choony locked eyes with Jaz and suddenly felt the full weight of his exhaustion. All he wanted to do was sleep for a week, but this appeared important. "Jaz, we have to alert Clanholme of this and pass this intelligence on to Ethan."

Even to his own ears, Choony's voice sounded frail and faint. He was definitely at the end of his endurance. He also wanted to reach out and comfort Jaz, as she had endured a horrific ordeal herself, one which Choony had been forced to watch. He couldn't imagine that she would ever be the same again, and his heart broke to think of it.

Andy said, "But anyway, we're going to rig up a stretcher and get you two home to Hoboken now. If you ever need to get in touch with me again, you can send word through the guy selling alternators at the north end of the market zone."

Choony nodded, but his thoughts were whisked elsewhere, anticipating getting home. A shower, a meal, and antibiotics—that sounded as close to heaven as he was ever going to get in this world. Choony smiled and reached out to take Jaz's hand.

Jaz leaned over to embrace him, and into his ear, she whispered, "You're going home."

* * *

0600 HOURS - ZERO DAY +643

Sitting at his desk, Taggart looked up from the three sheets of paper the messenger had handed him in a sealed envelope. Choony and Jaz had apparently been aided by some unnamed outside force, although he didn't yet have all the details, and Choony was refusing to say anything about the people who helped them.

The Intel they sent painted a very scary picture. The Maryland invaders were aggressively setting up intelligence rings in New America and hiring traitors from among Taggart's own people, and this new Intel filled a gap in his understanding of what was going on with the 'vaders. Two days ago, his scouts had retrieved some Maryland spy's logbook, communiqués, and several photographs that had truly raised an alarm in his mind. Those other photos had been taken from overhead, and the tiny printed writing on them indicated they were satellite photos. The Southern Cantonment didn't have any way to get such photographs, as far as he knew, which meant they got them from somewhere else. Probably that bastard, General Houle, in NORAD.

Those photos were now on their way to Ethan in Clanholme, his unofficial spymaster. Maybe he could make sense of them.

So now, Taggart had a much fuller picture of what was going on. The North Koreans were aggressively establishing ground assets—people—to gather intelligence, and working in cahoots with someone who had access not only to satellite photographs, but also high-quality, large-format printers.

From the reports he received from Ethan, that someone could only be the mysterious character, Watcher One. Taggart asked himself why Maryland would want to hijack the Clan's diplomats to New America, but the answer was pretty obvious. They were attempting to destabilize their enemies, the timing of which meant something big was coming. It was now only a couple months before the largest food harvests began, and his imagination immediately leaped to invasion scenarios.

Taggart thanked the messenger and said, "You're free to go."

He watched as the messenger left, and leaned back in his chair. Crossing his leg, he thought about sending Jaz and Choony a get-well package. They were friends as well as being representatives of the Clan and the Confederation. Also, he would have to send an order to double the guard put on their house. It was clear to him they were still in danger.

* * *

Jwa's senses came fully awake from the light dozing he had been doing while the wagon bounced back and forth. He'd been inside the covered back for two days, shackled to the interior with nothing but a bucket for his personal needs. Some fresh air would be nice, but they never let him out when the wagon stopped. He didn't dare to hope that this time would be any different.

Shortly after the wagon came to a complete stop, he heard voices talking, just as he had with every other stop. This time, however, he heard more voices. New voices. He began to feel uneasy. No one had told him what was going to happen to him, and although he would face it bravely as a soldier of North Korea should, that still didn't mean he was eager to die. And he sure didn't want to be tortured, although he had done his fair share of that to Korea's enemies over the last two years. If they did torture him, he was certain he would have deserved it, but he still would prefer to avoid that.

Then the wagon was moving again, albeit more slowly. He felt it wind back and forth, turning left, right, then left. It rolled onward, now moving straight again for another few minutes before coming to a halt.

Through the thick canvas walls of the covered wagon, Jwa heard a bit of a commotion. Lots of voices that, unless he had lost his mind, seemed to include both children and adults. Perhaps the wagon had stopped at a settled waypoint. Whatever the case, it didn't have anything to do with him, so he leaned back on the bench and closed his eyes to try to doze again.

The canvas door flap at the back of the wagon was abruptly thrown open. Through the opened flap, Jwa saw a man standing just outside, staring at him as though sizing him up. He probably was, Jwa realized, because he had the build and the bearing of a military man. Unlike most of the

Americans he had seen, and definitely unlike the filthy sand-eaters he had been forced to fight alongside, this man was clean-shaven, and his hair was cut very short. Beyond short. It had been cut in a military style. His posture, his direct gaze, his tidy appearance—Jwa realized this was possibly an American Marine. Those were just about the only true warrior troops the Americans had, according to everything he had been told, although he had never faced them in battle, nor had he wished to, given that the American Army troops had been far tougher than his leaders led him to believe before the eve of invasion. American soldiers were as tenacious as veteran Korean soldiers—how much more so would their Marines be?

Jwa kept his face passive, and he simply stared back. Eventually, someone would tell him what to do, but in the meantime, he wasn't about to disgrace himself by backing down. Especially not to a fellow soldier, and an enemy one at that.

The seconds ticked by interminably.

Finally, the well-built man nodded once and threw the door flap closed once again. Jwa closed his eyes as the seconds continued to march on.

* * *

Ethan spun in his chair when he heard the door opening, and a few seconds later, Michael came into view. "Sieg heil, mein general," Ethan said with a grin.

Michael rolled his eyes. He stepped into the bunker's office area, grabbed the other office chair, and straddled it to face Ethan. "Just so you know, most Marines would punch your goofy face for saying that. It's insulting. How are you holding up, buddy?"

"My vision's much better, and the ringing in my ears is

pretty much gone, but I find myself jumping at every damn noise, which is funny, considering everything we've been through so far."

Michael nodded and eyed him appraisingly. He said, "There's a world of difference between going into battle surrounded by your team and a one-on-one, life or death fight that ends with you being captured. I'm glad to hear the flash-bang didn't screw you up more permanently."

"Thanks." What else could he say?

Michael said, "Now that's out of the way, it's time to get down to business. The wagon we have been expecting just arrived. I thought you would want to know."

Ethan felt a bit of shock, his scalp tingling. One of *them*, here in Clanholme... It didn't make him comfortable, although he understood why it was necessary. At least, he understood why Cassy thought it was necessary. He would have rather just put a bullet in the man. "So we're really going along with Cassy's crazy plan?"

Michael nodded, but Ethan saw that his lips were pursed. "She leads the Confederation. She makes the policy, and it's our job to execute it."

Ethan snorted and said, "I'd rather execute the prisoner."

"So would I," he said, "but for now, that ship has sailed. We have a job to do. Whether we like it or not, I expect you to do your job, and do it well."

"Of course. And I do trust Cassy's judgment, but do you really think this wild plan to win over an enemy combatant is going to work?"

Michael's face went stony, which it always did when he thought someone was being insubordinate or disrespecting a superior officer, and Cassy was the Commander-in-Chief of the Confederation, as its chancellor. At least he didn't look angry, Ethan noted.

Michael replied, "She certainly made it sound

compelling. It may or may not work, but if it does, we're far better off than we would be if we simply put a bullet in him. Besides, if he stays uncooperative, she will eventually let me apply the old, tried-but-true methods of getting information out of him."

Ethan said, "Yes, but if her plan works, then it opens up some fantastic opportunities for—"

His HAM radio crackled to life, interrupting him with its loud squawk. He wheeled his chair over to the radio. "Oh goody, incoming traffic." He plugged the stage mic into his laptop and set it down in front of the HAM radio unit, then picked up the handset and said, "Go for traffic."

The radio squawked some more, and Ethan watched as the microphone recorded the noises into his laptop, where the binary code was compiled and then decrypted. The encryption on it confirmed the traffic was from New America, which drew his attention immediately. "It's from Taggart," he said, looking at Michael.

"Yeah? What's he say?"

Ethan glanced at the monitor and watched the hourglass spinning as his laptop went to work deciphering the file. "Damn, man, give it a chance to decipher. It's a file, not a voice transmission."

They sat in silence for twenty seconds while his laptop chugged away. When it dinged, task complete, Michael leaned forward to eagerly await the verdict.

Ethan opened the file, anxious to find out what was within. Usually, Taggart sent text files, which downloaded and decoded quickly. A few seconds at most. This had taken nearly half a minute.

"Weird. They're graphics." He double clicked the first one and saw a picture of Jaz and Choony standing in the market, their faces circled. The next was an overhead shot, clearly from a satellite, while the third was a typed .txt document. He double clicked that and skimmed it, then let out a low whistle. "Michael, come look at this."

He got up out of his chair so that Michael could sit to read the file, and read over his shoulder, checking it out in more detail. It was an Intel report from Taggart, relating some rather horrific recent events with Jazoony, but with reassurances that they would both recover. Physically, at least.

The Intel report concluded that the invaders were receiving outside help from somebody with access to satellites. There was a query as to whether Ethan might have inadvertently delivered such assistance to them. He knew damn well that he hadn't, however; this was the work of Watcher One. He had no doubt in his mind.

After Michael finished reading it more carefully, he continued to sit motionless, staring at the monitor.

The seconds ticked by, and Ethan eventually said, "I know it's rough. Are you all right, Michael?"

Michael nodded, his jaw clenched tightly. His knuckles, wrapped around the chair's armrests, had turned white from the force of his grip. "Save your concern for Jaz and Choony. I'm simply trying to restrain myself from going out topside and eliminating our invader guest in a rather spectacular fashion."

Ethan didn't respond. There was nothing he could say that could make the situation better, so he simply rested his hand on Michael's right shoulder.

He really, really wished that Taggart had sent that POW days earlier so they would have had the chance to get familiar with him *before* receiving this news. Or that Taggart had waited another week so that emotions in Clanholme could level out. Damn Taggart and his timing.

* * *

Choony sat in his recliner. He had it fully extended so that he was almost lying down. It was the most comfortable position he'd found, given his injuries.

The pain in his hands and feet from his shattered metatarsal and metacarpal bones was excruciating, and the surgery to set and pin some of those broken bones before putting on his partial casts didn't help.

His ribs, however, were the worst. They hurt every time he took a breath. It felt like someone was stabbing him repeatedly with a fiery knife. Taking shallow breaths helped, but then he had to breathe faster. The pain from that dwarfed the others.

Frankly, his favorite time of the day was after he received his injections of morphine and Dilaudid—the hazy sleep that followed had at least relieved his pain for a while. He wasn't due for more drugs in his IV for another couple of hours, however.

The only thing that made his agony bearable—and worth it—was the sight of Jaz sitting on the couch nearby, alive and well.

She was the most beautiful thing in the world, he mused, even as damaged as she had been, even as damaged as she was now. The new blemishes to her aura only inspired a deeply protective instinct in him, not revulsion or pity. The last thing in the world that Jaz needed now was pity; things happen, and pity was the reaction of those who resisted life's events. To Choony, they simply existed, and he would move on as best he could, and help her to do so as well.

"What are you thinking?" she asked, although her voice sounded flat and lifeless. She had been in the same spot the last time he went to sleep, just as she had been when he woke up a few minutes ago.

He thought about shrugging, but decided not to risk the pain. He said, "I was just marveling at your beauty. Even now, as hurt as we are, I prefer the sight of you to the most perfect lotus flowers." It wasn't a lie, of course, because he never intentionally lied—the disruption to his inner harmony simply wasn't worth it—but it was an omission of sorts.

A faint smile appeared on her face, but it was halfhearted at best and never did reach her eyes. Normally, she would have lit up brightly, hearing those words from him. There was nothing normal about her anymore, after what she had been through, and he wondered what the new 'normal' Jaz would look like when her inner wounds had healed.

"That's sweet, Choon Choon. But I don't feel especially lovely, and definitely not perfect." She took in a deep breath and let it out slowly.

Choony could hear the frustration in that sigh, but there was nothing he could do to fix her. Nothing so fast and easy as waving a magic wand, but he would keep looking for other, more realistic options.

"I'm only glad that I found you. It was worth it."

She looked away, then, jaw clenched. "It was too high a price. Totally too high."

"No. It would have been worth it even if they had killed me, just so that I could spend my last moments with you. And now, free again, life continues. I will never leave your side, Jaz."

When her gaze clicked to him, he met her eyes without flinching. He had told the truth, and there was no shame in that. No awkwardness, not for him. He only hoped that, however incapable she might be right now of accepting the truth of his words, her spirit would at least feel their truth. He thought of love and energy pouring from himself into her through that gaze, even though it felt silly. His mind rejected the very idea of something like that working, but his heart knew he had to try.

A knock at the door interrupted his thoughts and her

reply. She almost jumped from her seat, startled, then groaned from a sharp pain; she leaned forward, bending over with her arms crossed over her lower belly.

Her voice tight with pain, she called out, "Come in."

The front door opened, and he could see one of the soldiers who guarded them was at the door, holding it open. He motioned to someone just out of sight.

In walked Doug Holloway, New America's Secretary of State. As always, he was immaculately dressed in an expensive suit, this one a dark blue. He nodded in greeting as he saw Jaz and Choony, and walked toward them without another word to the soldier who had let him in. Choony noticed that he carried a small, decorative paper bag in his left hand.

When he had crossed through the entryway and into the living room, he beamed a well-rehearsed smile at both of them, reminding Choony of a shark. It was an apt comparison.

Doug said, "Good day to you both, heroes of New America! I am so thrilled to see that you are both alive, and I'm told you will make a full recovery. So how have they treated you since your return? I'm told you received the finest medical care."

Jaz simply stared at him, so Choony replied stiffly for them both, "Thank you."

Doug set the paper bag down on the table in front of Jaz, unbuttoned his suit coat, then sat in the other recliner. He sat ramrod straight. "I feel bad that I neglected to give you a proper housewarming gift when you first moved here, but I brought something to rectify that. Just a little something from me to you, in recognition of your deeds and your triumph."

Jaz shifted her gaze to the paper bag, face expressionless, but didn't move or respond.

Choony smiled warmly, feeling somewhat better about the man's thoughtfulness for having brought a gift.

Doug continued, "You know, you two have created quite a stir in the capital. Everyone is talking about what happened. Politicians and citizens alike have a lot to say."

Jaz looked at Doug. "I was under the impression that the politicians governing New America *are* its citizens. Was I misinformed?"

Doug smiled, his eyes crinkling. "No, of course we are citizens. I just mean the everyday people, the ones without the training and experience to properly run things. What happened to you both has caused quite a bit of fear. I believe that's on account of the fact that we have no wall between us and the wastelands to our immediate north. I'm sure you'll agree with me that it would be much better if we had a way of controlling the traffic leading in and out of civilized Hoboken."

Choony shrugged, ignoring the pain that he knew it would cause. "Actually, I don't believe a wall would have helped us. Jaz's kidnappers were apparently in Hoboken on legitimate business. Maybe some system of identification might have helped. Showing papers, perhaps."

Face neutral, Choony peered intently at Doug, gauging his reaction.

"Great minds think alike, they say. Yes, that is precisely what I have been pushing for with our president for several months, now."

"You think that would have made a difference?"

"If I had my way, I believe this would have been prevented entirely."

"What has Taggart said about it?" Choony asked. He hoped he was right about Taggart.

"Our president is more concerned with other issues right now, quite rightly, and he has much on his plate. That's why

I was selected to be the Secretary of State, of course, so that I could help him with these day to day small decisions."

"So, did he say no, or did he not yet reply?"

Doug frowned. "I don't think he gave it proper consideration. So, my hands are a little tied for the moment. I've been organizing a grassroots campaign to raise awareness of the benefits of such a system, though, hoping our president will listen better to the voice of his citizens than to one humble servant like me."

Choony always had a bad feeling about Doug. The man was a perfect example of the old world system, and how he had survived the Dying Times was a mystery. The world had an opportunity now to move beyond the petty, zero-sum political games of the past and truly focus on the welfare of its citizens. Doug Holloway was definitely not that proper leadership. It hadn't taken long for him to show his true colors.

Doug continued, "I know you, of all people, will understand the wisdom of this. We have to protect our citizens. We have to keep out those who would harm us, just as we should have done with those who wished to harm your lovely, very-capable fellow ambassador, here." He looked to Jaz, giving her a warm smile, but instead of smiling back, she rolled her eyes. He looked back to Choony.

Choony slowly shook his head. He could hardly believe what Doug had said, and yet he knew he shouldn't have been surprised. People like Doug were everywhere in every culture, he knew; Doug's soul was unenlightened, and in the end, it would drag him down. He was the sort whose Karma would be reborn again and again, never finding sanctity in the Peaceful Lands. And there was nothing Choony could do about it, for the world was full of dogs like him.

Choony felt suddenly exhausted. The effort of this conversation had drained him too much to care for diplomacy any longer.

Choony opened his mouth to speak, but Jaz cut him off. "If your goal is to limit people's movements as you increase your control over them, we won't be a part of that. I despise the fact our tragedy would be used as a catalyst for yet more government control."

Doug's smile melted from his face. "More of a government might have saved millions of lives."

"No," Jaz said. "Over the last two years, all the people who once relied on the government are gone. They starved, or they killed one another. More of what killed them isn't needed. Only those who could think for themselves, who could adapt to the changing situation... only they survived."

Doug leaned toward Jaz with a pleading look on his face, but when Jaz clenched her jaw, Doug halted. He took a deep breath. "Listen, you can't know that because, after the EMPs, there was no government. The old one failed its duties. We have the chance to make a new one, a stronger one. We can save lives!"

"You can create a dictatorship, Doug, but in this lifetime, you will never create the kind of big government we once had. Those glory days are thankfully gone."

Doug's firm control of his friendly mask slipped for an instant, but he quickly recovered. He kept that mask plastered on his face like a mannequin. "You wound me, miss. You misinterpret my motives. There really are people out there who would harm us, people who would harm you, as you have seen, to your sorrow. The biggest shame out of all of this tragedy is that it could have been prevented. Who wouldn't give up an inch of freedom for a mile of security?"

"There's no inches with your kind, Doug. You're a parasite who killed its host and is starving for power again. You just want to feed off America's corpse."

"Dammit! Why can't you see what I do? A better future.

Sure, less freedom—the freedom to starve, to get killed by your neighbors. You—"

Jaz snapped, "I won't help you kill this new America. I sincerely hope that wasn't the only real purpose of your visit because that would be, like, a total waste of all our time. You need to leave, Doug. Choony is exhausted, and you aren't helping him."

For once, Doug completely lost his famous composure, and his face grew slack with shock, jaw dropped as he stared at her incredulously. Then he cleared his throat, cheeks flushing, and replied, "Ordinarily, I'd have you two disrespectful little shits on the first wagon back to the Confederation, authors of your very own diplomatic incident. At the end of the day, your so-called Confederation is nothing more than a state within New America. I had hoped that some good could come from the evil that happened to you, that you might help me prevent this sort of thing from ever happening again. I'll be back in a couple of days to see how you're doing. When I return, I will expect you to have remembered your mission here, your role, and your damn manners."

Choony said, "You sure like to hear the sound of your own voice, don't you?"

Doug stood and re-buttoned his suit coat, then straightened his tie. Chin in the air, he gave a stiff, slight bow and left without another word, closing the front door behind him.

Jaz turned to Choony and stared.

Part of him wanted to explain the error of what she had done, but he could see from the fire in her eyes that this was the wrong time. Instead, he focused on her well-being. She was obviously out of sorts, and given the trauma of what she had recently gone through, he had no way of truly knowing how deep her anger ran.

He smiled at her and said, "I do appreciate your honesty, Jaz. Given what he said, I'll support whatever you want to do about it."

His words had an immediate effect on her, as the reddish hue and heat left her face and the corners of her lips lost their snarl. He would never lie, not to anyone and especially not to her, but what he said was true. Perhaps that feeling of having somebody at her back, someone to keep her safe, helped offset the rage she had felt at the threat Doug represented.

Or perhaps he was overanalyzing it, and he should just be happy that she had calmed down. He was a bit surprised at how radically different Jaz's speech had been from her usual way of talking, though. That was new.

* * *

Jwa slowly paced just outside of the wagon. They had attached a long runner chain to his collar, which allowed him some limited freedom of movement. Every step hurt, his muscles cramping after having been cooped up inside the wagon for so long with no opportunity to stretch. He felt his muscles slowly begin to unwind as he walked back and forth. He knew from experience that they would soon be more or less recovered, yet it would be a day or two before his full strength returned.

As he hobbled to and fro, he carefully examined his surroundings. He didn't even want to think of escaping yet, both due to his condition and because he had no idea where he was. He believed they had traveled west, rather than north or south, which might place him somewhere in Clan territory. He couldn't be sure, so until he got a better sense of where he was, he wouldn't run. Not as long as they weren't torturing him, at least. If that happened, all bets were off.

The first thing he noticed were the guards. They wore field camouflage, and the emblem on their hats identified them as U.S. Marines. At his best, he would be evenly matched against them one-on-one, but there were four here watching his every move. They stayed out of striking distance, not that he would have attacked any of them. Not here, not now.

The second thing he noticed were the plants. They surrounded him, and they all grew seemingly at random, no two adjacent plants of the same species. He also noticed that all the trees were fruit or nut varieties, except for a few willows and birch trees; in other words, all useful for something. Between the trees, shrubs grew at a variety of heights. Most of those were also fruit bearing. Then, around the shrubs, all sorts of other plants grew. He couldn't identify most of those.

He remembered previous Intel reports he had read that discussed this sort of arrangement, and noted that the Americans had called it 'permaculture.' It seemed very inefficient, but he knew that New America was also implementing the style of farming, if you could call it farming.

He wondered how many people it would take to harvest all of that, and his mind swam. It would require an inordinate number, and even with the two hundred and fifty or so people that had lived in the Clan settlements he'd raided previously, he imagined that at least half of all this produce would simply go to waste, landing on the ground in this feeble, fake forest. Leave it to Americans to devise a system that required so much labor, yet wasted so much produce at the same time.

He shook his head in disbelief. This bounty of produce would certainly feed everyone in this settlement, wherever he was, but how many half-starving people could have been fed with what the system must waste? How many of those who starved to death over the last two years might have been saved if the Clan had shared their excess?

Yes, Americans truly had no concept of working toward the good of the People. It had been the reason for the invasion in the first place. That, and their intolerable abuse of power on a global scale. The world's invasion of the United States may have drawn to a standstill after the second round of EMPs, but that didn't matter—they had killed America the mighty, slain the 'sleeping giant' that Japan had failed to defeat sixty years ago, and proved forever and always what a house of cards Capitalism had become.

He looked up through the trees and saw the sun's position, which told him it must be about 1400 hours. Normally, this would be the time when he and his troops ate, but he'd had virtually nothing to eat for at least two days now. His stomach cramped terribly. At least it no longer growled as it had on the second day, his body getting used to the starvation.

Would his captors allow him to starve to death? He doubted it. For some reason, they were treating him far better than a POW had any right to expect. While he was grateful for that, he certainly didn't trust their motives.

He resolved himself to resist any questioning, to offer no answer to any of their queries no matter how nice they tried to appear.

Jwa heard footsteps and looked up. Walking toward him was the same huge American who had opened the wagon flap earlier. He was probably a Marine like the ones guarding him, since he now had confirmed their presence, which validated his earlier assessment. Jwa stopped pacing and turned to face the new arrival, waiting placidly.

The man stopped within striking distance and looked him in the eyes. Oddly, the man didn't seem to be trying to intimidate him, he noticed, but was simply observing him. Evaluating.

After perhaps five seconds, the man nodded once, ever so faintly, seemingly approving of what he saw. Then the man said in English, "My name is Michael. While I would have preferred to simply kill you, my leaders have decided to keep you alive, for now. They didn't bother to explain why, and my job is simply to obey my orders. For now, then, you get to live. What's your name?"

Surprised, Jwa raised one eyebrow before he caught himself, and he cursed. He had just given away the fact that he understood English, assuming this soldier was at all observant, which he had every reason to believe. A faint smile grew on Michael's face, proving Jwa's assessment to be correct.

He let out a faint sigh and said, "I am called Jwa." There was no way he was going to reveal his rank or offer up any other useful information, but he couldn't see the harm in giving away his name. "Where are we? What place is this?"

Michael said, "You have the honor of finding yourself in Clanholme itself." He didn't offer any additional information.

Jwa was surprised to hear that, but this time he caught himself before he could give his reaction away. Why would the enemy bring him to Clanholme? That was like bringing a wolf into the sheep's pen on purpose. "I see. Please be advised that I will not betray my country nor my leaders. I have received extensive training in how to defeat interrogation attempts, however direct." He wasn't sure that was the right way to say it in English, but it had to be close enough that the American would understand his meaning.

The man named Michael nodded slowly, seeming neither disappointed nor angry. He simply took in Jwa's words without comment. Jwa couldn't tell whether he believed it or not. Well, if they tried to interrogate or torture him, they would find out how truthful he had just been. The Great Leader had seen to it that his honored troops sent to America had all received at least a bit of resistance training, and Jwa had received a whole lot more of it due to his role. That was only natural; special forces troops always received the best of everything, including training. *Especially* training.

Michael walked around Jwa, but his posture was one of supreme confidence, as well as complete readiness. Jwa suddenly decided that this Michael must surely be special forces also, though he couldn't have said why he thought that.

Once Michael got behind Jwa, he leaned against the back of the wagon and crossed his arms over his chest. "Have they told you yet how many of your men died during your raid at Ephrata?"

Jwa eyed him, looking for hints, but the man was unreadable. Was he being taunted, or was it a genuine offer of information about his men? It could be either because Michael was clearly a military man. There were certain professional courtesies that might be extended. Jwa shook his head. No, he hadn't heard.

Michael's face showed no sign of joy as he said, "I'm told your squad was all killed. Most were killed by mortars, the rest hunted down as they ran. The damage to the town was extensive, although mostly because of their own mortars."

Jwa simply nodded. That was no surprise—he had expected to hear they were all dead. Ephrata's defenders had accurate mortar fire and lots of it. They also had cavalry, so although he hoped his final stand would allow at least a couple of his men to escape, it had been a long shot, and he knew it even then. The news was not welcome, and Jwa averted his gaze, looking at the forest floor. Truly, every Korean lost was a tragedy. They couldn't be replaced, and they would have to kill ten Americans for each Korean lost, in order to destroy the American defenders.

Michael said, "I have been instructed to treat you well. That's not my preference, but that decision is above my pay grade. So, are you hungry?"

"Yes. I haven't eaten in days." He wasn't complaining, of course. It was just a simple statement of fact.

Michael launched himself away from the wagon he had been leaning against and turned to look at one of the guards. "Private, go check the kitchen and see if there were any leftovers. Make this soldier a plate, and bring it to him."

Jwa resumed his pacing while he waited, full of conflicting emotions and confused thoughts. If they thought they could buy him for the price of a plate of leftovers, though, they were sadly mistaken.

- **21** -

0900 HOURS - ZERO DAY +644

TAGGART STARED AT Doug and fought the urge to start shouting. "Let me get this straight. You want to wall off the reclaimed area of Hoboken and require people to show papers to get in or out?"

"Yes, Mr. President. The safety—"

Taggart interrupted, "And I suppose we'd charge a fee to pay for the manpower that would be required to build and then enforce, and for the added burden on our skeletal court system?"

"Of course. It's only right that the people pay for their own—"

"And you want to force this on our people even though they're overwhelmingly against the idea, right?"

Doug's lip curled up in anger. "They don't have any idea what's best for them. These morons only survived this long because their betters told them what to do. The ones who couldn't listen up died."

Taggart's eyes narrowed. This pompous, bureaucratic asshole! "Doug, you either represent the people or you rule them. These 'morons' are alive because they're self-reliant.

You are alive because you kissed the right asses and stole the property of other people during the Dying Times, and if I had my way, I'd have you tried for looting in wartime, because of it."

"You can't be serious. It was vital to keep people like me alive. Someone had to rebuild. Who would do that, Hick Jones the Farmer?"

Taggart took a deep breath, trying to restrain himself from demolishing this guy. He said, "People like you served no purpose before the EMPs, and you're a parasite even now."

"How dare you. I'm the damn Secretary of—"

"No, you aren't," Taggart said.

"What are you—"

"Listen Doug, you're hereby relieved of all governmental and regulatory duties, as well as the income and property you received thereby."

"I don't answer to you."

"You have twenty-four hours to be out of the SecState house. Leave the food in it, or I will have you shot for looting. Now get out of my sight before I forget the dignity of my position and snap your fucking neck, civilian." Taggart rose to his feet as he said the last, leaning forward to rest his fists on the table.

Doug almost stumbled in his haste to back away from Taggart's desk. He fumbled for the doorknob, pale white with fear and red-cheeked with rage.

As Doug backed through the doorway, he paused to glower at Taggart. He said, "Fine. See how well things run without me."

Doug slammed the door behind him, leaving Taggart standing behind his desk with his fists at his sides.

"Eagan."

The side door opened, and his cohort emerged, grinning widely. "Yes, sir?"

Taggart rolled his eyes. "Shitbird, what kind of trouble do you think that guy can stir up for us?"

Eagan stopped, and his face fell, crestfallen. "I hate to say it, but he can do a lot of damage. And didn't you choose him for the SecState slot because of his backers? We need them. They're the biggest, most influential farmers and merchants, engineers... everyone we really need supports him or supports the people who do support him. It's every single other person who hates him as much as we do."

Taggart frowned. This was getting out of hand, frankly, but to the core of his being, he detested what Doug Holloway stood for and the measures he was trying to put in place. Nor would he be backed into a corner by that piece of crap. He was the one who had fought those desperate early battles, had led when no one else could or would. He built New America on the bones of loyal troops and patriots. Really, there was only one way out of this.

"Eagan, I need you to get the Philadelphia envoy here in my office. Be discreet."

Eagan stared at him for several seconds before a slight grin cracked his face. "You bet, boss-man. I'm pretty sure I have something to do elsewhere after I get him for you, though, so you'll have to take your own meeting minutes."

He fought the urge to grin. Eagan, who was almost like a son to him by now, was quick on the uptake. "Stop standing there, shitbird, and go do something useful."

Eagan nodded and left him alone with his thoughts. Philly might just be useful as a neutral power after all. He only wondered what this was going to cost him if they agreed to his plan. He knew they would, though. They were pragmatic, and this was going to be in their own best interests.

He was reminded of the old saying about diplomacy being just 'sublimated warfare.' Well, it was about to get a lot less 'sublimated.' He reached into his desk drawer and stared at it for a long moment. At last, though, he removed the manila folder that lay at the bottom. It was an Intel report on Doug Holloway and all of his backers and followers that had so far been identified.

* * *

Ethan took the folder with his printed notes and slammed it down onto the desk.

Michael let out a deep breath and then reached for it. He opened it and, as he began reading through it, his eyebrows began to climb slowly up his forehead.

Ethan said, "You see? You're our defender. You keep Kaitlyn and the other kids safe, you make sure Amber and the other parents can sleep at night, safe in the knowledge you're out there defending them against everything that has ever been thrown at us."

"Quit buttering me up. I know what I do, and I know why I do it. So what is it you're asking of me?"

Ethan paced back and forth in the tiny computer room, down in the bunker. He could only take a couple steps before having to turn around, but he couldn't help pacing. He was too agitated to sit still, so he was basically spinning in circles in there. "There is a war coming, Michael. Whether we want it or not. You can sit here and prepare our defenses, but you know damn well their spies know all about our secrets and tricks. Our planes, our battlecars, our drones. Now they know we have radios."

"And?" Michael leaned forward.

"And then the whole thing with Jaz and Choony. Listen, New America has its own problems going on. Rumblings of war to their north, problems with Philly to their south. What's Philly going to do when the Maryland invaders are busy dealing with the Confederation? They're going to be freed up to be a major thorn in Taggart's side, that's what. You know it, and I know it."

Michael put his thumb and forefinger to the bridge of his nose and closed his eyes. Ethan saw the tension in him—Michael looked ready to explode.

"Dammit, Ethan. Don't try to sell me on it. Just tell me what you want."

"What I *want*," Ethan replied, leaning forward until his reddening face was only a foot away from Michael's, "is to deliver a knockout blow to their Intel, get a monkey off our back, and remove a thorn from our side. All in one fell swoop. What I *want* is for you, me, and your best SpecOps people to take the war to them while we do that. We have to kill Watcher One. He's too dangerous, and you know none of us will ever be safe with him out there."

Michael nodded, but said, "None of us is safe. Least of all you, right?"

Ethan stood bolt upright. His face felt hot, and he was sweating beneath his shirt collar. "Fuck me, Michael. I don't give a damn about *me*." He took a deep breath and backed away from Michael, who hadn't seemed to even notice his outburst. "I'm not angry at you. But putting the Clan in danger... yes, Watcher One is a bigger thorn in my side than any others'. But I am not suggesting this to save my own ass. I'm safe down here, now that the other access door is secured instead of just hidden."

Michael nodded and stood. "I know. I just had to be sure where you were coming from, but it wouldn't have affected my decision, except about whether to bring you."

"What?" Ethan looked at Michael, confused. "You have to bring me."

"No, I don't. But it'll be much easier getting inside his bunker if you come, and your talents are useful in so many other ways, too. But I wouldn't bring a coward, nor someone only out for themselves."

"That's not me. It never has been." Ethan felt his indignation rising, but squashed it. His feelings didn't matter, only the results of this little clandestine meeting.

Michael took a step toward Ethan, cornering him. He narrowed his eyes and, almost in a whisper, said, "I've always had my doubts about what happened when Jed died. You were the only other one there, and your story was weak. Jed was my best friend. But I let it go because I didn't have proof. And I let it go because you were valuable to our survival. But don't think for a minute I intend to let that happen to me."

Ethan backed away from that intense fire, but there was nowhere to go. He couldn't meet Michael's steel eyes, and looked away. How could that come up now, two years later? That was ancient history. He thought that incident with Jed was buried deep inside, but his own feelings of guilt surged up into his throat, bringing bile with it. He swallowed hard and, still looking away, said, "It should have been me that died out there, but Jed died a hero. He—"

Michael slammed his fist into the bulkhead next to Ethan's head. "Just be sure that I have my eyes on you. Whether it happened the way you said it did, or not, I do not intend to be another convenient accident. Got it?"

Ethan's shock began to wear off. "I got it, but just so you realize, you'd be wasting precious time and energy that should be directed toward this mission."

Michael took his fist off the wall and stepped back. He said, "I know. But when we leave on this secret-squirrel mission, I'm giving my troops orders to kill you if I die for any reason."

Ethan's jaw dropped, but he snapped it shut. If Michael

wanted that safeguard then fine. He couldn't even really be too angry about it anyway, considering what had really happened to Jed on their journey to Clanholme, but he'd take that to his grave. He looked up and met Michael's eyes once more. "Fine. So let's stop wasting time and let's work out the details."

Michael's body seemed to loosen a bit, and he nodded. He took his seat again as Ethan continued, "Who's coming on this mission, and when do we leave?"

"At least a couple weeks. We need to gather maps, Intel, gear. We need to do some field training and get your fat ass into shape, too."

"I'm not fat."

"You'll have to keep up with me. Does that put it into perspective for you?"

"Alright," Ethan said. "Let's get me shaped up."

Michael nodded.

They spent the next hour brainstorming details for the mission and taking notes. It was a very real possibility that the survival of the Clan and the Confederation depended on the outcome of their mission, and Ethan would leave nothing to chance in planning it.

* * *

1700 HOURS - ZERO DAY +648

Cassy sat on the couch and looked around the room. There was Frank, sitting on the recliner, in the Clanleader's position of course. One chair was empty—Grandma Mandy's. They'd left her chair empty ever since she passed away, a reminder to everyone of the moral compass she'd once provided. In a way, that empty chair still did provide that compass, as everyone present could practically hear in their heads what Mandy would have said on any issue.

Normally, there would have been three chairs empty—Mandy's, Joe Ellings', and Choony's—but their Korean-American friend had returned home to recover from his wounds in safety. It was so good to have Choony back—he'd always been her sounding board and counterbalance, and she felt more whole with him around.

Ethan and Michael rounded out the Council's presence here tonight since Joe was still in Philly. They hadn't heard word from him in a while, but that was normal.

"So," Frank began, "thank you all for joining us." Frank turned to Choony. "Glad to see you're feeling well enough to join us, Choony."

Choony nodded from his wheelchair, acknowledging Frank, but didn't say anything. His patient smile said enough.

Frank continued, "First, my update. No word from Joe in Philadelphia, but no reason to worry. A merchant caravan should be passing through from there in the next few days, and we hope to get a letter from him then. I'll open the floor to you all to report, now."

Choony raised his hand, but didn't stand as was the custom. With his injuries, everyone had agreed that it was fine for him to stay seated. He said, "You've all read my report about what happened to Jaz and me, and I expect no sympathy or empty words, but I think it would be prudent to first ask everyone here if they heard from Jack. If someone has, we can go from there. If they haven't, then we should put out an alert to be on the lookout for him, just in case he tries to come back here. He had some friends in the Clan, after all."

Frank nodded and Ethan typed furiously on his laptop. Cassy agreed it was a good idea. Jack had become a menace to them all and needed a good hanging for what he'd done to Jaz and Choony.

They discussed the wording for the alert, which only took about ten minutes. It was pretty straightforward.

Once he'd finished typing, Ethan stood and Frank acknowledged him. He set his laptop down, glanced at Michael rather oddly, then looked at Frank. "We have confirmation that Watcher One, the man responsible for blowing up that poor young Clan girl with a drone, is now providing Intel and even satellite images to the Southern Cantonment. That means he's had to print them out and have them delivered, since Maryland's invaders don't have any working computer gear or network that we know of."

Frank took a sharp breath and said, "That's terrible. They can get aerial photos of all our positions with only a day or two's delay. Michael, order cammo netting over all emplacements and supply depots small enough to hide."

Ethan continued, "We also have confirmation that when Jack kidnapped Jaz, he didn't only have personal reasons. He has become an agent for Maryland at some point since we failed him on his Clan probationary period."

Cassy perked up at that. "How do you know he became an agent after? If he had been a spy all along, that would explain how their death squad learned of the bunker's hidden escape route."

Ethan visibly shuddered. "Good point. Frank, I'd like to begin quietly questioning all the people he associated with during his probationary period."

Frank nodded. "Good idea. Now, what do we know about the increased activity with our southern neighbors?"

"Well, we have a list of their raids and the results. Analysis shows no obvious patterns to their attacks so far, and the battalion that raided Ephrata was their largest incursion before or since. They lost a lot of men, guns, ammo —and they didn't get the supplies they were after, which was mostly food."

Michael stood and said, "I believe they're just testing our defenses and positions. Mapping out incursion routes in advance of a major attack, perhaps, but not as intensely as I would expect to see if the invasion was imminent. Perhaps war is not inevitable."

Frank snapped his fingers and leaned forward. "Damn, I hope not. Should we redirect Joe Ellings down there, from Philly?"

Cassy frowned. Not all of Frank's ideas were good, after all. "No way. Philadelphia is a huge wildcard. If we can get them to join our cause, even at a steep price, it radically changes things for the Southern Cantonment. They'd have to keep troops in reserve to defend against a possible attack from there, which means fewer troops attacking us."

Frank agreed and told Ethan to consider who to send south as a diplomat. Then he turned to Cassy and said, "What can you tell us about Confederation overall readiness?"

Cassy stood. She had some good news, for once—her plan to lure the invaders into a trap, cementing Ephrata's return to the fold within the Confederation, had worked thanks to Michael's usual battlefield brilliance.

"The raid on Ephrata woke everyone up. They've realized that they can't just leave us to deal with the wolves alone, not if they want to survive. It was a fresh reminder of strength in numbers because Michael's counter-attack there sealed the raiders' fates. It was a PR coup."

She sat down, and Frank nodded. "Good, good. Let's get a list of available troops, transport, materials, and so on. Cassy, that's your job. Michael, what do you have for us?"

Michael stood again, and as usual, his expression was inscrutable while he was 'on duty.' "Our troops are ready, but not at full alert. We doubled our outlying scout screen and increased the number of radios Ethan and our redneck engineer Dean Jepson rigged up. We'll be able to react to any major incursions. Liz Town remains a problem, in that their Packs are eager to fight, but Carl is still basically hermiting in his mansion."

Frank grunted.

What else was there to say? Carl was a shell of the man Cassy had once known.

Michael continued, "One other thing to report. This stays here, in these council chambers. This information is highly classified."

"We understand," Frank said. "It is so noted. Continue, please."

"Watcher One has become an existential threat to the Confederation in general and the Clan in particular. I have just finished putting together a SpecOps team and, over the next few weeks, we'll be training hard for a mission."

"What mission?" Frank leaned forward, looking fairly alarmed.

"Ethan and I, with my hand-picked team, are going to locate, enter, and destroy Watcher One's bunker, with a secondary priority of eliminating Watcher One himself."

Frank jumped to his feet, face turning pale. "No. That'll be impossible. We need Ethan to manage our intelligence ops, and you're the damn general for the entire Confederation. What are we supposed to do without you two while you're off on some wild goose chase? Do you even know where his damn bunker is?"

Michael didn't look alarmed or upset. Cassy thought he looked more like a patient parent explaining things to a child as he said, "Ethan has trained a replacement who is fully capable of running the message operations that are his primary duty. And Carl's still not ready to fill my role, so I have a replacement XO who will continue preparing our defenses, which is something any highly-trained, intelligent monkey could do. Sorry, Frank, but I'm vetoing your veto. You're right, I am the general for the whole Confederation, and this is a Confederation-level decision. I'll make sure you're in good hands while we're gone, though. I promise."

* * *

Two hours later, the meeting split up, and everyone left but Choony. He was staying in Cassy's house until he recovered, unwilling to spend time in his earthbag dome home without Jaz. Not that they'd spent much time in Clanholme in the last year. Besides, the Complex was a long way away in Choony's condition, and they'd have had to spare someone to help him every hour of the day.

Anyway, Cassy was happy to have him stay on her couch. She handed him a cup of nettle tea. He adored the stuff, and it was practically a superfood. She took her own to the other end of the couch. She sat, crossed her legs, and smiled at him.

"So," he said, "what do you think of Ethan and Michael's idea?" He sipped the tea and scrunched his face up as the bitterness hit him.

Why he liked this stuff, she had no idea, but she had gotten used to it. "I think there's nothing much we can do to stop them. That's what I think."

Choony chuckled at her. "I've rubbed off on you. That's a very Buddhist way of looking at it. It's also quite true."

She pursed her lips. She hated bringing up a sensitive subject but had to know. "Please don't take offense to this, but why is Jaz staying behind in Hoboken? If it's too personal, just say so. I just—"

He waved his hand dismissively. "No, it's not too personal. She seeks the one who did this to us. While I had hoped she could let it go and accept what happened, it seems she cannot. Perhaps hunting that demon down will make her feel whole again, but from what I've seen, revenge never heals those old wounds."

"Still, Jack is a traitor to New America, his new home, and still a threat to you and Jaz as long as he lives. It's not pointless for her to hunt him down."

He shrugged. "I disagree. Others are already hunting him, and as long as he is on the run, he is harmless to us. She could have returned with me to begin her own healing process, but you know how Jaz is."

She reached across the couch and put her hand on his arm. Her heart had pretty much broken to hear what those two had endured. What they'd been made to watch as each endured. Jack was evil. "I'm grateful you are back alive, and will recover. If you or Jaz need anything or need someone to talk to, I'm here."

He took a deep breath, set his tea on the table, and leaned back into the couch, stretching his arm out along the top toward Cassy. He met her gaze directly and said, "She and I are safe. I am more immediately worried about this war coming up."

Cassy took another sip of the bitter draught. "You heard Michael. Their raids are uncoordinated."

"What do you mean?"

"Well, they haven't really done anything more than they've always done. They've just been doing a lot more raiding in this past month or so. There's no guarantee a war is coming. For all we know, their leader is just bleeding off his disgruntled soldiers in suicide missions, or getting them out of town on raids so that they can't stir up trouble. We just don't know."

"I hope you're right, Cassy. You usually are. For now, we can sit back and enjoy our hard-earned freedom. We're more or less at peace, no matter what storm clouds lurk on the horizon. I'm alive and healing, and Jaz is alive, healing in her own way. With her hunt, she's taking back the power, I think, and I can't blame her."

Cassy nodded slowly, just taking his words in. "You know what? Memorial Day is in a couple weeks."

"I almost forgot."

"You'll be here for that, right?"

"Yeah," Choony said, "and Jaz might, too, if she finishes up before then."

"I don't have anyone to go with since Frank is going with Michael and Ethan. They have this thing they do on the old holidays, very hush-hush. So I need a date. You game?"

Choony smiled, as she had expected him to. Life went on, and he was always the first to point that out, the first to enjoy life's smaller pleasures that went unnoticed by everyone else, including by Cassy herself. He said, "I'd be delighted. I find myself needing a date since I'll be here for it this year. Whatever will people say, though?"

Cassy laughed out loud. "The same thing they've always said. I am apparently a cougar, despite my face scars and advancing old age."

He shook his head and let out a melodramatic sigh. "You were beautiful before the scars, and you're more beautiful now that your insides are as gorgeous as your outsides. And you're what, thirty-five? Something like that? Supermodels have been your age. And all that work on the farm... You are, as they say, smoking. Let them talk."

She laughed again. He was full of crap, but pleasantly so. "You make a lady feel young again. Anyway, it's going to be a big celebration this year, since the Clan is playing host for the Confederation. Apparently, people like our apple cider. Who knew that would become our main export?"

"You mean besides knowledge of how to farm well without fertilizers, tractors, balers, and big delivery trucks?" he replied, smirking.

"Our cider is the best around, though. At least east of the Mississippi, which is all we've had the pleasure of tasting since the war began."

"Regardless, we should enjoy this time, Cassy. We have peace right now, more or less."

"Certainly more of it than we've had at any time before the Mountain War."

"Yeah, so enjoy it. Spend time with your kids, bake pies and share them. You know... really live."

Cassy lay her head back against the couch's backrest, looking up at the ceiling. He was right, of course. And if he could say that with everything he'd just been through, then surely she could say so, too.

"Thanks, Choony. I'm going to bed. For once, I'm going to sleep like a baby, too. Let tomorrow bring its woes tomorrow, right?"

Choony didn't respond, and Cassy looked over at him only to find his eyes were closed, a faint growling snore escaping him. She smiled and got up, grabbed his blanket from behind the couch, and covered him up with it.

She padded quietly to the stairs leading up to her loft bedroom and blew out the lantern they'd attached to the wall like a sconce. "Good night, Choony," she whispered, then climbed up to her own room.

Tomorrow's problems weren't real yet. She would take his advice, and worry about tomorrow when it happened.

* * *

"Not a chance in hell," Janice said, looking up at Mark from her desk.

Mark frowned. He hadn't expected her to jump at the chance to spy on the CIA even more than she already did, but he hadn't expected her to shut him down completely. She had no way to get top-secret information directly, but she knew people. Not all information passed through official channels, especially among those spooks.

Ignoring her refusal, Mark said, "I'm thinking the CIA director's civilian aid would be your best bet. Harry trusts you, and you haven't ever given him a reason not to. I think this is important enough to risk it."

"Mark, for all you know, Operation Raptor is only some new push on hygiene to get everybody to brush their teeth more." She furrowed her eyebrows at him.

He shook his head. There was no way she believed that any more than he did. "You've seen a lot of the same reports I have. I just ran the most recent batch of reports through OCR software and analyzed them with word cloud and keyword density check programs—this new operation was named multiple times. If it wasn't classified Top Secret, I would've received a copy already. We both know this is some secret squirrel op."

His primary concern, other than her flat out refusal, had been her safety and not blowing her cover. If it became known she leaked information to him, she would be cut off, and could even be executed for espionage. This was, after all, Martial Law in a time of war. Hell, he could be executed too.

"Have you heard any word about my family?"

"The same as last time. But I promise you, we'll keep looking."

Janice closed her eyes and let out a long, slow sigh. "I have an idea on how to get that information from Harry Emerson. Just leave it to me and don't ask too many questions. Also, I suspect you're going to owe me a big one."

Mark turned his head to look at her directly. "Of course. Do what you have to do, and I'll make it right in the end."

* * *

Mark had taken steps to ensure he wasn't followed or seen, and he wore a hoodie to hide his face from random people and cameras. Anyone who looked hard enough through the security camera system would be able to figure out where he came from, and therefore who he was, but a casual glance at the cameras wouldn't reveal it. This was a top secret journey after all—he had just received Janice's text that simply read "Successful." Now, he was about to find out the details on Operation Raptor.

He knocked on Janice's door and waited.

A couple seconds later, she opened it and waved him in. Closing the door behind them, she said, "Have a seat."

Janice sat on the recliner across the living room and took a deep breath. With one hand, she reached into her pants pocket and withdrew a folded piece of paper. "Here's what you're looking for. I read it already. Wish I hadn't," she said, her voice sounding uneasy as she handed it to him.

Mark unfolded the sheet and looked it over. A second later, he felt his jaw drop. He had to reread it to make sure he hadn't misunderstood.

He felt his heart beat erratically, like he was about to pass out. He didn't want to believe that Houle would do such a thing, but Mark knew he would if pressed. He obviously felt pressed now.

They sat in silence for a long moment, and Mark felt a cold chill run up his spine.

His mind reeled. In his hands lay the General's orders in black and white, direct from General Houle himself. The orders were simple: Gain control of several nuclear missiles and use them to "cleanse" the United States from the traitorous influences of New America and the remaining invaders on the Eastern Seaboard.

Basically, a large chunk of the eastern states would soon be turned to an irradiated wasteland.

Suddenly, an image of his estranged brother flashed through his mind—the last he heard, he was out there on the East Coast. But if anyone could survive the hell going on out there, it would be a person as deadly as his brother.

Mark gazed at Janice—the woman who was now the only hope for millions of innocent Americans who had no idea their lives were teetering on the edge.

"Houle has to be stopped," he heard himself say, almost as though someone else had spoken.

"How?"

"I don't know," Mark said, his voice barely audible above the deafening pounding of his heart. "But whatever I come up with, I'll need your help."

# # #

To be continued in Book 8...

About the authors:

JJ Holden lives in a small cabin in the middle of nowhere. He spends his days studying the past, enjoying the present, and pondering the future.

Henry Gene Foster resides far away from the general population, waiting for the day his prepper skills will prove invaluable. In the meantime, he focuses on helping others discover that history does indeed repeat itself and that it's never too soon to prepare for the worst.

For updates, new release notifications, and more, please visit:

www.jjholdenbooks.com

Made in the USA
Columbia, SC
01 December 2020